The Thieves of Heaven

The Thieves of Heaven

Richard Doetsch

A DELL BOOK

THE THIEVES OF HEAVEN
A Dell Book

Published by Bantam Dell
A Division of Random House, Inc.
New York, New York

Title page art from a photograph by Nick Jones
Book design by Virginia Norey

ISBN-10: 0-7394-6657-7
ISBN-13: 978-0-7394-6657-5

Printed in the United States of America

For Virginia,
My best friend
I love you with all my heart.

There is a comfort to love that only those that truly know it feel. It is warm and secure, free of anger and jealousy. It is euphoric and renders one immune to life's cruelty. It is filled with never-ending hope, undying appreciation, and true selflessness. It is the rarest of gifts.

Acknowledgments

It is my distinct pleasure to thank the following people:

Gene and Wanda Sgarlata, without whose friendship and assistance you wouldn't be reading these words; Irwyn Applebaum, for opening the door and giving me this opportunity; Nita Taublib, for closing the deal and making my dream a reality; Kate Miciak, for your unending patience, guidance, and confidence; Joel Gotler, for doing the impossible; Maria Faillace and everyone at Fox 2000, for creating the initial excitement.

And above all, Cynthia Manson. Thank you for your innovative thinking, unending faith in the face of adversity, and true friendship.

Thank you to my family: Richard for your curiosity, wit, and strength; Marguerite for your humor, your heart, and your beauty; Isabelle for your smile, your laugh, and your innocence. Most important, thank you, Virginia, for putting up with my 3:00 a.m. workaholic ways. You are my inspiration, my laughter, my joy; you are the reason for everything good in my life.

Finally, to you, the reader, thank you for taking the time to read *The Thieves of Heaven*. In this day and age where people choose their entertainment in two-hour movies, half-hour sitcoms, and three-minute videos it is nice to know there are still individuals who choose to read and let the story play out in their imagination.

Richard

The Thieves of Heaven

Nighttime NYC

Michael St. Pierre flipped the Steiner night vision monocular down over his left eye, loosened his grip on the rope, and continued his descent from the fifteenth floor. The darkened alley, now rendered green, was his landing site. He was careful not to look toward the big city lights in the distance; he couldn't afford blindness at this moment in his life. The alley below was clear except for a few bags of garbage and a couple of rats on their nocturnal prowl. A thirty-yard jog across the street would put him over the ten-foot granite wall into the nighttime safety of Central Park. He stayed in the shadows of the buildings around him. He wasn't worried about getting caught: the hard part was over and this particular corner of the world was deserted.

He was sixty feet from touchdown when out of his left eye—the enhanced one—he caught a glimpse of flesh. Soft, naked flesh. It was in the adjacent building, a town house, fifth floor. The dark, nobody-home, adjacent building sitting just off Fifth Avenue. He swore he could make out a breast. He averted his eye; he wasn't a Peeping Tom. But it was a nice sight. A stone's throw away. He never would have known, but for the night vision. He wasn't worried, though: she couldn't see him, of this, Michael was sure.

He continued his descent through the hot sticky night.

But, like a siren, the vision pulled him back, if only for a second. Yes, it was a breast. Two, in fact. Well proportioned above a trim waist, the whole scene bathed in green. God, he did love the view up here. The woman lay on her back. He couldn't really make out her face but it was an exceptional body. He watched as it writhed in passion. *Think of the job,* he reminded himself, fighting the momentary lust.

He released his guideline, continuing his descent. He had invested too many hours to risk it all now over stolen glances at unsuspecting lovers. He would be home in no time flat if he stuck to the plan, safe in the embrace of his bride, who was far more alluring than this woman before him. *Though she did possess a body like none he had ever laid eyes upon.*

Without warning, as if reading his thoughts, the woman's head snapped left toward the window. Michael froze, holding fast to the line, not a sound, not a breath. Had she seen him? Impossible. He was dressed for concealment; the area around him couldn't be darker.

And then his insides turned to water.

She wasn't looking at him. She couldn't. Her eyes were covered with a dark cloth; in her mouth was a ball gag. The twisting of her body was not passion but terror. He looked harder. She was bound spread-eagled to a table and she was in pain. A sudden rage filled him as he saw a figure poised at her side; the man's face was obscured but the gun in his hand was not. This wasn't a game: the woman was being taken against her will. And it was all happening less than twenty feet away from him.

He looked down. Only fifty feet to go. Freedom. He felt the small pouch on his back shift its weight. Six months of planning for that pouch; it was his future. He wasn't going to let it slip through his fingers. This was no time to be a hero.

But she was still there, the green hue of the nightscope painting her skin, her body straining against its bonds. Michael didn't need to hear to know she was screaming behind the gag in her mouth.

⌘

Summertime on the Upper East Side. Most had abandoned the city for the Hamptons, for Greenwich, for their little piece of what they called the country; their apartments left dark and dusty until September. The kings and queens abandoned their castles for greener pastures and fresher air, leaving behind Silicon Alley fiefdoms and Wall Street empires. It was a concentration of wealth unlike any in the world, allencased behind thirty blocks of limestone facades and hulking Irish doormen.

The imposing embassy was originally the home and offices of J. S. Vandervelde, an oil baron whose empire rivaled those of Getty, Rockefeller, and Carnegie. The Akbiquestan government bought the building in the early seventies not for her ornate beauty but for her impenetrable exterior structure: walls three feet thick, massive doors, bulletproof windowpanes. The Vanderveldes had known their place in the world: they knew their enemies better than they knew their family and so had their home designed accordingly. Johan Sebastian Vandervelde had constructed his fortress—eight floors of mansion, seven floors of office—in 1915, moving his family uptown from their Greenwich Village home on Fourth Street. Running afoul of his workers had grown commonplace with Johan Sebastian and there was a price to be paid. It just wouldn't be paid in blood on his own doorstep.

The Akbiquestans also knew their place in the world and knew they needed a bunker more than an office building. They had upgraded Vandervelde's former home since moving in, plumbing, electric, heating, and security. The only way in was through the front door, if you were willing to endure guards, scanners, guns, and the like.

But people tend to think in two dimensions, not three. An assault from above was never considered a threat, even when the Akbiquestan ambassador was in residence. The roof was outfitted only with standard alarms on the roof doors, windows, and skylights.

It had taken six months of planning. Michael knew every corner of the building better than its longest resident. The Landmark Preservation Commission had been extremely accommodating in providing full plans and specs on the property. When they heard he was writing a book on the history of the most famous avenue in the world, they dropped everything they were doing to assist the nice young man in the Ralph Lauren suit. Not only did they provide info on the building in question, but on each of the adjacent structures. Forbes Carlton Smyth—Michael chose the alias for its implied pedigree—assured every commissioner he would receive an acknowledgment for his assistance. The building's American security system was easily identified and access codes were purchased from the manufacturer for a nominal fee, as U.S. sentiment didn't run deep for the Akbiques.

Like every good businessman, Michael was thorough in his work, dotting every i and crossing every t. He was every bit the professional. No stone left unturned in his planning, no detail overlooked in his research. Every foreseeable scenario was played out and provisioned for. But unlike other businesses his was a firm of one. No R&D staff, no secretarial pool, no VP of human resources. Michael always worked alone; in an untrusting field, you can't be the trusting kind. Always performing below-the-radar lifts: governments, criminals, the over-insured. Nothing could or would ever point to him. Always in and out in minutes, never a mistake, never a trace, never a clue, and, most importantly, never caught.

The embassy was down-staffed now that the United Nations was on hiatus. Two guards on duty per shift, a handful of daytime secretaries, and that was it. Everyone else had returned home to enjoy the mountainous desert land they represented.

The ambassador, Anwar Sri Ruskot, was a well-respected general who excelled at diplomacy, but that talent ran a distant fourth to his greatest skills. General Ruskot was well-known in the black markets as a top courier, fence, and merchant specializing in the movement of antiques, jewelry, and paintings, all the while hiding behind his diplomatic credentials. As far as the general was concerned, the diplomatic pouch was an invention greater than electricity, the light bulb, and women combined. Rumors of his activities ran rampant in law enforcement circles but the FBI and Interpol were powerless. If they shook the tree, the State Department would have a major crisis on their hands that could swiftly escalate to bloodshed between the not-exactly-friendly countries.

When General Ruskot was in town, he ran his enterprise from the fifteenth floor of the embassy, well out of reach of his guards, councilors, secretaries, and busybodies. His office was on the top floor, where only he was allowed. Ruskot claimed that it was here he conducted his country's most sensitive dealings and that if those dealings were to be prematurely exposed, the impact would be catastrophic to world diplomacy. Nobody ever entered fifteen, under any circumstance.

Michael was the first to see the ambassador's true operation. He hung in the middle of the room on a Kevlar wire, five feet off the ground, shining a small penlight. The study was large, a cross between a gentleman's library and an opium den. A massive masculine desk surrounded by high-back red leather chairs was positioned against the rear wall, while on the opposite end was a nomadic sitting area of thick deep pillows centered around a *hookah,* its stale opiate smell still clinging to the air. Among the host of Eastern antiques and master paintings, Turkish rugs and tapestries, there were ledgers, files, and computers detailing each shady transaction, each illicit payment, every underhanded deal. While most of the criminal element was discreet about record-keeping, that was a worry Ruskot would never have: the general wasn't on American soil, this was pure Akbiquestan ground protected by the Vienna Convention.

Michael had entered the alley shortly after midnight to begin his ascent. The four-story boutique sat just off Madison Avenue, its granite-block face a climber's dream. On his back he carried several lengths of thin kernmantle rope; at his waist, carabiners, clamps, and a tool kit—all taped to avoid jingling. From the shadowed alley he began his climb, his fingers clinging to the impossibly narrow lips between the building's granite blocks. As if out for a stroll, he scaled the boutique in seconds, then cut across the roof and headed up the adjacent eight-story apartment house. Possessing the style and strength of a master, he moved building to building toward Fifth Avenue, rising higher in the city as he went. Michael loved climbing buildings more than rocks. They possessed a greater challenge, a greater sense of accomplishment for him. He'd gotten hooked on man-made facades back in college: the Towers dormitory was his first Mount Everest. He had worked his way up to the twenty-second floor of the dorm, slipped in and out of a student teacher's window without so much as a sound; all for want of a test paper. The adventure didn't have the payoff he was hoping for—the girl he stole it for had still failed the exam.

Michael descended to the Akbiquestan Embassy roof from the adjacent eighteen-story condo. The skylight, installed in '68, was alarmed but easily defeated through a few choice splices. He removed the glass, looked about the dark room through his monocular, then lowered himself down. Hell of an apartment, hell of an art collection. Michael had studied the plans like a playbook and could easily redraw them blindfolded; he knew every inch of the place long before he set foot inside.

Through his various sources he was aware of a considerable amount of uncut diamonds on the premises and his contacts were proven correct when the six-foot-high 1908 Wells Fargo safe swung open under his knowledgeable fingers. There were diamonds, all right. He unfurled the black velvet jewelry roll and there they sat like stars against a night sky, winking and sparkling up at him. Enough to fill a cookie jar. Thirty million black market, untraceable dollars. What made the job even sweeter was no one would ever report these diamonds missing. They were surely stolen, illegally insured, their existence known to only a select few. The ambassador would never send out an alarm. Too many questions would be raised as to their origin. Under no circumstance was anyone entering the fifteenth-floor suite to inspect the scene of this crime. No police, no investigation, no problem.

⌘

At the same moment as the safe door swung open, Cpl. Javier Samaha was growing restless at his post by the embassy door. The guards had drawn lots to see who would rotate home and Samaha had gotten the proverbial short straw. The monotony of twelve-hour shifts was making his feet throb and his head ache. It was a quiet night, a Thursday, and nothing, as usual, was happening. Besides eating, reading, and cards, there wasn't much else to do. Despite all the fears of being a stranger in a hostile land, there had never been an incident at the embassy or against any of his countrymen. Samaha thought the ambassador's paranoia unfounded and the man's precautions over the top. This was the twenty-first century, the age of tolerance, and the embassy sat in the most diverse, liberal city in the world. Besides, it was the middle of the summer, all the radicals and college kids were on vacation, nobody was going to stage even a protest until at least September. Samaha turned to the desk officer and told him he was going to make his rounds early, he needed to stretch his legs and clear his head. He usually started on the second floor and worked his way up, but exercising what little authority he possessed, tonight he decided to start at the top.

⌘

Michael closed the safe and stuffed the diamonds in the satchel, throwing it over his back. He took a brief moment to admire the artwork, confident that no one would be entering this restricted area, and noticed a jeweled cross in the corner. It was nine inches high and encrusted with a host of sapphires, rubies, and emeralds. He had come only for the diamonds, but the cross just screamed to him, he didn't know why. It wasn't in his plan and he hated deviating; he was always extremely fastidious in his work. He knew the key to success—which translated to not being caught—was to stick to the plan. But after all, this would be his last job.

He threw the cross in the bag and was out of there in 93 seconds.

⌘

The elevator door opened on fifteen. Corporal Samaha knew the restrictions but tonight curiosity had gotten the better of him. No one was around to catch him, so what harm would it do? He checked the only apartment door on the floor—the only door the guards didn't have a key for—and, confirming that it was securely locked, headed for the fire stair, a bit disappointed. Then he turned and looked back at the carved mahogany entrance to Ruskot's sanctuary. The corporal didn't have much respect for the paranoid diplomat, but it was his sworn duty to protect the general and to uphold the dignity of his country. Samaha resigned himself to never knowing the truth up here and turned his thoughts to coffee. He'd opened the fire door and stepped into the stairwell when he heard a sharp *click* in the silence. He stopped, focused his hearing. The sound came from the apartment. He heard it again. Not as loud this time but it was definitely a click, and it wasn't natural. He retraced his steps and checked the door: locked. He placed his ear to the polished mahogany, listening intently. He was sure he heard something. He thought of the implications, of his duty to his country; he considered the general's violent personality and he considered the general's violent personality again.

Throwing caution to the wind, he kicked in the door. The apartment was dark but for the light pouring in from the hall and the little bit of glow coming from the skylight. The corporal noted the roomy study was finely appointed, better by far than any other room in the embassy. A palace in the sky. He took a moment looking about. Nothing appeared out of place. He took particular notice of the large safe; pondering its use, he checked the lock. Secure. He turned to leave, deciding the sound he'd heard was probably just a settling noise from the air duct. But then he noticed the wall.

It seemed like a water stain, an outline of dust. Samaha moved in for a closer look at the wall, stepping over the pillows and casting a disparaging glance at the *hookah*. Though the apartment was deep in shadow, there was just enough light to make out the shading. The corporal ran his fingers along it, tracing its outline. Sunlight had, over time, discolored the wall but one single area still retained the vibrant green of its original application, a small area in the shape of a cross.

⌘

And so Michael hung fifty feet in the air with his guaranteed future in the satchel upon his back. Five stories to freedom. A tortured woman before him about to die. His bad feeling, the one in the pit of his stomach, the one that usually told him to run the other way, was almost overwhelming. But it was nothing compared to the fear he felt for the innocent victim he'd glimpsed.

He raced up the rope, hand over hand, made the hundred-foot climb in seconds, and leaped the parapet. Twenty feet away and nine floors below was the six-story town house. He scaled the adjacent condo, dug his fingers into the brick face and shimmied his way across, affixed and played out his rope, then lowered himself down.

He liked a carefully thought-out plan, always had one, always had a backup, and always had a backup to his backup. Flying by the seat of his pants was something he preferred to avoid. He was running on adrenaline and now would have to rely on instinct. He reviewed what he knew: the town house was held in a corporate name, some European textile firm, it was usually occupied by a husband, wife, and a little schnauzer, and it had a cheap and ineffective alarm system. This building had been part of his planning; it was a fallback position, he had studied it well.

Thoughts raced through his head. Where was the husband? Who was the perpetrator? Was it the husband? Was this how this couple got their rocks off? No time for questions, only facts: the woman's body language had pleaded to God for help—she was about to die.

⌘

It really wasn't much of a decision. Samaha explained to the desk officer that he'd heard something on fifteen and despite his orders not to enter the floor, had felt it was his sworn duty to protect his country. He explained that he checked the rest of the building and felt someone may have been prowling about the roof. Nonsense, was all the duty officer said. Samaha suggested calling the NYPD to have them do a drive-by and to keep their eyes open for anything suspicious. It was a good cover story—let the police comb the area; if the thief was still about, the cops would catch him and Samaha would be credited with quick thinking. He might even get a commendation. And if they didn't catch anyone? General Ruskot and his wicked temper were due back in two weeks. Going AWOL in a city like New York was not that bad an alternative.

⌘

Michael entered the town house silently through the top floor window. He had no gun; he hated guns, never had a use for them and wouldn't know what to do with one if he had it. But he did have his knife; he held it in his hand, the handle smooth, comforting to his touch, its blade reflecting shards of light off its deadly edge. He rolled it back and forth in his palm, saying a silent prayer he wouldn't have to use it; its honed metal was unfamiliar with the suppleness of skin.

He flipped down his nightscope, painting the rear guest bedroom in its eerie green glow, then stepped in the hall. Subtle sounds of thrashing, naked skin screeching against a table, a low whine drumming behind it, combined to shiver his soul and strengthen his resolve. At the end of the hall, just outside the door, lay the schnauzer, motionless in a pool of blood. Michael inched his way down and peered into the room. It was a pottery studio: racks of drying clay pots lined a wooden shelf; various paints, thinners, and glazes on a desk; a large kiln in the corner, he could hear its exhaust fan venting intense internal heat. The smell was moist and earthy, mixed with an unnatural hint of jasmine. Scraps of dried clay littered the floor; wooden tools were strewn about, as if a whirlwind had whipped through the place. He saw the table where the work was done, where the clay was pounded and molded, cut into pieces and formed into art. But it wasn't clay being worked tonight.

The woman was blonde, on the closing end of her thirties. A thin layer of sweat coated her body as her breasts heaved in fear. Even naked, you could tell she was of exceptional wealth, her body toned like an athlete, her face chiseled to perfection by a Park Avenue plastic surgeon. Her pedicured feet hung over the edge, tied to the legs of the table, her arms were secured above her head, a black scarf covered her eyes. The tearful moans coming from behind the ball gag chilled Michael's heart, but at least they confirmed one thing: the woman was still alive.

Upon the windowsill was what could only be described as a nineteenth-century medical kit, a sawbones's menagerie of crude antique surgeon's tools: knives, scalpels, and bone saws.

He looked everywhere—there was no sign of the woman's assailant. Ripping off his nightscope, Michael flipped on the light and raced to her side. Her skin was unmarred; whoever had done this had not yet started to work. He quickly began cutting her from her restraints. She kicked and let out a muffled shriek, unaware that Michael was her savior.

And that's when the steamroller hit him square in the side of the head. Michael tumbled backward, dazed, losing all sense of time and reality. He glimpsed a shadow, its face obscured by a scarf, holding a sculptor's mallet in its right hand and in its left a large gun. Michael's head throbbed as he fought to hold on to consciousness. He never imagined death as an option when the night started, but now . . . Not a word was said as the cold barrel of a gun came to rest against his forehead. The madman thumbed back the hammer then paused, seeming to draw joy from prolonging the moment. Michael squeezed the hilt of his knife, taking comfort in the fact that it was concealed. Then, without a moment's hesitation, he thrust his blade upward into his attacker's wrist, buried to the hilt, the bloodied tip jutting out the back of the man's forearm. The assailant fell backward, tumbling against the kiln. He landed shoulder-first against the twelve-hundred-degree metal as his gun skittered away. Instantly, the stench of scorched flesh filled the air.

Michael stumbled to his feet, trying to get his bearings, his head still a jumble from the brutal blow. He grabbed the table to steady himself and finally got a good look at his attacker. The man's eyes were cold and dead as smoke rolled off his seared shoulder and blood poured from his arm, dribbling down the handle of Michael's blade. Oblivious to the pain, the man ripped the knife from his mangled wrist and charged, jamming the knife into Michael's shoulder, tackling him to the floor. The madman grabbed the knife handle and, like a dead pig on a hook, dragged Michael by the hilt across the room, dumping him by the kiln. With a snarl of rage, the man kicked the blade; agony shot through Michael's body.

Teetering on the edge of blackout, a loud radio squawk startled Michael. A police monitor. It was his attacker's. Michael could barely make out the words: *"Possible robbery at the Akbiquestan Embassy, car in route."*

Michael lay there, his body heading into shock from the pain. The woman on the table shrieked a strangled scream through the gag in her mouth; she would surely be seeing death now. Michael's thoughts ran to his wife. How would she ever understand? He pictured the police explaining his death to her; how he was found; how he was murdered. Could she please help them with their investigation? Help them to explain the stolen diamonds in the satchel on her husband's back. Did she know the dead naked socialite? Were her husband and the woman having an affair?

Against any rational thought, Michael reached up and in one mighty pull ripped the knife free from his shoulder, the pain so intense it sucked him instantly toward darkness. He was close to blacking out when a flowing liquid shocked him back to life. The solvent ran along the floor, spreading everywhere, burning his nose, scorching his skin as it seeped into his open wound. For the first time in his life, the realization of his mortality was upon him. If he didn't move—and now—not only would he die but so would the woman.

Standing in the doorway, the madman drew back his arm, the wick of a makeshift Molotov cocktail ablaze. Michael struggled to his feet as the man hurled the flaming bottle straight at him. The paint-thinner bomb floated through the air for what seemed an eternity before arcing downward, finally exploding on the red-hot kiln. Fire mushroomed up, racing out along the floor. The madman disappeared as the doorway burst into flame.

Michael, fighting the agony of his throbbing shoulder and what was surely a concussion, scrambled across the room through the thickening flame and smoke. From a shelf he grabbed a tarp and threw it over the stunned woman. He tore away her mask and gag. She saw the flames and shrieked, on the border of hysteria. Tying his rope to the table leg, Michael hurled a chair through the window and, immediately behind it, the rope. He clipped on his harness and grabbed the lady. She didn't need to be told where they were going: she held on.

He hurled himself and his burden out the window as the room erupted. Together, they tumbled down through the summer air as the table skidded along the floor, finally slamming home against the window. They jolted to a halt—stories above the alley below. Flames licked out the window only yards above their heads.

They touched down on the sidewalk just as the town house windows exploded, flames and plumes of smoke curling up into the city sky. The interior of the town house glowed orange as the sixth floor became fully engulfed. He lay the woman down. She was whimpering incoherently as she pulled the tarp tight around her naked body, shivering and weeping.

Michael tore off his belt, throwing the tools in the bushes, and checked the diamond-filled satchel on his back. Still there. The blood poured from his shoulder, his dark shirt had gone crimson. He hoped the blood loss wasn't fatal; he didn't have time to deal with dying right now. He leaned over the woman. Life was returning to her eyes. She smiled, as the tears rolled down her face.

Sirens blared and within seconds three police cars screeched to a halt across the street. Michael looked across Fifth Avenue toward the wall to Central Park. He touched the pouch on his back; it was his future. Freedom was only twenty yards away.

He could still make it.

Chapter 1

Stained glass—they don't make it like this anymore: brilliant purples, deep rose, rich gold, all melded to depict the Gates of Heaven, the centerpiece of an old-fashioned, whitewashed church. The morning sun filtered in, casting colored shadows upon the host of parishioners, some there because they wanted to be, most because they had to be. And like in any house of worship, no matter the denomination, there were the people who sat in the front pews as if their proximity to the altar made them closer to salvation. The ladies in their fine dresses, the men cologned, blazered, and adorned in their best silk ties, all thinking it was the clothes that made the saint.

Behind the pulpit stood Father Patrick Shaunessy. His close-cropped hair was pure white and in sharp contrast to his stern black eyebrows. His stubby arms, buried deep in the folds of his voluminous green cassock, moved with the Irish lilt of his voice. For years he had preached to his flock, many hours spent on his words of wisdom, but he never failed to wonder whether he had ever gotten through to a single individual. Now, just as in his youth, there was a constant rate of crime, adultery, and a general exodus from religion. People, it seemed, put their faith in technology, science, and sex, believing only in the tangible. If you can't stroke it, don't believe it. Not sure why, Father Shaunessy preached on with the hope that he would save at least one soul from this world gone to confusion.

The priest may have been a slight man; some would say he bordered on puny—he had had fleeting dreams of being an equestrian legend, racing for the roses at Churchill Downs—but his voice, that was his gift, for his voice was as large as his body was small. And it was this voice that now boomed out over his congregation.

"You cannot steal salvation, like a thief in the night. For it is not perfection of life on this earth for which we strive, but perfection of faith. Faith in God will provide us eternal life, faith alone is the key that will grant us eternal salvation."

He gathered up his papers and, as if for emphasis, murmured, "If you open your missal to 'Morning Has Broken,' page one hundred and three."

The congregation joined in song, and while it wasn't Cat Stevens, it was on-key and hopeful, filling the air, echoing off the rafters.

Near the rear of the church, tucked away in the back, almost as if in hiding, sat Father Shaunessy's greatest fan. If the woman was trying to hide, it would be a daunting task; the auburn curls spilling down her back like liquid fire made her impossible to miss. With an air of confidence and a missal in hand, she sang quietly to herself; an action that stood in stark contrast to the rest of her life. She had been hard to contain for more years than anyone could remember. Since the age of thirteen, she had been one of those contradictions—learning of the seven deadly sins at Catholic school during the day, then running around at night, trying to commit all of them. And though the years brought temperance and a sense of responsibility, she would never totally abandon her wild roots. Saturday night usually found her out dancing, but almost every Sunday, no matter the weather, no matter her health, no matter what, she could be found in the same seat at eleven a.m., her head bowed, quietly thankful for everything in her world. Although she didn't always agree with the Church and her manner would never get her nominated for sainthood, Mary St. Pierre's faith in God always rang true.

Beside her in the pew her husband sat silently, his lips tight in protest as he contemplated the singing congregation. A shock of unkempt brown hair framed a strong face, striking, yet worn beyond its thirty-eight years. The man fidgeted. You could see in his dark eyes that his mind was already at the exit. To date, Michael St. Pierre had never told his wife of his diminishing faith, and now was definitely not the moment to do so. They already had enough issues to deal with.

⌘

Mary and Michael exited the church amidst the throng of parishioners all angling to shake their pastor's hand, hoping against hope that maybe some of the priest's holiness would rub off on their own souls.

Father Shaunessy went through the motions with a cordial nod to each, thanking them as they complimented his sermon, his slight smile hiding the question in his mind: *If quizzed, could anyone of them repeat a single sentence, let alone the daily moral?* But then his face lit up, for he had caught Mary St. Pierre's eye.

"Beautiful sermon, Father," Mary said, looking down on the little priest. It was almost as if she was talking to a child, the disparity in their heights was so extreme. Concerned her size would make him uncomfortable, she was always careful never to wear heels to church, but even in her flat shoes she pushed five feet nine.

"Thank you, Mary." He clasped her hand in his. "I can always count on your smile when I'm at the altar." Father Shaunessy didn't acknowledge Michael. It was as if he wasn't there at all. Sensing her husband's discomfort, Mary smiled, pulling him close.

Finally, as an afterthought, not wishing to offend Mary, the priest nodded to Michael. "Mike."

"Patrick," Michael begrudgingly mumbled back.

The line of glad-handers behind Mary was growing long and impatient. Reluctantly, the priest released her hand. "Peace be with you, child."

"Thank you, Father. And you."

The St. Pierres headed down the tree-lined walk toward the parking lot as Father Shaunessy continued to greet his well-wishing flock.

⌘

The '89 Ford Taurus pulled out of the church lot and headed east. Its dinged and pinged body may have been old but it was clean. Michael drove, silent, focused on the horizon, lost in thought. Mary knew Michael was hurting again. Her husband was retreating to that world where he shut out everyone to tackle his problems all alone. It was a wall she always fought to break down, and each time required a new strategy. Her eyes twinkled and she smiled, reaching out to touch him.

He glanced over. "What's up?"

"Just brushing something off your shoulder."

"Dandruff?"

"No. The chip."

"What?" Michael was genuinely confused, moving as if he had a spider on him. "What chip?"

"The chip on your shoulder."

Michael grimaced, trying to hold on to his bad mood.

"Pat is not a bad guy," Mary said.

"He looks down on me, like I'm going to infect his congregation or something. I thought priests were supposed to be forgiving." There was bitterness in his voice.

"It's pretty hard for a man that short to look down on you, Michael."

"Take a look at the world through my eyes, Mary." Michael's eyes never left the road.

Mary hated when he snapped. It wasn't often, only on Sundays and generally within an hour before or after Mass. She knew it was difficult for Michael but it was only an hour out of his week. She did see the world through his eyes; it was something she was always able to do, and as far as she was concerned, he could use a little peace in his life. "Why do we have to go through this every week?" Mary rested her hand on his leg in reconciliation.

An uncomfortable silence filled the car.

Cars by the dozens lined the sides of the road. Music, sounding like Springsteen, blared from somewhere. The roar of the ocean was not far off; a sea breeze filled the air with that unmistakable summertime smell. Mary walked up the slate path to a weathered gray Cape Cod house with Michael an obvious five steps behind her, still silent and stiff. She rang the bell. No answer. She rang again as Michael finally caught up. Mary grabbed the handle, opened the door—

"I don't know if I'm really in the mood for this," Michael warned.

"What are you in the mood for?" she demanded, her patience seeming to wear thin.

Michael said nothing.

"We'll say our hellos and good-byes within a half hour and be home before two."

She took his hand and led him inside. The rooms were dark, suspiciously empty. Mary wound her way toward the back of the house, through a simple living room, past the dining area, muffled noise growing with every step. She came to a sliding glass door, a large curtain across it.

"Remember to smile," Mary whispered.

She pulled back the curtain to reveal a party. Not just any party—this was a party to end all parties. A sea of people filled the back terrace, spilling out onto the beach. Three barbecues blazed, their flames licking the sky. If there was any meat on their grills, it had long since been cremated and returned to the gods. Large speakers spewed "Candy's Room," Springsteen's wailing voice having a hard time competing with the festive uproar.

Mary tugged Michael's hand and they dove into the mayhem, squeezing their way through the drunken throng. As she tugged Michael to breathing room at the back of the terrace, they spotted a huge bear of a man walking toward them. People parted, as if out of respect for royalty, nodding and slapping his enormous back as he went by. He was a heavy man, not fat but not muscled, either, just big and burly. At six feet five, he towered over everyone. His sandy blond hair reminded you of a surfer but they probably didn't make boards big enough for him. Mary was instantly swallowed within his girth as he hugged her tight: a gentle giant caressing a dove.

"The party can now officially start," the big man growled. He released Mary from his clutches, turned and embraced Michael, who couldn't have been more embarrassed as the wind was crushed out of him. "As usual, you're late," he roared.

"Church," Mary defended.

The giant looked right into Michael's eyes and asked: "Bubby?"

"I was praying for that large, whiskey-pickled soul of yours."

The big man's eyes became stern. "Excuses, excuses." He grabbed Michael's head in his enormous hands and pulled him close. "They're just like assholes—everyone's got one and they all stink." He planted a noisy kiss on Michael's forehead before releasing him. "Glad you made it."

Michael finally relaxed.

Paul Busch didn't drink to excess except when he had a really good reason—which was rarer than rare—didn't smoke, and drugs had always been his enemy. In fact, other than a weakness for junk food, Paul was probably one of the cleanest-living men you would ever find. Except for once a year. Once a year around this time, Busch had his Memorial Day weekend blowout. Everyone he had ever met, spoken to, beaten up, kissed, coached, hugged, or married was invited to help him kick off the summer. This was his appreciation-of-life festival and thank-you to all the living, and since he paid the freight he felt entitled to partake in everything, including the alcohol. Hence, his current clumsy, grinning state.

The sound of giggling, screaming children rose above the pounding music drifting over the crowd, the noise getting closer by the second. And suddenly they were there, as if materializing out of thin air, a boy and girl no more than six, Irish twins. Robbie—older by eleven months—and Chrissie Busch, a pair of towheaded blonds with smiles that could warm the depths of the ocean. Charging through the partygoers, they leapt into Michael's waiting arms.

"Come on the trampoline—" Robbie shouted, pulling Michael left.

"No! Sand castles!" Chrissie tugged to the right.

"Hey, guys, how about a hello?" Busch admonished his children.

"It's OK," Michael said, loving the attention.

"Give the man a break, let him at least get a drink." Busch tried to pull his kids off.

"But, Daddy . . . he's the only one here that'll play with us," Robbie pleaded.

Busch looked his son straight in the eye. "That's because he's the only one here with your advanced level of maturity."

"It's OK," Michael repeated, crouching down to the kids.

"Dad, please . . ."

Busch may have been a strong man, probably the strongest you'd ever meet, but when it came to his kids he was more than weak, he was putty. Throwing up his hands, he turned to Michael. "Suit yourself, but if they kill you, don't come crying to me." Busch grinned and put his arm around Mary. "Care to have some fun, beautiful lady?"

And they vanished into the crowd.

Michael and the two children sat down right in the middle of the party crowd as if they were sitting in their own private playroom, and in a magical fashion Michael raised his arms and waved both hands, showing they were empty. The two kids looked confused, exchanging glances. Then he reached behind their ears, pulling from behind each a small stuffed elephant. The smiles couldn't have been wider.

⌘

Sitting among a coffee-klatsch of women, Mary listened to the mile-a-minute chatter. The women had gathered, sipping umbrella drinks and gorging on chips and salsa. The conversations ran from gossip to their disappointing marriages back to gossip, none of which Mary could relate to. Next to her was a woman who had no patience for the pretentiousness of these ladies. Jeannie Busch sat back watching the diverse cross-section of her husband's friends and their wives mingle, chat, and drink, all the while barely concealing her contempt. Jeannie hated parties. All the phony smiles and insincere gestures seemed to dissolve to truth as the alcohol washed away the carefully constructed facades. Not that she didn't enjoy the company of her girlfriends, but this was her husband's party and she chose to keep her friends away, not wishing to expose them to the lunacy—that is, all her friends except Mary. Mary was Jeannie's anchor, her rock. She would help her keep her lip in check lest she pop off in her tough, take-no-prisoners fashion to one of Busch's inebriated buddies or boss—or worse, his boss's wife. One's true character was usually laid bare by drink and in general Jeannie didn't like what she saw—but she wore her smile and nursed her water every Memorial Day, because Jeannie hated parties but she loved Busch.

"How's the new school, they treating you all right?" Her husky voice cut through the banter.

Mary nodded, her hair glowing like embers in the midday sun. "I've got twenty-six of the cutest kids you've ever seen."

"Couldn't take that many," Jeannie remarked, pulling her sandy brown hair into a ponytail. "My hands are full with my two munchkins from hell."

Mary smiled. "I'd be happy to take them off your hands."

"Just wait until you have a set of your own, you'll see." Jeannie paused as she momentarily caught sight of the tops of her children's heads before the pair vanished in the throng again. "You think they are all cute, peaches and cream, but after sundown . . . they're nocturnal, you know, up all night. They come alive just when you're ready to collapse. Oh, they may hug and kiss you but it is all just a front, it's a big kid conspiracy. They turn on you like animals."

Mary let out a soft laugh but her attention was waning. Her emerald green eyes were following a beachside football game. Jeannie followed Mary's gaze to Michael. She smiled, leaned forward, and waved her hand before the younger woman's face. "Hello? Earth to Mary . . . ?"

Mary snapped back to the moment, smirked in embarrassment, and rejoined reality. "Sorry," she said, as she stole another look at her husband.

"Honey, never apologize for lust."

⌘

A football game was in full swing, bare feet cutting through the hot white sand. The tipsy athletes were over-the-hill wannabes reliving past revelries and triumphs from their youths. But to Michael, they all looked like they were about to explode, heaving for breath, faces on fire. Of course, they were real men, so pain was not a factor, at least not in front of friends.

Michael took the snap, faded back, and threw deep, the ball gliding through the clear blue sky. Paul Busch may have been a large man but his size certainly didn't weigh him down as he sailed across the sand for the goal line, leaving his pursuers in the dust. The ball arced inward, picture perfect, landing right in his palms. Touchdown. Busch danced in the end zone, spiking the ball and thumping his chest. He charged back to the huddle slamming high fives as if the score just put them ahead at the Superbowl.

"Way to go, Peaches!" Michael called, tickled with their teamwork.

One of the guys on the other team, hearing Busch's nickname, threw a look at Busch.

"Don't ask." Busch glared as he brushed his straw-colored hair out of his eyes.

They lined up six on six as Michael kicked off, sending the ball tumbling end over end into the end zone: touch back. They slowly huddled up, chatted about the latest greatest beer commercial and, clapping in unison, they broke. Busch crouched down, knuckles in the sand, looked left then right, and finally at his opposing man. Jason was half his size, the top of his bald head burned and beginning to blister, but the pain was mercifully dulled by his beer intake. He looked Busch in the eye and in a mocking tone crooned, "Peaches? What's up with that?"

The blood rushed to Busch's face. Time seemed to slow as the big man snorted like a bull, deep and rhythmic. And the ball was snapped. Busch, a taunted raging beast, violently plowed the smaller man over, burying Jason halfway in the sand. He triumphantly stood over his dazed and confused opponent. "Sorry," he crooned back, gleefully.

⌘

The sun had set hours ago, taking the warmth of the late spring day with it. The party was finally breaking up. Empty beer bottles were strewn everywhere; the last wisps of smoke floated up from the grills. Most of the crowd had long since passed out or been carried home. The kids were the only ones left with energy, still charging from room to room.

Michael draped has blue sport jacket over Mary's shoulders. She pulled it tightly around herself to ward off the evening chill. They gathered up their things and headed for Jeannie, who manned the front door. "I have to grab some stuff from the shop," Michael told Mary.

"At this hour?" Mary just wanted to get home to bed.

Before Michael had a chance to answer, Jeannie leaned in, kissing Mary's cheek. "Thanks for coming, guys."

"Thanks for having us," Mary replied warmly.

"Leftovers, take 'em." Jeannie handed Mary two bags. "They'll last you at least till Thursday, and you'll be helping me stay in my size sixes through the summer."

"Mike?!" Busch's slurred voice echoed from some other room. Michael headed to the kitchen, leaving the two women by the door.

"Lunch Tuesday?" Jeannie asked.

"Ooh, doctor's appointment," Mary said. "Wednesday?"

"Mulligan's?"

"Twelve o'clock," they agreed simultaneously.

Busch, a little more than drunk, slumped over his kitchen counter and pulled out some papers. "Just need your Johnson Hancock-owitz."

Michael took the pen. "Thank for everything. It means a lot."

"You'd do the same for me." Busch nursed a Scotch.

"The kids don't know about me, I mean, do they?" Of all people, Michael would be devastated if Busch's children were to find out the truth.

"No way. And they never will."

Michael continued flipping the legal-looking pages, signing as he went, ignoring the document's content; he already knew its purpose. Coming to the last page he gathered them all up, stacked them neatly, and pushed them toward Busch. "Can I ask you something?"

"Anything," Bush said, pouring himself another drink.

Michael thought on this a moment. "Any others here tonight?"

"Man, I told you, I invited you here for you, not this." Busch pointed at the papers. "Our friendship isn't a ploy. It's usually the kiss of death but hey, what's life without risk? Pat Garrett was friends with Billy the Kid. Besides, who else would want to be your friend?" He emptied the entire glass of Scotch. "But I do have to be honest with you—you're cute, but I think Mary has a much more fantastically splendid derriere." Busch grinned and burped. Getting out of his chair, he threw his tree trunk of an arm around Michael and led him out of the kitchen.

Tomorrow, as he had done for the last twenty-four months, Busch will file the forms Michael has just signed: one copy for the courts, one copy for his commanding officer, and one copy for his files. They were official, the state emblem along the top. In big bold letters the heading read: *PAROLE BOARD STATE OF NEW YORK.*

Chapter 2

Michael dug through a desk in the repair area of his anally organized security-and-alarm shop. Safe and Sound was fastidiously arranged. Electronic components lined the Peg-Board wall; security monitors, switches, and control panels filled the shelves. Several empty desks lined the back wall—provisions for future success. For now, Michael was pretty much on his own. Out front was a state-of-the-art showroom, gadgets for every imaginable security need: miniature cameras, bulletproof vests, bugging devices, special watches, lie detectors, hidden safes. Most went unsold; it was really the security installation systems that drove his business, and that was where his talent lay. Michael felt at home here. It wasn't much, but he had built it from the ground up; while they still counted on Mary's weekly paycheck, he was determined that someday he would make enough money that she could stop working to raise a family.

Unbeknownst to Michael, a man stepped through the doorway. The newcomer was handsome, in his mid-sixties. His long white hair was pulled back in a ponytail; dark eyebrows framed his earthen-brown eyes. Wearing a long dark raincoat over a fine European suit, he smelled *rich*.

As Michael straightened, he caught sight of the man and nearly jumped out of his skin. "Jesus Christ!"

The man let out a soft laugh. "No." His voice had a hint of a German accent. "Hardly. But thank you for the comparison. I didn't mean to startle you." The stranger's warm smile exuded confidence and charm. He was definitely the charisma king.

"We're closed." There was an uncomfortable pause.

"I'm terribly sorry to bother you—"

Michael, searching the top drawer, pulled out a set of blueprints. "I'm in kind of a rush."

"I'll be brief." The stranger handed Michael a business card. "I think we could help each other." He walked about the office, looking, assessing. "I could help you solve your problems and you could help me solve mine."

"Problems? I'm sorry, Mr."—Michael glanced at the card— "Finster." He stuffed the card in his pocket. From a cabinet he grabbed an envelope marked *Proposal* and tossed it, along with the blueprints, in a briefcase. Clipping his keys on his belt, he looked directly at the man. "I don't have any problems," he said tersely and led the way out of his shop.

Michael set the alarm, pulled down the security cage, locked up tight, and started walking through the mini-mall parking lot. Finster fell in step beside him.

They were silent for about ten paces until, "I could compensate you very—"

Michael put up his hands and stopped. He knew exactly where this conversation was going. "What, did you read it in the paper? You some kind of groupie?" He shook his head. "I'm on to a different career now."

"Circumstances change," Finster suggested.

"Not mine." Michael couldn't be clearer on this point as he walked away.

"Call me if they do. That's all I ask." Finster watched Michael stride toward his car. Seeing Mary sitting in the front seat and watching their exchange, he smiled at her. "Please don't lose that card," he called cheerfully.

"Don't wait for my call," Michael shot back, not bothering to turn his head.

Mary looked at Michael and then curiously at Finster. She smiled and nodded at the white-haired stranger.

Finster returned the gesture as the St. Pierres drove off.

⌘

The door opened to a nice, modest apartment. Nothing fancy in this two-bedroom, but Mary had made it cozy and warm. The third floor of a middle-class apartment building suited them just fine. As Michael and Mary entered, a huge drooling Bernese Mountain Dog came galumphing into Michael's arms. "Hey, Hawk! Keep them bad guys out?" Michael collapsed to the floor, rolling around with the black, brown, and white dog, two kids at play, neither sure of who the master really was, neither really caring.

"I gotta walk him," Michael told his wife.

"Coming to bed?" she said hopefully.

"Little while. I just have some things to take care of." Michael didn't even look at his wife as he grabbed the leash off the foyer table.

"Not too late, OK?" But she knew her words were falling on deaf ears.

⌘

Michael was back in fifteen, the walk doing them both good.

"Michael?" Mary called from the bedroom.

"Yeah?"

No response.

"Mare?"

Michael stepped into the darkened room; he couldn't see his hand in front of his face. He looked around. It was too quiet. "Mary?" He tried the light switch—no good, the light must have blown. "Come on, Mare, quit screwing around."

He checked the bathroom, nothing. Tried the light switch one more time, still no good. "All right, this isn't funny."

The bedroom door slammed shut.

Michael reflexively crouched: if he wasn't on guard before, he was now. Instinct took over. It had been over five years, but the muscle memory was still there, his hyper-keen senses intact. He moved back one step and was immediately jumped. His heart leapt and he moved to strike but he instinctively pulled the punch. The figure spun him around, threw him on the bed, dove on top of him . . . And ripped open his shirt, the buttons flying everywhere.

Michael's shock was wearing off as Mary whispered, "You forgot to kiss me."

⌘

Mary, lying in a sea of pillows, the sheets in disarray, stroked her cat, CJ, as Michael pulled on a pair of shorts. It was the moment after, and you could see it in their eyes: despite the earlier tension, these two were still in love—as much as they had been six and a half years ago when they'd met.

She'd been twenty-four, just finishing her master's degree in education. She had been offered a teaching position at the upscale Wilby School in Greenwich, Connecticut, one of the finest elementary schools in the country. Although Michael was eight years her senior, from the moment they set eyes on each other, there were undeniable sparks.

It was a fluke meeting. Mary had backed her car into Michael's, and the fireworks instantly flew. It was passionate. However, it certainly was not romantic. They'd argued for twenty minutes about whose fault it was, trading verbal jabs and punches, both refusing to back down, neither willing to admit defeat. There really wasn't any damage to either car, but that wasn't the point. It was the principle. The funny thing was neither could remember fighting like that with anyone in twenty years. They were both known pacifists, the settlers of others' arguments. But not this day. This was war. Even the policeman who stopped by gave up after threatening them both with arrest. The cop was actually the first one to know it: these two people were made for each other. The fight was at a full-tilt pitch when out of exasperation Michael declared he would only give in under one condition. Of course, that sparked another argument, but after five minutes Mary surrendered. Dinner. Michael couldn't for the life of him imagine why he had asked, it was just one of those spur-of-the-moment impulses. And to this day, Mary couldn't imagine why she had said yes. No one had ever gotten her Irish up like this man.

After a two-month courtship, they eloped to the U.S. Virgin Islands where, barefoot in the sand with the sunset at their backs, they were married by a local priest. There was no need for flowers, friends, or the "Bridal March." As far as either of them was concerned it was the perfect ceremony, for they each had found their perfect match. The witnesses who stood in as matron of honor and best man were an eighty-year-old couple they had met on the flight down. Neither bridegroom nor bride had family they wanted to include in the celebration and the only one to express annoyance at the happy news was Jeannie Busch—Mary hadn't even introduced Michael to her until they returned with rings on their fingers. But after Jeannie popped off, flipped Mary the bird, and stormed out of the house, she returned with an armful of wedding gifts, a smile, and a big hug for Michael, welcoming him to their world.

They settled into Michael's summer house in Bedford, which Mary promptly transformed into a home. Accustomed to eating out for most of his life, Michael was initially uncomfortable without a dinner reservation, but that soon changed. Mary loved to cook. Michael was quickly spoiled by her culinary talent and soon had to add an additional mile to his daily runs to ward off the extra calories. And Mary discovered Michael's talent with his hands, immediately enlisting him in her never-ending remodeling schemes. He had a way of looking at problems—physical, mechanical, even emotional—and making them disappear. They looked at the world a bit differently than everyone else and because of that, they had an even greater appreciation for each other. While most people spent their dating years falling in love and then, once married, watched their love slowly decay, Michael and Mary turned the premise on its head: every day they discovered something new about each other. They not only fell deeper in love but they became even closer friends.

Chapter 3

It's silent. The air is musty and stale. Suddenly, a grate swings down from a ceiling, swaying on its hinges. A figure in black drops from the opening, landing panther-like on the floor of an old-world museum. Vast, stretching out for what seems like miles. High ceilings, marble floors, and columns as far as the eye can see. Room after room filled with paintings next to sculptures next to ancient artifacts. Every period from the early ascension of man to present-day computer art is represented; a time capsule of history itself. In daylight, this would be a magnificent palace to man's accomplishments, but daylight has long since passed. What little glow filters through the medieval-style windows creates a surreal effect, thrusting everything into shadow.

The figure in black moves with pure grace, down corridor after corridor. In his hand he twirls a knife, more out of nervous energy than deadly purpose. The carved ivory handle is wrapped in leather, its blade reflecting intermittent beams through the darkness. The figure clutches the knife as if it is a talisman warding off spirits or, at the very least, curious, unseen security guards.

He glides through the armor exhibit passing battlewear from every nation and from every time period. Each piece mounted in a fighting pose or upon horseback as if the souls of their owners never had the frame of mind to vacate and were still waiting for the order to be given. Past the Anasazi Indian display, fragile bones unearthed from cliff dwellings, small identification cards informing on the correct location of an ancient tibia or mandible. Egyptian sarcophagi line a wall; mummies lie in vacuum-sealed glass tombs awaiting an afterworld that has eluded them for three millennia, their golden jewelry, gifts to appease the gods, never delivered. Each artifact—armor, flesh, bone—the possession of someone long since dead, radiating an aura that seems to permeate the enormous rooms and long cold hallways. This is a celebration of the dead, of lives invaded, of eternal rest violated. These were items not meant to be disturbed yet they were pillaged, stolen, dug up for fortune, glory, or vanity. We can't help wondering what was dug up with them and brought to this museum, for although there is not a soul in sight, the sense of an angry presence is everywhere.

The figure pays no mind to the riches in his midst as he races up a grand staircase, across a balcony, to arrive finally at a circular room. In its center stands a large glass case. A single ray of light shines down on its contents. The figure cautiously approaches the case, circling it as if in reverence. He spins his knife in his palm, twirling it through his fingers. He waves his hands over the case as if stroking the air, testing its will. As he steps back, we finally see within. Resting upon midnight-blue velvet are diamonds. Old, stunning, priceless. Jewels for which love was promised, battles were fought, empires laid ruin. Undoubtedly the riches of a long-lost kingdom, for no individual could possibly have possessed diamonds of this size.

Again the figure moves toward the case, obscuring it. Motionless, he stands, his hands remaining at his sides, his breathing imperceptible. Waiting. Seconds, then minutes, tick by. He remains steadfast. The air still, dead. Silence permeates the halls. Finally he steps back, and . . .

The case is empty.

⌘

The figure effortlessly climbs a thin nylon rope back up through the grating into the air duct. It's a tight fit as he shimmies through the tin can, the dim light through the grates bathing him in an eerie glow. If the halls below seemed endless, these ducts are downright interminable. But he is comforted by the fact that the difficult part is behind him; he can now breathe a little easier, for his prize is safely tucked into his pouch.

Suddenly, there is a noise somewhere behind him. It's distant but it's approaching. His confines are tight, he can't turn to see what is back there, so he continues on through the duct . . . a little quicker. It's probably just the expansion and contraction of the tin duct as it cools after a hard day's work, he reasons. Nothing to be concerned about, his mind settles down, he'll be home soon.

Again, he hears the sound. This time louder, definitely closer, and it's not the contraction of the duct. It's not a sound you would expect to hear in an air-conditioning shaft, nor is it a sound you would expect to hear in a vacant museum. It continues to move closer. No, it's definitely not a man-made sound, it's animal-like, guttural, vicious. His heart starts to pound in his ears, a cold sweat creeps up his spine as he quickens his pace. The sound continues its approach, rumbling louder like a distant storm. He can now feel the mass of his pursuer pounding in the shaft, its weight flexing the tin. By the sheer volume, he knows: whatever's coming, it's huge.

Every contingency was planned for: the guards, the alarms, the lights; every foreseeable variable anticipated. Timing was laid out to the second: even in the event of little glitches, this was to be a job by the book—and he wrote the book.

The deep growling grows more distinct: it's not far off now. Whatever it is, it is moving faster, breathing hard, its weight thundering the metal; it's beyond deafening. The whole building feels like it's shaking.

It's a race against hope through a cacophony of ear-shattering sounds. Passing over another grate, Michael's face finally catches the light. His eyes focused and determined, sweat pouring down his brow. He's flying through the air duct now like a gerbil in a Habitrail. His flight would almost be comical to an outside observer but there is nothing comical about impending death. This isn't about the jewels, and it's not the latest gadget against crime. Whatever is in this duct with Michael shouldn't be here, it shouldn't be anywhere.

Wishing he could just pick up and run, Michael grows more scared and frustrated, his muscles aching as his sweaty palms slip on the two-foot wide surface. The pain is crippling his joints and muscles; his eardrums are ready to burst from the train-like roar of the approaching beast. It's like being trapped within a drum, with a musician relentlessly pounding out a death march.

And then there is nothing. Pure silence. He stops. Listens. Nothing. His mind racing, wondering if his pursuer is coiling up, waiting to spring its attack—or did the creature miraculously fall through one of the grates? His ears strain; he thought the noise was bad, but the silence is excruciating, leaving a question mark on the next few moments of his life. Claustrophobia sets in. Fear locks up his body. Maybe the beast has lost his scent, his direction. A single breath could tip it off. What is it, where is it, how can he possibly defend himself in this cramped box? His thoughts whirl back to Mr. Buffington's biology class, fight or flee, survival of the fittest.

He takes off. Never did he think his body could move this fast. Desperate, all his efforts going into escape, into survival. Better to die from a heart attack than in the jaws of his pursuer. Oblivious of his bloodied hands, his bruised legs, he would welcome a year of pain if he could get out of this duct, out of this building.

And now with a vengeance the sound returns, roaring down the shaft, growling, throbbing, the mass of its approaching body forcing a clammy death-like gale to rush past Michael. Worst of all, Michael can now smell it. Vile, putrid, like rotting flesh, it violates his senses. His eyes water from its stench.

Then he sees salvation, up ahead, fifty yards: hope. The proverbial light at the end of the tunnel: the shaft exit. With every resource he can muster he hurls his body toward the light. Twenty-five yards. Soon relief will be in his grasp and as if sensing this, the ugly sound of the beast stops completely, like it was never there at all. The sound, the smell—all vanish into the ether.

Twenty yards from freedom, Michael stops: the beast is gone. It's the light. Slithering back to its shadow world, away from the light, that's the only explanation. But before that sigh of relief comes, the light up ahead is obscured. Michael's racing heart stops as he realizes: There is more than one. Now, in front of him, a pair of predatory eyes glow. Feral eyes, the eyes of something utterly evil. They narrow as if contemplating an attack.

And once again, from behind, he hears the growl of his pursuer, its foul breath heavy upon him. He is frozen, unable to turn, unable to see behind him or in front of him. He's trapped. The moment hangs over him, his heart has surely stopped, his mind is numb. His attackers wait, invisible yet there. Their breathing: heavy with anticipation. The stench overwhelming, turning his stomach. He is on the verge of passing out or maybe it is death that he is feeling, his body's response to pending doom.

The breathing stops; could they have changed their minds and fled? But the odor of death is still there, all around in the darkness. The waiting tortures his very soul.

Then in a flash, whatever is behind him grabs his foot and jerks his body backward. Michael is paralyzed with fear, a scream that will never come caught in his throat. And then swifter than anything humanly possible, he is silently ripped backward at an appalling rate. Back through the duct, back into the blackness.

⌘

Mary bolted upright in the bed, struggling to breathe. She looked for Michael. He wasn't there. In fact, he hadn't been in bed since they'd made love. Her heart hammered, her worst fears seeming to lurk in the deep shadows. CJ was spooked, arching upward, hissing at Mary as if at a stranger. Mary flew from the bed, not bothering with a gown. She raced out of the bedroom, into the living room: empty. To the kitchen, a half-eaten sandwich on the counter, then through the hall, no sign of Michael. She saw the closed den door, light streaming from under the doorway. She grabbed the handle, praying to herself, *Please, not again,* and barged into the den.

Michael was working at his desk, Hawk, asleep at his feet. Startled, he spun around.

Mary stood there staring at him, her eyes begging the question. Then she collapsed in his arms, panting but relieved. The tears flowed.

It was just a dream.

"Honey . . . ?"

"Promise me something, Michael?"

Michael held her tight. "Anything."

"That you'll never go back, that it's all in the past . . ."

Michael looked her in the eye and spoke to her heart. "I promised you two years ago, never again . . . I swear to you, Mare, never again."

Chapter 4

Noise. Lots of it. All walks of life in and out of the main precinct of the Byram Hills Police Department. Built in the twenties, this precinct had seen the city grow twentyfold; the force once numbered five, but last year they broke the hundred-man barrier. Drunk and disorderly used to be the arrest of the week and it was always on pay day. Now, well, it's the new millennium and each cop would give his left testicle to avoid another homicide.

Cops coming and going like the wind this morning, the occasional criminal being marched through to booking and then on to the basement holding cells. The young patrolmen in their blues congregate at the worn marble stairs sipping coffee, munching bagels before their morning tours of duty.

The detective area on the second floor is one step above uninhabitable, fifteen desks crammed into a five-desk room. Paul Busch, in a rumpled sport coat and jeans, was filling out paperwork at his desk. It was organized mayhem, files upon files upon files all ready to tip into confusion. His first soda of the day was halfway gone. Busch prided himself on his lack of addiction to coffee and donuts. Of course, his daily Coke-and-Oreo breakfast didn't make him a candidate for any National Institutes of Health awards. Fifteen years he's been here, five as detective. He used to hate the job but now he has settled into going through the motions, biding his time until March 18, five years from now, pension time. He came in like all the guys, young and eager, ready to clean up the town, bring justice to the people of this fair city. But the crimes wear you down. No matter how much you do, there will always be another skank waiting in the wings to victimize someone else. What really made Busch sick, though, was the number of convictions. As a young idealist, he always believed an arrest would lead to a conviction and remove the scum from the world, but half of them walked and all too soon would be practicing their trade all over again. And while his attitude changed along with his outlook on life, his code never did. He always thought of himself as an unwavering enforcer of the law, a tool of the justice system. His job was to gather the evidence and catch the criminal: what happened afterward was someone else's job. He never once was compromised, his values and his approach to the law could not be purchased, could not be deterred.

One time his wife was racing their son, Robbie, to the hospital, the boy's arm fractured while skateboarding, and she was pulled over. The officer was a cocky son of a bitch out to make his monthly quota and he wasn't giving an inch, even after seeing the child's pain. The ticket was for doing sixty in a thirty zone, the two-pointer, five-hundred-dollar kind. All the begging in the world wouldn't change that cop's mind; he didn't even offer to help them to the hospital. Jeannie requested, then recommended, then demanded that Paul take care of it; bury the ticket, work some magic with his police brethren. But Busch would have nothing to do with it; even though the ticket would double their insurance rates, he flat out refused. "The law is the law," he kept saying. Jeannie didn't forgive him for two weeks, refused to have sex with him for a month. She told him, "You got laws? So do I."

Next to Busch's desk sat Johnny Prefi. An unlit Marlboro hung from his mouth. His black spiky hair stood straight up—not from hair gel but from a four-week lack of soap and water. His sleeveless T-shirt read, *Fuck you. Keep staring and I'll kill you. Have a nice day.*

It was easy to understand why he was wearing handcuffs.

"Johnny, seeing as how you're an arsonist on parole, anything more than a barbecue is a parole violation," Busch said.

Johnny just stared back at Busch as if he didn't comprehend the English language.

"And torching a warehouse for someone is a little more than a seaside cookout."

"Hey, nobody got hurt," Johnny said with a sincere snarl.

"Hey, you're missing the point. Fire—"

"Scared of the flame, huh?" Johnny taunted him; he'd hit a nerve.

"If I liked fire"—Busch was beyond pissed—"I would have been a fireman." He went back to his paperwork.

Johnny was thinking; a wicked little smile creased his face as he tilted up the unlit cigarette pinched between his lips. "Got a light?"

Busch stared in disbelief.

Captain Robert Delia, Busch's by-the-book boss, interrupted before the big cop could explode. "Paulie, say hello to Dennis Thal. Thal's gonna be tagging you."

Busch rose to greet a mildly handsome man of thirty. Light brown hair receding just a bit. Nice suit, firm handshake. Thal's body language screamed arrogant enthusiasm—shoulders back, left hand in his pocket, head tilted just a bit to the side.

"Glad to meet you."

"Glad to be here." Thal's voice was smooth, subtle, just above a hushed tone.

"No offense," Busch said to Thal as he turned to Delia. "But I don't have time to play nursemaid, Captain."

Delia may have been half a foot shorter than Busch, but in his mind, the captain could crush this man under his boot and had no problem reestablishing the chain of command. "Listen to me, Paulie, *Detective* Thal's got nine years under his belt. He's on loan from *State* to help us cover our staff problems. They wanted him to work the rounds with our best but they are all on vacation so he's stuck with you. *Capisce?*"

Busch knew when to fight and when to stand down. He nodded.

"In addition to his detective responsibilities, Paul here handles our parole program on behalf of the courts," the captain continued.

Busch looked at Thal, decided babysitting him was a discussion for another day, and took on a serious, Walter Cronkite air. "I'm sure the captain told you about our wonderful working environment. Some call it Oz—I call it Eden and all the parolees we deal with are one hundred percent reformed."

Delia grunted, turned to Thal, and led him away. "Let me show you your desk before he poisons you on the whole law enforcement profession."

"See you around," Busch called out, not particularly liking his boss today.

Thal turned and with a finger point and a wink said, "You will."

Busch turned away, and said quietly to no one in particular: "Dweeb."

⌘

Mary was the teacher you always wanted. In a blue train-engineer's cap, she led a conga line of five-year-olds around the classroom, all rapping military style at the top of their little lungs.

"When you ride our choo choo, one plus one is always two. Our engine makes a mighty roar, two plus two is always four. To the station we are never late, four plus four is always eight."

Her classroom was a superbly organized child's dream, with lots of toys and learning stations. Since being hired two months ago to fill the position of a teacher who'd never returned from maternity leave,

Mary had won not only the respect of her fellow teachers but the love and admiration of the children. They adored her.

She was offered the kindergarten class, her favorite grade, young minds like unformed clay, young hearts still pure. Greenwich Country Day paid slightly better than Wilby but it was the allure of these five-year-olds that captured her. She had been teaching fifth grade, children on the verge of junior high; she loved them but felt she could contribute more if given the opportunity to provide a foundation early on. She couldn't deny herself; their innocence was closer to her optimistic view of life.

Quietly, the principal, Liz Harvey, her gray hair swept up in a bun, stepped into the room smiling at the shouting children. Instantly, the classroom fell silent. Liz handed a piece of paper to Mary. Mary glanced at it, her face hard to read.

"Everything all right?" Liz put her hand on Mary's shoulder.

"Fine." Mary smiled back, still looking at the message from her doctor.

"Good news, I hope. This classroom has a way of enhancing one's fertility." Liz was already thinking about where she would find another replacement. This would make the fifth kindergarten teacher in three years to go out on maternity leave and find the joys of motherhood too compelling to return to work. "If your husband isn't around I'd be happy to drive you."

"Don't be silly. You sure you don't mind covering for me?"

"Not at all."

⌘

Michael stood behind the counter of Safe & Sound, smiling as he stared at a small handwritten note. It simply read: *Hi, sexy*. Mary had stuck it in the pocket of the blue sport jacket she wore the other night, the same jacket he was wearing now. She continually played this game with him, leaving notes and little presents in the pockets for Michael to find when he finally got the clothing back. It was a silly thing but he loved her all the more for it.

"Did you hear what I said?" A gruff elderly man by the name of Rosenfield was chastising him as the man's beautiful trophy bride stood several subservient steps behind him. "I just want it fixed." Rosenfield's slow-play security VCR sat on the counter for the second time in two weeks.

"I'll fix it."

The wife, unbeknownst to her husband, was seductively looking at Michael. Michael tried hard as hell not to notice but was sucked in. She was too gorgeous and her smile too bright. He subtly scratched his nose with his wedding-ring finger, in the hope she would get the message. But she simply smiled and raised her two-carat diamond in response.

"My home's security is crucial. The installation work was fine but this equipment . . . your choice of suppliers leaves something to be desired—" Rosenfield saw where Michael's attention was focused. "You're not even listening to me."

"Sorry, Mr. Rosenfield." Michael snapped back to attention. "I said I'd make it right and I will."

"I want action, not words." Rosenfield paused and finally softened. "I like you, Michael. But maybe you should consider another field."

"Nah, I like this one. I'm good at it."

Rosenfield didn't seem to believe it. "Do you have any other skills?"

"Nothing legal." Michael grinned.

"Nothing legal?" Rosenfield headed for the door, laughing. "I like that. I expect the VCR back by the weekend." He hooked arms with his wife and continued out the door, chuckling. "Nothing legal."

His beautiful wife looked over her shoulder at Michael with a smile. Michael couldn't help smiling back; it was any man's reaction to flirtation.

Mary, still wearing the train-engineer's cap, walked in the shop, brushing by the exiting Rosenfields.

"Loyal customer?" she teased.

"Huh? No, no. Disgruntled, maybe a little horny."

Mary wrapped her arms around him. "What if I said I was a disgruntled, horny customer?"

"Then I'd have to check out your entire system," Michael was choosing his words slowly, carefully, "strip it down, examine everything, use only the finest tools. But most important, make sure you're completely satisfied when you leave so you become a repeat customer."

"Can I keep my hat on?"

"We'll see." Michael kissed his wife deeply, completely seduced. Jealousy was obviously not a factor in their relationship. As the kiss dissolved, something occurred to him. He glanced at his watch. "Shouldn't you be at school?"

⌘

Michael sped through the center of the city, white-knuckling the wheel. His mind was racing as fast as the car. Mary sat next to him, her hands folded calmly in her lap.

"How could you hide this from me?"

"I wasn't hiding anything from you, Michael. I just didn't want you to worry."

"What did they say?"

"They want to see me about my tests."

"And that's *nothing*? What kind of tests?"

Mary could hear the fear in Michael's voice as she stared out the window.

"Mary, what kind?"

She took a breath. "Ovarian."

Michael gripped the wheel even tighter as he struggled to breathe. He couldn't turn his head toward her, afraid that doing so would somehow make this nightmare come true.

"I'm sure it's nothing, honey. Hey, it's not like I'm dying—"

"Did the doctor say that? I can't believe you had these tests and didn't tell me."

Mary remained calm, always the optimist; everything would be all right, she was certain of it, it was her mantra. "Hey, look at me." She touched his face gently. "I'm not going anywhere, Michael. We're just getting our lives back on track. If I'm not worried . . ."

"I think we can treat it," the doctor said.

Michael kept rubbing Mary's back, as much an effort to calm himself as to calm her. Dr. Rhineheart took on a fatherly tone. "We're going to treat it. We've a very high success rate and your condition doesn't seem to have spread beyond the ovaries."

They were sitting in a typical, sterile doctor's office, oak desk, two guest chairs, a two-picture frame containing images of his middle-aged wife and two kids. Dr. Phillip Rhineheart, forty-five, balding and gray at the temples, stood leaning back on the front of his desk. He always found it too formal to sit behind it and discuss people's lives as if they were just business. Michael and Mary St. Pierre were trying to be stoic for each other but Rhineheart saw through them. The doctor had seen it too many times: the hideous disease that eats away not only the human being but the human soul, wreaking havoc, infecting all the loved ones with a sheer sense of dread. "I know this is hard—"

"What about children?" Mary's voice was distant.

Rhineheart shook his head. "Both ovaries are invaded." He took a deep breath. "We're going to have to remove them." This was the worst part of his job and it had caused him many a sleepless night. "I'm sorry."

Mary placed her hand upon her husband's as he continued to rub her shoulder. Both of them strained to avoid eye contact, for to look at each other would surely shatter what little composure they had remaining.

"This treatment—how much does the—what does it . . ." Michael couldn't finish the question.

"You can relax about that. It's covered by insurance."

"How much?" Michael pressed, afraid of the answer.

"Mary's cancer is in an advanced state. It could cost upward of two hundred fifty thousand, depending on the regime we prescribe. Relax. It's nothing experimental. Insurance covers all the phases." Rhineheart paused to emphasize his confidence. "And I assure you our cancer facility is the finest."

The small room was closing in on him. In all his life Michael had never felt more powerless, more inferior than right now. He felt like the reluctant executioner at the switch, powerless to save the life before him. "We don't have insurance," he said, as if decreeing a death sentence.

This was happening too often, people living unprepared. Rhineheart was one of the few doctors who pressed for mandatory governmental coverage of all U.S. citizens, but that was just a dream. Not enough profit to make it "worthwhile." He turned to Mary. "What about the school? They should have an excellent insurance program."

"I've only been there two months. It's ninety days before you're eligible," Mary replied. The hope had slipped from her eyes.

"I see." Rhineheart exhaled slowly. He'd donate his services but the surgery costs, hospitalization, the radiation and chemo—the hospital wasn't a charity. Medicine was a for-profit business, the hospital had budgets to meet, shareholders to satisfy. Medicine was no longer about the patient; rate of return was the goal of medical care. He suddenly hated his job.

Finally, he stood up and said in a confident tone, "Well, I've got to get you started on some blood work, Mary, so we can design a treatment program. Michael, why don't you speak to your bank? I'd be happy to help you with the paperwork—I'm sure you can work something out."

Michael sat there, stunned.

Chapter 5

Michael emerged from the brass revolving door into the First Bank of Byram Hills' enormous rotunda and felt instantly dwarfed by its grand marble pillars and vast cavernous space. Businesspeople rushed by on all sides as he stood there in his only suit, feeling way out of his element. He was five minutes late for his appointment and made to wait twice as long before the bank officer grimly gestured him into a chair.

Kerry Seitz, a tight-jawed VP of the bank impeccably clad in a three-piece suit, scrutinized Michael's file. Seitz's face was impossible to read as he absorbed the material. Not a sound passed his lips for fifteen minutes as he picked through Michael's life from various sources: credit agencies, DMV, the state and federal court systems. Michael felt like a child in the oversized chair, trying to fit in, trying not to look desperate.

Finally, Seitz looked up. He ran his hand through his perfect hair and in the coldest tone Michael had ever heard said, "No. I'm sorry."

"What?"

"We can't help you." Seitz tossed the application in his out-box.

"You haven't asked me a single question."

"I've read your application. We would need to secure the loan with an asset." He had already put Michael's request behind him, busying himself with another document.

"My business is my asset," Michael protested, seeing through to the man's fearful stereotyping soul.

"Your background"—the words came icily—"for lack of a better word, Mr. St. Pierre, makes this impossible."

"I know I've made some mistakes."

"Yes."

"But you didn't have a problem when I opened my business account here."

"Holding your money and loaning you money are two entirely different things."

Michael jumped out of his chair, barely containing himself from flying across the desk at this man's throat. "I'll go to another bank."

"I'll save you the time," Seitz said, rising. The bank security guards were taking notice, edging closer. "Nobody is going to loan you a nickel. You're a convicted felon with a worthless business and no credit history. You're a risk that no one will take."

"You son of a bitch, my wife is dying!"

"I'm sorry, but that is a burden you will have to shoulder on your own. Good day." The guards arrived, flanking Michael. Without another word, he stormed out.

⌘

An obscenely white room. It's remarkable that in this day and age, with everyone running around talking about bedside manner, hospitals have stuck with antiseptic harsh white. All the studies about how blues and yellows relax the mind were apparently lost on the medical world. "Impersonal" was the operative word here, a cold approach to treatments, attitudes, and architectural design.

Mary and Michael were eating one of those hospital meals: pot roast in watery brown gravy, soggy beans spilling into the mashed potatoes that were thicker than mortar, and a slice of pear of unidentifiable color. The meal was the obvious explanation for the assortment of chips and cookies strewn along the bed. Mary was propped up, tubes running in and out of her body from the most uncomfortable places. Michael had pulled up a chair, using her bed as a table.

"Can I get you anything?"

"I'm OK. How was work?"

"Fine." He hadn't been to work in three days.

He reached over, scooped up some mashed potatoes, and inhaled them. "These aren't bad." An uncomfortable silence filled the room. Michael looked at Mary lying there in that skimpy white hospital gown with the embarrassing slit up the back and realized he'd give his soul to trade places with her.

"I'm sorry," she murmured.

"Don't be silly. There's nothing to be sorry about, you didn't cause this." Michael's mind couldn't seem to shake the thought that this terrible trial was a punishment for his past deeds.

"How are we going to pay for this?" she asked softly, knowing the pressure that just asking it put on Michael.

"Don't worry."

"Our savings are almost tapped out." Mary struggled to hide the desperation in her voice as she nervously fingered the gold cross hanging from her neck. It was a habit she had developed in her teens: whenever her stress level rose, her fingers would run to the little cross seeking comfort and protection, like it was some all-powerful amulet. Over the years the gesture had become an unconscious reaction and Michael was sure she was unaware of it even now. She'd had the cross since her First Holy Communion, a gift from a beloved uncle. She rarely took it off. It always bothered Michael when they were making love and she was on top, the moonlight catching it as it dangled from her throat. He found the cross as intrusive as if someone was spying on their intimate moments. Although Mary insisted that it had always protected her, Michael's doubt of that was surely confirmed by her current diagnosis.

"You just focus on getting better, Mare. I can finance it, not a problem." His stomach was in knots. Through all the years they had been together, through thick and thin and most particularly through his arrest and jail time, he had never lied to her, ever. Maybe a little fib here and there—*I love your haircut; I'd love to see that movie; she's not prettier than you*—but not direct, deceiving lies. Now, within two minutes, he had laid three at her feet.

"Michael?" Mary managed that smile that always warmed his soul.

"Hmmm?"

"We're going to be fine." And while she sincerely meant this, Michael couldn't shake the fear that the worst was yet to come.

⌘

Michael was trying to get comfortable in the most uncomfortable chair he had ever been in. Mary was tubed and wired from head to toe, restlessly asleep. Varrisa Schrier was the night-duty nurse and chief of the nursing staff, ruling her people with a strict German discipline. To say Varrisa was big-boned was being kind; her ample body strained her white uniform. And her face . . . Well, her visage was just about as harsh as her big hands. But her nature was far from strict, for compassion ran deep in her. She was always assigned the tougher cases.

"Mr. St. Pierre?" He could hear the concern in the nurse's voice as she poked her head in the room. "Go home, get some sleep, you need your rest just as much as your wife."

"I don't think I'll be sleeping for a while."

Varrisa nodded and stepped inside. Quietly, she went about cleaning up the magazines and newspapers, discarding the empty food bags and generally returning a sense of order and normalcy to the place. Michael looked at Mary and wished the industrious nurse could restore his wife's health as easily.

"Let's see what happens." Varrisa put her man-sized hand on his arm. "You're no good to her if you're not one hundred percent."

"Yeah, well, I don't think I've ever been one hundred percent for her."

"Now would be a good time to start," Nurse Schrier said matter-of-factly. She picked up Mary's chart and quietly made some notations. "You can't blame yourself for her condition. I've seen this too many times. Loved ones look for a reason for these tragic situations, and when they can't find anything logical, they turn to the illogical and blame themselves."

The large nurse knew too well that the immediate family needed as much support as the patient. She had spoken at length to Mary about Michael. Both women shared the same concern; he needed a friend, a confidant, someone other than his wife with whom he could share his thoughts and, more important, share his grief. With Mary's permission, the nurse had made the call an hour ago.

Silently, the door swung open. Standing there, taking up the entire doorway, was Busch.

⌘

Busch was shooting a lone game of pool on his favorite table, the green felt stinking of whiskey and practically worn through to the underlying slate. He sank almost everything he touched. One of the grimiest bars in North America, the Old Stand dated back to the fifties. Busch's father used to hang here shooting on this very same table. The place was alive at eleven thirty on a Wednesday night: a few blue-collar regulars arguing the pros and cons of unions and what they had done to their lives, while the jacket-and-tie bunch scoped the door for the girl of their dreams to walk in.

"Another drink?" Busch asked.

Michael, impassively throwing darts, didn't answer; he hadn't answered much lately. Busch waved to the bartender for another round. He had spent the car ride over and the last half hour trying to crack through, to get Michael to talk. He had seen firsthand what pressure did to cops, to criminals, to people in pain. They either exploded, hurting others, or shut down, killing themselves. But he knew, too, that until a person was willing to accept help, there was not much he could do.

"Life sometimes just sucks out loud," Michael finally said.

Busch lined up and sunk the two ball, clearing the table. "She'll pull through this. She's tough." He walked across the sticky barroom floor, reminding him of hot tar in summer, grabbed the triangle, and reracked the billiard balls.

Michael hurled a dart. "Two hundred and fifty thou. That's more money than I've ever had. Hell, I never even got away with stealing that much."

Busch ignored the comment. "How could you guys not have insurance?" he asked instead.

"We thought it would only be for three months. When Mary left her last job, the insurance didn't carry and we had to wait ninety days before it kicked in at her new school. The state made her old job offer Cobra coverage but we had to pay for it. It was too expensive. We didn't think much about it."

Busch understood; clarity always came after the fact.

"It was only going to be three months," Michael repeated. The barmaid set down Busch's Coke and Michael's Jack Daniel's and left.

"I got about thirty-five thousand dollars," the big cop offered.

"Thanks, but I couldn't take your money."

"It's not for you, it's for Mary, and you'll take it." Busch stopped his game and leaned back on the pool table. "Damn, though, thirty-five k is still a long way from covering your nut. You've got to be able to get something against your business."

Michael shook his head. "The banking community wasn't real helpful."

"Any family? There's got to be someone."

"Mary's mom was broke until the day she died. And my folks left me nothing."

"Did you ever think of looking for your real parents?"

"While Michael's last name was French in origin, it wasn't the name he was born with. All he knew of his real parents was that they were three-quarters Irish and, for some unknown reason, dumped him in an orphanage when he was barely a month old. Michael never went down the self-pity route of seeking out his birth parents. The way he looked at it, he considered himself lucky: the St. Pierres had chosen to adopt him instead of some other child.

"A little late for that," Michael answered. "I wouldn't know where to begin."

A couple of after-work softball players got rowdy celebrating a win, their whooping and hollering competing with the rock-and-roll jukebox. Busch was draining balls left and right, the cue ball always in place for the follow-up. He lined up the seven ball with the corner pocket, drew back his cue, and suddenly spun around to Michael. "Shit! You're not thinking what I think you're thinking?"

"I gave my word to Mary," Michael answered. Returning to a life of crime had definitely crossed his mind, but he would never break his word to his wife. "If I can't raise this money . . ." His eyes were grim.

"Hey, quit talking shit. There's always a way."

"Isn't fair," Michael said.

"Nothing is. God didn't create this world to be fair."

"I'm not really buying into the God thing anymore."

"I wouldn't let Mary hear you talking like that."

"Look, I did some things, paid the price, never complained." He was throwing the darts harder now. "But Mary—she's never wronged a soul. She's the essence of good. After everything I put her through— You know she never misses church? I can't believe there's a god that would let this happen to her."

"You're just looking for someone to blame." Busch ignored the fact that every dart Michael threw nailed a bull's-eye. "And hey, I can't say I'd be any different if I was in your shoes."

"I'm serious, Paulie. I see no evidence God exists. Explain Mary's illness. And don't give me any of that test-of-faith crap. My faith has been tested enough and every time it comes up empty. Mary has nothing but faith and look where she is."

Busch sat on the pool table. "We all need something to believe in. Doesn't matter what. God, Buddha, Elvis. We all need faith. That's what gives us hope, hope that there's something better out there, something to strive for. Hope is what drives you. Hope gets you out of bed, hoping you're going to make that big sale at work, hoping you get to make love to your wife at night."

"You can't get by on hope. It doesn't pay the bills and it doesn't save lives."

"You need hope and a simple code. A creed that guides you, compels you to go on. Mine's the law." Busch threw back the rest of his Coke.

Michael smiled, turned, and raised his glass. "Truth, justice, and the American way. Right on, Superman."

"Thanks, Lois." Busch forced a smile. He wasn't getting through. "How about you, what drives you?"

Michael paused a moment and then simply said, "Mary."

Before dawn, Byram Hills Memorial Hospital was a different world, no outsiders to deal with, no phony smiles or sympathy to help the confused and grieving. Visiting hours didn't start until nine a.m. The medical machine of nurses and doctors prepared for the coming day's business, scurrying about, filling out forms, prepping for surgery.

Like a ghost, Michael glided down the hall in the same clothes he'd left in, five hours earlier. He knew he shouldn't be there, but it was hard for him to stay away. Besides, a little sneaking around always seemed to get his blood flowing. A file tucked under one arm, a big shopping bag in the other, he snuck along the corridor, quickly ducking in a doorway to avoid the notice of a passing nurse.

Mary was scheduled for another battery of tests this morning and Michael wanted to see her before they whisked her away. The bills for the testing alone had swiftly drained what little funds they possessed. If he didn't come up with the money for her surgery and treatment soon, the hospital would discharge her to make room for someone else, and what little chance Mary had would surely evaporate.

Michael slipped silently through the door into Mary's room, careful not to make any noise. She looked so tired, sitting at the little table next to her bed. She was always an early riser, up before the sun, she'd say, when the world was fresh and new. Her auburn hair was perfect, as if they were going to a royal ball, but then again it was invariably that way no matter the hour. Mary had always taken care of herself, not out of vanity but for her husband. Whether it was staying fit, doing her hair, or fighting the desire to wear grungy sweats, Mary strove to remain pleasing to her husband's eye at all times.

Michael stooped to gently kiss her cheek. "Good morning."

"Hi," she answered warmly, kissing him back.

"How was breakfast?"

"I think it was reheated meat loaf in the shape of waffles."

Michael couldn't help smiling.

"Sleep OK?" she asked him.

"Bed's too big without you." He unloaded the bag: makeup; fresh clothes; bath towels, soft ones instead of the white sandpaper hospital standard. He pulled out her favorite book, *Oh, the Places You'll Go!* by Dr. Seuss.

"You are so good to me. I was reading this to my students before I left."

"I know." Michael pulled out a tape recorder and placed it on the table. "They would like you to finish it. Record at your leisure. Liz said she'd pick it up and play it for them."

"This was your idea, wasn't it?" she said, with a tear in her eye.

Michael said nothing, but smiled as he continued emptying the apparently bottomless bag. Last but not least, he pulled out the goodies: cookies, soda, Ring Dings.

"Are you trying to fatten me up? I'll never eat all that junk."

"Actually, it's for me." Michael gave her a sly look. He pulled out a file marked *School Work* and offered it to her.

Mary took the file and stared down at it, wishing she were in class with her children. A chill came over her as she looked at the dozens of pictures sent by her students; she was so afraid she'd never see them again. "I was thinking—now, don't get upset, it's really just a precaution . . ." She paused. "Maybe I should get my affairs in order."

Michael pulled a chair over to the bedside and sat down. "What?"

"I'm sorry, it's just that—"

"No! I don't want to hear that. We're going to get through this."

"I know, I know." She took his hand in hers. "I'm sorry. It's just so much money. . . ."

"Don't say that again. St. Pierres never give up." Michael was doing everything in his power to keep from losing control. "Never."

There was a quiet knock at the door and Father Shaunessy popped his head in. "Mike, Mary—is this a bad time?"

Michael glared at the priest. His timing couldn't have been worse.

"Could you come back in a half hour, Father?" Mary asked.

"Sure, sure." The priest nodded as he closed the door behind him.

"Why is he here?" Michael's anger was spilling over the surface.

"I thought—" But Mary didn't get the chance to finish her statement.

Michael stood abruptly. "Thought nothing. Don't even tell me you were doing the last rites thing."

"Michael, you're jumping to conclusions. I asked him here to talk and pray," Mary's voice was tight. She was now equally upset, but unlike Michael, she reined in her anger.

He paced the small room. "Pray? Do you really believe that if He was merciful He'd let this happen to you?"

Mary took a moment. She never thought she would have to defend herself, let alone her beliefs, to the person she loved more than life itself. Her anger dissipated as she answered quietly, "Michael, you have to understand something. There are two things I have always counted on to get me through hard times: you, and my faith in God. And right now, darling, I need both."

⌘

The hospital was abuzz with activity as Michael left his wife's room. On a crowded bench in the corridor among a cluster of older ladies sat Father Shaunessy. The women were chatting about forgiveness as he thumbed his rosary beads: they were almost worn down to the nub. Michael ignored him and continued down the hall.

"Mike?" the priest called out.

Michael stopped and turned; not a word escaped his lips.

"How are you?" Father Shaunessy asked.

"My wife is dying."

"You should have more faith, Mike, that is far from a certain conclusion. Come inside, we can talk. Pray with us." The priest waved a hand toward Mary's hospital room door as if showing the way to redemption.

Michael exploded.

"You got to be fuckin' kidding me! I've prayed nothing but unanswered prayers since I was a child. Spent more Sundays than I can count looking for answers and I got nothing but betrayal. And now, my poor wife . . . She put her faith in God—look where she is."

"Well, you're certainly not the answer. While you sat in prison, she waited for you. You wrecked her life and yet she always stood by you, always had faith in you. God knows what she sees in you." The little priest was shaking with anger. "Maybe you should stop being so damned selfish for once and stand by her. Help her, instead of feeling so damn sorry for yourself." The small man stepped into Michael's space. If he hadn't had his collar on, he would have reverted back to his days on the streets and slammed Michael in the jaw.

"Sorry for myself?!" Michael shouted back. "The only person I feel sorry for is you and your misguided beliefs. You're leading my wife down a path where hope doesn't even exist." He turned and stalked away.

The rage Father Patrick Shaunessy felt was like nothing he had ever experienced before. And yet he couldn't help feeling that he was watching Michael's soul slip away down the cold white hospital hallway.

⌘

Michael slammed out of the hospital, his brain a jumble, his hope falling away. He had always been a problem solver, a fixer, and not just of mechanical objects. He was superb at seeing things from a different perspective, stepping out of the box and coming up with solutions. The talent had saved him on more than one occasion and served his former career well.

That career was not something he had aspired to, desperation had not driven him to be a thief nor had a lack of abilities in more legal arenas. It was something discovered through a selfless act to help a friend.

At the age of seventeen, while Michael was still looking for his purpose in life, his best friend, Joe McQuarry, had already found his. Joe was the one with the natural athletic ability; the one with the scholarship and early acceptance to college to play baseball. Joe found his talents young and knew how to exploit them. Humor and sports. The sports got him popularity and girlfriends while his humor brought him charm and trouble. Joe was the good-natured kid who could never seem to get out of his own way. His idea of fun usually consisted of pranks and laughter at the teacher's expense. Because of it he had his own seat at Holy Father High School; it was reserved especially for him in the principal's office.

It so happened on one Friday, Joe found himself in his special seat while the principal, Father Daniels, lectured him on the downfall of society as a result of the lack of respect. Father Daniels detailed how Joe's life, while all rosy with his sports scholarship, could easily turn on a dime and evaporate. The principal's limit had been reached. Joe's two suspensions had left Daniels with no choice but to expel him for another incident. Daniels tried to put it into terms that Joe could relate to: one more strike and the teenager was out. And if Joe thought he was so brilliant, so much smarter than everyone else, he should just test him. Daniels proclaimed a week's detention and told Joe not to move until he returned.

Joe sat there stewing, wondering who this man thought he was. In three weeks, Joe would be gone from this school, moving on to greater heights, while Daniels would surely remain stuck here for years to come. Joe sat there staring at an award on Daniels's desk. The statue was dated from fifteen years earlier recognizing the priest for his outstanding influence on the lives of his students. As Joe waited for the principal to return, his emotions began to get the better of him. The more he thought on it—*outstanding influence*—the more indignation he felt.

Joe sat staring at the small statue for nearly an hour before Daniels's secretary came in and told him that the principal had been called away and wouldn't be back till Monday. Joe nearly boiled over as the secretary left the room. But, instead of erupting, he gathered up his things and he did something that would have lifelong implications, implications that he could never see coming.

He took the brass-and-Plexiglas award that sat on Daniels's desk.

That night, as Joe, Michael, and their friends hung out at the lake tearing into a six-pack, Joe showed off the small statue he'd stolen.

The boys all howled in laughter at his derring-do, their faces glowing from the fire they had stoked up for warmth. They clustered around Joe as Michael took a Polaroid of the thief with his spoils. Joe popped open another beer and they all raised a toast to him as he ceremoniously tossed the statue in the fire.

But as midnight rolled around, Joe's bravado began to evaporate. Reality started to sink in as he realized that come Monday morning Father Daniels, upon finding his statue missing, would have only one suspect to point the finger at.

Strike three.

Michael watched the panic seep into his friend's eyes. It had been ten years since they met as altar boys on a cold Sunday in February and in all that time, Michael had yet to see his self-confident friend so desperate. Joe kept up his tough-guy routine but Michael knew there would be no talking his way out of this one. Neither the school nor Joe's parents would forgive this. And being expelled would render his college acceptance null and void. The night had started out as a celebration and ended like a funeral. The six boys all headed home feeling sorry for their friend. And no one was more sorry than Michael, who could see his friend's crushing remorse.

Arriving home, Michael walked into the garage which his father had converted to a wood and metal shop. It was his dad's hobby; he built everything around their house, and when Michael was a child his dad taught him much of his craft. But, like most kids hitting their teen years, Michael rebelled and steered clear of his father's interest.

Michael looked at the tools before him, then pulled the Polaroid out of his pocket. For the next thirty-six hours, with the Polaroid propped on the workbench for guidance, he worked without a break. It took him sixteen tries to shape the Plexiglas statue; another eight to create the engraved wooden base. At 11:50 on Sunday night he headed through the woods to the high school. Up a tree and onto the roof, he made his way to the bulkhead door, which hadn't been locked in thirty years. As Michael's heart pounded in his ears and the adrenaline rushed in his veins, he felt a sense of confidence in himself that he had never before experienced. As wrong as what he was doing was, it just somehow felt good. . . . It felt *right.*

On Monday morning Joe sat in the principal's office. He had been summoned first thing and knew he would be facing the ruin of his entire life. Father Daniels sat there silently for what seemed like eternity. Joe waited for the end to begin. But then the priest stunned him: he apologized. It was a side of Daniels that Joe had never seen. Father Daniels apologized for losing his temper and for rushing out on him on Friday and leaving him there alone. He told Joe that was enough detention; he wished him luck in college and said he was free to go.

As Joe left, he looked at the award on Father Daniels's desk and decided he must be dreaming. He was certain that he'd seen it burn.

Chapter 6

Michael sat slumped in a booth at the local diner, two cups of coffee on the table; neither had been touched. His eyes, red and swollen from lack of sleep, fought to stay open. With the sun long set, he braced himself for another endless night. The exhaustion was already dragging at his mind like a lead weight. He nervously flicked a business card as his eyes darted around the diner. He'd violated her trust; he'd lied to Mary three times. And now this . . .

He had run out of options. The hospital was demanding to know how he would pay for the surgery, how he would pay for her follow-up treatment. In three days, he had already run up over twenty thousand in bills. Tests, tests, and more tests. Each more painful and expensive than the last. Dr. Rhineheart had tried to pull some strings, but there were no more strings to pull. The head of hospital administration had laid it out most clearly: if Michael couldn't pay for the treatment, his wife, unfortunately, would have to leave the ward. Mary and Michael were stuck in the middle—not enough income to pay for the treatment but just enough not to qualify for aid. Michael was reduced to begging, pleading with anyone he knew. Busch would get him the thirty-five thousand as soon as he liquidated his pension. That crushed Michael but he accepted the loan; he had no choice, his pride be damned. The money wouldn't be available for three weeks, though, and even then it wouldn't be close to enough.

The final humiliating blow struck yesterday. It had been the last place to turn. Michael had exhausted every avenue, every possibility. He sat in their office and accepted their tea, not wanting to appear rude as he had so often in the past. He explained the problem: if he didn't get money, his wife would die. Father Shaunessy and the parish council listened with nodding heads and sympathetic ears, not saying a word until he was finished.

And then the Church which Mary so believed in simply said no. "We do not have the resources to provide funds for our parishioners." But they would be happy to remember Mary at Sunday's Mass.

Michael sat in the booth stirring his cold cup of coffee, staring at the other patrons. There were only three. They sat on the other side of the diner quietly laughing about who knew what. He couldn't help but stare, wishing he had paid attention to those moments, those times that lives were lived carefree, when he'd been unaware that it could all wash away with a doctor's diagnosis. Why hadn't he paid attention to those moments, absorbing them, appreciating them? Most of all he wished that he could somehow get back to those times. It seemed so long ago that he had felt unburdened, yet it was less than a week. Five days ago, he and Mary had been hobnobbing at Busch's party, oblivious to what was to come. He knew there was no way of going back, but what frustrated him was he had no means of moving forward.

From out of nowhere, Finster arrived, impeccably dressed in an Armani sport coat, his white hair pulled back tight in a ponytail. As he sat down, Michael noticed that Finster was much older than he had appeared when he'd first shown up at Michael's business. You could see it in his eyes, ancient and hardened as if he'd been through life more than once.

"You look like you could use a friend," Finster remarked.

"Circumstances change."

"I'm sorry about your wife," the German murmured with genuine sympathy.

"Yeah, well." Michael was hesitant, the words came hard. "You wanted to talk?"

"How are you?"

"Time is short."

"I know that you are out of the business, I respect that." Then Finster seemed to have a change of heart. He leaned back, shaking his head. "We don't have to talk about this now. Perhaps later, when you are in a better frame of mind."

"No, it's now or never." If he didn't hear the man out at this moment, his nerve would be lost and so would Mary.

"All right. But if you're not interested, I will understand, and we can part as friends."

Michael stared at the older man. He knew that anyone dealing in his former trade was questionable at best.

"I am prepared to take care of all of your wife's medical expenses no matter the cost—"

"For what?" Michael cut to the chase, aware this was no minor job. Two hundred and fifty thousand dollars—the estimated cost of Mary's treatment—was danger pay.

"There are two objects I desperately need to acquire. Both are in a minimum-security building. No armed guards, easy access—"

"I'm on parole."

"The job is in Europe. You wouldn't be breaking your parole here."

"Actually, I would. But more importantly, I'd be breaking it *here*." Michael tapped his heart. "I promised my wife."

Finster leaned forward and rested his arms on the table. "Situations change, Michael. Your wife's life hangs in the balance. Would you have made such a promise to her if you knew it meant the difference between her life and death? Of course not."

Finster was right. Michael knew it. He would never have made the promise if he'd known it would put Mary's survival in jeopardy. "I need more details," he said as he sipped his cold coffee.

"Good. At least you're thinking about it. Unfortunately, that is all I can tell you now. If you choose to accept the job, I will give you all the details. But once you accept . . ." Finster let it dangle.

Michael knew now there was no turning back. "I always finish what I start."

"One thing; maybe important, maybe not. This job may be in conflict with your religious beliefs." It was an offhand warning but a warning nonetheless.

"Go on."

"The job is in a church."

Michael let out a chuckle, "Ah, one of life's little jokes." He leaned back in the booth, picking up his coffee again. "I don't believe in God. Do you?"

Finster seemed taken aback by Michael's comment, his lack of faith. "With all my heart. After all I've seen . . ." He pondered his own faith for a moment. "There is no question in my mind."

A waitress arrived and gave them a coffee refill. She flashed Finster a smile.

He nodded. "Thank you."

She brushed the hair shyly out of her middle-aged eyes and left.

"Think about my offer." Finster stood and threw some money for the coffee on the table. "I must be on my way. I have other business to attend to."

"At this hour?"

"Haven't you ever heard the expression, 'No rest for the weary'?"

"You mean the wicked?"

Finster flashed his dazzling smile, then shook his hand. "I hope you make the right decision, Michael."

⌘

Hawk raced for the door the second the knob started to jiggle. CJ could care less. The little cat sneered at the big dog and curled back up on the couch. Michael walked in and Hawk was all over him licking and slobbering, jumping and whining. On most days, Michael would be on the floor soaking up this unconditional love but not today. He gave Hawk a quick pet, then shushed him over to the corner.

Michael headed into his study and from the center drawer of his desk he pulled a large manila envelope, opened it, and withdrew a set of papers. He spread them out on the desk blotter and for the thousandth time he read:

> *Having served 3 years 5 months and 22 days of a 10-year sentence for the crimes of grand larceny, possession of stolen property, and burglary, Michael Edward St. Pierre is hereby granted parole. This conclusion has been drawn by the Parole Board of the State of New York on the basis of fact that Mr. St. Pierre has been successfully rehabilitated and hereby has fulfilled his term of the sentence imposed upon him by the State of New York.*

PAROLE GRANTED had been stamped in an officious red ink across the document.

Five and a half years ago, the call had come in the middle of the night. Mary rolled over on the third ring and sleepily answered the phone. Michael was in jail, suspected of things she couldn't fathom he was capable of. It was a shattering betrayal. Her new husband had hidden his life from her.

They had caught him at the Central Park wall. He was almost over and probably would have made it if it weren't for the blood loss from his shoulder. The two NYC cops tackled him hard, slamming him into the granite wall. He was cuffed and bagged before he could say a word. They roughed him up pretty good; he didn't blame them. The woman was lying naked in the street, covered in blood, incoherent, half-insane from her ordeal. The cops didn't know the blood on her was Michael's—they assumed it was a brutal rape and they didn't take kindly to that. It was two days before she was lucid again. She gave a brief statement confirming Michael's innocence and valor. He was a hero. But in this day and age, heroes only last a week. In this case, he didn't last an hour. The fact that he'd rescued her never even made the paper.

Ambassador Ruskot flew in and declared he had never before seen the thirty million dollars in diamonds they'd found in Michael's backpack. The general couldn't afford the questions or the scandal. Thirsty for revenge, he pressed the DA's office to prosecute to the fullest extent the thief who violated his country's sovereign soil to steal the jewel-encrusted cross. He claimed it had enormous cultural value to his nation and that he personally viewed the crime as an affront to his deep religious beliefs. Truth be told, Ruskot had bought it behind the Iron Curtain years back for a pittance and hadn't gotten around to selling it yet.

The State Department knew full well of the ambassador's side business but was powerless against him. Instead, they pressed the district attorney's office to ensure a conviction. Relations were shaky with Akbiquestan and the United States government needed to show a sign of good faith in protecting the interest of their foreign "friend."

On the first day of the trial Mary sat stoically in the back of the courtroom, but she never met Michael's eye. Michael wrote her a note and had his court-appointed attorney pass it to her. She crumpled it up and stuffed it in the bottom of her purse without even looking at it. She would play the part of the dutiful wife throughout the trial, she told his lawyer, but when it was over, they were over. For three days, Michael walked in and out of the court, his hands cuffed, desperately looking to her with sorrow. Throughout the trial, she never once made eye contact.

Michael had no defense to offer; his attorney was barely two hours out of law school and it was only the boy's third case. They tried to introduce Michael's heroics in saving the beautiful Helen Staten—the jury learned that she was the blonde trophy bride of James Staten, a seventy-five-year-old industrialist—to mitigate Michael's situation, but they had no witness. Mrs. Staten had had a nervous breakdown; the gibberish she babbled was incoherent at best, and it was believed the rape had mercifully slipped out of her mind. To compound the matter, there was the death of James Staten, her husband, two days after the break in. There was no one left to speak on Michael's behalf.

Guilty. The verdict came back within an hour of the jury's convening.

The State took their summer house in Bedford, Michael's bank accounts, Mary's bank accounts, every asset they had to pay court costs and his three-hundred-thousand-dollar fine. As there was no evidence that Michael had ever earned a paycheck, held a legitimate job, or filed a tax return, the prosecutor tried to tie Michael's assets to other thefts. He failed. Fortunately, Michael had never left a trail until that fateful night.

Sing Sing in Ossining, New York, would be Michael's home for the next three and a half years.

Mary received the petition for divorce a week after the criminal trial ended. She read it through twice and, her religion be damned, she would go through with it. She called her lawyer. He told her to sign the papers and he would have them served on Michael at prison. She was digging through her purse for a pen when she came upon the note Michael had written her at the beginning of the trial.

Mary,

Please do not torture yourself by sitting through this trial. The shame I have brought upon you is burden enough. Marriage is about trust, marriage is about faith in one another. And after what I have done, I know you will never have faith in me again. You must move on with your life. I know you will find someone else to love and care for you.

M.

She arrived at the prison at nine a.m. the next morning with the divorce papers in her purse. He told her everything. He explained it all: how he never really had a consulting business, that his income was actually from prior thefts. How he had decided when they met that he would hang it up. There would be one last job and he would make it count. After that, he would be able to provide for her for the rest of their lives so she could stop working and concentrate on raising their family. But it had all fallen apart over a stolen cross and a thoughtless act of bravery. He finished by telling her that he would not contest the divorce.

But it was her simple reply that made it all clear to him. "I never cared for money, for fancy clothes or cars, Michael. Those things just grow old and are discarded. The greatest treasure to me is living and growing old with you, together. I love you, Michael, and you love me. That's all I need."

Mary visited every Saturday and Michael called every Monday and Wednesday. Over time they reforged their relationship. For better or worse, she was devoted to him. And he vowed he would never again betray her.

When he was released three and a half years later, Michael had become the epitome of a reformed man. He started his own legitimate business, paid his taxes, and reestablished his marriage. And perhaps most surprisingly, he became best friends with an officer of the law. Paul Busch's wife and Mary were old friends and Busch had actually asked for the assignment. Paul was never just a parole officer to Michael; he had become and would always be a friend. An unspoken bond developed on the day Michael was released, and its strength had grown tenfold since.

Betrayal weighed heavy on Michael now as he stood in his study and the memories coursed through his mind. The words of the parole board rang in his ears: "*Do not so much as contemplate a felony, particularly burglary, for if you do, never again will you see the outside of these prison walls.*" His betrayal of Mary was only the beginning; while the guilt would never wash away, he could only hope that, someday, she would understand the actions he contemplated now. But Busch . . . Michael knew that accepting Finster's proposition would not only destroy their friendship but would turn them against each other for life. Busch's commitment to the law would blind him to the dilemma that Michael and Mary faced.

It was now clear—in that karma kind of way—that Michael's current circumstances were his true sentence for his transgressions. He had desperately racked his brain for another option, for some miracle solution, for some simple alternative that had eluded him.

Michael slipped his parole papers back in the envelope, dropped it into the desk drawer and, leaving the drawer open, walked over to the bookshelves. Novels of every genre crammed the top shelves: Dickens to Dickey, Conrad to Cussler. The bottom shelves held his old research books: texts on alarm systems and jewelry collecting, art history and magic, European museums and photography. The middle shelves were reserved for their mementos: seashells, stuffed animals, postcards. Things that kindled memories; things that sparked love. Reflections of their lives collected in their travels. Some of the *tchotchkes* dated back to their courtship days: goofy photo-booth pictures, handmade plaster cats, a caricature of the two of them dancing in the surf. And while some of the items had grown embarrassing with time, he and Mary always agreed that they would never put them away. For they were reflections of moments, the things that they had held near and dear throughout their life together. Taking them down would be like rejecting their past, his and Mary's denying themselves.

Among their most treasured possessions on the wall was a crucifix given to them on the occasion of their wedding. A simple cross, nothing fancy; in fact, Michael didn't even remember who gave it to them. Made of plain simple wood with a plastic Jesus stapled to it, it was like something you'd find by the thousands at any flea market. He and Mary had joked that whoever had given it to them must have stolen it off the rearview mirror of a New York City taxicab. Now, with the events of the last few days, the sight of it had become unbearable. While Michael knew he was betraying Mary and Busch, he also felt that he, too, had been betrayed. All his years of devotion, all his years of prayer had led him here to this moment, alone, with no alternative.

And with that final thought, Michael reached out and removed the plastic crucifix, the symbol of his now former faith. He walked back to his desk, placed it with his parole papers, and closed the drawer tight.

Chapter 7

Michael sat at Mary's bedside all night, leaving before she awoke. The pain medication was only allowing her a few hours of lucidity a day, and while it hurt him not to hear her voice, he knew it was best, for the powerful medicines coursing through her veins helped her avoid the increasing pain of her illness. Studying her face, ghostly pale under the blue lights of the monitor, only strengthened his resolve. If she didn't undergo surgery immediately he would lose her. And to be trapped in a world without her would be a prison far worse than any he had ever faced.

All this raced through his mind as Finster fixed him a drink from a polished maple bar. The two men were alone in one of the finest hotel suites in the city. Crystal carafes and aged liquors lined the mirrored wall. Rich leather sofas bordered a seating area whose centerpiece was an enormous fireplace. A Bosendorfer grand piano sat in one corner while a grand Louis XIV desk sat in the other.

Finster handed Michael a crystal glass. "Chivas, it's always been my favorite." He picked up his own drink and raised it. "May our next drink be to success."

Michael ignored the toast. He was not a man for formalities or fancy Scotch. He had always worked alone. He had never pulled a job for anyone else: and he knew that, for this one, for the first time in his life, he wouldn't be making the rules.

"But enough civilities. Please sit," Finster requested in his slightly accented voice. "I will of course provide anything you require—money, personnel, equipment."

Michael took a seat on the couch, placed his glass on the coffee table, and leaned forward. "For?"

"Two keys."

"Keys," Michael repeated, confused. "What do they open?"

"They are antiques, one gold, one silver, dating back two thousand years." There was a shadow of excitement in Finster's voice as he sat down.

Michael remained stock-still, appearing emotionless. But inside it had begun, his heart was pounding, his pulse racing; he couldn't help it, that sense of excitement was back, the beginnings of an adrenaline rush. He knew, however, that he had to keep his emotions in check; this job was not for him, it was for Mary. "Where?" he asked.

"Italy. Rome. It should not be difficult for a man of your talents."

"How do you know of my talents? I was always low-profile."

"Reliable sources."

"Who?" Michael knew the devil was in the details.

Finster smiled. "You'll have to trust me on that, Michael."

"No offense, but trust is something that doesn't exist in this business."

"As a show of good faith, I will wire one hundred thousand dollars into your account within the hour so your wife may begin immediate treatment."

"You could have me killed upon completion of the job, renege on payment."

Finster rose from the couch like a noble knight to his king. "Michael St. Pierre, I give you my word, no harm shall come to you and the final payment will be made upon delivery. I am a man of honor."

Michael was unimpressed. "Honor among thieves is an oxymoron."

"I have never broken a promise or backed out on a deal. Ever. If I did, I couldn't do business."

"You never mentioned your business." The way Finster answered the question would be just as telling as the response itself. Michael already knew the answer from his preliminary research on his new associate. With his record, Michael couldn't afford being set up by some overzealous cop. He had verified Finster's identity and business before coming here.

"I'm in various industries. Retail sales, that kind of thing, all on a worldwide basis." Finster looked Michael straight in the eyes. "You have my word, sir."

Michael wasn't sure just how good that word was. He decided he would test it later, but right now his curiosity was piqued. "So, which church in Rome?"

"A church per se." Finster paused. "The keys are in the Vatican."

Michael took a deep breath, absorbing this. "The Vatican. You want me to steal from the Vatican? That's a bit of information that you should have made me aware of up front."

"I'm sure you can now appreciate my need for utter secrecy. Are you backing out on me?"

"No. It's just pretty bold. If"—Michael emphasized the *if*—"it can be done, this will take considerable planning. Such a high-profile trick would be extremely dangerous. It leaves no room for error. That's not a low-security building; it's one of the highest-security principalities in the world. And the guards? Don't let those foofy blue outfits fool you. The Swiss Guard are one of the most efficient, highly trained military outfits in Europe. But more important, they possess something you can't train into a soldier: they are one of the most loyal forces on the planet."

In all the years he practiced his trade, there was one emotion that never entered Michael's mind, but it did today. Fear. It was nipping at his heart, causing it to skip a beat. He had bargained himself into a very dangerous position, a road he could not turn back from. This had just turned into a job that could leave both Mary and himself dead at the end if he should fail.

The art of this deal was what he was *not* being told and, in his estimate, that was a lot. This wasn't about keys or antiques. There was something more. But whether it was some quirky collector's obsession or a means to an end for Finster, Michael didn't care. He never involved himself in the politics of others and he knew that if he busied his mind with trying to judge this man's motives, he would not be able to focus on the job at hand. To him this was a theft, the only job that would save his wife. Finster's interest in these keys was not his concern. All he knew—all he cared about—was that by stealing them, he would be stealing life for his wife. That is what he would focus on, that is what would drive him to success, despite the mounting odds against it.

Finster handed Michael an overflowing black leather briefcase. "This contains information on the keys, their exact location, and the layout and details of where they are kept." He walked back to the window and looked out at the city. "You understand that I am putting my trust in you as you are putting your trust in me." It was a moment before he turned back to Michael. "We have only just met but I believe we have come to an understanding, have we not?"

Michael nodded his head slightly.

"But there is one thing above all else that I need you to understand." Finster walked toward Michael, speaking slowly for emphasis. "Do not betray me. Do not try to take these artifacts elsewhere to a higher bidder. Do not try to switch them. I will know if they are not the true keys, Michael." The white-haired man stood only a foot from Michael, looking down at him. "I will know," he repeated.

Michael slowly rose from the couch with the briefcase in his hand, never breaking eye contact. "You didn't answer my question. What do these keys open? A chest? Some kind of safe?"

"No. Nothing of the sort, probably just some old doors long gone."

⌘

The following morning, one week after her doctor's appointment, Mary was in surgery. The tumor was bigger than Dr. Rhineheart expected, but after eight hours in the operating room he thought they got it all. It had wrapped itself around her left ovary and fallopian tube and was beginning to invade the right. Rhineheart was the premier cancer specialist in New York. He had graduated top of his class and was one of the few doctors who hadn't become an automaton. He still cared. It was a personal loss every time a patient was consumed by this disease. He had lost his mother to breast cancer when he was fifteen and he fought for each patient with every resource in his power. Each fight was a renewed battle in a war that he was determined to win. Each patient was someone's sister or wife, father or brother. Each patient was his mother again and again.

The combination of chemotherapy and radiation treatment he prescribed was to eradicate any remaining cancer from Mary's body. It was a heavy regime that would require all her strength. Rhineheart explained to them that he always found it to be a paradox: he needed to poison his patient in order to rid her body of an even deadlier poison. It was a delicate balancing act, he said, but it had proven successful so many times before that he had the confidence of Mercury in the hundred-yard dash.

Michael sat at Mary's side in the recovery room, her hand clasped in his. The color was drained from her face, and while this was to be expected, her pallor still shocked him. He couldn't shake the feeling that she was dead. She needed him now more than ever, he reminded himself. She would rely on his strength to carry her through this ordeal, the way her strength had carried him through his imprisonment. Mary had saved him and by God, he was going to save her.

⌘

Paul and Jeannie Busch left the hospital; not a word was said the whole ride home. They had waited with Michael the entire time Mary was in surgery. The eight hours seemed like twenty. It took everything they had to keep the conversation upbeat and encouraging. Busch found it difficult to be so positive on the outside while his heart was filled with dread. He and Jeannie were closer to the St. Pierres than anyone in their lives and this cruel twist of fate was tearing him apart. What bothered Busch the most, however, was that a terrible question kept cropping up in his mind.

He and Michael had become more than friends. A trust had developed between them that Busch didn't share with anyone but his wife. Michael had been there for him when Busch had difficulty in his marriage. He had become distant from Jeannie, mostly due to his job; it wasn't something that was heading for divorce, it was more like one of those blips in a relationship, the peaks and valleys of love. But Michael had listened and that was what Busch had needed. Busch had always found it hard to open his heart, he had been taught since childhood that emotion was a feminine trait and woe to the man who displayed soft feelings. As Busch poured out his heart, Michael never once made the conversation uncomfortable and spoke only when Busch needed it. The situation had resolved itself, but it was Michael's friendship that had helped him through.

And Michael had trusted him. He was always forthright in their discussions of his criminal past; how he had found burglary to be an art, something practiced by craftsmen, how he found prison to be a punishment worse than Hell. Michael had always included Busch in his plans for reforming his life, looking for a respectable job, starting his security business. Busch was the first person Michael turned to when Mary's illness was revealed. Though stoic, Busch could see the helplessness in his friend's eyes, his inability to raise the money necessary for her treatment. Two hundred and fifty thousand dollars.

Again the question posed itself, a question Busch had pondered all day: *Where had Michael gotten the money?*

⌘

Michael sat at his dining room table, the contents of the black briefcase strewn out before him. Maps and books, charts and documents. Michael was doing his homework.

The Vatican was vast, a country unto itself. A sovereign state within one hundred and nine acres. Her main protection was provided by the Swiss Guard. They were a small army entrusted with guarding the Pope and protecting the Apostolic Palace. The Swiss Guard wasn't an army in the traditional sense: they wore no fatigues, carried no M16s draped over their shoulders. It was more like an ancient security force. Their brightly colored uniforms were contemporary—if you lived in 1589. A puffed tunic with brilliant blue and gold striping, matching pantaloons, spats, and black slippers: an outfit more befitting a Shakespearean actor than a military officer. Their three-point peaked hats reminded Michael of salt-and-pepper shakers with red feathers stuck on top. Carrying eight-foot staffs called halberds, these soldiers were more equipped for slaying dragons than defending a country. In principle, their function was more like that of an ancient honor guard, the laymen thinking, Who would ever lay siege to the Holy See? But the Church knew better; the Vatican had been under attack for centuries from many corners, known and unknown. Some attacks were by direct physical assault; some were the intellectual assaults of science attempting to explain away a higher order, while some came from unexplained spiritual forces. And that is why, under their fanciful outfits, these men possessed the requisite skills of a superbly trained military unit. Their function may have been traditional; but their ability was ultramodern. Each was skilled in weaponry, hand-to-hand combat, and counterterrorism. Each knew that an attack on the Church could come at any time, and from any source, and each man was prepared. And while the halberd appeared ceremonial, it was, in fact, a razor-sharp scythe expertly used by the Swiss Guard since they were brought to the Vatican by the Warrior Pope Julius II, on January 22,1506.

II Corpo di Vigilanza was a squat stone building on the northeast corner of St. Peter's Square. It was not an especially remarkable structure. Underneath it, however, was a different story. The situation room beneath II Corpo di Vigilanza was similar to something you would find within the bowels of the Pentagon. Here two worlds collided: high tech and high art. High-speed Cray computers next to Bernini sculptures, electronic maps above Raphael paintings. It was a time machine gone wrong. This room was the home of the Papal Gendarmes, the Vatican Police. Working in conjunction with the Swiss Guard, they were in charge of the security of the palace and the gardens. While the Swiss Guard was drawn exclusively from the Swiss army, the Vatican Police were all former Italian army. The combined force of the Swiss Guard and the Vatican Police was ready twenty-four hours a day to meet any assault and, unlike the security forces of other governments, theirs was a loyalty not just to their nation but to God. Any fanatic willing to die for his beliefs in an assault on Vatican City would be met by an army equally willing to give up their collective lives for a more powerful belief. No more allegiant force could be found in the world. No power on earth could deter them.

Of course, the Vatican was home to the Pontiff, the Pope, the leader of the Catholic Church. And since the attempt on Pope John

Paul II's life in 1981, the security around the Pope and the Papal home had tripled.

Michael's objective lay within one of the world's largest museums. And while the Vatican Museums contained many religious treasures, on the face of it, the museums' security seemed almost carelessly minimal: cameras, alarms, and the occasional guard. The real security, however, was tenfold. All manner of entrance and egress contained expertly concealed metal detectors; radioactive isotope scanners; olfactory filters capable of detecting the chemical signatures of accelerants, combustibles, and toxins; instruments capable of identifying everything from nuclear devices and plastic explosives to the common gunpowder of a firecracker. Cameras were hidden everywhere, their monitors in the situation room attended constantly by keen eyes. Undercover security roamed the grounds, providing an up-close human observation of all activity.

Finster had provided the exact location of the two keys, allowing Michael to concentrate on his method for procuring them. But Michael had been in this business long enough to know that you trust no one but yourself. While he had already committed to the job, it didn't mean he trusted Finster for one moment.

Before agreeing to the heist, one of the first things Michael did was look into the German's background. What he found would impress most. Finster was a billionaire who'd come out of East Germany a decade earlier, a Midas-touch industrialist who dabbled successfully in several fields. Michael used his sources to confirm Finster had no legal affiliations nor altercations in his past. Finster, it turned out, was your typical overly successful European who wanted what he couldn't attain. The ultrarich always seemed to crave that which was just out of reach and would go to any length to get what they thought they deserved, believing they were above not only the common man but the law.

And while Finster checked out, that didn't raise Michael's level of trust. He would check and recheck all of Finster's Vatican information, relying on none of it. Research was one of the keys to success, and he would be thorough in confirming every detail that his employer provided. But all the books and all the maps in the world wouldn't tell him the routine of the museum, the ebb and flow of the tourists, of the priests, of the guards. If he was to prevail, he had not only to overcome the Vatican police and Swiss Guard security measures, he would have to become one with their routine.

Michael reached for a large accordion envelope. It had arrived that morning, hand-delivered from Finster's hotel. From it, he pulled a small box and, opening it, found an iridium satellite phone inside. The phone was larger than a regular cell phone: eight inches by two and a half wide and an inch thick. Michael opened the back and pulled out the battery. It was heavier than he expected; its size was the obvious reason for the phone's bulk. The phone may have been oversized but it had its unique advantages: it was capable of calling anywhere in the world from anywhere in the world. The attached note read: *It is secure; you may contact me at your leisure in order to keep me apprised of your progress. But more importantly, you may use it to speak to your wife because, after all, that's what this is all about.*

In the envelope, Finster included ten thousand dollars in U.S. currency, twenty-five thousand euros, and three platinum credit cards, each matching a different alias. If something were to go wrong, Michael would have more than enough money and resources to purchase his way home.

There were three passports with the three different aliases. Michael's real passport had been revoked in accordance with his probation. He had posed for the new passport pictures before leaving Finster's hotel one week ago, allowing Finster to take care of the rest. Michael didn't want to get picked up for the simple crime of passport falsification. That would end his journey before it began.

He spilled the remaining contents of the envelope into his hands: a plane ticket to Rome, another from Rome to Finster's home in Germany, and a third for the return flight to New York. An itinerary was attached. He would be staying at the Hotel Bella Coccinni overlooking the Tiber in Rome.

He had seven days.

⌘

Mary, dressed in a pair of khakis and a floral blouse, lay in her hospital bed. The standard hospital wear had grown tired and embarrassing after a week, and it felt good to be back in something resembling healthy normality. Although still in considerable pain, she was relieved the surgery was behind her. She didn't tell Michael but she was terrified of being put to sleep; she feared she would never wake up. Between the cancer and her nightmares, it had been weeks since she had felt well-rested.

Over a month ago, she'd awakened, her belly just a fraction distended from its usual taut appearance, her period six weeks late. She'd been filled with an almost overwhelming sense of joy as she drove to the pharmacy to get one of those early pregnancy tests. For years, she and Michael had wanted children. They had tried and tried.

After Michael's release from prison, they had both undergone multiple tests; they were both found to be fertile as rabbits. But nothing. The world told them to be patient, it would happen. Two months, then two years, had gone by. No specialist, herbalist, or prayer had cracked the problem.

But now, she was certain, things would be different. Everyone was right, it had happened. Mary felt life growing in her womb. All the way home from the pharmacy she planned how she would surprise Michael. Over a quiet dinner, maybe giving him a gift-wrapped baby rattle, or doing the traditional knitting-a-baby-sock routine while relaxing in a rocking chair. A special present was called for, one that was meaningful for both of them.

She finally settled on Dr. Seuss. She bought *Green Eggs and Ham* and had it wrapped in bright paper decorated with baby elephants. She would give the book to him that night in bed. She was bursting to tell him, to surprise him at work, but she wanted this to be memorable. Michael loved children. Together, they were going to raise a healthy brood. It had been a long road, but now they were on their way. This child would be the first of many.

Mary got home, opened the pregnancy test, and headed to the bathroom. It was a messy process, one she had done countless times before, but this time it would be different.

She waited the requisite five minutes. Nothing. She thought she had made a mistake, and reread the directions. There was a second test included in the box; she would wait an hour and take it, making sure she followed the directions to a tee.

It was negative. She felt like sobbing. Why had she allowed herself to be so hopeful? Michael would understand, but deep down, she knew, he would be disappointed. She threw the Dr. Seuss book in the garbage. She decided not to tell him. Why burden him? One broken heart per day was enough.

Now she sat in her hospital bed staring at the things Michael had brought her on his visits before the surgery. There among the cookies and flowers was a gift Michael had bought for her, thinking it would cheer her up. The tears welled in her eyes; it was *Green Eggs and Ham.*

⌘

The television was on mute; Jerry Springer's flailing arms didn't have their usual impact without his raging voice to back them up. Michael bent down, kissing Mary's lips. "I've got to go away for a few days."

"Where?" she asked, with a smile. She masked her disappointment well.

"Down South. I've got to sign some papers and do some work for Rosenfield, the guy who helped me cover these expenses."

The lies were coming too easy and that worried Michael. Rosenfield may have liked Michael, but people didn't invest in personalities. While the old guy had sympathy for Michael and Mary, he didn't have enough. Rosenfield had said he was sorry, he couldn't lend Michael so much money, he couldn't take the risk.

"Did he just give you the money?"

"I told you before. It's a loan, against the business and future work."

"I still can't get over that. I didn't think there was anyone left with charity in their heart." Mary scratched absently at the bandage that covered the shunt in her arm. "I don't know how I could ever thank him."

"I thanked him." Michael took her hand in his. She had no idea that the security shop was just getting by. All she knew was that Michael was bringing home a paycheck every week and for that she was proud of him. For her, he had built something from nothing. "I've got to leave tonight."

"Do you have to?" Her chemo was scheduled to start this afternoon and from what she had learned, severe side effects were ahead: she dreaded facing them alone.

"There is no place I would rather be than here with you."

"Can I go, too?" It was more of a joke than a plea.

"I wish," Michael said.

"I wish, too."

"You have to start treatment."

"I know." She nodded, a shadow of disappointment in her eyes. "Just looking for an out, I guess. How long will you be gone?"

"About a week."

"Hurry back," Mary whispered as he held her in his arms. They were each facing the challenge of their lives, yet neither showed fear. Each concerned more about the other than themself.

⌘

Dennis Thal entered the locker room. The young cop had soaked through his sweats as if he had jumped into a pool and was looking forward to the ice-cold shower. His one-on-one game of basketball with John Ferguson, a rookie detective, had ended in victory for Thal despite a crippled pinky and ring finger on his left hand; he never lost. Thal hated losing.

Busch stood at Thal's locker, waiting impatiently.

Thal was in good shape, his body lean and cut. Busch was envious but knew it was the blessing of youth. In time, the younger man would succumb to the effects of french fries and gravity like everyone else. Thal seemed like a clean, straight-as-an-arrow kid raised with a silver spoon in his mouth. The word around the station was that he was wealthy, had a substantial trust fund, and was doing the law-enforcement thing for kicks. Busch was doing some checking of his own, and if this was true he'd request that the kid be transferred. Law was something that wasn't enforced for fun or an adrenaline high. If Thal wanted to get his blood flowing, he could do it on someone else's dime. Extreme law enforcement wasn't a sport, it was Busch's job. He wasn't about to end up dead because some dude was looking to get his rocks off.

"What's up?" Thal asked as he opened his locker.

"You were supposed to meet me upstairs fifteen minutes ago."

"Oh, hey, I'm sorry; I didn't mean to screw you up." Thal swiped his sweaty brown hair out of his eyes. "Let me take a thirty-second shower and I'll be right up."

Busch walked out of the locker room, calling back to Thal, "You've got three minutes."

Thal looked around; no one else was in the area. He pulled off his dirty sweats and tossed them on the floor, throwing his towel over his right shoulder. He hopped in the shower, soaped up and, true to his word, was out of the icy water in thirty seconds. Efficiency was his motto. No need to waste time when there were more important things to attend to.

He combed his hair and threw on his pleated pants. Buffed up his shoes with his wet towel and grabbed his freshly pressed white shirt out of his locker, hastily putting it on. Thal wasn't a modest man, he just didn't want Busch (or anyone, for that matter) to see his right shoulder. Dennis Thal knew that, despite the Ralph Lauren shirt and Cole Haan loafers, he wasn't what he seemed.

Thal knew the "tattoo" would set Busch off. The black skull with roses growing out of fractured bone would just confirm the big cop's beliefs. It had been the foolish move of a sixteen-year-old, a way to be cool and fit in. In Thal's case, it didn't work. Costing three hundred and fifty dollars, the tattoo was a thing of hip beauty on the day it was done, but it no longer had the luster and the fine artistic lines he'd paid for. The scar tissue from a burn had distorted it to a grotesque horror that he couldn't erase.

If Busch saw his tattoo, it would raise too many questions, questions that Thal could never answer. He had worked hard at polishing his lily-white image and something so incongruous would surely raise more than curiosity in a veteran cop like Busch. And Det. Dennis Thal hadn't gone through all this trouble being assigned to Busch to be found out—he had a job to do and he wasn't about to let his employer down.

⌘

The files on the left side of the desk stood eleven inches deep, a good three inches shorter than the stack on the right. For the last five minutes the piles alternated in height as Busch aimlessly pulled a case folder, pretended to review it, then shifted it to the other side of his desk. His parolee was fifteen minutes late; it wasn't like the man, and Busch was growing concerned.

"Isn't it a violation of parole to miss a required meeting?" Thal asked as he sat ramrod straight in Busch's side chair.

Busch didn't bother answering: he called the shots, not Thal. He was about to put him in his place when from somewhere under the papers came a muffled ring.

Busch pushed files aside and answered his phone. "Busch."

"Hey, it's me." Michael sounded out of breath.

"You OK?"

Thal looked at Busch, his brow furrowed in question.

Busch quickly changed his tone. "You're fifteen minutes late." He wasn't about to let Thal know of his friendship with Michael St. Pierre. He sensed that Thal would somehow turn it around and use this knowledge against him.

"Sorry, I had to take care of some things for Mary."

"How is she?" Busch asked, a little curtly.

"She's hanging tough, she starts chemo this afternoon." It finally occurred to Michael: "Someone's with you."

"Yeah." They were now on the same page. "Listen, you've got to get in here, we had a formal meeting scheduled to review your rehabilitation; skipping it is not an option."

"I didn't mean to put you in a tight position." Michael paused, then said, "I've got to go away for a few days."

Busch's blood ran cold. "How many days?"

"A week."

Busch was afraid to ask the question but he had a job to do. "Why?"

Michael was in his apartment, cradling the phone to his ear, staring at the Vatican plans spread out on his dining room table. "It has to do with the financing of Mary's treatment. I've got some security work to do."

Busch wasn't buying it. Friend or no friend, he knew he was being misled. He'd get his answers but that would have to wait until he shook Thal.

"When?"

"I have to leave tonight."

"Not until we meet." They both knew Michael couldn't leave the state without Busch's permission.

"I don't know if I'll have the time."

"Make the time." Busch was real clear on this. He had never spoken to Michael in this tone before. Busch wanted answers, Michael could tell, and he owed him an explanation. He'd meet him, but the truth would have to wait. Michael was sure the last thing the truth would do in this case was set him free.

⌘

Busch and Michael stood behind the fence of a Little League baseball game, the bats bigger than the kids. Busch was the coach; he loved any and all sports, and he would pass what he knew on to his son. Robbie Busch played second base; down and ready, the boy was determined not to let a ball get by his pint-sized body. Neither man looked at each other. Instead, they kept their gaze on the kids on the field.

"So, where are you heading?"

"Virginia. Fredericksburg."

"Seven days?"

"Yeah."

The batter stood in the box, his three-and-a-half-foot body crouched and ready for the pitch. And though the pitcher didn't have a prayer of throwing within the child's diminutive strike zone, it didn't matter, these kids swung at everything. Three pitches, three strikes, and the first batter was out.

"Let me go with you, I've got some time coming. Four hands do twice the work in half the time."

"No, that's all right, it's mostly tech stuff, installation work."

"Hell of a time to be going."

"It's the deal I made."

"And what kind of deal is that?"

Michael looked at Paul; the subterfuge was killing both of them. "Standard contract."

A squirt of a kid smacked the ball to third. The third baseman tried to make the throw but it fell short. The runner rounded first heading to second. The skinny pitcher picked up the ball and tossed it to Robbie who made the catch and raced for the bag, neck and neck with the runner; he reached out with all of his eighteen-inch arm and made the tag.

"Great job, Robbie!"

Robbie grinned wide at his father.

As the next batter came to the plate, Busch turned to Michael, getting serious. "Where did you get the money for Mary's treatment?"

Michael kept his eyes on the game. "One of my clients." He paused; he didn't like being backed into a corner. "The one in Virginia."

"Who?"

Michael ignored the question. "He gave me some work and helped me get a loan."

"Thought you said you had no credit." It was turning into an interrogation.

"I don't."

"Then how does someone without credit get a loan?"

"They get a benefactor." Now, Michael looked directly at Busch. "Someone who has faith in them. Where are we going with this?"

"You tell me, Michael. Where *are* we going with this?"

Michael just stared; it was all he could do. He knew if this went on any longer he'd slip up, if he hadn't already. He had to stay focused. Ninety-nine percent of the job was not getting caught and Michael was afraid that was about to happen.

"Will you look in on Mary while I'm gone?"

"You know I will," Busch snapped. He was beginning to seethe. Michael was hiding behind his wife.

Michael turned to leave.

"Michael—don't make me do my job."

Michael said nothing as he got in his car, started it up, and pulled from the curb.

⌘

Michael drove down Maple Avenue. He had packed light, a carry-on with summer-weight clothes and the overstuffed black briefcase. He would pick up his tools and supplies once he landed in Italy. There was no sense being subjected to unnecessary questions at Customs.

Michael had tried to reach Mary before leaving but she'd been asleep. The medication they gave her helped the pain not only by numbing it but by helping her sleep through it. Although he had said his good-byes earlier, he longed to hear her voice before he was airborne. It would be the first full night they'd spent apart since he'd been released. Michael's heart was breaking. He had left Mary alone for three and a half years while he was in prison. He'd sworn he would never do it again. And yet here he was, abandoning her in her most desperate hour. *But, this job is different,* he reminded himself. *This job isn't for personal gain or ego challenge.*

He had asked their neighbor, Mrs. McGinty, to feed and walk Hawk. The old lady was more than happy to help. She'd even refused the money that Michael offered for her services. She was glad to keep CJ in her apartment for the week, glad to have the cat's company since she had lost both her own cat and her husband, Charles, in the last six months. It was good to have a purpose again, she told him.

Michael pulled into the long-term lot and paid for seven days in advance. As he locked the trunk, he noticed a green Torino slow up outside the parking fence. He had spotted it back on the highway; he had always had a fondness for muscle cars, so this one had easily caught his eye. Those big engines were a thing of the past, rarely seen in anything but police cars these days. He hadn't paid it much mind as it exited the interstate behind him but now he watched it continue past the lot.

Michael locked up the car and headed for the terminal. He didn't see the Torino again and breathed a little easier as the large sliding doors of the airport came into view. Paranoia, he told himself. He had been out of practice for almost six years now and was probably just being overly cautious. He stepped up to the airline check-in counter. No one on line. A pretty lady with a Southern accent took his ticket. "Will you be checking any luggage today, Mr. McMahon?"

"Just carry-on, thank you," Michael replied, checking in under an alias. His first crime committed, he had just broken his parole. The airline attendant handed Michael his boarding pass, thanked him, and directed him to the security checkpoint.

⌘

Paul Busch was beginning to feel terrible. He had followed Michael, never knowing his intended purpose, never knowing what he would say when he caught up to him. Michael had followed procedure and it was Busch's call whether or not to let him leave the state. As he walked through the doors of the airport terminal, he decided he would just see Michael off, granting him his permission to go. He would put his faith in him.

Busch had sent his son home with Jeannie, telling her not to wait up, then borrowed the assistant baseball coach's Torino. Since the birth of their children, Jeannie had one rule. It was reasonable and, in this day and age, it was prudent. There were too many horror stories and she refused to let her family be a statistic. No guns around the kids. And so, Busch had left his gun, along with his wallet and badge, in the safe at home before the baseball game. He hadn't bothered to pick them up on the way to the airport; he didn't see the need.

⌘

Michael walked through the airport, his carry-on bag slung over his shoulder, slapping his thigh as the bag bounced with his stride. The black case he carried in his right hand was heavy. He flashed his ticket at the security gate, emptied his pockets, and placed his bags upon the conveyor belt. As he stepped through the archway, the alarms sounded. Michael froze. Flashbacks of being arrested coursed through his mind. They must be onto him, he thought; he was doomed. Before he left his apartment he'd made sure that there would be nothing incriminating in his bags or on his person: now he couldn't fathom the problem. The guards moved forward to pat him down. He rechecked his pockets and sighed with relief as he found a stray nickel. He stepped back into thc archway. This time, he was clear and free to go.

⌘

As Busch reached the security checkpoint, he caught sight of Michael heading quickly down the hallway toward the gates. Before he could decide on his next move, the guard asked him for his ticket. Of course he didn't have one. Busch asked to be let through: he was a police officer on official business. The guard asked him for his ID, but of course he didn't have that, either. Busch watched Michael blend in with the sea of outbound passengers. He looked around for a solution and decided he would continue to give Michael the benefit of the doubt; he'd speak to him when he came back in seven days. But then, he saw the sign: *INTERNATIONAL DEPARTURES.*

Michael had just become a fugitive.

From the tarmac, in the shadows, a figure watched the 747 climb into the night sky. The man was alone and he wasn't an airline employee. He walked back toward the hangar door passing the maintenance crews and luggage carts; no one paid him any mind, it was as if he belonged or had a special pass.

The figure stepped through the door and headed down the security tunnel. A guard stood at the exit. The guard looked up, puzzled at the unfamiliar man walking his way, but when the figure flashed his police badge it instantly became clear. Dennis Thal smiled as the guard bid him good night and walked out the exit.

Chapter 8

The raven-haired waitress placed the cappuccino on the table next to Michael's work papers. It was Michael's second cappuccino and his new favorite drink. Starbucks didn't hold a candle to the original made in its land of origin.

The cafe, Bourgino's, was just outside Vatican City on Via del Campiso, an ancient Roman street of rutted cobblestone. For the past two days, it had been his destination of choice: tiny, off the beaten path, and completely absent from Fodor's tourist guide. The clientele was a mixture of locals and expatriates, his presence was not even questioned. Fortunately, he was mostly black Irish. With his brown hair and tanned skin, he easily passed for Italian.

He had spent his first day in the city learning the narrow streets and alleys, his flawless memory his greatest tool. Committing buildings, security systems, and routes to his personal brain trust allowed him time to work out the intricate problems and details of his trade.

Michael had pored over every renowned work on the Vatican and its contents, but nothing he read had prepared him for the grandeur that met him as he walked up Via della Conciliazione. The massiveness of St. Peter's Basilica dwarfed the images in his mind. The Piazza San Pietro's width was just shy of three football fields: it could hold three hundred and fifty thousand people for the Pope's Masses. It was framed by two vast semicircular colonnades that reached out from the basilica like welcoming arms. The 284 Bernini-designed Doric columns stood forty feet tall and ran four deep around the entire ten-acre open space. As Michael looked up, he couldn't help but feel he was being judged by the scores of marble saints perched atop the colonnades, all staring down into the square.

In the center of the enormous piazza rose the obelisk brought to Rome by the Roman emperor Caligula, in AD 37. Capping the eighty-five-foot structure was a cross and golden ball rumored to contain the remains of Julius Caesar. While such an ancient obelisk in any other city would have been the center of attention, here it was simply an afterthought. The Vatican was another world, a remnant from a nearly forgotten history, a fairy tale out of the past. This holy city was beyond the imagination of any one man. Rather, it was the magnificent achievement of some of the greatest artistic minds that ever lived. While Michael had researched its history, inside and out, he hadn't grasped until this very moment its astonishing breadth. Back in the U.S., he had stayed intensely focused on saving Mary's life, treating this mission as just another building to overcome, another security system to defeat, another police force to outsmart. He was unprepared for the grandeur of the world he now entered.

The dome of St. Peter's Basilica reached up to Heaven, like an enormous bejeweled crown. At the foot of the wide entrance steps stood the enormous statue of St. Paul. He held a sword, defending the Church against those who wished to bring her harm. On the left stood an equally massive marble statue of St. Peter, the first Pope, in his hands a cluster of keys.

Looking in every direction around him, he saw nothing but architectural genius, not only in form but in function. The Vatican City's immense, imposing wall ranged from forty to over one hundred feet in height, its medieval design capable of repelling even a modern-day military strike. Vatican City held everything you would expect of a country, even one that was only a little over one hundred acres—banks, post office, radio stations, a newspaper, and even a helicopter pad. It had its own currency and judicial system, and it was presided over by Europe's only true absolute monarch, the Pope. While the Vatican welcomed the public into certain of its areas, the majority of the Vatican was isolated within the walled enclave. Access to this area was permitted only to a select few.

Michael spent two days in the more public areas of the Piazza San Pietro, the Sistine Chapel, and the host of museums photographing and observing, learning and planning. He hadn't realized until he commenced his research the breadth of the Pope's cultural domain. The Vatican included a twelve-museum complex; one, some claimed, was the largest in the world, a title debated by both the Louvre and the Smithsonian. The Vatican Museums encompassed fourteen hundred rooms. They stretched along corridors totaling over four miles. A sightseer could spend an entire year there and still not see the vast collection, one accumulated over two thousand years. Every interest could be satisfied: Etruscan art, classical statuary, archaeology, Middle Eastern artifacts, Renaissance paintings, books, maps, manuscripts, tapestries, furnishings. Treasures that no one man could imagine and precious items collectors everywhere coveted. From the three-hundred-and-sixty-foot-long Gallery of Maps to the Gallery of the Candelabra overflowing with Roman classical sculptures to the mummy- and sarcophagi-filled Egyptian Museum, every square inch of the museum complex held some of the world's most irreplaceable objects.

While most had heard of Michelangelo's masterpiece, the ceiling of the Sistine Chapel, the side walls of the chapel itself were masterpieces in their own right. Here, the greatest artists of their age—Perugino, Botticelli, Ghirlandaio, and Rosselli—had created magnificent frescoes that spanned the entire length of the chapel. In other halls could be found entire rooms painted by the likes of Raphael, Pinturicchio, and Signorelli, And though the Sistine's ceiling cast its shadow over the other works, their perfection was never in dispute.

The great collection had initially overwhelmed Michael, but he had forced himself to focus. Now he paid particular attention to the Museo Storico-Artisticoe e Tesoro. Known as the Sacristy and Treasury Museum, the ten-room complex was adjacent to St. Peter's Basilica and housed many of the greatest relics of the Christian empire and Papal State; the Crux Vaticana, containing fragments of Christ's cross; innumerable reliquaries; the diamond-encrusted Stuart Chalice donated by England's King Henry IV. Manuscripts and decrees passed down from pontiff to pontiff, staffs, crucifixes, and weapons. And of particular interest to Michael, a section devoted to the first Pope. Here, too, were artifacts from the days St. Peter himself walked the streets of Rome: a copy of the Chair of St. Peter; the rusted chains that had bound him prior to his crucifixion at the hands of the Roman emperor Nero. But of greatest interest to Michael was a hallowed corner where stood a single display case. Its pedestal was made of ebony, the dark wood merging into the surrounding shadows and yet standing out in sharp contrast to what it supported. The glass case that sat upon it was two feet square, the glass an inch and a half thick. A ceiling-mounted, pencil-thin spotlight cut through the gloom to illuminate the purple velvet pillow upon which sat the targets of Michael's mission here. Their design was simple, reflecting their two-thousand-year-old age. They were given to St. Peter by Jesus and were the origin for the symbol of the Pope. Their image was reflected frequently throughout the Vatican, most particularly in the Vatican's crest. To millions of people they were the true symbol of St. Peter and his Papal heirs, the leaders of the Church Christ himself had founded. To Michael, however, they held a different meaning: the one chance he had to save his dying wife.

Their design was simple, slightly larger and thicker than one would expect today. And though they did appear to serve a function at one time, today they were clearly displayed to inspire awe. They were the gold and silver keys; the keys to Mary's survival.

⌘

It was estimated that within these walls, there was in excess of forty billion dollars in art, antiquities, gold, and jewels, along with titles to the Catholic Church's vast holdings throughout the world. No other country concentrated their assets in such a small area. And because of it, there were security measures with no equal in the world.

Every doorway was monitored personally and electronically. The modern-day architects of the Vatican rivaled the fabled masters in their creativity. Their security designs—while cutting-edge—were, for the most part, out of sight so as not to diminish in any way the grandeur of the structures they protected. Metal detectors were concealed, so were radioactive sensors and electronic bomb sniffers. Hidden or not, all were in constant search of the next threat: knives, guns, explosives, even nuclear material. The precautions taken were proactive.

The Swiss Guard were stationed at every entrance and checkpoint, but they were not the ones who gave Michael pause. It was the contingent of Vatican Police wandering and intermingling within the crowds—the guards without uniforms. Their haircuts, the way they walked and positioned their bodies evident only to the practiced observer. These men floated in and out of the crowds seemingly at random, but upon closer scrutiny, a pattern was revealed. Each museum was always covered by at least two Vatican policemen. As one left, another arrived. Their timing was synchronized down to the second. And they were all watching. They were all waiting for any conceivable threat to the security of this unique kingdom.

Within the Sacristy and Treasury Museum were nine stationary cameras, their observation span covering every angle around the gold and silver keys and the entire range where Michael planned to operate. The cameras were superbly concealed within the walls so as not to interfere with the art and ambiance, but as Michael committed the room not only to memory but to film—never taking more pictures than the average tourist—he knew the hidden video cameras monitored his every move. And he realized this job would require more than experience and creativity. It would require ingenuity and a resourcefulness unlike any he had ever possessed if he was to overcome the impossible and save his wife.

⌘

"Hello." Mary's voice was as clear as if she were next door, her greeting sweet to Michael's ear. The satellite phone Finster had given him was amazing; bulkier than a cell phone and quite noticeable when in his pocket, but the reception was perfect as he walked the streets of Rome.

"How is it going?"

"You first. Are you OK?"

"I'm fine."

"How's the treatment?" She'd started chemotherapy the day he left. But for the past four days she had been too weak to do more than whisper into the phone. Today, for the first time, she sounded like herself.

"It turns out it's not really that bad." Her tone was upbeat and filled with energy. "Now, tell me—are you OK?"

"Fine, things are going great, I'm actually ahead of schedule. I should be able to get home a day or two early." Michael was relieved not to be lying for once.

"I was hoping, when you get back, maybe we could get out of town for a few days, maybe just be alone."

"I would love that. Are you getting everything you need?"

"Jeannie comes every day. She brought all your favorite junk food and a collection of literary smut. And Paul stopped by today. He brought some pictures that his kids made and was nice enough to drop off some of my schoolwork."

"How was Busch?"

"Fine. Why?"

"I think I pissed him off."

"Michael . . ." She sounded like a disappointed mother.

"He offered to come with me and I turned him down."

"Why?" There was a tinge of sadness in her voice. "He was just being nice."

"I think he was having second thoughts about what I was doing and wanted to keep an eye on me."

"You're paranoid, he seemed fine. He said he couldn't wait for you to get back, said your team took a beating—twenty-one to six—due to the lack of their star quarterback and that he was going to take his anger and frustration out on you."

"I'll bet," Michael said.

"Michael, Paul is your best friend, he trusts you."

⌘

While Mary, the eternal optimist, was fighting for her life, she had actually begun to think of death as an escape from the devastating feeling that wracked her body. She would never admit to Michael what she was going through. The pain from the chemotherapy was more than she ever imagined. But each time she thought about dying, she quickly said a prayer and asked for God's forgiveness. There was nothing she wanted more than to live. To live and enjoy life, experience the world, appreciating all those things she took for granted when she'd so carelessly thought herself immortal. Michael was fighting for her life as much as she was and she viewed her terrible thoughts as a betrayal. She was determined to make it through this wretched journey; she wouldn't let Michael down.

⌘

The garage smelled of grease and oil. It had not only stained the air but the concrete floor as well. Two dismantled Fiats were in the corner; their engines hung from chains in the ceiling. Michael was in the back near an open window; it helped to carry away the fumes as he cooked over a Bunsen burner. The fumes weren't toxic but their sweet smell was in stark contrast to the odors emanating from the car repair shop and he couldn't afford the attention. He had picked up his supplies at the supermarket, an art supply shop, and nearby drugstore. Mothballs, Epsom salts, paint, sugar: everyday items with everyday purposes. Michael combined and heated the mixture to 137° Fahrenheit. He formed the thick paste into malleable balls, and painted each brown. He poured them into an empty Milk Duds box and placed it next to a box of Good & Plentys.

He'd located the garage before he even left the States. It specialized in Fiats and Alfa Romeos, and its sixty-five-year-old proprietor was of the highest reputation—particularly when it came to erasing the ownership history of a vehicle. Michael had gone straight there after landing. He found the owner, an old-style grease monkey, working on a transmission in the driveway. Attilio Vitelli stood there silently in his blue coveralls as Michael explained his desperate need for a metal lathe and some tools. He had some very expensive video equipment that had been damaged by the careless luggage handlers at Rome's airport. The parts he needed would take a month to arrive from Japan and if he missed his fast-approaching deadline he would lose his job. Michael wore a green windbreaker and a New York

Yankees cap. His small gold-rimmed glasses gave him an intelligent, inoffensive appearance.

Vitelli studied him for almost a minute, wiping his greasy hands on an old rag. Michael feared that maybe the old Italian's English was not as fluent as he had bragged.

"You know how to work a lathe?" Vitelli said.

"Yes. So, you think I could use some of your tools?"

Vitelli looked at Michael again, then climbed back under the hood, resuming his work without replying.

"I'll pay you five hundred euros. It shouldn't take me more than five hours," Michael added. He wasn't about to offer an outrageous amount, as it would raise even more suspicion than the crafty Italian already had.

Without looking up from his task, Vitelli replied, "My mechanic rate is one twenty an hour."

"Fine."

"You only work while I am here. And if I need to use any of my tools you defer to me." He popped his head out from under the hood. "Camera equipment?"

Michael pursed his lips as he nodded. "I promise, I won't get in your way."

⌘

On the worktable in Vitelli's garage sat Michael's notebook computer. On its screen a digital grid overlay various images of the two keys, their display case, and the room in which it stood. Next to the computer were Michael's creations from the day. He had worked the metal and plastic upon the lathe to perfection. Each piece honed and polished. Each device flawlessly constructed. His talent had developed considerably since his youth. Using metal and plastics, he was capable of fashioning almost anything, from fake jewels to intricate mechanical devices. Mary always bragged to her friends, *Michael is so good with his hands.*

Vitelli had only stepped into the garage twice, both times to silently get tools. He'd ignored Michael as if the American was an employee and let him go about his work undisturbed. In all, Michael fashioned five items, each ordinary in appearance. But their function went far beyond their appearance.

⌘

"Professor Higgins?" Michael rose from the couch, extending his hand. The man he'd greeted slowed and stared at Michael, ignoring both his hand and his greeting. He finally continued on and away from Michael without a word.

"My name is Michael McMahon. I left a message for you earlier?" Michael hurried to catch up to him.

"If you'll excuse me," Higgins said curtly, not bothering to look at Michael. He kept walking across the elegant marble lobby to the elevator and hit the button.

"The Vatican Office of Scholarly Advancement gave me your name—"

"I'm sorry, Mr. McMah—"

"It's Professor. Actually Doctor," Michael said, feigning modesty. "But I don't really brag about it—"

"You just did. Please excuse me." Higgins tried to turn away, growing jittery, nervously tapping his right foot as he waited for the elevator.

"I just thought as a fellow American, and seeing we will be together on the Vatican tour tomorrow . . ."

"Who sent you?" There was a paranoia in Higgins's eyes.

Michael looked at him, confused.

"If you are trying to dissuade me . . ." Higgins's foot-tapping was growing louder, echoing off the marble walls. "If you are here to challenge my theories, go write your own book."

"Sir, you must have me mistaken for someone else. I actually don't disagree with your theories. In fact, if you have time for a drink, I'd like to tell you how I concur with several of your ideas." Michael stood there, a smile on his face, hoping that the bait would be snatched up.

Higgins looked around the hotel lobby before finally turning back to Michael. It was a moment. And then he stopped tapping his foot.

⌘

Michael never finalized details of any job until he arrived at his location. He needed to mold his plan to fit the environment. With Higgins as part of that environment, the last piece fell into place. Two days earlier when Michael had shifted his research from escape routes to the mysteries of the Vatican, he had identified the members of the various scholastic tour groups through the Vatican Office of Scholarly Advancement. All it took was a simple phone call explaining his desire to touch base with other visiting academics who would be touring the Vatican and its museums. As Michael used his various resources to review each academic's background, he zeroed in on Professor Albert Higgins. Higgins was almost the same height and build as Michael and his hair color was close enough, but that wasn't what excited Michael. For Michael, Higgins's open disdain for the Catholic Church was nothing short of a windfall.

The professor had traveled from New England to do some final research on a book he was writing about the history of the Vatican and the influence it had exerted on shaping society. Michael picked him up and had tailed him earlier in the day during his museum rounds. He had taken an immediate dislike to the man, particularly the condescending way he spoke to people and his generally superior air. Higgins was a WASP in every sense of the word, looking disparagingly down his aquiline nose at all other races, creeds, and religions as he constantly flicked back his greasy brown hair over his swollen head. Here was a man with perpetual blinders on, finding fault with all theories but his own. For years he'd clung to his hypothesis—one he was certain he would prove soon—that the Catholic Church had been the downfall of all societies and was responsible for the Holocaust, Communism, AIDS and—worst of all—the withered condition of the British Empire, home of his ancestors.

The more Michael learned of Higgins, the less conflicted he felt about what tomorrow's tour would bring the unsuspecting professor.

⌘

Busch was sitting at his desk, wondering where the hell Michael was. Somewhere abroad, which could be anywhere, and anywhere non-USA was a direct violation of his parole. Busch had kept it quiet for the last four days. He didn't dare mention it even to his wife. Jeannie would have said something to Mary and that was the last thing anyone needed.

Busch had visited Mary again this morning and was increasingly disturbed by her appearance. She put up a good front but he could see she was in terrible pain. He had asked her about Michael, when he would be back, small talk really. She'd told him that Michael's job was going smoothly and that he'd said he should be home in a few days. She had gone on to express her gratitude for the generosity of a Mr. Rosenfield—a man she had never met—who had paid for her treatment.

Michael had lied to Mary and to him. Busch had been down this road before. The lies floated on the surface, always masking something more disturbing, something deeper, some graver dishonest fact. Michael had fallen. He had gone back to the other side. It was the only explanation. And yet, for the first time in his thirty-nine years, Busch was torn.

Michael had been reformed, cured of his illegal desires, yet he'd been hit with a devastating dilemma. Whatever he was up to, he was doing it for Mary. Busch couldn't help but believe that Michael was a victim; he'd done nothing to deserve this. He'd been forced to cross the line because of his love for his wife and Busch supposed that if faced with the same situation he would do the same. Love has driven many a man to many a desperate, foolish act.

Nevertheless, Busch was a man of the law. Upon Michael's return, he would have no choice: he would arrest him.

Chapter 9

The dome of St. Peter's Basilica soared 390 feet into the air, designed by Michelangelo. It had taken forty-four years to complete the Italian master's staggering vision. This was the literal golden crown of the Church. As the tour group of six academics rounded the cathedral's altar, Michael glanced upward, amazed at the 415-year-old craftsmanship. Michael was dressed in loose-fitting clothing, a tan vest over a white oxford shirt, a pen-filled pocket protector in his breast pocket. He carried a small leather satchel that held, among other things, two notebooks, a camera, another collection of pens, several books on the Vatican, and two boxes of candy, which he pulled out and placed in his pocket. The round gold-rimmed glasses he wore gave him the distinct air of an academic.

After a one-hour lecture on the detailed history of what they were about to see, their tour started at precisely 9:15. The tour was designed as an overview and precursor to the more detailed lectures they would partake of in the afternoon. It was scheduled to take three hours and would conclude in the Sacristy and Treasury Museum at 12:15. Michael had no intention of sitting through the afternoon lectures. At the time his group would be sitting down in the lecture hall, Michael would be sitting on a plane flying out of Rome. He looked at his watch and hit the timer. He had lined everything up. Barring any unforeseen event, his mission would be complete before noon. He had three hours.

⌘

The group Michael was with was more scholarly in nature than the tourists he had grown accustomed to seeing in the past four days. Sisters Katherine and Teresa had pooled their meager savings and escaped from the Cenacle Convent in Ireland, where they helped to instruct future nuns in Catholic history. The two nuns traveled under the guise of education but were actually looking forward to tomorrow's Mass celebrated by the Pope in St. Peter's Square. The two women were like Dead Heads: groupies following their favorite rock star. They had attended three of the Pope's Masses and were so touched by his presence that they would pack up in a VW bus, don potato sacks, and sell T-shirts just to hear one of his sermons. There were two rabbis in the group: Abramowitz and Lohiem from Brooklyn. The two older men were more than pleasant, finding joy in every breath of life, their youthful spirits belying the twilight of their lives. Many of the tourists found it strange to see Jewish men of the cloth. They did not realize that though the Jewish people did not believe Jesus Christ to be the messiah and savior, he was a teacher and Hebrew, living his life as a model Jew and rabbi. And Peter, in whose name this great city was built, was considered the apostle to the Jews.

Finally, there was Professor Albert Higgins. He and Michael had shared a bottle of wine the evening before, while Michael listened to him espouse his nouveau riche divinity theories. Michael was sure the man could talk about himself for weeks on end. Michael had excused himself after an hour, stating that he needed to have all of his energy for the following day's tour. That morning, when the tour group greeted one another outside the Vatican offices, it was as if Higgins had never met Michael before. The professor barely acknowledged him. The man was only aware of what he wanted to be aware of.

The tour was led by Brother Joseph, a member of the Vatican staff and a student of its history. What little hair he possessed had gone to gray early but his cherubic face still held a hint of boyishness. He wore the traditional brown pants and white-collared shirt of his order, having left his stylish designer clothes in the past. Joseph Mariano, a professor of Vatican history at the University of Rome, had lost his wife three years earlier in a car accident. Losing all sense of direction and the will to live, he'd immersed himself in his work and received the calling. Not sure whether to commit to the priesthood, he found a compromise in the brotherhood; he would give it three years and if he still felt the pull he would commit the rest of his life to God. Brother Joseph was assigned VIP tours as a result of his knowledge and ready smile, which combined to make him the ideal ambassador. He took his job very seriously, and even though he possessed that sweet smile, he had no need for those who didn't follow the Vatican rules.

Michael's face was curious and responsive to Brother Joseph's walking dissertation. But it was all a mask. Michael's mind was two hours into his plan. When he awoke at dawn, he had reviewed every detail of the heist again. He had contemplated each unforeseen obstacle and its resulting contingencies. He had found a greater focus than he had ever experienced in all of his years. In the past stealing was always selfish, it was always for himself. But not today. This was for Mary. Every detail was contemplated, constructed, set up, and in motion. Everything was on schedule.

⌘

At ten a.m., Attilio Vitelli peered out from underneath the Alfa Romeo and chose not to run. The four cop cars pulling into his driveway were nothing new to him. The Italian autos in his possession were—for the most part—legal. And the ones that weren't had already been stripped, refurbished, and had ownership titles, leaving nothing to tie them to their former owners. Nine gendarme diligently surrounded Vitelli, waiting for him to speak first. But the old man didn't even look at them until the heavy, bald man in charge poked his head under the red auto's hood.

"It's not about the cars this time, Attilio," the officer said.

And that got Vitelli's attention. "Social visit, Gianni?" he asked.

Investigator Gianni Francone never had anything solid on Vitelli; it was always innuendo and assumptions. He knew about Vitelli's underground business, he just couldn't make anything stick. So when he received the anonymous call about someone planning an assault on a Roman landmark today before noon, someone operating out of Vitelli's garage, Francone couldn't pass up the opportunity to search the place.

Three policemen fanned out around the yard while six entered the three-bay auto garage.

Francone sat on a Fiat Spider, his weight severely testing the suspension. "So, my friend, any visitors lately?"

⌘

"In fifteen forty-six, Michelangelo Buonaroti took over as chief architect of St. Peter's Basilica, redesigning many of its elements including the grand dome above us, but sadly, he did not live to see its completion." Michael and the group remained tightly bunched around Brother Joseph so as not to miss a word. "The artwork here was obtained from many sources. Some was donated or purchased, some created specifically for the Vatican, and some was found underneath where we now stand," Brother Joseph explained in his thick Italian accent. He stopped in front of a forty-foot-tall marble statue of a man holding a spear. "You will note that the four magnificent statues of saints within the dome support columns surrounding the Papal altar. This is called the Loggias of the Relics. This figure of Longinus"—he pointed to the spear-holding statue—"was created by Bernini, while the three others were crafted by his students. Each of these statues was built to contain relics. St. Longinus was the centurion who pierced the side of Christ upon the cross to prove He was dead. The statue was designed to hold the tip of what some refer to as the Spear of Destiny." Brother Joseph turned. He led his group over to the statue of a woman holding an enormous cross. "The statue of St. Helena, the mother of the Emperor Constantine, who discovered the actual cross of Christ, at one point contained nails and sections of the True Cross of our Lord." He turned to a statue depicting a woman holding a wind-blown veil. "St. Veronica, who offered her veil to Christ to mop His brow as He carried His cross to Calvary, commemorates the actual veil which our Lord returned to her imprinted with His features. You will note her pose: in bullfighting, the most classic movement is called the Veronica. It is when the toreador swings his red cape slowly before the face of the bull, like Veronica wiping Christ's face. It's so named for this statue."

Brother Joseph led them to the fourth and final statue. "St. Andrew was the brother of St. Peter and he, like his brother, was crucified. He was tied to an X-shaped cross and died in Greece. His head was in the possession of the Vatican until 1966, when it was returned to the Greek city of Patras—where he had died almost two thousand years earlier—as a gesture toward improving relations with the Greek Orthodox Church. But for the head of St. Andrew, each of the relics I have referred to is here. All are kept in the chapel above St. Veronica."

They began walking down elaborate marble steps adjacent to the statue of St. Longinus. Michael had successfully passed himself off as Professor Michael McMahon from the University of St. Albans. His forged letterhead introduced him and asked for assistance on matters regarding the origin of the original Vatican. When the Office of Scholarly Advancement called for verification, they were told by the university that Professor McMahon was on sabbatical conducting research around the world for a textbook he was writing. If they would like to get in touch with him they could leave a message, as the professor checked his voice mail at least twice a month. The university administrator explained that due to the school's limited funds, McMahon's sabbatical was for only one semester; any help that could be extended to the professor would be appreciated and returned in kind by St. Albans.

There really was a Professor Michael McMahon at St. Albans. Michael's simple Google search revealed those vainglorious ones who not only announced in print their paid leaves of absence from school but foolishly laid out their itineraries. McMahon was writing a book and traveling the world; only he wasn't in Rome at the moment, he was in a remote section of Tibet communing with some Buddhist monks.

Michael's group stood in an area directly under the Basilica, an area rarely seen, off-limits to most of the outside world, reserved by appointment only for scholars and archaeologists: The Sacred Grottoes. It was a dark and ominous place, befitting its name. The soft glow of hundreds of candles danced off golden wall sconces and polished marble walls. The group walked past ornate sarcophagi that seemed to stretch on forever, the final resting places, Brother Joseph revealed, of not only most of the Popes since 1549 but also emperors and queens, VIPs, and dignitaries.

"One hundred and fifty-three Popes are buried here," the brother's voice echoed off the marble tombs. "And there is room for hundreds more, of course with the hope that their service in Christ only comes to an end after a long and productive tenure in His service."

"Speaking of tenure, care to comment on those whose tenure was abbreviated by murder?" Professor Higgins cut in.

Brother Joseph hated being interrupted, it was written all over his face. But he acquiesced cautiously. "Pope John VIII was murdered in his sleep in eight eighty-two. Then there was Pope John XII, who was eighteen when elected Pope. He was murdered in December nine sixty-three—"

"I was referring to more recent events." Higgins's condescending smile was as sharp as an accusation.

Brother Joseph stared at Higgins for what seemed like an eternity, clearly doing everything to contain his anger. An uncomfortable hush fell over the group. "Yes, well, we have had our share of intrigue. In nineteen eighty-one, when Pope John Paul II was shot, Colonel Alois Estermann was the first person to our Holy Father. The colonel shielded the Pope with his body from further harm. Through the years, the Pope maintained a very close relationship with Estermann and in nineteen ninety-eight, Colonel Estermann was nominated by our Holy Father to be the commander of the Swiss Guard. Tragically, less than two hours after Estermann's nomination, he and his wife were murdered in their apartment—"

Higgins interrupted. "When it was found he had been a spy for the East German secret police, the Stasi—"

"Incorrect." Brother Joseph cut him off. "While you are a guest of the Vatican, Professor, I must ask that you please refrain from repeating innuendo. The Estermanns were shot by a disgruntled member of the Swiss Guard who then turned the gun on himself. So, yes, there was a murder at the Vatican in ninety-eight—"

"Actually," Higgins again interrupted, "I was really referring to the murder in nineteen seventy-eight." Higgins looked pointedly at the tomb of Pope John Paul I.

"You are out of line, sir."

"I'm not saying anything that hasn't been published." The group watched with mounting interest as the challenge was thrown down. "My understanding is that he was poisoned. The Pope's housekeeper found him dead sitting up in bed. He had only been Pope for what? Two weeks?"

"Myocardial infarction," Brother Joseph said through clenched teeth. "Our Holy Father had a heart attack."

"But there was no autopsy—"

"Professor Higgins, if you wish to be escorted back to your hotel, I could gladly arrange it. Otherwise, this discussion is at an end. We are not in the habit of being insulted by our guests."

Higgins opened his mouth to speak again but thought better of it. Nevertheless, his dark eyes sparkled a bit brighter over his victory of getting under the brother's skin.

⌘

The police team was talking in earnest inside Vitelli's auto shop. Before them, on a workbench, lay a pile of metal and plastic shavings; three smoothed-out, formerly wrinkled pieces of blank paper; and an empty air cylinder. A thin detective, who looked no more than twelve, handled the blank pieces of paper with surgical gloves. He took a long piece of graphite and ran it lightly over the paper. "We can see here the outlines of the writing on the paper that had laid atop this piece."

"And . . . ?" Investigator Francone prompted him.

"Schematics of some kind."

"Yours?" Francone turned to Vitelli, who was calmly smoking a cigarette.

"No. I don't need drawings. Everything I need is up here." Vitelli tapped his forehead.

"Then whose drawings are they?"

Vitelli knew he should have charged that American more money for the use of his tools. "He was an American. Said he needed to borrow my tools for a bit."

"You let anyone use your garage, huh? A law-abiding guy like yourself. You surprise me, Attilio."

"I surprise myself sometimes. The guy seemed harmless. And he paid in cash."

Investigator Francone had initially doubted the anonymous call placed to the station but now, as he looked at the rubbing, he was glad he hadn't ignored it. He was unsure of what the schematics were for but his gut was telling him people don't build innocent things in chop-shop garages. "Well, it looks like your American friend is up to something. And if he is up to something, and we don't stop him before he pulls this something off . . . After all these years, Attilio, of being such an *honest* businessman, you may end up in jail as an accessory."

"Accessory to what?"

"That's what you are going to help us figure out." Francone looked at his watch. It was 10:32. "And you better start thinking fast or you just may have *fixed* your last car."

⌘

The four continued through the Vatican catacombs. The verbal sparring between Higgins and Brother Joseph left an anxious silence on the group that had yet to break. They eventually arrived at a black iron gate set in granite, flanked by two Swiss Guards. Brother Joseph handed over his credentials along with a letter of authorization. The guards studied the papers as well as the faces of Brother Joseph's charges before finally allowing them to pass.

After inserting a series of keys, Brother Joseph pulled open the entrance to a set of wide stone stairs. The group walked two abreast, speaking in hushed tones, aware they were descending through time with each step they took. They came out in an area that confined them under a low earthen ceiling. After fifty yards through the stony caves—some natural, some man-made—they arrived at a large blue plastic tarp. Joseph pulled this aside and they all stepped through into a musty area. It appeared to be a traditional archeological dig; dirt floor, dimly lit by a string of construction lights, the ground terraced in three-inch increments, each step labeled. The dig had gone on for seventy-five years under the direction and watchful eye of the Church. While their faith was the purest of the land, the Church hierarchy was keenly aware that controversy always lay inches below the soil. One never knew what artifacts could create unwanted debate.

"Welcome to the Necropolis." Brother Joseph paused, allowing everyone to absorb the improbable sight before them: an ancient city street. But where there should have been sky above they saw nothing but the foundation of the basilica. "What you see is the coming together of two worlds, of two beliefs. This is a place of burial, both Christian and pagan."

The confined space in which they found themselves was an actual street no more than six feet wide; on either side were structures made of brick and stone, doorways covered in ancient carvings. The poorly lit road jogged left and right through shadows before falling into total darkness. "This section, excavated over a thirty-year period, contains dozens of elaborate mausoleums, all of which are pagan—except one. The entire area predates Constantine, actually going back two thousand years. Necropolis is a pagan word meaning 'city of the dead,' whereas the Christians preferred to call it a *coemeterium*—where the modern word cemetery comes from—which translates to 'place of sleeping people.' "

Brother Joseph walked up the gently sloping street. The group followed, awestruck at this pagan secret deep below the seat of Christendom.

"This necropolis was explored and excavated by a team of Vatican archeologists beginning in nineteen thirty-nine at the direction of Pope Pius the Twelfth." Brother Joseph came to an open section. Debris was scattered about here; wall footings poked up through the dirt. "This is all that remains of the first church of St. Peter, our first Pope. The original church, dating from AD one fifty, was buried to make way for the first basilica, which was built by Constantine in the fourth century. It was during recent excavations that the most compelling evidence of St. Peter's life was found."

The brother pulled a small flashlight from his pocket and shined it just left of where they were huddled. The beam illuminated a large pane of glass set in the granite wall. Beyond lay a room. The bones were hard to distinguish at first, the color not the milky white of TV forensic shows but much darker. The light picked out a tibia, a fibula, and a femur; while the mandible was not attached to the skull and the teeth were scattered about, you could clearly make out the shape of the head: only then did you realize that this pile of bones was once a living being, the warrior saint who was the first leader of the mighty Church.

No matter the backgrounds or religions of the group, it was hard not to be in awe, staring at history, at a life that two thousand years ago was persecuted and brutally ended for its beliefs and teachings, a man who was ridiculed and mocked in death like his teacher before him for his unwavering faith.

Brother Joseph continued in a whisper. "If you were to go straight up from this point, you would be in the center of the Basilica. Four hundred feet above that is the exact center of the dome. The Lord's Church, literally built upon His most devout disciple, Peter, a name derived from the Latin *petra*, meaning rock."

"Were there any other bodies found?" Sister Katherine asked.

"He was found alone. His wife's tomb was never found."

Everyone appeared surprised except the rabbis.

Brother Joseph smiled. "St. Peter was a married fisherman before his brother Andrew introduced him to Jesus; the celibacy edict didn't occur for another thousand years. There are remains in the other mausoleums down here but within this particular sepulcher, there were no other bodies. St. Peter's tomb had rotted away, along with most of the original church he was buried in. But, as you will see, there were many other items that stood the test of time down here. Most are on display upstairs. Peter's chair, the chains that bound him, parchments in his own hand, some clothes, textiles, clay pots, and the keys . . ."

⌘

The actual museums were crowded. Brother Joseph deftly led them through the strangling throngs at the Gregorian Museum of Etruscan Art, his commanding demeanor parting the crowds as he continued his lecture. Their tour through the various museums was brief, as their focus was not art but rather the intertwined history of the Church and the Vatican. Still, Joseph allowed them brief stops to absorb the magnificence around them. The two nuns were drawn to the ceiling paintings, the rabbis to the sculptures, while Michael and Higgins stopped to peer into the glass display cases containing books and artifacts.

Within the Gregorian Museum, Michael was drawn to the Room of the Jewels. The large cases here displayed priceless jewelry and artifacts. He took a particular interest in a large gold medallion, the face of which depicted a man and woman entwined in each other's arms. It had been dug up from the necropolis of Vulci and the image of the couple was as pure and detailed as the day it was created some twenty-five hundred years in the past. It was as if the couple's love had survived undiminished for two millennia. As Michael looked upon them, he felt for the briefest of moments the possibilities of the life that lay ahead for him and Mary. If he could just get through the next hour . . .

And then Michael reached into his pocket. It was a natural movement, not unlike someone reaching for a tissue, or some money. But

Michael was reaching for neither. He palmed the item as he leaned over the display case, apparently admiring the golden medallion one last time. He affixed the brown malleable ball under the case. It was a simple movement, natural, unannounced, and undetected. And it was the same move he performed on four other cases as they made their way through the Gregorian Museum.

⌘

At eleven a.m. the main number of the Vatican was called. A woman refusing to give her name and not allowing the attendant a moment to speak stated that she had it on good authority that an abortion rights protest was going to be staged soon in St. Peter's Basilica. Young university students looking to protest anything until dinnertime, when their convictions would be replaced with hunger pangs. The Vatican, like every country, received such threats on a daily basis. Most turned out to be hoaxes but it only took one ignored caller to end up with a crisis. The head of the Swiss Guard, Colonel Enjordin, was entrusted with the direction of both the Guard and Papal Gendarme and hence the safety and protection of the small nation. He was technically the head of both the military and the police. He was the man in charge. Enjordin treated each threat as if it was real, and reacted to this one accordingly. He had never shut the doors to the Church or her museums based on a threat and he wouldn't today. But he did decide to increase the number of guards, both uniformed and undercover. He had a new contingent in training. A precautionary exercise like this would be a good test of their diligence. He dispatched thirty-five supplemental Vatican Gendarme to wander the Vatican.

⌘

As Brother Joseph's group stepped into the Sistine Chapel, Michael reached his point of no return. It was 11:16, they still had one hour left before the end of the tour and it would be at least half that before they arrived at the Treasury Museum. Michael would use the time to focus his mind and clear it of any other thoughts: failure, Busch, Mary. He needed all of his concentration to ensure success. He had run the plan through his head over and over to the point where his mind and body would be on autopilot, acting and reacting just like a dancer upon the stage. Through each section of their tour he noted the movements of the guards, both uniformed and undercover. Their routine and timing was as precise as he had noted over the previous days. He knew their patterns, he knew their faces, he even knew their names. Now he noticed that their numbers had increased; there were new faces supplementing the guards and gendarme. And these men looked worried.

The grand masterpiece of the Sistine Ceiling depicted scenes from the Bible, starting with the creation story and working its way through the Great Flood. In 1508, Pope Julius II had commissioned—what in those days was a commission would be considered conscripted slavery today—the artist Michelangelo to create this masterpiece to God. The youthful genius, who was all of thirty-three, was more than reluctant to take the commission. He viewed painting as a less noble pursuit than sculpture, but Michelangelo's hand was forced both by politics and by inflexible Papal decree. The work would cover over three thousand square feet and ultimately contain over three hundred figures in a room based on the dimensions of Solomon's Temple. Through appalling conditions Michelangelo had labored nonstop on his back upon a scaffold eighty-five feet in the air. Despite extremes of hot and cold, his inspiration never wavered.

At the front of the chapel, behind the gold and marble altar, was a fresco greater than the ceiling above. Filling the entire wall, it was much darker, more somber, and grimmer in its vision than the illustration overhead. Called The Last Judgment, it pictured God as uncompromising and pitiless, visiting His harrowing vengeance on a degenerate humanity below. In 1534, Pope Clement VII had conscripted Michelangelo for this work. Though Clement was to die shortly thereafter, both his championing of Michelangelo and his will could still be felt to this day. At the same time, the Pope had Michelangelo redesign the Swiss Guard uniforms to incorporate the gold, blue, and maroon colors of his family's crest. Clement came from the family known as the Medicis; the Italian family of renown; the business and political deities of Renaissance Italy.

Michelangelo had spent four years on the chapel ceiling, a work representing faith and hope; the Supreme Being portrayed as a living, merciful God. But the Last Judgment—which took nearly seven years—could only be viewed as terrifying.

Here, God was depicted as merciless, vengeful. The central figure of Christ was surrounded by humanity, the righteous summoned to Paradise on the left, their bodies floating up from their earthen graves. On the lower right, Christ consigned the damned to Hell, where they were pulled irrevocably down by cloven-hooved beasts. Below the earth, the dark evil eyes of Lucifer gazed with hunger upward at his reluctant minions.

This was not a work of art but rather a work of warning: those who sought to betray God would face His unquestionable wrath.

On the lower right side of the painting, a figure could be glimpsed, his body being dragged to Hell by an unholy creature. Ultimate horror twisted the face of this damned soul as he approached his doom. It was the only figure among the three hundred to look outward from the fresco. This lost soul knew it was beyond redemption, its eyes seemed to plead with Michael for understanding.

The entire image cried out to Michael that his actions would reap only grave consequences, consequences that couldn't be reversed. His mind was suddenly fogged as to his purpose and goal. But he quickly suppressed this confusion, His welfare was of no consequence, only Mary's. And the next few minutes would determine her future. He had already gone too far. Like the lost souls before him, he was beyond redemption.

Chapter 10

Brother Joseph led the group through the throngs of St. Peter's Basilica to the Sacristy and Treasury Museum. This was the final museum of their private tour. Fifteen minutes to go before they would retire to a lecture hall for questions.

The Treasury contained paintings primarily concerned with St. Peter, the Apostles, and their influence throughout the ages. Cases containing Bibles, books, and manuscripts occupied the center of the hall, just a smattering of the Church's enormous library. Most of the volumes were contained in the Vatican Archives, which was off-limits except when a special papal grant was given for access. Several of the cases contained artifacts dating back to the time of Constantine, while others reached back to the time of Christ Himself: chalices, pottery, coins, scraps of clothing, and tools from an age long since vanished. Significant artifacts required and received their own cases and in many instances were mounted in separate areas. Most were unimportant to Michael.

Michael reached into his bag and pulled out two notebooks. Holding them in his right hand, he reached into his pocket and pulled out his wallet, holding it in his left.

"Albert," Michael said to Higgins. "Could you help me out here? Could you hold this?"

Higgins's breath of exasperation was audible. He looked at Michael with disdain as he took the notebooks from his outstretched hand. Michael dug deep into his bag and pulled out a red pen and slid it in his breast pocket. He took his items back from Higgins, who stormed off in the direction of their group. "Thanks," Michael called after him.

Michael checked his watch: 11:59. He leaned over the last display case—palmed something from a pocket—and placed it underneath the case. A small brown object with a pink confection stuck in the middle, affixed out of sight.

He caught up with the group again as they continued to a wall case where a set of old rusted chains was displayed. The brass placard read: *We gratefully acknowledge the generosity of San Pietro in Vincoli for the honor of displaying The Chains of St. Peter.*

"Before his death, Peter made a pilgrimage back to the Holy Land to the Mount of Kephas. There he prayed a fortnight asking his Holy Father for guidance. Some scholars speculate that he returned to the Holy Land to pay homage, but a select few believe Peter had a premonition of things to come, including his death, and was returning something to the land of his God for fear of it falling into the hands of the evil emperor of the Roman Empire, Nero. During his journey, a great fire consumed over two-thirds of Rome, killing thousands and laying ruin to many sections of the great city.

"Upon his return to the city, Peter found his fellow Christians mercilessly persecuted at the hands of Nero, who had laid the blame for the city's devastation upon them. Peter was bound in chains"—Brother Joseph indicated the chains upon the wall—"and tortured for his beliefs. After being held nine months in the Mamertine dungeon in the dark with St. Paul, Nero ordered Peter's execution. Believing the Apostle to be nothing more than a usurper of his power, the emperor commanded Peter to be crucified, deliberately mocking the crucifixion of Jesus. Peter, not wishing to draw comparison to his Savior, asked and was permitted to be crucified upside down."

As everyone listened intently, Michael drifted toward the glass case in the corner. Lit by the single beam of light, the case was set on the onyx pedestal that stood three and one-half feet tall. A velvet rope barrier supported by three stanchions cordoned off onlookers. Michael didn't bother looking in the case; he had inspected it three times in the last two days. Inside it, the two ancient keys rested on the plush purple cushion.

Brother Joseph continued his story about the upside-down crucifixion of the saint at the hands of the emperor. "Nero was the wicked ruler of Rome, made famous by his notorious circus, where he would loose lions on criminals and peasants for the sheer enjoyment of seeing them torn apart. His drunken orgies were world-renowned in their day and his decadence has yet to see its equal in the two thousand years since his demise. He was as depraved as they come, rivaling Hitler, Pol Pot, and Genghis Khan for the worst in history." In his years of teaching, Brother Joseph had developed a talent for keeping his students' attention. No one ever nodded off in his classes at the university. His current group clustered closely around him so as not to miss a word.

And it was this level of concentration that had caused each of them to jump in fear at the muffled sound of an explosion somewhere down the hall.

⌘

There were three hundred and sixteen cameras, handled by thirty-six monitors; the six images per monitor cycled by in four-second intervals and could be locked at the flick of a switch. Each grouping of monitors, tucked between rose-colored marble columns, was individually manned by three shifts of guards. Fifteen-minute breaks were required hourly in order to keep the eyes of these guards fresh. There had not been a major incident in the Vatican in over three years. The last had been a lunatic brandishing a gun and demanding to see God at once or he would start shooting up the Sistine Chapel. The incident barely received mention in the news. The apprehension of Juan Medenez was credited to one man. That man was promoted for his fast action to the rank of colonel and was appointed personally by Pope John Paul II to head the Central Order of Vigilance. Stephan Enjordin, at thirty-one, had become the youngest director in the history of Vatican security. Respected by his underlings yet equally feared, Enjordin did not hesitate to mete out punishment in his quiet baritone voice for indiscretions, incompetence, or insubordination. When he had first arrived at the Vatican, he'd become one of the most well liked of the Swiss Guard for his broad smile and sense of humor, but as his responsibilities increased, he shed his charm as he felt it an impediment to the chain of command. He walked about the situation room below II Corpo di Vigilanza overseeing the forty-three men crammed in the high tech, Renaissance-decor space. Like each of the Swiss Guard, he was unmarried—there would be time for that later in life—and had a focus unmarred by outside interests. He was a soldier whose direction was always clear, always on the side of good, unhampered by changing politics or administrations. Enjordin's mission was unambiguous: protect God, the Pope, and this one-hundred-and-nine-acre country.

He prided himself on being a techie, always up on the latest technology, and he had a knack for assimilating it into Vatican security. The chemical and bomb "sniffers" were tuned to the high-tech devices used by military, terrorists, fanatics, and pranksters. The body scanners recessed in the doorway arches were far superior to anything found in an airport, embassy, or even the White House. Countless guns had been confiscated from tourists who, while innocent and more than willing to cooperate, were stunned at the unobtrusive detection of Enjordin's team.

Colonel Enjordin had taken the surprise factor out of his enemy's hand, for without the element of surprise, you always saw your enemy coming. That was why his eyes were glued to monitors six and seven, every muscle in his lean body flexed. He couldn't believe what he was seeing.

⌘

Woomph. A low rumble emanated from the display case in the center of the Treasury. The underside of the case started to billow smoke. Thick dense smoke, the kind that could disorient in seconds. A huge cloud rose and spread through the Treasury Museum.

And then the other display cases rattled in succession, a series of similar low *woomphs* occurring underneath each. What initially seemed to be a minor incident was swiftly escalating into a danger-filled situation. The explosions started at the far end of the long hall and worked their way forward like a series of dominoes falling. As the room filled with smoke, confusion reigned. Everyone dissolved in panic. Tourists screamed, mothers grabbed their children, a fire alarm blared. Over its deafening clang, no one could hear the instructions to stay calm or how to get to safety. The terrified public, easily numbering two hundred in the Treasury alone, charged the exits. The smoke was now thicker than molasses. People pushed and slammed into each other blindly as total mayhem took over.

Almost simultaneously, in the Gregorian Museum, the same muffled explosions were occurring. Thick smoke filled the halls and rooms as the panicked tourists charged for the exits. Four more cases began to bubble up smoke, sending the masses into utter confusion.

Without warning, steel plates crashed down in front of the wall-mounted artwork throughout the entire museum complex, sealing each masterpiece from destruction. The books, manuscripts, and artifacts were vacuum-sealed in their display cases under one-inch alarmed glass, protected from any intrusion of the outside world. These frescoes and oil paintings, books and artifacts were cherished works created in the name of God. All were irreplaceable, so the modern world moved swiftly to protect the precious past.

⌘

Brother Joseph was the calm within the storm, telling each of the members of his group to hold hands and he would lead them out. His eyes stung, tears ran down his cheeks, but nothing could wash away the determination in his eyes. The nuns and the rabbis found the moment rather exciting and figured it a bonus to their day. And though they had a burning in their eyes and a hacking cough in their throats, never once did fear replace the excitement they felt.

That wasn't the case for Professor Higgins. He hadn't come here to die, and God be damned if he was to die in this house of worship. What would the papers say, what would his colleagues and detractors say? He wouldn't be remembered for his great work, he would be remembered for the irony of his death: *another death at the hands of the evil Catholic Church, they finally got him, too.* And then someone grabbed his neck. He felt a pinprick just below his ear and he became suddenly dizzy. He panicked, picturing his own death, and pulled away from his assailant. Then he started to run, charging into what he was sure was the exit. He didn't have time to realize how wrong he was. He was out cold before he hit the floor, having crashed into a marble statue of St. Thomas Aquinas, patron saint of academics.

The crowds poured from every exit, quickly filling the Piazza San Pietro. People cried, someone started the rumor that this great institution was going up in flames. Brother Joseph led his group calmly to a remote corner before collapsing with relief. They were all too busy talking to notice that they had lost Michael and Professor Higgins.

⌘

Within the museum, the oily smoke had thickened, wafting upward and then curling back down on itself. Never mind seeing your hand in front of your face, you were lucky if you saw your nose. The sounds of panic diminished, most of the crowd having fled the building. All that remained in the hall was Michael St. Pierre and the unconscious figure of Professor Higgins.

Michael had less than thirty seconds. It wouldn't take long for the Vatican Police and fire department to arrive. Michael had planned everything out; his timing was precise. The smoke bombs he had concocted at the car shop out of sugar, mothballs and Epsom salt had worked like a charm. The pink and white fuses were the key: once stuck into the brown concoction, the coating dissolved and when the contents of the two items mixed, the chemical reaction was swift. The white confection was two centimeters thicker than the pink and acted as a fuse lasting forty-five minutes. The pink confection was a fast-acting five minutes. There had never been any risk of fire. Michael wasn't in the business of killing people.

He grabbed Higgins by the feet and dragged him across the floor toward the key display. Sometimes fortune smiled. The smoke was at its thickest. Michael looked around, listened. Satisfied he was alone.

He reached in his bag, pulled out the objects he had crafted in

Vitelli's garage, and quickly assembled a hammer. Raising it high above his head, he slammed it with all his strength into the two-by-two-foot case. The glass didn't break, not even a spiderweb crack. But the diamond needle-nose hammer, its point thinner than a lock of hair, pierced the one-inch glass. As the case was punctured, compressed air rushed from the handle through the needle and exploded the glass case's seams from within. Another alarm sounded. It blended with the fire alarm and created even greater confusion.

⌘

Colonel Stephan Enjordin and two Swiss Guards raced through the Basilica as the remaining stragglers rushed by to safety. Enjordin had dispatched the fire department and they were less than a minute behind him. Security ratcheted up to def-con one; thirty-six guards converged on the exits to supplement the forty already in place.

Enjordin and the two guards worked their way into the Treasury Museum through the blinding haze calling as they went, wary that something might be occurring that had nothing at all to do with the fire.

⌘

Michael stood at the shattered case. He reached in and removed the keys. Fourteen seconds to go. As he could barely see the end of his arm, he was certain that no one would be able to see him. He quickly dismantled the hammer—the handle of which held eight liters of compressed air—back into its three components and placed them in Higgins's bag. The diamond-tipped needle tucked nicely back into a pen, the head of the five-pound hammer was disguised as a camera body, and the handle looked like the spine of a textbook—all of which fit nicely in Higgins's satchel. Michael looked carefully at his fingertips. The painted-on latex skin was indistinguishable from his real skin but for the lack of fingerprints. Without hesitation, he peeled the clear latex off his fingers, rolled the pieces up into a small ball, popped it into his mouth, and swallowed it.

⌘

With the doors open and the air vents at full blast, the smoke was slowly beginning to dissipate. Enjordin led his men at a sprint through the Treasury Museum, coughing, waving in vain at the smoke, trying desperately to see. They were well trained and knew the difference between the two alarm sounds: a robbery was in progress. Never had there been a theft from the Vatican and it wasn't going to happen on their watch.

All at once they were upon the key case; they saw the broken glass but couldn't see inside due to the lingering smoke. Enjordin turned and was shocked to see a man standing there. In Italian, he demanded to know what the man was doing. Michael had limited knowledge of the language, but he knew what he was being asked.

"What are you doing?" Enjordin demanded, this time switching to English.

"I . . . I—" Michael sputtered.

"What are you doing? How break the glass?" one of the guards cut in. Vernea was the largest of the three, bursting through his blue and gold uniform, he would get answers, no matter what method required. He wasn't about to let his superior down.

Michael's breathing quickened as he mutely stared up at the guard.

Vernea's powerful hand clamped down on Michael's shoulder, dragging him toward the case. "Where are the keys?" This was an assault against God, a blasphemous act for which no punishment could be too brutal. But then . . .

The smoke around the case started to clear. Just a bit at first. Vernea looked closer as Colonel Enjordin leaned in. He reluctantly released Michael's throbbing shoulder.

There, on their purple velvet cushion, lay the two keys.

"Pardon, I'm sorry, sir. I did not think—" the large guard began.

Michael waved him off. "No, please, please, I'm sorry. I couldn't see through the smoke. This man . . ." He pointed at Professor Higgins facedown before him. "I didn't see him, we ran into each other, but the case . . . The case was already broken."

Enjordin ignored the American's explanation, assessing the situation. He studied the damaged case as if it would tell him what really happened and then, stepping back, took in the other nearby display cases and artifacts. He was digesting everything—the damage, the smoke, these two suspects, committing it all to memory. After a moment, he crouched over Higgins, rolling him over. Enjordin patted down the unconscious professor, finding only his wallet and hotel keys. He rifled the brown book bag at Higgins's side, pulling out two books; he passed these to his subordinate. He dug deeper finding three pens and an assortment of anti-Church flyers. Grimly, he continued his search, his hand falling on something that took a bit of effort to pull from the leather satchel. The camera was heavier than any camera he had ever held. He turned it over in his hand, amazed at its weight—at least five pounds. He glanced through the anti-Catholic leaflets, his face reddening. He looked to Vernea and then turned his contemptuous smile on Higgins. He had noticed the man earlier in his monitor; he'd been easy to spot, that arrogant air, the obvious disdain and contempt on his face as he argued with Brother Joseph. This tourist had no respect for the Church. It took every bit of his enormous strength to restrain himself from beating this man so badly he would never wake from his unconscious state.

"Are you hurt?" Enjordin asked Michael, but his question was perfunctory. He never turned to Michael, his eyes remained glued to the man still lying at his feet.

"Just shaken up. The fire—"

"We'll show you out." Enjordin cut him off, turning to the guard. "Reiner?"

⌘

Corporal Reiner took Michael by the arm and led him through the clearing smoke. The sound of their lone footsteps was loud in the eerily deserted museum. Like ghosts materializing from the walls, the Swiss Guard and the Vatican Police had taken up silent position around every case, artifact, and exit; their halberds had been traded for rifles and sidearms. As Michael looked back at the crime scene, he was amazed at how swiftly and efficiently they had responded to the threat. Enjordin controlled the room and his people as if they were extensions of his own body. Higgins was slowly waking up, his head bobbing, his eyes unfocused and lost as Vernea yanked him to his feet. Michael ached for the chance to be a fly on the wall at Higgins's interrogation; how the arrogant bastard would explain the items in his bag would be priceless. There was nowhere he could hide, Higgins's hatred for the Catholic Church was well-known and published; it would be an easy leap of faith to ascribe the blame for this incident to him. It was a quirk of fate. His life had been spent in an attempt to tear down the Church and now, because of simple bad timing, it would be the Church that would burn him down.

"*Un momento!* Wait!" The voice was loud, booming off the museum walls.

Michael turned to see Colonel Enjordin charging down the hall toward them; his heart froze. He looked back at Reiner, whose cheerful demeanor instantly dissolved as the guard assumed his military stature at his commander's approach. Michael glanced over Reiner's shoulder: at the distant doorway, three Swiss Guard had snapped to attention, blocking the way. No matter how hard he ran, he was trapped.

Enjordin came to an abrupt halt, speaking in quick bursts of Italian; Reiner mechanically nodded his head at the furious volley. Then both men turned their attention to Michael.

⌘

Three black Suburbans, sirens flashing, screeched to a halt in front of the hotel. The concierge came running out but was nearly trampled by a swarm of Vatican and Roman police. They charged up the stairs leaving behind a contingent to block all exits. The concierge ran behind calling for them to stop. He waved his pass-key to no avail.

The security force, weapons drawn, charged onto the third-floor landing and without a moment's hesitation broke down the door to room 306. The winded concierge stumbled through the doorway still clutching his pass-key.

The guards' weapons weren't necessary; there was no one inside. But more importantly, they didn't need to tear the room apart. It was all there on the table: maps and charts of the Vatican, pictures of the museum, a recipe for smoke bombs.

Moments later Investigator Francone strode in with two of his men and Attilio Vitelli in tow. Francone had heard the dispatch and rushed to the site. While en route, he explained what he and his men had uncovered at the garage to Colonel Enjordin of the Vatican.

"Anything look familiar?" Francone asked Vitelli.

Vitelli looked at the items on the table; the silent TV with images of the smoking Vatican; the packed suitcases. His eyes finally fell on the Yankees hat hanging from the bathroom door handle. He thought, *Only an amateur American would wear something so . . . American.*

The concierge finally caught his breath and, with his eyes wide and arms askew, turned to one of the policemen. "What has the professor done?" he pleaded.

⌘

Michael pressed each finger into the designated sections of the paper, rolling them as instructed. Reiner gave him a paper towel to wipe his hands of the excess ink while a guard photographed Michael from all sides. He stood in his underclothes in a small antechamber off the Piazza San Pietro that contained only a table and two lamps. The door was closed and had been locked from the outside. The contents of Michael's bag—his notebooks, his sunglasses, his books on the Vatican—were spread out on the table. Next to them lay his clothes and the contents of his pockets—his wallet, money, passport, key ring, PalmPilot, and the iridium cell phone.

"And you're staying at the Hotel Bella Coccinni?" Reiner asked in clipped English as he concentrated on the nearly completed form.

"That is correct." Michael crumpled up the paper towel and threw it in the trash can, careful to keep his smile in place.

An investigator in a Vatican Police uniform stood over Michael's effects with an electronic security-wand, passing it back and forth. It rang as it passed over the keys, PalmPilot, and phone. He picked up each article scrutinizing them in detail. Then he removed everything from Michael's wallet—from credit cards to little scraps of paper—reading each with a careful eye. He turned on the PalmPilot, scrolling through the programs, verifying its functionality, and placed it back on the table. He picked up the phone, surprised at its size and weight, and looked at Michael with a question in his eyes. Turning the phone over in his hand, he opened the back and removed the large black battery. "An iridium phone," he said in a thick accent.

Michael smiled. "Amazing reception."

The investigator examined the phone in detail as if it was a fine piece of jewelry; Michael knew that it wasn't out of admiration but suspicion. The technician put the battery back in and turned the phone on. He gestured to Michael. "Do you mind?"

"Please, feel free."

The investigator dialed the phone and after a moment the cell phone in his pocket rang. Satisfied, he put it back on the table. He turned to Michael and ran the wand over Michael's entire body. He gave no indication of a pass or fail and put the wand away. He turned to Reiner and gave him an unspoken look.

Reiner handed Michael his clothes and pushed his possessions across the table. Michael remained silent as he began dressing.

"You understand, Professor McMahon," Reiner began as he studied Michael's passport, "with a breach such as this, we must pay attention to even the most insignificant of details." Reiner placed his pen down on the table and spun the paper around, indicating the line for Michael's signature. "No one is a more thorough investigator than Colonel Enjordin. The colonel may need to reach you if any further irregularities should arise."

"Of course." Michael finished dressing and quickly signed the release.

The door opened abruptly and Enjordin stepped inside. The door slammed shut behind him and the lock fell back into place. Ignoring Michael, he turned to Reiner and the Vatican policeman. "We have been to his hotel."

Michael's face was a mask although his heart felt like it would burst in his chest.

"Everything was there—maps, pictures. This *professore* was not smart."

Enjordin looked Michael up and down, assessing him. Without turning his eye, he snatched Michael's passport from Reiner and stared at the travel document as if memorizing it. Switching to Italian, he spoke in rapid bursts to Reiner who remained silent—though his eyes kept darting Michael's way.

A moment of silence hung over the room and then . . .

Enjordin handed the passport back to Michael. He thumped the door three times. The latch was released.

⌘

As they emerged into the light, an ambulance rolled in, coming to a halt next to several fire trucks. A host of Swiss Guards checked the exiting crowds, frisking and questioning them. The guards looked at Michael but turned their attention to the next group once they saw he was being escorted by Corporal Reiner.

"That was scary," Michael commented.

"Sorry for the inconvenience," Reiner replied. "Are you sure you are not injured?"

"Just a little shaken."

"Do you wish a doctor?"

"No, really, I'm fine. I just need a drink."

"Please do not let this discourage you from visiting us again." Reiner nodded, then hurried back into the museum.

The crowds had not yet begun to disperse; the confusion would last a bit longer. Michael turned and headed for his hotel, thankful that no one was hurt and the only thing people would be walking away with today was a good story. As he crossed the Piazza San Pietro, passing the towering obelisk and the enormous colonnade, he looked back at the Basilica. While its grandeur hadn't diminished, he no longer felt the intimidation he had felt when he first looked upon the ancient city.

Michael reached in his pocket and turned on his phone; he needed to hear Mary's voice. He needed to tell her that he loved her and that he was coming home. Michael walked out of Vatican City at exactly 1:00 and smiled, knowing that Mary's chances of survival had just risen.

He had the keys.

Chapter 11

Michael was packing. The room at the Roman Traveler's Inn he had paid for in advance barely had enough space in it for the bed but comfort was not a factor, never had been; he had booked this room for its view. From it he could see the Vatican perfectly. And more important, he could see the myriad intersecting streets below and would know which one to take if escape was in order. While he had checked into the Hotel Bella Coccinni, it was merely for cover; this small hotel was his true base of operation.

On the TV screen was a shot from earlier in the day of smoke billowing out of the Vatican Museum, the tourists scattered about, coughing. The announcer from the CNN Italian bureau spoke over the footage, *"evacuated with only minor injuries sustained."*

Michael sat down at the small corner desk and plugged a memory stick into his notebook computer. Suddenly, numbers started flashing by on the screen. In thirty seconds, the computer was thoroughly wiped of all memory.

The computer had acted as the perfect partner, performing timely and without error. At ten a.m. it auto-dialed the police station through the untraceable cell phone Michael had attached. Recognizing a live human voice, the computer activated the preprogrammed twenty-two-second message leaving the tip about Attilio Vitelli's garage. The computer had modified Michael's prerecorded voice and his rapid speech didn't leave room for a response before the line was disconnected.

At precisely 11 a.m., the computer had dialed the Vatican Police. Michael's voice, now modified to a feminine timbre, warned of the impending protest. It was all a screen, a matter of misdirection, leading investigators on a trail that bore certain truths but not the whole truth, while at the same time creating chaos.

Michael flipped over the computer and removed the hard drive, running a magnet over it repeatedly. Though an auto virus had infected the computer at 11:17, destroying any evidence, and he had just deleted all of the computer's memory, Michael didn't think it was possible to be too cautious. He preferred the belt, suspenders, and parachute approach. You could never be too sure.

Michael was glad nobody was hurt—except maybe Professor Higgins's ego and his head, partly from kissing the statue of St. Thomas Aquinas and partly from the sodium amytal that prolonged his slumber. The anti-Catholic leaflets Michael had placed in his bag blinded the guards with rage, fogging their minds to rational thought as they raced off to Higgins's hotel. The hotel was only three blocks from the Hotel Bella Coccinni. As it only had a single concierge on duty, it had been absurdly easy for Michael to slip in and out of Higgins's room that morning on his way to the Vatican, leaving just enough evidence to further support the Swiss Guard and Vatican Police's theories and suppositions.

It wasn't one piece of evidence that helped to seal the Vatican Police's conclusion, it was the collective: the items in his bag, his blind hatred of the Church, the items in his hotel. The fact that nothing appeared stolen kept their focus on an anarchist vandal, not an opportunistic thief. The truth only emerged as the sodium amytal wore off. But nobody would want the truth; they had already made up their minds about Professor Higgins.

Michael pulled out his iridium phone, opened up the back, removed the battery, and replaced it with the fresh spare.

"The cause still remains a mystery," the CNN reporter continued. *"And the museums remain closed for the first time in forty-five years."*

Michael peeled up the label on the top of the battery, revealing the battery's seam. With his knife, he sliced along the seam and opened the battery. The battery's insides looked like pitch; Michael dug into the black putty-like material and there sat the two keys, buried in the tar. On the north edge, where the contacts were, sat a small battery within the battery. The power source was fully operational; the phone worked just fine, it simply had a life expectancy one-tenth that of a regular battery. It was Michael's Trojan cell phone.

It was the first opportunity Michael had to examine his prize up close. He pulled out each key, placing both on the bed. They were covered in the black gunk of the battery, but as he wiped them off, the precious metal began to shine through. He picked up the silver key and, with a towel, he wiped off the remaining tar and buffed it to a high sheen. He picked up the gold key and began to clean it. And then something caught his eye. His heart froze.

Michael hurried into the bathroom. He held up the keys.

"A rumor persists that several smoke bombs detonated in the Sacristy and

Treasury Museum and the Gregorian Museum of Etruscan Art but no one was hurt." The TV reporter could be heard from the next room.

He looked at the key closer, then turned on the tap and ran the key under the hot water, dissolving the remaining tar-like substance.

"Fortunately, it has been confirmed, nothing was stolen." The TV voice echoed off the tile walls.

The sink turned to black—and the key turned to gold.

Michael examined it closely. In tiny lettering, almost imperceptible to the eye, was an engraving. Michael strained to see but he wasn't mistaken. Etched on the side was *585*.

Michael looked up from the key, placed it on the edge of the sink, stared into the mirror, and ran his hands over his face. "Shit," he groaned.

The satellite phone rang. Michael ignored it. His heart was thundering in his ears.

He closed his eyes.

The phone rang again. And Michael exploded, sweeping his arm along the medicine shelf, sending toiletries and water glasses crashing against the wall.

Michael ran out of the bathroom, picking up the phone on its third ring. "Hello."

"I'm watching the news," the voice said. "Great thing, this worldwide television, I wonder if CNN is for sale."

Silently, Michael watched the television coverage of the Vatican. Finster's warning the week before echoed in his brain. *"I will know if they are not the true keys, Michael. I will know."*

"Well?" Finster asked.

"Well, the Vatican isn't stupid." Michael tried to restrain his anger. The inscription, 585—14K in the U.S.—was the European designation for 58.5 percent pure gold, a designation that did not appear on gold two thousand years ago.

"And . . . ?"

"And . . ." Michael was at a loss, his head was spinning, he couldn't afford failure. He had to succeed. Mary's life depended on it.

"What do you mean, Michael? Do you have them?"

No response. Michael was lost in thought, staring at something on his bed.

"And what, Michael? What's going on?" Finster's voice sharpened.

On the bed was Michael's stack of research books. One in particular caught his eye: *THE VATICAN—Its Politics and Territories.* On the cover was the simple picture of an old stone church. The simplicity and logic were suddenly obvious to Michael, but then the past is always clearer than the future. Misdirection. Michael's specialty. Like a magician: have the audience stare at your right hand while your left hand deceives them. You look here, so I can accomplish the impossible over there. And people tend not to question fact, particularly when they confirm it with their own eyes. Everyone, look at my empty hand while I pull a coin from my pocket; everyone, look at Higgins, the enemy of the Church, while I just borrow these keys; everyone, look at these genuine keys in their case while we hide the true keys somewhere else.

"Michael, what's going on?"

"Things aren't always what they seem," Michael said more to himself than to Finster. "Plain sight. It's so simple. Why didn't I see it before?"

"What are you talking about?" Finster's voice was brittle.

"I should have started at the beginning." Michael was suddenly intensely focused. "I'll see you in a couple of days."

Finster's protest was cut off as Michael absentmindedly hung up the phone.

⌘

The walls were covered in Crayola masterpieces. Bright pictures of clouds and dogs, stick figures and flowers. Jeannie Busch had picked them up from school. The children worked so hard when they heard that Mary "had a bit of a cold" and wouldn't be back before summer vacation. Many of the children cried. The classroom seemed to have lost its sense of balance. Mary had been their center, their surrogate parent, and she was gone. Mary had plastered the pale walls hoping to cover up not only the sterile atmosphere of the room but the sterile feeling in her heart.

She sat in a chair, dressed, pretending to read. She had been tested so many times before, but never like this. The treatment was not only draining her strength, it was draining her will. She longed for Michael's return, knowing that he would be the catalyst to spark her recovery.

"Hey, Mare," came the whisper. Mary didn't react at first, lost in thought behind her book. He stepped in closer. "Hi."

Mary jumped, startled at the voice, but all that washed away when she saw his face. "Paul." Her smile was genuine.

"You look terrific." He had actually expected her to look worse. "How are you?"

"Fine. They're making a big deal out of nothing."

Busch leaned in to give her a kiss. He had come straight from work and his suit was wrinkled, his tie askew, but at least he'd taken the time to comb his tangle of blond hair. "You've got to hurry home, Jeannie is driving me crazy. I need you to keep her in check, make her laugh once in a while."

"You do a good enough job at that yourself."

"Yeah, but she's laughing *at* me, not with me. I brought you some cookies and magazines." Paul placed a package on the end table. The stacks were growing, the end tables overflowing; it would take her a year to read through everything.

"Thank you. How is Jeannie?"

"Insane," he said with not much humor. He looked around the room at the crayon drawings. "Got a lot of fans."

"Yeah, my flock."

A long, uncomfortable silence followed. Busch busied himself, pretending to look at each picture one by one.

Mary closed her book, gathered her thoughts, and smiled. "Thanks again for helping Michael out, letting him go down South and all."

Busch turned to her. "Hey, you know, sometimes you've got to bend the rules." It killed Busch that Michael had lied to Mary. He didn't have the heart to tell her that her husband had left the country.

"I don't know how we can ever make it up to you."

"Just get better."

"Promise me when Michael gets back, we can all go out to dinner. OK?"

Busch reached out and gently touched her hand; it took all his effort to smile. He hoped against hope that she would take his tender smile and touch as a sign and let the question slide. He couldn't answer her question; he couldn't lie to her, too.

⌘

Mary settled into bed. She could barely keep her eyes open during Busch's visit. He had always watched out for her, particularly during Michael's incarceration. Paul had never made it difficult, never made her feel uncomfortable. When he'd quietly volunteered to be Michael's parole officer, it was a surprise to both Mary and Jeannie. He had helped Michael get back on his feet and the fact that they became such close friends seemed more than Mary could ever ask for. She was thankful that Paul was such a big part of Michael's life.

Chapter 12

An open field in the middle of nowhere. Scrub grass for as far as the eye could see. In the distance was a small range of mountains. Michael crested the hill and threw down his canvas satchel, taking in his surroundings. He had been walking for hours. No road had been laid here, only a few scattered cart paths cut through the vegetation. It was hard going, but he reminded himself that it was only a fraction of what Mary was going through. He pressed on.

The foothills of Mount Kephas were an uncontested barren place, bearing no political or religious significance. On the other hand, if you were to travel three miles south to Jebel et-Tur, also known as the Mount of Olives, the significance was dramatic. The stories of the Mount of Olives had been chronicled and passed down through the ages, the location taken as gospel: it was where Jesus rose to Heaven. But the Mount of Olives is in fact a range of twenty-five hundred-foot hills.

Among the research books Michael acquired was one on the vast holdings of the Catholic Church. He had read that within the confines of the Vatican, among its great treasures, was a file of deeds, a file room containing all of the real-estate ownership documents for all of the Catholic churches spanning the globe. The book had listed tens of thousands of churches under the leadership of the Pope and he had taken special note of one in particular. Throughout the world there were thousands of sanctuaries called the Church of the Ascension—in fact, the one of greatest renown was only three miles away on the Mount of Olives—just as there were many St. Patricks, St. Augustines, and St. Michaels. But there was only one Church of the Ascension on Mount Kephas in Israel. It was a gamble, but too many of the facts pointed in this direction. Brother Joseph had said, "*Before his death, Peter made a pilgrimage . . . Some scholars speculate that he returned to the Holy Land to pay homage, but a select few believe Peter had a premonition of things to come, including his death, and was returning something back to the land of his God . . .*" Peter had nothing of value, having forsaken possessions. The one thing that he valued was the Word of his

Savior and *that* he had sworn to protect with his life. The only true physical connection that Peter had was the keys, and he would protect them at all costs from the Emperor Nero, who sought to destroy anything to do with the hated Christians. And so, Michael reasoned that Peter, whose name derives from the Greek word *petros,* or rock, made a pilgrimage to the true mountain where Christ rose to Heaven, a mountain named Petros or, in the Aramaic tongue, Kephas. The Vatican, by displaying St. Peter's keys in the Vatican Museums under tight security, was confirming to the world their validity. As a result, the true keys could be kept where Peter intended, with little fear of theft. For who would go looking for Christ's keys in a non-Christian part of the world, when the keys were already on display for all the world to see?

Michael had wasted no time booking a flight into Tel Aviv from Rome. He headed into the city, made his rounds purchasing supplies, took a car to the foothills in Jerusalem, and began his trek. As he ascended Mount Kephas, his thoughts were on Mary. Soon they would be together again, his journey would be complete, and for once he would have used his innate talent for good.

At the top of the last rise he caught sight of it: an ancient stone church. A simple wooden sign indicated Sunday services. Across the field, stretching to the horizon, was an enormous cemetery. Not a soul was in sight. Not a town or any civilization, for that matter. The Church of the Ascension was a relic of an age gone by. It was obvious, in this primarily Jewish part of the world, Mass was seldom attended, if at all.

The orange glow of sunset bathed the church as he pushed open its door. The interior was spartan, constructed of timber and fieldstone. No windows, only slits in the thick stone walls. The fading rays of the sun illuminated a crucifix over the altar. There was no sense of time within the sanctuary. As far as Michael was concerned, it could have been millennia ago. The central altar table of weathered wood and rock was covered with a white cloth decorated with the Papal symbol of two crossed keys. Two carafes, one filled with wine, the other with water, were set next to a tin bowl. On either side of the altar table were two candles, their flickering light reflecting off an old chalice. It wasn't lost on Michael that someone maintained the candles.

He walked around the altar, feeling the walls, the priest's chair, the small tabernacle that was set off to one side. He had brought his tools but he doubted he would need them tonight. He was not in some high-security museum but a simple, antiquated church whose function was not to keep people out but draw them in. This was a place where crime was clearly never given a second thought, except in forgiveness and sermons.

Michael crawled under the altar table and lay on his back. The underside was thin and solid; there wasn't enough room for what he was looking for. He rolled over. The floor of the altar was built up about six inches from the rest of the church and was made of an ageless beech wood. Michael tapped the floorboards, working his way across the four-foot area. Directly beneath the altar, a hollow sound echoed back. Like an artist, he pulled his knife, inserted it, and pried up the plank.

Six inches down, there was nothing but dirt floor. He pried up the two adjacent boards: again, nothing but dirt. Michael sheathed his knife and stood. He took a seat in the first pew and thought. The Catholic Church made it a practice to place holy relics within the altars of each of its churches, imbuing all of them with a sense of the presence of God. In fact, there was a section of the Vatican called the Relics Library, a macabre chamber filled with nothing but the bones of saints and ancient artifacts. Its librarian's job was to fill tiny boxes and envelopes with such relics and send them on to churches across the world for safekeeping within their altars. Michael stared at the simple altar before him. Surely, this church would not be an exception to the rule.

He moved back to the altar, drew his knife, and again crawled under the table. He studied the compacted dirt, patted it, dug at it with his fingers, but nothing seemed out of the ordinary. Then, taking his knife, he raised it high and in a single swift motion stabbed it into the earth.

Michael's arm reverberated in pain as the knife came to an abrupt halt. The six-inch blade pierced the dirt . . . but only to five inches. He withdrew the knife and stabbed again, a foot to the left. Again, the blade went only five inches deep. A third stab, two feet to the right: again the hilt stopped an inch shy of the earth.

Michael frantically started digging with his blade. The ground was hard-packed as if it hadn't been disturbed for centuries. His arms grew tired as he worked away, loosening the earth and then digging it out with his hands. Every few minutes he would stop and peer outside. The solitude was getting to him, it was beyond quiet. Even his digging seemed to be silent. Until he hit metal. It was a distinct *ping,* the knife squealing as it skidded across the unseen surface. Faster, he pulled the dirt away, the pile next to him growing higher by the minute.

Slowly, the obstruction started to come into view. He cleared it off, swiping the last bits of earth away. It was metal, pitted, and very old. Its hammer-worked surface was dull and marred. And it was hollow. Michael's heart beat faster. He was correct: something of value lay just within.

His fingers found the edge of what was now clearly a metal box, about four feet square. And there was no lock, no handle, no way in.

Michael pulled from his bag a portable oxyacetylene torch and lit up; the blue flame danced shadows across the walls. He adjusted the flame to near invisibility and went straight for the edges of the box, the thinnest part, the twelve-hundred-degree flame wasting the welds quickly. He cut the flame just short of circumnavigating the perimeter of the box, pulled a small crowbar from his bag, and inserted it in the broken seam. The top of the box creaked as he pried it up. Peering inside, he could barely make out another container about four feet below. Hopping in, he crouched to find it was a small metal chest. He hoisted it out of the hole and himself right behind it. There was no lock on the chest, merely a simple latch, which he raised.

He reached in and pulled out a small wooden case. This was the size of a cigar box, ancient, ornate gates carved in its top. Michael laid the box upon the altar and opened it. Inside was an old white cloth, tattered and worn. Michael removed this and reverently set it down as he had done so many times in the past. It was always a spiritual experience when it was diamonds or artwork, but this would be different. Not a holy experience, not a divine or blessed event, but an achievement unmatched by any conquest in his life. The contents of this cloth, he knew deep in his heart, would be the resurrection of life for his wife.

He unfurled the cloth and out tumbled two simple, tarnished keys. Almost exact replicas of their stand-ins from the Vatican. These, too, were slightly larger than a modern-day key; each thick and almost four inches long. One silver in appearance, the other gold. As Michael rolled them in his palm, the weight told him the truth: they were not made of precious metals; most likely they were brass and iron. These were the objects he was searching for. He rolled the keys back up in the cloth and returned them to their case, wrapped the case in his sweater, and threw it in his satchel.

Michael stepped from the church. The sun had long since set.

Only its faint glow remained, painting the horizon of the early summer sky purple. In the distance, a low fog was rolling in. He started down the path, comfortable in the growing darkness. Darkness was his friend. He always enjoyed the cover of night, knowing that while he couldn't see he, in turn, couldn't be seen. He felt an elation; he was done and on his way home.

"Excuse me?" a voice called out.

Michael strained to see through the darkness. Wary, he slowed his pace.

"Can I help you?" The voice came from somewhere up ahead. The darkness refused to give up the stranger. The speaker's accent was not Hebrew, not Middle Eastern. It was Italian.

Michael came to a complete stop. "Show yourself."

"Unfortunately, I am without light. Perhaps you have one."

Michael pulled out his flashlight and shined it down the path, sweeping it back and forth. And while it was a powerful lamp, he could see no one through the thickening fog.

A cold chill ran up his spine, instinct took over; he held the light as far from his body as his arm permitted. He was being set up—the light was a bull's-eye and he was the target. As he squinted to see—

KPOW. The light flew out of his outstretched hand, blown to bits.

Michael took off, cutting through the open field. The darkness and fog had combined as one; he had no idea where he was going; he knew only that he was heading away from the report of the gun. Michael was flying, but his pursuer was still closing.

All the preparation for the Vatican theft had been a waste. He had timed that sleight-of-hand operation and performed it smoothly, which only emboldened his ego. He'd been vain of his expertise and it had blinded him: this evening's job was an amateur theft and he made an amateur mistake.

His heart pounded in his ears as he ran from the unseen threat. While he had lost his faith in God, it crossed his mind that right now might be a good time to regain that faith, to kneel down and pray. But he was sure of one thing: he wasn't on God's top-ten list at the moment. Then he saw it. Up ahead, through the fog, gravestones . . . the cemetery.

Michael pumped his legs, straining, panting, only ten more yards. If he could make the graveyard he would have a chance. He was so close to success, so close to bringing home the job, so close to saving Mary. Too close to fail.

He cut into the graveyard, dodging ancient headstones, leaping footstones. Though his sight was impaired by the night and the weather, what he could see—all that he could see—was tombstones, thousands of them, stretching in every direction. He cut deeper into the cemetery. The fog hugged the ground here like a down blanket, creating a knee-high covering as thick as milk. He was moving at top speed, ignoring the obstacles hidden in the mist. Then he tripped on a low-lying grave marker. He tumbled headlong into a tombstone. Dazed, he tried to shake off the pain.

His pursuer was there. His footsteps were careful, evenly paced, the footfalls of a hunter closing in relentlessly for the kill. Michael couldn't pin down his location; he sounded as if he was everywhere. The mist obscured sight while its water droplet components dispersed the noise in every direction, amplifying distant sounds.

Michael was being stalked.

He was faced with two options: run or hide. He risked the possibility of giving himself away if he was to run but was equally challenged by hiding without defense. He never carried a gun. Guns were against everything he stood for. He had always considered himself a gentleman thief. He never stole from anyone who couldn't afford it, or wasn't insured. Most of his jobs were from museums and galleries, well-insured institutions. He wasn't in the business of taking life. Right now he was in the business of giving life—Mary's life—but if it came down to the stranger or him, Michael was prepared: he would kill.

"I will find you." The voice seemed everywhere.

Michael hugged the ground, hiding at the foot of the tombstone of Ishmael Hadacas. Born 1896, died 1967. The markings said that he had died in the war for Israeli freedom, a Coptic Christian giving his life for the land of the Jews. *He must have been a brave man,* Michael thought; he wished Ishmael was here now. He could use an ally.

"You do not know what you have wrought if you continue," the Italian voice called out. Whoever was out there was scared, Michael sensed it. Perhaps a guard who had fallen asleep on the job or a police officer who had grown overconfident from years of tedium.

Michael remained silent, looking around. He didn't dare move.

"I ask you for the sake of Christianity, for the sake of all peoples." The even-toned voice was almost a whisper, filled with desperation. "If you do not relent, I will have no choice, I must kill you."

Michael knew the man's words to be true. Slowly, silently, he began crawling. He strained his eyes around each headstone. He hoped he was crawling away from the voice. In his estimate, he was crawling south, back toward the village path. He checked his watch; it had been ten minutes since he last heard the man's voice. Maybe his pursuer had given up, had gone away, accepting failure. But these were false hopes. The man was still there somewhere. It had become a waiting game. Patience would win the day.

Then he got an idea. Michael removed his dark coat and draped it on a crumbling tombstone. He crawled twenty yards and propped himself against another headstone.

Michael gathered some stones, laying them out before him. He could barely make out the jacket-covered gravestone in the distance. He hoped it was convincing, giving the appearance of a man seated on the ground. He listened. Nothing. He looked around: the man was still out there and Michael was about to find out exactly where.

He gently hurled one of the stones at the jacketed grave marker. Silence followed. He picked up the next stone, lobbing it. As soon as it hit, a shot rang out. Michael's coat crumpled along with the tombstone.

Michael's heart was in his throat; the flame of the barrel had been only a few feet away. He didn't breathe. He could see his pursuer now. The figure stood over six feet tall. His head swept side to side as he raced toward the remains of his crumbled target. The way the man moved, the way he carried himself, terrified Michael. This was a hunter who would never give up the chase. Michael's new fear sharpened his resolve. He was up against a professional. The man was military.

Michael picked up another stone. With all his might, he hurled it as if it was a football. The rock sailed at least seventy-five yards before landing against another headstone. And in a fraction of a second, another shot rang out. A second tombstone shattered. The report of the gun echoed for miles. But to Michael's surprise, this flash was farther away than the last one. The man had silently worked *away* from Michael.

Michael was up and running into the thickening fog. Shots exploded behind him. The shots continued, evenly spaced, methodical, but coming from a greater and greater distance each time. Michael didn't look back. He just kept running.

Chapter 13

The great Bavarian mansion stood at the top of the mile-long drive. Made from fieldstone, it was nearly two hundred years old, built for some long-buried member of the German royal family. One hundred and thirty kilometers outside of Berlin on a thousand-acre parcel, the big house was rumored to contain over one hundred rooms, but the house staff was never able to find more than eighty-four. The host of elegant cars in the garages never saw much use. The staff mechanic was the only one to drive them, keeping them tuned, oiled, and ready should their owner ever decide to get a license.

Rumors prevailed of the wild doings of the current inhabitant within the confines of the great wall that circumnavigated the entire property. From a security standpoint, it was on a par with any U.S. Embassy. The grounds staff alone totaled twenty; their two-thousand-euro weekly salary was not only for their special skills but also assisted in keeping wagging tongues at bay. Each had his specific chore: gardening, lawn care, masonry—but these were skills learned only in the recent past. All had spent their prior lives in the military. As a whole they loved their jobs, it was easy work, excellent pay, and never once did they have to call upon their talents with weapons. Though they couldn't understand why a legitimate businessman would need his own private army.

The entrance hall was spectacular, reaching up three stories; the leaded glass windows positioned to capture light all day. The interior was grand, with deep rich tones, dark mahogany walls offset by maroon and green curtains. The furnishings were a mixture of the ages, tapestries older than the cornerstone of thc house, furnishings representing all periods. The wealth on display was inconceivable. And one thing stood out above all else, it was obvious: there was no lady of the house. This was the home of a gentleman. No light airy floral prints in the living room, no breezy yellows in the parlor. Everything was masculine, right down to the interior house staff.

The butler was a kindly old man with deep-set eyes lost in an ancient, wrinkled face. Charles ran the house; his word was the rule.

The butler knew the master better than anyone: his needs and wants, his travels and tastes. And while the master was quiet and reserved, Charles knew, too, that if you crossed him you would never return. No one would impede Charles from pleasing the man who ruled this vast house; that was how he was trained, how any good butler was trained, and he would be damn sure not to fail.

Charles bid Michael welcome. He showed him in and silently led the way to the library. He did his butler's duty, offering to take Michael's jacket and satchel, but Michael refused, holding tight to the leather bag on his shoulder. He wasn't letting go of it until the deal was done. Charles poured Michael a drink and then excused himself, telling Michael to make himself comfortable.

The enormous library was filled with books, thousands of titles. Michael had always felt a man's books were a representation of his mind and his soul. This man had everything. Michael walked past the car-sized fireplace, past the wingback leather chairs to a bookcase ladder. It soared to the top of the room, twenty feet up, and slid on its own track. Michael could spend a lifetime here and never even get to the second level of volumes. He pulled out an old, leather-bound book on geology and walked toward the windows for better light. He was about to look through the text when the doors opened.

Finster stood there, dressed in a tweed sport coat, a smile on his face.

"One of my favorites." Finster's eyes twinkled as he approached Michael. "Written in nineteen twelve by Alfred Wegener. One of the first to pose the theory of tectonics. You are holding one of only three volumes in existence."

"I'm sorry." Michael clutched the book, unsure what to do with it, like a kid caught with his hand in the cookie jar.

"Nonsense. You are a guest in my home; I am honored by your presence. While you are here, you may avail yourself of anything you wish. Please, keep it, it is an excellent read."

"No, that's all right."

"Please, a book, once read, is merely a trophy. I have no use for it anymore."

"Thank you, but I couldn't."

"If you change your mind . . ." Finster relented. "Let me show you around."

"I can't stay—"

"Another drink?"

At that, Charles appeared with a silver serving tray, two champagne flutes balanced upon it. Finster passed a glass to Michael and raised his own. "To your wife's good health."

"Thank you," Michael said as they chinked their glasses.

"Can I persuade you to stay for dinner?"

"I really can't."

"Certainly, you'll join me in a cigar?" Pulling out two cigars, Finster offered one.

Michael raised his hand in refusal.

Finster smiled. "I have too many vices: liquor, cigars, women. Unfortunately—what is that saying? The spirit is willing . . ."

". . . but the flesh is weak. I'm sorry, Mr. Finster—"

"August," Finster insisted.

"August. I'm sure you can understand, I really wish to finish our business and get back to my wife."

"Of course. But tell me, what happened in Rome? I haven't heard from you since you left Italy and you were extremely cryptic when last we spoke."

"Rome, the Vatican . . . it was a decoy." There was a weariness in Michael's voice. "The keys were on the outskirts of Jerusalem."

"Jerusalem?" Finster's interest intensified. "Where in Jerusalem?"

"A little out-of-the-way church."

"Interesting. Guards?"

"One."

Finster pondered this a moment. "And? Did you dispatch him?"

"He tried to 'dispatch' me."

"What did you do?"

"I ran."

Finster smiled and nodded. "Could you describe this guard?"

"It was dark," Michael answered uneasily. "Why do you ask?"

Finster seemed lost in thought. He turned and opened the doors to the hallway. "Let's talk and walk, shall we?"

Michael set the book on the table and followed Finster.

⌘

They walked together through the grand house, past billiard rooms and game rooms, ballrooms and parlors. Finster lit his cigar, drew a greedy puff, and slowly exhaled, the smoke lifting into a rich gray cloud above their heads.

"Life's simple pleasures." He savored the moment. "I read a study once that said the indulgence of a vice can be healthy. After all, what is a vice but something we find pleasurable, irresistible? Do you have a vice, Michael?"

"Not anymore."

"Of course." Finster nodded in understanding, his white ponytail bobbing against his shoulders as he did so. "You are a reformed man. I, on the other hand—let's just say I've yet to meet the person who can convert me from my ways. I couldn't live without my"—he held out his cigar and drink—"*weaknesses.*"

"Never know unless you try," Michael replied.

"Ah, but what is the reason? I've earned the right. I have the power to quit or continue and that is what's important. The power."

"Obviously, you've never been married."

Finster laughed heartily, patting Michael on the shoulder. "Come. I'd like to show you something."

They stopped at a heavy wooden door, the earthy brown wood older than the ages. It seemed oddly out of place in the elegant home surrounding it. Finster reached out and opened the behemoth. Its hinges squealed in protest. Ahead, a long set of stone stairs faced them. A musty smell wafted up. Michael couldn't pinpoint the odor but it conjured unpleasant memories of prison. The stairs wound down, spiraling into darkness, like something out of a Boris Karloff movie.

"A little dramatic."

"I thrive on drama," Finster replied cheerfully as he led the way downward.

The inky blackness instantly engulfed them. Michael loved the dark, always had, it had been his friend. But not this dark. The odor hit him again, musty and raw, the sour smell of jail cells, solitary confinement, death row. It was the smell of hopelessness. Their footsteps echoed off the walls. Michael closely followed Finster, who remained strangely silent, giving no details or guidance.

It had been at least a two-minute walk down stairs and through caverns; never once did Michael catch a glimpse of light. The moisture had grown in the air the deeper into the earth they traveled; it felt cold, clammy, unnatural. It occurred to Michael that Finster could kill him now and there'd be nothing he could do about it. This was one of the reasons he never did third-party work: you never really knew your employer or their motives. And murder was only one step away from grand larceny.

With a flash, the lights blazed on. Michael's eyes burned at the sudden glare, white spots dotting the back of his eyelids. Instinctively, Michael shielded his eyes. As the seconds passed, his vision returned and he began to look around. In that moment, he wished he was back in the dark, for while the blackened passage had scared him, that had only been his imagination running wild. This was real.

Before him was an assortment of artifacts, some ancient, some of a far more recent vintage. Stone pottery, medieval armor, African wood carvings, Oriental pictographs. Each as different from its neighbor as possible except for one thing: they were all religious in nature. This was an ominous gallery of religion, fear, and horror. Stacks and stacks of paintings were piled against each other. Faces seemed to cry out for mercy as if they were somehow trapped in the canvas.

"What do you think?" Finster asked with pride.

"Unique," was all Michael could say, doing everything in his power to mask his fear.

"Charles, my butler, calls it the dungeon."

"It captures that quality." Michael hoped the humor would mask his alarm as he unconsciously clutched the key box through the leather satchel. He couldn't understand it but the box seemed to be the only thing giving him comfort as he looked out at the chilling cavern spread before him.

"Thank you." Finster pointed down an aisle between the artwork. "This way."

The hall—the entire space—was like something out of the Dark Ages. It was enormous, of this Michael was sure, for the light trailed off into blackness before the far wall was evident. The house was centuries old but this place . . . this place had been around for far longer. This was another world deep below the surface. Finster had claimed it as his own, filling it with a macabre collection that would never be part of any auction at Sotheby's.

Was this merely the warped collection of an eccentric or was it something more, something worse? As Michael passed each piece, he thought maybe he was jumping to conclusions. Maybe this was just a warehouse for weird objets d'art. Stuff Finster didn't deem appropriate for display in his home. Maybe it was like the attic of every grandmother: crammed with wondrous frightening things, items collected over a lifetime's journeys, things that appeared scary on the surface but deeper down held a much more innocent meaning. Like an old china doll with a missing eye or the dusty steamer trunk filled with moth-eaten old dresses.

They arrived at a huge wooden door set in stone. Its ancient lock's black color was deeper than night. Finster withdrew a set of keys from his pocket, unlocked the door, and opened it.

This room was small, about ten by ten; there was no artwork here.

The solid stone walls had recessed shelves carved in them five feet off the ground. The room was virtually empty but for a mahogany pedestal standing in its exact center.

"My latest acquisitions go in here for my private enjoyment." Finster used his cigar to light a candle on a shelf and smiled. "Sets a mood, doesn't it?"

Michael watched as Finster continued to light small candles along the perimeter of the chamber. He found this room more comforting, no strange carvings or statues staring back at him, no suffering eyes peering out from the shadows. The walls were now bathed in candlelight; it was almost peaceful after the macabre collection they'd just passed. Michael said nothing as he reached into his bag, pulling out the carved box.

"Beautiful." Finster stared at his prize.

Michael held out the box.

But Finster stepped back, raising his hand in protest. "You should have the honor of placing it on the display pedestal."

Michael, a bit confused, acquiesced. He opened the box, uncovered the two keys, and stepped forward for Finster's inspection. Finster glanced at the keys but again backed away.

"Is something wrong?" Michael asked.

"Breathtaking. Their beauty leaves me . . . in awe." Finster steadied himself in the doorway. Michael reached in the box, pulled out the silver key, and passed it toward his host. But again the German raised his hand. "No, no." Finster was trembling. Michael was reminded of a housebound mother of three who'd won a car on *The Price is Right.* Like her, Finster's mind seemed to be on overload as he struggled to comprehend his good fortune and what was now his.

Michael smiled. "It's not going to bite you."

"Never know," Finster joked. "I prefer to examine my possessions privately. Taking my time. When I obtain something I have desired for so long I'm sometimes"—he paused—"overcome."

Michael turned back to the pedestal, hoping against hope that Finster hadn't seen his face. For, suddenly, Michael was now even more scared than when he'd entered the outside chamber. Finster had hired him to steal these keys and now the man was more than afraid of them; he was clearly terrified. He was refusing to come in contact with them as if they carried the plague. Suspicion raced through Michael's mind; now that he had completed his mission, was he in even greater trouble than he previously imagined? Was there more to these keys than he knew? And if one of the most powerful men in the world was so frightened of them, why wasn't he? Michael wanted out, to be back outside, back in the light of day, back home with Mary. Anywhere but here.

He placed each key on the pedestal's velvet cushion, setting the box beside them. Stepping back, looking at the keys here in this room, he sensed deep down that this was a mistake, that he had violated something beyond the law.

"The money has already been wired, along with a bonus of two hundred and fifty thousand dollars for you and your wife to enjoy once she is better," Finster said, pulling Michael back to reality.

Michael turned and faced his employer. As wrong as this was starting to seem, Michael reminded himself that the theft was enabling him to provide the treatment that Mary so desperately needed, the treatment that would save her life. And in the same way that we justify just one more drink, just one more cookie, convincing ourselves that it won't do us any harm, he eased his mind and his conscience, and shook Finster's hand.

"Thank you," Michael said as Finster handed him the wire transfer confirmation.

"Thank *you*. I truly wish your wife a speedy recovery so you can both get on with this business of living."

Finster led the way out of the room and as he was about to close the door, he looked in on his new prize. A smile crept along his thin lips. It wasn't a smile of joy or happiness: this was a smile of triumph, the smile worn by a general who has just taken the hill, eradicating his enemy. The smile of a battle-weary emperor who, near defeat, has just obtained the one weapon that could not only save him but turn the tides of war.

Chapter 14

Morning light filled the room. It had been a rough night; they all had been since the treatment started but last night particularly so. The vomiting and diarrhea wracked her system, sapping her energy. Pain literally seemed to rise up from the marrow of her bones. She was exhausted, drained of what little will she still possessed.

As the sunlight touched her eyelids, Mary stirred. The solace of sleep would elude her for another day. She rolled over and her mind leapt, a joy racing through her body as she saw him. For the first time since her diagnosis almost three weeks ago, she felt rejuvenated. Now that he was back, she would defeat this monster that had challenged her, beating it back down to the horrible place from whence it came.

"Good morning," she whispered.

Michael was arranging flowers. He had cleaned and freshened her room. The disorganization and clutter were gone from her life. The curtains were pulled back for the first time in days and Mary stared at the blue sky as if for the first time.

"Morning," he replied as he leaned in to kiss her passionately. Mary admonished herself. Her dreams of danger and death were nothing but senseless worry; Michael had come back to her, just as he had promised.

"I missed you," she murmured as she sat up against the pillows.

"I missed your smile. How're you feeling?"

"Much better."

"I'm glad." Michael knew she was lying but he wouldn't call her on it, he knew she was being strong for him.

Mary nestled herself in Michael's arms. Of all the thoughts and prayers, of all the medications and good wishes, this was what she really needed. To be held. And to hold. To her it wasn't just the receiving of love, it was the giving. It was like an elixir to them both. The anxiety that Michael had felt since he left the country was gone, left somewhere back in Germany.

"I was thinking maybe"—he pulled back, looking into her eyes—"we could head out to the Cape for a week, stay at the Ship's Bell Inn."

"Make love in the dunes . . ."

"Mmmm. Eat Portuguese soup . . ."

". . . fresh lobster."

Michael paused. "Did they say how much longer?" He couldn't wait to drag her away from this place.

"Another week. They're doing some more poking and prodding tomorrow."

"I'd like to do some poking and prodding of my own."

"We could arrange that," Mary said as she nuzzled into his neck. She had always loved his smell, it comforted her, secured her. Though she had tried to push the thought out of her mind, she'd spent the last seven days thinking he would never return. It was the one thing that truly scared her: she was terrified to die alone. "How was your trip?"

"A little longer, a little harder than I thought." Michael began rubbing her back, working from the shoulders down, the way she liked it.

"Paul was looking for you." She closed her eyes and laid her head upon his shoulder.

"Did he say what he wanted?"

"Wanted you to call him when you got back, said you have a game Saturday."

That was bullshit. Busch was going to string him up alive. But Michael would deal with that; after what he had gone through these last few weeks—Mary's illness, the Vatican, Israel, Finster—he could handle anything. No, he wouldn't call Busch yet. Busch could wait.

"Did you finish your job?" Mary asked. Michael was not telling her everything, but she knew whatever he had done he had done for her. Now was not the time to question him on it.

"Yes." He held her tightly. "I won't leave you again."

"I know."

For the first time in a long time, they both believed that everything finally would be all right.

⌘

Michael entered his dark apartment, throwing the mail on a side table. He popped his head in the bedroom calling, "Hawk?"

He checked the answering machine; the little red light read thirteen messages. He pushed the button. *"Message number one,"* the electronic female voice droned.

"Michael? It's me, call me." Busch's voice came over the machine. Michael hit the button, going to the next message. "Call me, Michael."

Again Busch. Again, Michael pushed the button. "Michael, I know you're back, don't make me come and get—" He hit the button, cutting off the message. He turned off the machine.

"Hawk!?" He checked the kitchen. Maybe Mrs. McGinty had the dog out for a walk. Michael realized that CJ was nowhere to be seen, either. He actually hated the cat, he had always hated cats, such a fickle breed of animal, he never understood their attraction. But it was Mary's cat and if she loved the little beast, then . . . he could at least pretend to love it. Mrs. McGinty had probably kept CJ in her apartment since he left. Michael would have to remember to get her a gift for her troubles.

He scooped up his mail and, opening it, wandered into the den. Turning on the light, he nearly jumped out of his skin.

Sitting in his favorite chair was a man, powerfully built, hair black as pitch, eyes like blue slate. Weathered face and hands, definitely someone who'd been through the world a few times. The stranger was dressed in black slacks with a black shirt; his black sneakers were worn down at the soles although the black uppers were surprisingly clean. His age was impossible to determine: he could have been anywhere from a worn-out thirty years old to a vibrant fifty. In his lap stretched Mary's cat. He stroked CJ as if she were his own. Hawk was sprawled out at his feet, asleep.

"Mr. St. Pierre?" His accent was Italian.

Michael instantly recognized the voice. "Get out," he ordered.

The man sat there.

Michael reached for the phone. "You've got thirty seconds," he said and started dialing.

"And what would you tell your policeman friend?"

Michael slowed his dialing.

"That the man whom you robbed is sitting in your apartment?" The foreigner didn't appear to even breathe.

Michael hung up the phone.

"You didn't think I'd let you get away?"

"Who are you?"

"My name is Simon," the man answered.

Tension crackled in the air between them like lightning. Michael could hear the blood rushing in his ears as he tried to focus on what to do, how to react.

"I would like my keys back," Simon said.

Michael knew that no job was ever really over. The specter of being found, of being arrested, perpetually lingered. "I'm not sure what you are talking about," he evaded.

"Really?"

"Really." Michael crossed the room toward the seated stranger and quietly called out, "Hawk?" His voice filled with frustration and anger. Hawk woke and, looking at his master, rolled onto his back looking for a rub. Michael crouched down and scratched his belly. "Some watchdog," Michael whispered to the air as much as Hawk, all the while assessing the mettle of the man still seated before him.

"Let me see if I can refresh your memory," Simon said. "A little short on cash, wife gravely ill, you running around the Vatican setting off smoke bombs." He made a gesture with his hands. "Stealing a couple of decoy keys, hopping a plane to Jerusalem, climbing Mount Kephas, stealing two more keys from a church." He paused for emphasis. "My bullets missing your head by inches," he added.

"You're full of shit."

Simon didn't break his stare as he pulled a pistol from his jacket, resting it on his leg. He slowly inched it over, coming to rest on the head of the sleeping cat. His eyes betrayed nothing. "I believe this is your wife's pet."

Michael was beyond furious: this guy was flat-out threatening him and there was nothing Michael could do about it.

"Tell me where the keys are." Simon looked at the cat, at Hawk, and then back at Michael. "The three of you can live if . . ." Chillingly, he let the ultimatum hang. "Maybe I could visit Mary; it would be a shame—all that effort, and she ends up dead because of your ineptitude."

Michael's work never had put Mary in peril; never would he have allowed that to happen on any job.

"The keys are gone," he said curtly. "I sold them."

"To?"

"A man."

Simon exhaled. "Name?" he asked softly.

Finster's guards numbered twenty, that was Michael's count. And the stolen keys were underground in what Michael knew was an impenetrable room. No one was going to get to them. Not Simon, not anyone. "A German industrialist. August Finster," Michael replied. The words rolled off his tongue; he felt no remorse at betraying his employer. August Finster understood when you played with the big boys sometimes the big boys hit back—sometimes the jaw, sometimes the heart.

With the grace of an animal, Simon stood. CJ leaped off his lap. The man was tall; at least six-two. "You have no comprehension of what you have done," he said.

"I saved my wife's life—"

"—And damned the world."

The statement hung in the air, leaving Michael speechless.

"What? What the hell are you talking about?"

"Do you believe in God, Mr. St. Pierre?"

"Not at the moment."

"So, you once did? Well, you better start believing again."

"I'll say a prayer of thanks when you leave."

Simon stood his ground. "In the year of Our Lord thirty-two, Jesus said to one of His disciples, 'Thou art Petros and upon this rock, I shall build My Church. . . . And what thou bind on earth shall be bound in Heaven.' And he gave Peter two keys to symbolize his power to absolve or condemn. The power to control the Gates of Heaven."

There was a coldness to this man like Michael had never seen before. He wouldn't stop at Michael's death or Mary's; he was acting on a deeper belief, one usually reserved for terrorists and fanatics.

"I think it's time for you to go," Michael insisted.

"You still don't understand, do you?"

"Understand what?"

"You have stolen the keys to Heaven."

This guy was insane. Whatever credibility he had just flew out the window as far as Michael was concerned. Michael's faith had waned and this only proved to amplify his resolve. He had assumed it was a money issue for this guy's boss, but no, it was one of those Blues-Brothers-mission-from-God routines.

"Now, I'm really calling—"

"Heaven is closed, Michael—"

"Get out now." Gun be damned, he was going to hit the lunatic if he didn't shut up.

"You don't even realize who you sold those keys to, do you?"

Michael grabbed the guy's arm but Simon was bottled lightning. He spun Michael around so fast, Michael didn't know what day it was and then slammed him down into the chair. CJ yowled and fled. Simon leaned in and in a clear, even voice, declared, "We are going to get those keys back."

He turned and left the room.

Michael got to his feet and fell in step close behind: no one violated his home and no one ever told him what he was going to do.

"*We* aren't doing anything." Michael struggled to control his voice, the adrenaline making it tremble. "I have a wife to care for."

"Do you value her soul?" Simon didn't wait for an answer. "If you do, then you'll help me. Otherwise, Mary, like all of us, is damned." He opened the front door. "We leave in two days." Then, turning back, he demanded, "How stupid could you be? You really have no idea who Finster is?"

Michael was silent, still in shock; he had never seen anyone move so fast in his entire life.

"Look it up," Simon said as he slammed the door.

Chapter 15

Dean McGregor was a three-time loser who was doing everything in his power to go straight. Paul Busch met with Dean the third Wednesday of every month. Dean was the kind of happy-go-lucky guy who would always be in the wrong place at the wrong time, with the wrong friends and all the wrong intentions. His first robbery was a small liquor store, not a lot of cash in a liquor store—certainly not enough to give up five years of your life over. So, weren't Dean and his pals surprised when they pulled their guns and the clerk handed over twenty thousand dollars. Of course that twenty thousand was narc money, the place was under surveillance for the distribution of marijuana, and that twenty grand was being closely monitored by three DEA agents sitting in a Ford across the street. When they busted Dean and his hoodlum friends, their six-month operation went up in smoke; the DEA made sure the DA threw the book at the boys.

Dean was only out five months when he tried to knock over a gas station. His wife was pregnant and he wanted to buy her some nice things because she was awfully depressed over her escalating weight. Using his usual plastic toy gun he hit up the gas attendant, finding the register half full, with maybe four hundred bucks in it. What he didn't know was that the gas attendant's wife was also pregnant and the guy was a moonlighting cop trying to provide a nest egg for their unborn child. The attendant's service revolver was sitting under the counter due to the fact he came straight from work, his third double-shift in a week. Officer Paul Busch pulled out the revolver; Dean wet himself right on the spot. Busch read him his Miranda warnings. While they waited for a patrol car to pick up Dean, they got to talking about their unborn children. For the first time, Busch could see that while committing a crime is always wrong, what motivates a criminal can sometimes have a certain degree of nobility to it. Of course that wasn't an excuse—the law was still the law—and Dean went right back to prison, sentenced to a fifteen-year stretch.

So it came to be that Busch and Thal were sitting in a coffee shop six years later running down the usual questions with the recently released Dean McGregor; he'd got out for good behavior after serving a third of his sentence. Busch shook Dean's hand warmly, greeting him with a smile. The man paid his dues, served his time as the court had seen fit, and that was fine with Busch. His job was not to pass judgment—just to enforce the law.

Dean extended his hand to Thal, who just stared at it without moving. The younger cop's glare sent Dean into a nervous twitch that lasted throughout the entire interview.

They spent the next thirty minutes running over the usual questions: How you doing? How's the family? Is the job we got you working out? Are you showing up for work on time? The usual adjustments-to-life-on-the-outside questions. Busch took the lead, guiding the conversation in the direction he wanted. He didn't like his charges feeling anxious or nervous around him. Being comfortable at your parole meeting was important because when the ex-con was relaxed he would open up, be honest about his acclimation back to society. It was when an ex-con got scared or desperate, feeling that he couldn't cope with the outside world, that a parolee reverted back to crime. Busch's job was to keep them on the straight and narrow. It was his failure as much as theirs if they fell back into their criminal ways.

Busch's cell phone rang and he excused himself from the table. He allowed Thal a little leeway to ask some questions but told him to wrap up and set Dean on his way. Thal's first question about Dean's dreams and nightmares seemed innocuous enough, but it went downhill from there: antagonistic, browbeating, confrontational statements.

"You dream about the money, don't you, McGregor? Tell me the truth. When you lie in bed at night, you can't help but think of the easy way to put food on the table." Thal smiled. "How many years before we pick up your kids following in Daddy's footsteps?"

Dean sat there in shock, sweat beginning to pour down his face.

"I used to believe in reform," Thal continued relentlessly. "I used to believe in forgiveness. But you know what, Dean? I don't think you're reformed and you certainly shouldn't be forgiven."

Dean's nerves were fried in the two minutes he spent with Thal. He was more afraid of this guy than anyone he'd ever met in prison. And it wasn't the young cop's words: it was his tone and the way his eyes glittered when he spoke.

Thal placed his hand on Dean's shoulder as if he was a child. "You disgust me, McGregor. You're a waste of space in this world. You better pray that I don't catch your ass in my gun sight committing a crime. Because if I do, I'll splatter your brain all over the pavement, scrape it up, and deliver it to your wife."

Busch's return abruptly ended the inquisition.

"Dean? I'll see you in three weeks," Busch said. The emphasis was on *I'll.* He walked the shaken Dean McGregor to the door, calming him with an arm around the other man's shoulders.

Busch returned to the booth. Sat down. Sipped his lukewarm coffee. Added more sugar. He let the minutes tick by and as they did Thal started to squirm. The anticipation of the ass-chewing was making the younger man nervous.

Finally, Busch leaned in and, raising one finger, quietly said: "I'm going to tell you once—one time only—that if you ever conduct yourself that way again with a parolee, a suspect, a human being, I will not only personally make it my mission that you are removed from this profession, but I will have you brought up on charges. As far as I'm concerned, you don't even hold a candle to that man." Busch paused, struggling to regain his composure. "I will work with you, guide you, for one more month. But from then on out I will see to it that we never cross paths again."

"Hey, I was shaking him up, maybe he'd let slip some job he was planning—"

"We don't shake 'em up. Ever."

"How do we know that man isn't scheming to bust his parole?"

"Believe me, if he did, I'd know it." Busch gathered up his papers on Dean McGregor, dropping them into his briefcase.

"So, if you knew that someone broke their parole, you'd bust them right away?"

"Without question."

"And how strict are we? The letter of the law on each?"

Busch looked up. "What are you talking about? This is the law. We enforce the law."

"Remember, I'm new at the parole thing. I'm just trying to model myself after you."

This pissed Busch off no end; there was nothing he despised more than being condescended to. "Ignorance is not an excuse when it comes to breaking the law, no fucking way around it."

"So what do we do if someone violates their parole?" Thal asked again.

"Bring 'em in."

"Send 'em back to prison?"

"That's up to the judge."

Thal pondered this a moment. "Without exception?"

"No exceptions," Busch said.

"So we should bust that guy St. Pierre. He left the country. According to you, we gotta bust him." Thal was gleeful in his ratty sort of way.

Busch was caught totally off-guard. Realizing he had been trapped by this little shit, he snapped, "How do you know this?"

"Reliable source."

"Reliable source—bullshit! That's not going to fly with the judge. You better come clean." Busch knew full well Michael left the country. He'd seen him vanish into the International Departures terminal, but he thought maybe there was an explanation and he'd be able to deal with it in his own way. But now . . .

Now it was Thal who leaned in and, raising one finger, calmly said: "I'll get you proof."

"Don't talk to me about this again until you do." Busch grabbed his briefcase and stood. "Anything else I can *teach* you today?" he demanded with utter contempt.

Thal sat there a moment; although it may not have seemed so on the outside, he felt he had won the conversation and he was dying to place the icing on the cake. "Why do they call you Peaches?"

Busch lunged across the table into Dennis's face and made his point real clear. "You——never——call——me——Peaches."

The hospital library was tiny but it had a book collection that covered at least the basics that a patient might be looking for. The atmosphere was collegiate and quiet as could be expected but that disinfected hospital smell still prevailed, always reminding you where you really were. Beyond the selection of medical books, periodicals, and theses, there was a good selection of both current fiction and nonfiction. The encyclopedias and reference manuals had been donated by a benefactor who'd lost his mother to heart disease.

Michael was thankful for the man's generosity as he found the latest edition of *Who's Who in International Business*. Most of the players had a blurb that lasted maybe a couple of paragraphs; August Engel Finster had his own page.

Michael had looked into Finster before he accepted the assignment; there was nothing that gave him pause then. Now it was Simon who was giving him pause. Michael wasn't sure who to be afraid of: Finster or Simon. And he wasn't sure what he was looking for now as he stared at the same page he had read almost three weeks earlier.

August Engel Finster had emerged from the Eastern bloc after the fall of the Wall. His buying sprees were legendary. He'd spent over three hundred million deutsche marks a month in the building of his empire. The origin of his financing was a mystery, though, as was that of many of the financial titans who'd emerged from East Germany. Many, if not all, Michael knew, had been involved with the Communist government in one way, shape, or form in their prior lives. While unsavory ties were suspected of these elite, how could they be criminals in a land where the law was at the whim of their bureaucratic brethren?

Finster had amassed an empire of textile mills, mining companies, and munitions firms—most acquired through the privatization of the former government's businesses. These corporations had gone on to great success, which was credited solely to Finster's business acumen. He was an extremely private man, few knew his strategy for success, and those who worked for him were tight-lipped and invisible. Universities and his competition tried to crack his formula but no one ever succeeded in re-creating the Finster business model. Finster had never failed. Yet. And that was the mantra: everyone crashes and burns at some point. One day, it would be Finster. People always cheered, reveled in, and rallied to the side of someone on the ascendance, the underdog reaching for the top, for the golden prize. But when a man attains it, the tide turns and people begin to look for faults. A winner was no longer like them, struggling against the odds, fighting the masses. A winner was successful where they were not and this didn't sit well. It was human nature really. You couldn't rule the world for too long, if at all. It happened to everyone. Bill Gates, the computer nerd who took on IBM, came out of nowhere to create the computer industry. Then watched as the states and governments tried to tear apart his empire. Michael Jackson, the king of pop, the little kid who conquered music and remade the entertainment business. The feeding frenzy for his songs shifted to the feeding frenzy for his blood. Even the real King had been torn down by his fans. Elvis was done in by first the Beatles, then Woodstock, and later drugs, and everyone said, you see, I told you so. Soon, everyone said, it would be Finster's turn.

No information existed on him prior to 1990, and to race to a net worth of over thirteen billion U.S. dollars in ten years' time from nowhere boggled Michael's mind. The lengthy article told of all of Finster's business conquests but of his personal past there was nothing: no father, no mother, sisters, or brothers. No wife, children, or dogs. Or maybe there was information and Finster was able to hide it in an expert fashion, the way he hid his business strategies. For the past three years he had lived the high life in the public eye, chronicled like a movie star's dossier. Racing from meetings to dance clubs to gala social functions. The pictures were exactly as Michael had seen him. His long white hair pulled back in a ponytail, dark eyebrows accenting the brown eyes of this white-maned lion. Finster was rarely without a beautiful woman on each arm, none of whom were above the ripe old age of twenty-two. His charisma was evident even in photographs, Michael could feel it flowing from the page.

But still . . . no background whatsoever.

Michael flipped the pages to other German industrialists and that eased his mind somewhat. The other East Germans were also lacking in background. It was like a little club. You don't tell, I don't tell. They had all done something in their past that would damn them and they would just prefer that it be forgotten. All wanted to put their former lives behind them. After all, East Germany had been Communism at its worst. Food was short while oppression was rampant, the public consigned to a world of misery. Everyone watched each other, fear being the order of the day. Brother would turn in brother for even innocent words against the malevolent government. And those who cried out had vanished into the prisons of East Berlin, never to be heard from again. There were rumors, whispered in alleys, bars, and basements, that not even the souls of the dead could escape the Berlin Wall. And then the Wall came down in a tumble of rubble and cheering . . . and from its ruins emerged Finster.

All the information ever compiled was in the book before Michael, and he was still at a loss. The German industrialist was successful, Michael imagined ruthless—you can't swim with sharks unless you have the teeth—and private, but he didn't seem the threat that Simon had suggested. Finster was eccentric, Michael had seen this firsthand, but that surely came with the incredible wealth and power that the man had. The German's strange collection of artwork stored away in his medieval basement was sick, but it was merely art. And that is what Michael suspected the two keys he'd stolen to be: an old possession, something to be kept hidden in Finster's private museum. Maybe the keys did have the historical significance that Simon had alluded to, but how did that matter? No magic here. No special power over the souls of all humanity. Heaven was a concept Mary might believe in but Michael still had trouble with it.

"Did you find what you were looking for?"

Michael looked up to see Nurse Schrier—the big German nurse from Mary's hospital floor—looking at him.

"I'm not sure," he answered.

"So, who are you looking for in the *Who's Who?*" she asked.

"Actually, I found who I was looking for."

The nurse looked over Michael's shoulder at the picture of the white-haired man. "Finster?"

"Yeah. You know him?" Michael asked, half-joking.

She laughed off the remark. "Nah, not personally."

Michael closed the book, rose from his chair, and placed it back on the shelf.

"The name really fits him, wouldn't you say?" Schrier asked as she picked up a stack of magazines and headed for the door.

"Whose name?"

"August Engel Finster. All that money, all those women."

"I'm not sure I follow."

"If it was my name I would have changed it. All the joking as a child must have been hard. Still, I guess he grew into it—it fits him."

"You've lost me."

"His name"—the nurse opened the door and smiled at Michael—"means great angel of darkness. Just like Satan."

⌘

Michael headed down the corridor for Mary's room. His mind reeled. Was this a joke? He ran everything over in his mind from the moment he'd met Finster to what Simon had said to what the German nurse had just revealed to him. Great Angel of Darkness? Of late, Michael had trouble with the whole concept of God: now he was being asked to examine his belief in the possible existence of the devil. Finster's manner was contrary to what Michael would imagine in anyone evil, the man had actually cared and tried to help Michael and Mary.

No.

It was only coincidence, a convenient coincidence planted in his head by that lunatic Simon. No, Finster couldn't be. They weren't the keys to Heaven, it went against logic. The keys to Heaven were surely myth—like the Holy Grail—something dreamed up by some long-dead priest to inspire faith and fear. Michael's mind was set.

His heart was a different story, though. It was racing and a sweat was breaking out on his brow. There was no such thing as coincidence. When too many factors pointed to something, it wasn't by chance. Sherlock Holmes said it best: "When you have eliminated the impossible, whatever remains, however improbable, must be the truth."

The memory that kept rearing its ugly head was the way he'd felt standing in Finster's dungeon. The cold fear that had iced his spine. He couldn't put his finger on it then, but it was becoming clear now. It had been there in the shadows, in the paintings, and in the man who'd led him into the clammy darkness. And the only comfort he'd received had been from clutching the box which held the keys. He didn't understand it then but maybe it was making sense now. He had seen evil in a few of the inmates in prison, the ones who had no feeling, the ones whose only desire was to torment and destroy others. But he avoided it, he avoided them . . . but he couldn't avoid it now. It was everywhere in that lower level of Finster's house, he smelled it, felt it crawling over his skin, it was there in the silence: evil.

Michael was completely lost in thought, so lost that he ran headlong into Dr. Rhineheart.

"Michael? Good. May I speak to you for a moment?" Rhineheart asked grimly.

⌘

The rain had started at midnight and showed no signs of letting up. Combined with the cold winds slicing out of the north, it had pulled the temperature fifteen degrees below normal. To make matters worse, a thunderstorm had rolled in that morning. Mary was staring out the window watching the lightning bolts dance across the horizon, counting the seconds until the thunder shook her hospital room. The room had grown cold, the world a little duller in the last few hours, and it wasn't on account of the storm. Mary didn't know how she would tell her husband. He had worked so hard and, she suspected, sacrificed so much to provide the care for her. She had forever been the optimist, the one to lift the spirits of those who faced their darkest hours, she was invariably the shoulder to cry on and the person to impart hope. But that was always for others; now, even when she dug deep down in herself, she found nothing. The words of optimism weren't coming this time.

She wasn't ready for him when he walked in. She stuttered in spite of herself, "Mm-m-Michael?" She couldn't meet his eyes, "I'm sorry . . . I'm so sorry."

Michael took her in his arms. "Hey, shhh." He held her tight. "Those doctors don't know what they're talking about." His voice was strong and confident. "We'll get another opinion; we'll find a way . . . St. Pierres never give up." His heart felt like it had shattered into a thousand pieces when Rhineheart broke the news. He'd held back his tears then; he would now. He'd never let Mary see them.

"Michael . . ."

"Listen, we haven't gone through everything that we've gone through to lose. We've always made things work. You've stuck by my side and made a life for me to return to. It works both ways, you know. I refuse to give up and I don't expect anything less from you. We are going to beat this"—he stepped back, put his hands on her shoulders and looked directly into her eyes—"*together.*"

Mary found strength in his words, just as she always had. "There are other doctors," she said, trying to sound convincing.

"Exactly. We'll find the best."

"I have heard of a number of treatments which haven't yet been approved. . . ."

"We'll try them all." The tide was turning and they both felt it, feeding off of each other's optimism.

"Herbalists, some newfangled methods," she added, half-joking.

"Precisely, a little whacko, but we'll try them all." He was smiling. "I'll try them with you. We never really did the drug thing when we were younger, maybe it'll be fun."

Now Mary was laughing and that was how Michael liked it, her smile was back and her shoulders were held a little higher. "Whatever it takes, we'll beat this together," she told him.

"Amen to that, darling."

As they fell silent they were both lost in the same thought: they always thought alike and now was no different. Despite their little upbeat rah-rah fest, there was the very distinct possibility that Mary would not survive. Her body was riddled with cancer. It was everywhere and there really was not more than an extremely slender hope of beating it. As the silence drew out, each sensed the other's thoughts and it only made the words come harder.

"What if . . ." She couldn't finish, she couldn't think of how to phrase it; but Michael knew.

"You're not going anywhere." He said it as firmly as if his words would manifest themselves into a cure.

There was another painful pause. Michael looked around at the children's pictures, at the flowers everywhere—they were so inconsequential, they brought no comfort. Flowers only served to fill the florist's pocket and provide a fleeting sight and scent of what was blooming in the world outside the hospital. They were a cruel reminder of what the patient was missing. He kept staring at the bag of Oreos he'd brought Mary; he didn't know why, he just kept staring at that blue package as if it held a solution. That commercial kept bouncing around in his skull, *Kids eat the middle of the Oreo first and save the chocolate cookie outside for last.* He decided that he hated that song.

Mary could see the panic setting into his eyes. "It's going to be OK," she murmured, touching the cross she wore around her throat. Now, she was doing the comforting. "Even if— We'll be together again."

"Don't talk that way!" Michael shot back fiercely, instantly regretting it. As with many men, he'd turned his fear into anger and he'd lashed out at the person he loved most.

Mary took his hand. She stared out the window, at the rain streaming on the glass like a waterfall, distorting the views into a palette of washed-out grays. She whispered, "What do you think it's like?"

Michael had no idea what she was talking about, his brain felt like mud. All he had gone through, everything that he fought for in the prior weeks, was now for nothing. They'd lost their battle. *He'd* lost their battle. He'd failed her. Again.

"Heaven." A comforting peace overcame Mary as she answered his unasked question. She continued looking out the window as she whispered, "What do you think it's like? Do you think it's beautiful?"

The shock rippled through Michael's body like the lightning on the hills. Simon's words echoed in his mind: *You have stolen the keys to Heaven. . . . Heaven is closed.*

Michael knew at that instant that Mary would not survive the cancer. Everything Simon had said was true. He turned back to Mary, pulling her to him, holding her close, desperate to protect her from the killing horror that raced through her body, that was stealing her from him. He couldn't look at her, hiding himself in their embrace as he whispered back, "I'm sure it is."

⌘

A half hour earlier, Dr. Rhineheart had explained Mary's condition to Michael.

While they had removed her ovaries and fallopian tubes, knocking out the cancer there, it had metastasized into other areas of her body, worst of all to her kidneys and brain. The symptoms weren't evident yet, but they would be soon. It was like it had been beaten out of the bush where it was feeding upon its kill, only to settle into a new nest for a new feast. The cancer was aggressive. It was multiplying at a fantastic rate.

And would kill her within six weeks.

Chapter 16

The Old Stand was packed. Wall to wall, shoulder to shoulder. The weather had rained out every men's league softball game that evening. So, tonight, no excuses, just drinking, and drinks were flowing into every glass. Shouting was the only means of communication and if you came here to think, forget it.

Michael was tucked in a booth in the back, waiting. He had been there for over an hour, nursing the same drink. He had left Mary's room, left her sleeping, and pulled out his cell phone. Busch answered and the swearing didn't stop for two full minutes, the volume close to the bar's current decibel. Michael took it in stride; he was hurting and had nowhere else to turn, he needed a friend now more than any other time in his life. Busch screamed about trust, loyalty, and friendship; truth, betrayal, and lies; but mostly he screamed about the law and the position that Michael had put him in. When he'd finished, Michael asked if they could meet. Oh yeah, they could meet. Michael was told to be at the Old Stand by nine o'clock and he had better not be late.

So, Michael waited. He knew that he would have to own up to Busch for violating his parole. He had taken advantage of their friendship and abused it badly. But while the guilt for betraying his friend weighed heavy, the guilt he felt for betraying his wife was tenfold. Over and over he kept running what Simon had said in his mind. If Heaven was closed—and that possibility seemed to have increased throughout the day—then he had destroyed her hope of eternal life, a violation of her core beliefs that was beyond comprehension. His brain was a jumble of incoherent thoughts that drowned out even the racket of the rowdy bar.

A very anxious and angry Busch squeezed into the booth across from Michael. The big cop was doing everything in his power to keep his fury in check. Michael said nothing, eyes cast down. Finally . . .

"Where the hell were you?"

"I'm sorry."

"Don't even go there; I'm not in a forgiving mood. Where were you?"

"I had some stuff to take care of."

"Stuff? That's a load of shit, Michael. I want to hear it from your own lips—where the hell have you been these past ten days?"

Michael stared at him, not knowing what to say: all he wanted was to get his ass-chewing over with and move on to Mary.

"Do you realize the position you put me in? I've been covering your ass for almost two weeks, buddy, and I don't cover anyone's ass but my own, you understand?" Busch was beginning to lose control; he glared at the wall, breathing hard, struggling to gain equilibrium. The seconds ticked by.

"I just came from the hospital," Michael said quietly.

Busch looked up, the anger wiped clean from his face. "And?"

Michael's expression said it all. Busch didn't need the words; Michael's eyes were those of a wounded child. Busch had never seen Michael this way. Sure, Michael had been down over Mary's illness, but there was always that shadow of hope. "How bad?"

"It's everywhere."

This was the last thing Busch had expected; he was revved up to tear Michael down. Now, he forgot all about his anger. "Oh . . . Mike. What can I do?"

Michael just looked at him, no answer, his eyes filled with remorse and fear.

"I know you're hurting—"

"I've done something," Michael said softly, his head bowed in confession.

"What?" It was a question Busch no longer wanted answered. "What did you do?"

"I've damned her."

Busch's eyes narrowed, confused. He wasn't just worried about Mary anymore.

"I've destroyed everything she believes in."

"What are you talking about? This cancer isn't your fault."

"They say our loved ones always pay the price for our sins."

"That's a load of shit; Mary's condition has nothing to do with who you are, with what you did."

"Why couldn't it be me in that bed?"

"Hey, you bury that thought right now, this is a tragic thing but you didn't cause it. Things happen in this world that we can't control. They just happen."

"I wish I could take it back."

"Take what back?" Busch couldn't be more lost. "Mike—what the heck have you done?"

"I went to Europe." Michael paused. "And I stole two keys."

Busch closed his eyes. He knew Michael had gone abroad. His intention tonight had been to get Michael to admit to it, but not this way. He had hoped against hope that there was a reasonable explanation, for if the purpose of Michael's trip was to commit a crime, Busch would be in the worst of all possible positions. "Don't be telling me this—"

"I stole the keys to pay for Mary's treatment."

"Shit, I knew it. You promised me!"

"Yeah. I promised a lot of things."

The volume of the bar seemed to grow with the intensity of their conversation. Busch found it hard to believe that all the merriment could be occurring around them as his best friend's life was crumbling. "Michael, this is serious—"

"I sold them to a man named Finster—"

"This is a lot worse than breaking parole. I—"

"He's the Devil, Paul. I sold those keys to the Devil." Michael said it quietly, still not wanting to believe his own words.

"Mike—?"

"I sold them to the Devil; they were the keys to Heaven. The keys to the Gates of Heaven."

Busch sat there, stunned, totally unsure how to deal with this nervous breakdown happening before him. Michael was going to pieces before his eyes and he didn't have a clue what to do. "You're talking shit here, Mike." Busch sat forward. "Look at me. I know the strain you're under—"

Michael looked him straight in the eye. "I'm telling you the truth."

Busch saw it; Michael believed what he was saying. That scared him. He had dealt with the criminal element that was classified as insane, he knew how they believed in their own world, in their own definition of right and wrong, good and evil. "You sincerely believe you met the—"

"It doesn't matter what I believe," Michael interrupted. "It's what Mary believes. I've taken the one thing she values more than anything: her faith, her eternal life."

As much as he hated himself for it, Busch was deeply terrified; his best friend had gone over the edge. Busch had no idea how to handle this, it was Jeannie who always dealt with the delicate issues. Busch wasn't delicate. So, he ran to the one place he always did before panic set in, hoping to jar Michael back to reality. "Look, buddy, we've got another problem."

Michael leaned forward.

"You busted your parole. We've got to deal with that."

"That's the least of my worries."

"No, it isn't. You might be going back to jail."

"I told you this in confidence. As a friend."

"You are my friend, Michael. But the law is the law. If anyone finds out you left the country, and they will," he added, remembering Thal's inside info, "we're both fucked. It's the law, Mike, and you busted it . . . deliberately."

"I've got to rectify what I've done." Michael wasn't even paying attention.

"You're delusional, Michael. You're just blaming yourself for Mary's illness."

"I have to go." Michael got up from the booth and looked at Busch with accusing eyes. "Thanks for all your help—"

His sarcasm stung Busch. "I can't let you go, Michael." The big cop stood, authority in his voice.

"What are you going to do, throw me in jail while my wife is dying?"

Now Busch was back to pissed, back to the mood he carried when he came into the bar. Michael had successfully turned the blame and guilt around and placed it squarely on his shoulders. Busch was seething. "Damn you to hell—"

But Michael walked away, uttering under his breath, "I've already done that."

⌘

The Busch children were screaming like banshees. The two kids had an unnatural bond for a brother and sister and were seldom apart. As they sailed around the kitchen with Playskool tomahawks and lightsabers, they exhibited an energy seldom seen in anything short of a cheetah racing for the kill.

As if in a soundproof bubble, Busch sat silently picking at his dinner, oblivious to his shrieking brood. He didn't feel like talking; he didn't feel like doing much of anything right now. He was losing two of his closest friends: one to cancer and one to insanity, and there wasn't a thing he could do for either of them. Never had he felt so helpless. And to make matters worse, Michael had turned his back on him. How could the man violate his parole, after all that Busch had done for him? It gave him such a hollow sense, it was like everything he'd fought for had been swept away abruptly by some swift summer wind.

Jeannie sat across from Busch. She, too, was silent. Paul had come home like this too many times to count, when the trials of his day had sucked the life out of him. She knew not to press the matter; if and when Paul felt like talking, she was there to listen. Getting things off his chest usually helped, but there were times when the pain of the retelling, of the reliving, was too great until the passage of weeks—sometimes years—acted as a safety net. Paul loved her and she him, that was the bottom line. Sometimes lives had to be lived separately on certain issues.

The children continued to circle and Busch's soundproof bubble was beginning to crack. Jeannie read his annoyance. "Hey you two, keep it down to a dull roar, huh?" she said, hoping to avoid the inevitable.

But of course, kids will be kids and they only screamed louder, running faster, pushing their lungs to the breaking point. And then without warning everything screeched into slow motion. Robbie's arm, swinging out, caught the glass pitcher on the table. It tumbled through space and shattered on the floor; lemonade exploded everywhere.

Busch erupted out of his chair. "Don't you listen to your mother? You have no regard for rules! I'm sick and tired of the lack of respect around here. Things are going to change, do you hear me?"

The youngsters froze in their tracks. Too scared to cry, they started to shake in terror. Their father rarely lost his temper with them but when he did, the punishment was usually so severe it would leave both in tears for hours.

Jeannie scooted the children out of the kitchen. "It's OK, kids, upstairs. Pajamas, brush your teeth, and you can watch a movie."

When she stepped back into the room, Paul was pacing, rubbing his brow, making a tight fist and then releasing it over and over again as if pumping some medical instrument. He could no longer hide the reason for his mood.

"It's Michael. He broke parole. He told me. Told me!" Busch shouted in disbelief. He sat back down, exhausted, as if the ten words were a marathon. He continued, softer now, "He stole something in Europe."

"In Europe? I thought he went down south . . ." Jeannie paused. "What are you going to do?"

What was he going to do? That was the question he dreaded answering. "I have to take him in." He knew all along what he would do but telling Jeannie had made it a reality. As the words left his lips, it was as if acid had poured over his tongue.

"I'm sure there's a logical explanation."

"He did it to pay for Mary's treatment."

"Oh, God." She couldn't imagine the pain Paul felt. He was about to take away the life of his best friend. And not just his friend—*their* friend. Her best friend's husband. And what would it do to Mary?

"I don't make the rules, Jeannie. It's not up to me to listen to explanations, that's the judge's job—"

"They'll put him away. And it will kill Mary."

"Jeannie." Busch paused. "Mary's treatment's a bust. The cancer has already spread."

Jeannie was a strong woman but not that strong. She remained motionless, in shock. Tears welled in her eyes. Mary had been her best friend since high school. "Are they sure?" Her voice cracked. "There has to be something. . . ."

He shook his head. He had no answer to give her.

They sat there silently for God knows how long, without saying a word. Jeannie had been with Paul for more than fifteen years. In all that time, he'd been a rock, the stronger of the pair. He had attended countless funerals: his mother's and his brother's three years ago, two months apart. He had died at the hands of a drunk driver, she of a lonely heart. Colleagues, friends, even a partner gunned down in the line of duty. In all those days gone by, she had never seen a tear from him. Until tonight. And when they came, it was as if all of his years of grieving flowed forth as one. Tonight, he never spoke a word. He just sat there, tears running down his face.

⌘

Busch stood in the doorway of his children's bedroom watching them sleep, tangled under their white summer sheets. So innocent, so optimistic. Life hadn't taken away their dreams yet. A parent always tries to protect his child's world from the harsh reality of adulthood.

Only a parent could understand the pain felt after scolding a child. Busch felt shame for lashing out at his son and daughter. They had done nothing more than act like children and that wasn't a sin. He had tried so hard to be different than his father. He'd devoted himself to be a real part of their upbringing, their coach, their friend. He had been determined to be everything to them that his father wasn't to him. And most of the time he was. But it was the slipups like this evening that gave him the real insight into his own father. There were always circumstances and secrets that were best kept from children. Things like cancer and prison. Busch saw now that what he thought to be his father's inattention was really preoccupation with the troubles of life.

There were always two perspectives on every situation. And he realized that was where the gifts of wisdom came from . . . a little bit at a time. He leaned over his children, kissing each on their rosy cheeks as he silently thanked them for helping him grow.

⌘

Michael grabbed two glasses and a bottle of Jack Daniel's and headed into the den. The room was in total darkness except for the light from the street lamp outside. Hawk slept curled up in the corner by Michael's desk.

"So, now you know," came the voice from the shadows.

Michael froze. After a moment, he put the glasses down, poured the whiskey, and passed a glass to Simon, who was seated behind the desk. He turned on the desk lamp and sat in the side chair. "I don't know what to believe."

For the past two hours, Michael had wandered the streets of Byram Hills, on the verge of madness. There could be no other logical explanation. The pressures he had placed upon himself had finally broken him. His life was becoming his dreams, his dreams nightmares, and his nightmares reality.

He'd left Busch in the bar, having destroyed his only real male friendship. He had left Mary in her hospital bed, knowing he had destroyed all that she believed in. *Insanity was an easy thing,* he thought as he walked. It had crept up on him unnoticed, much like the cancer had crept up on Mary, devouring his brain the way her body was being devoured. But the insane were never aware of their insanity—or so he had heard.

He wanted answers and there was only one person who could provide them. Simon alone could reveal the truth. Besides, he was the only one Michael had left to turn to. And Michael hated him for that.

"Remind me"—Michael's voice dripped with cynicism—"why I should have any faith in what you say?"

"You lack faith in yourself, so how would it be possible to have faith in someone else? Least of all me?"

"Try me," Michael challenged.

"Jesus Christ was preaching to His twelve disciples—you do know about His twelve Apostles?"

"Yeah, I went to Catholic school," Michael sneered.

"When Jesus came into the banks of Caesarea Philippi, He asked His disciples, 'Who do men say that I am?' And they answered, 'Some say you are John the Baptist; some, Elias; and others, Jeremias, or one of the prophets.' And Jesus said, 'But who do *you* think I am?' "

"Each of the twelve men sat there pondering the question but only one knew the answer. And this one disciple said, 'Thou art the Christ, the Son of the living God.' And Jesus said to His follower, 'Thou art Petros and upon this rock, I shall build My Church.' And He imparted to this renamed disciple—Petros—the power to condemn or absolve all those who wished salvation, saying, 'What thou shall bind on earth shall be bound in Heaven and what thou shall condemn on earth shall be condemned in Heaven.' He gave him the power to control the gates of eternal life. And He gave Petros two keys imbued with this power—one gold, one silver." Simon paused. "The keys to the Gates of Heaven.

"Upon the death, resurrection, and ascension of Jesus, this disciple, Petros—whose name translates into English as Peter—led the Church of Jesus Christ, Christianity. History has come to know Peter as the first Pope. This power that our Lord placed in Peter passes down to his successors. Along with the keys." Simon sat back, allowing Michael to absorb the story, waiting for him to comment.

"So, these two keys," Michael asked, "the Church has placed a great value on them?"

"A value you still can't begin to comprehend."

"And naturally you place something of such tremendous value, of such worth, in a dilapidated church in the middle of nowhere. How smart you must be. Do you know how easy it was? If this is true, if these are the keys that Jesus left behind—" Michael paused. "These keys are nothing more than a bunch of superstitious hocus-pocus."

"You may not share our beliefs at the moment"—Simon erupted out of his chair and began to pace—"but don't *dare* mock me." He stopped, dead still. "Those keys were placed by Peter before his death at the true location where Jesus rose to Heaven. A link between Heaven and earth. The place where the Church of the Ascension was built—"

"It's a myth! A fairy tale embellished down through the ages—"

"Peter decreed, and each Pope thereafter has agreed, that's where they should stay. As long as the keys were the property of the Pope and the Church, the link was preserved. The gates were open."

"Wait a minute." Michael raised his hand. "Those keys *were* protected. They were protected by you." He couldn't resist inserting the verbal blade. "And you *failed*."

Simon didn't answer. His eyes bored into Michael before looking away.

"And now you have to clean up your mess. Does the Vatican know?" Michael demanded. "I tend to doubt it, otherwise, there would be more of you."

Simon grabbed Michael by the collar, hoisting him from his chair, pulling him forward. "I should just kill you. Or better yet, maim you, leave you to reap the seeds you have sown. Finster will be back, you know. He'll be back for your wife and he will be back for you. And all you can think about is taunting me with your cocky bullshit. You would rather pound your chest at my expense, your scared mind trying to bury the real fear you feel. You would rather insult me than save your wife from damnation. Your arrogance disgusts me." He effortlessly tossed Michael to the couch.

"How could Finster be who you say he is? I see no proof—"

"Proof? You have your proof. August Finster bid you to steal; you were his pawn."

"Finster? He's a collector, a businessman, respected, extremely successful—"

"He's all that except for one thing: he is not a man."

"How do you know this about him? No. This is insane."

"His name repeatedly came up in connection with his interest in some of the more profane art produced against the Church. I wrote him off as sick, as did everyone else. But when certain pieces started to vanish into the black market, I decided to do a bit more checking on his background. Seems he has no background—"

"Neither do most people coming out of the Eastern bloc—"

"But he, unlike the others, was never *born*." Simon stared at Michael.

Michael laughed.

"You think it humorous?" Simon said. "You know nothing of the East Germans. They kept tabs on everyone, pretty much from conception. People think the records are gone; they're not, you just have to know where to look. And I looked. There is no record of Finster—anywhere."

"You're hanging your hat on that?"

Simon ignored him. "A couple of years ago, I paid our friend Finster a surprise visit in Berlin. No one had any idea of my itinerary yet there he was, waiting for me as I got off the train. Standing all by himself on the platform. I asked him point-blank who he was. His reply was: *Why do you ask a question to which you already know the answer?* I intended to accuse him of conspiring against the Church and against God. He denied everything. The only problem was his denials came before I even voiced my accusations. He knew absolutely everything

I was going to say. Next thing I knew, I woke up on the train heading back to Rome with no recollection of how I got there. And since that day, not a night goes by that Finster doesn't haunt my dreams."

"Dreams?" Michael shook his head. "You're basing this on—"

"He is the dark angel cast out of Heaven before time remembered."

"A very convenient tale meant to scare the world. Keep little children hiding under their beds. Mothers cowering in fear, begging for forgiveness. All running to their benevolent God to save them. To protect them from the evil of a make-believe Satan." Michael sat up, becoming more sure of himself as each word left his lips. "August Finster is an egotistical businessman with too much power, casting his spell over all of Europe and, it seems, you."

Simon sat down directly across from Michael. "August Finster is an extremely handsome, charismatic being; funny, appealing, warm. And he is the blackest evil. Everything about him is a facade. He appeals to your inner wants and needs. He knows what you desire; he knows exactly what terrifies you. He plays on this knowledge." Simon leaned in closer. Now it was his turn to twist the blade. . . . "*As he played you.*" His eyes were unwavering and cold. "How coincidental that the answer to your prayers arrives in your most desperate hour with the ability to provide that which you can not get from anyone else. All in exchange for a simple blasphemous task. *Who is the one who has failed here?*"

The room suddenly felt darker, the world more claustrophobic. Michael was acutely aware of the sounds around him: his dog's breathing, the cars outside, the tick of his watch . . . all seemed to accent the fear inside him.

"What does he want?" he asked Simon.

"What he has always wanted. Our souls. Barter one here, steal one there. No need now. He'll have them all. By controlling the keys, he controls the Gates of Heaven."

"Why doesn't God just reopen them—these gates? They were opened once before when Jesus hung on the cross. Isn't that what you believe?"

Simon hadn't feared anything since he was sixteen, since he'd endured a moment in life that struck him to his very core. His heart had died that day and with it, his emotions. He had not known fear—or any other emotion—since. Until now. "God would have to return, a fulfillment of the Scriptures, the end of the world, whatever you want to call it. Gabriel's Horn would be trumpeted across the lands. The sign that God is returning: Judgment Day. Michael, we must retrieve those keys."

Michael didn't know whether to laugh or scream. Everything that had happened in the last few weeks seemed to fall into place now. Every step he had taken had brought him to this moment. He had not only hurt and destroyed the lives of the ones he loved; he had trampled over the beliefs that sustained them.

"We must leave," Simon told him. "We don't have much time."

"My wife is dying. I can't leave her again."

"I'm sorry." There was no sympathy in Simon's voice.

"I can't leave, her life . . ."

"Her life is ticking down. There is nothing you can do to stop it. But if you value her eternal life, there is still time. Save that, Michael. Save her soul."

⌘

All night Michael tossed and turned. No longer able to sleep in the bed, he had reverted to the couch with its out-of-whack spring pushing up against his shoulder blade. He preferred its uncomfortable stabbing to the thoughts that had raced through his brain as he tossed alone on their king-sized mattress. Their empty bed stirred too many thoughts. This is what it would be like when Mary was gone. He wasn't ready to face that now. She was still alive. Of this he was sure.

It was the only thing he was sure of.

After Simon had left, he had walked the night streets. Aimlessly wandering until he had found himself at the hospital. He stood staring up at Mary's darkened window. He hadn't gone inside. If he did, if he saw her, his grief would overcome him again and he needed to think straight and true. If he was to leave with Simon, there was no telling how long he would be gone. Mary might die in his absence and how could he live with that? Michael could let Simon go alone but he would never know if Simon succeeded in getting the keys back. The torture Michael would endure for all the rest of his days—the uncertainty about whether Mary had gone on to a better place, a more merciful place—would be with him to his own grave.

Michael's faith in God had been destroyed, becoming nonexistent. Yet Mary's was stronger than ever. She believed in everlasting life, she believed in eternity, she believed in Heaven.

It came down to his shattered beliefs against Mary's unshakable faith.

His decision was made for him.

He would leave with Simon.

Chapter 17

Morning, Mike.”

Busch’s shadow loomed over him. Michael squinted as he rubbed the crust from his eyes. “How’d you get in?”

“You gave me keys last year, remember?”

“Seems I’ve been giving keys to all the wrong people lately.” Michael groaned in exhaustion.

As Busch stepped aside, the early morning sunlight slammed into Michael’s eyes with a vengeance. He regretted those last two shots of Jack as a hammer pounded deep in his brain. “Can I get you some breakfast?” he asked in a groggy voice, pulling a pillow over his head to block out the light.

CLICK. Something wrapped about his ankle. Michael lifted the pillow and looked toward his feet. He was greeted by the face of Dennis Thal. Busch’s new partner was adjusting a clip on the metal bracelet that now encircled Michael’s lower leg. Not cuffs, nothing restraining. Worse. Around his ankle was a security monitoring bracelet. The kind with a built-in GPS that could be tracked by a central station, reporting on his whereabouts at all times and sending off all sorts of bells and whistles for each and every time he strayed.

Michael violently jerked his legs up and away from Thal. The young cop smiled like the hunter who knew the hunt was over, knew there was no place his prey could go to escape.

“What the fuck?”

“Sorry.” Busch was unable to meet his eye.

“Sorry? What are you doing?”

“You’re a flight risk. I can’t take a chance that you’ll run.”

“Run?” The incredulity poured from Michael’s voice. “Run from what?”

“I had to report you to the judge.”

“I told you as a friend—”

“Makes this even harder.”

“My wife is *dying*, Paul. Do you really think I’d run? Do you think I’d leave her?”

“You can see her as much as you want. We just want to know

where you are. Don't want you leaving town"—Busch's pause hung in the air—"again."

"You son of a bitch! You're sending me back to jail!"

Michael jumped up, lunging for Busch, but before he could swing, Thal was on him. The cop hit Michael and hit him hard, pummeling him about the body before Michael even had a chance to react. As he fell to the floor, Thal drew back his right leg to strike Michael in the head. But he never got the kick off. Busch grabbed Thal about the shoulders and hurled him across the room.

Busch could hardly think straight, his emotions running the gamut as he looked at Michael rolling on the floor in pain.

Thal stood, dusted himself off, then turned back to Michael. "Scum like you belong in a six-foot hole. You're gonna rot there, you know. Your wife will die alone—"

Busch was back in his face; his whispered voice trembled with rage. "Wait for me in the hall," he snarled. "Now."

As Thal left, Busch tried to help Michael up. But Michael defiantly refused, pulling away.

"Mike, there's nothing I can do. Law's the law. I can't risk covering for you. I've got responsibilities, too."

As much as he cared for his friend, Busch had a wife and kids. He couldn't let them get dragged down. Even if he wanted to put his ethics on hold this one time for his friend, someone else knew that Michael had broken his parole. And as sure as the sun would set, Thal would turn them both in for the sheer pleasure of sneering at them.

"Mary's illness is pushing you over the edge, buddy. I'll explain it to the judge. He'll go light. I'm sorry."

"You have no idea what you have done." Michael's words cut through Busch like a razor through butter. Michael wiped the blood from his nose, and turned away.

Busch stood there, his breathing all but stopped, staring at Michael. Finally, without another word, Busch walked out.

⌘

Mary was sound asleep, nestled in Michael's arms. He had slipped into her hospital bed, ostensibly to comfort her but really more to comfort himself with her presence, to selfishly feel her touch again. He still hadn't figured out how he would tell her he would be leaving again. How could you tell the woman you loved you were abandoning her?

He had covered up the involuntary jewelry about his ankle with his sock and made sure to wear a pair of extra baggy khakis to hide the bulge. The gray box was a little larger than a pack of cigarettes. It was affixed with a plastic zip-tie and a security bracelet. Every step he took, he was reminded of its presence as it chafed away his skin. He was free to see Mary at his leisure as long as he called in to outline his itinerary each time. And that is exactly what he did before he'd left the house.

"Parole Monitoring and Tracking," the policewoman had answered.

"St. Pierre." Michael had called from his apartment. "Going to see my wife at the hospital."

"You are confirmed, Mr. St. Pierre. Please be sure to call us when you arrive at the hospital in accordance with guidelines."

So formal, Michael thought. The Parole Division would be monitoring his movements around the city. He was required to check in hourly when out of the house. If the clip was removed or damaged or he traveled outside the city limits, he would be subject to immediate arrest for parole violation. What would they do if they followed his movements onto a plane and out of the country?

He had arrived at the hospital to find Mary coming out of radiation. She and Michael had decided to keep up the treatments. If anything, they might at least buy a little more time. And you never knew, after all, miracles could happen.

They had a quiet breakfast of eggs and sausage that Michael had picked up on the way. Their words came few and far between. Michael was never the poker player, Mary could read distress in his face from a mile away, and that only served to thicken the air between them.

"Something's bothering you. I can see it in your eyes. Whatever it is, it can't be that bad"—she forced a smile— "all things considered."

"I have to go away again." His head was bowed in shame, no words had ever come harder. "It's only for a few days. . . ."

"That's what's troubling you?" Mary almost laughed. "I'll be fine, don't you worry. They take terrific care of me here." She took his hand. "You just come back to me."

"I will." Relief washed over him. He would come back.

"I know."

She kissed him. Michael could feel the slight trembling in her body. He took off his sport jacket and put it over her shoulders. She held the jacket tightly about her, absorbing his warmth, inhaling his smell. It seemed to revive her, the smell of his clothes; she had taken to wearing his shirts and jackets, always finding it like a security blanket.

Mary had seemed to slip a bit in the last twenty-four hours. It was as if knowing her prognosis had accelerated the symptoms of the disease.

And so Michael had spent the last hour lying at her side. "Only a few days," he whispered to his sleeping wife. She didn't move, didn't respond. Maybe it was better this way. Quietly, he continued, "I need you so much . . . I thought I was saving you . . . And I've done so much worse. I have to make this right . . ." He stroked her brow. "I just ask that you have faith in me."

She stirred, her eyes still closed, and ever so gently squeezed his hand. Nuzzling into his neck, she wrapped her arms around him, and whispered softly, "I always have."

⌘

"Nobody ever said anything about freezing to death," Jane Arlidge grumbled as she briskly rubbed her hands together for warmth. No one told her she would need a sweater in late June. You'd think when they issued her her uniform blues last week they would have at least given her a sweater.

"Fifty-two degrees, fifty-two ice-cube, snowflake degrees." The, perky young police officer sat before a host of monitors—there must have been thirty in all. Each one meticulously labeled with a vellum floor plan overlaying each screen, a little green blip moving about. A name, ID number, and status line appeared at the bottom of each. Jane Arlidge came to the police force straight from the academy, choosing to dive right into her career, unlike the other graduates who headed off for a week of celebration before their crime-fighting careers began.

She sat in a large windowless room. Along the back wall rose an array of computer mainframes. Wires ran haphazardly about the floor while the terminal lights blipped green, blue, and red. Only one desk approaching any level of comfort was available, its high-backed leather chair—occupied by Jane, now feeling frozen solid—vastly superior to the cold metal stools at the computer workstations. The computer room of the Byram Hills Police Station was not only cold in appearance but just plain cold. Fifty-two-degrees cold as prescribed by the mainframe manufacturer and the police IT department. The lucky rookie who drew monitoring duty inevitably ended up with a hell of a head cold that would last right through the dog days of summer.

The monitors Jane stared at were each assigned to a felon awaiting a court date, a prison cell, or the end of a sentence. Those granted house arrest with the sexy ankle bracelet were the lowest of the low-risk. These were the ones who knew remorse, who knew contrition; the chance of their running was slim to none. Hell, the bracelet really wasn't necessary; it was just a constant reminder that they were being watched. Jane knew this and so her diligence wasn't acute. The rookie had brought a couple of books as her predecessor recommended—he'd forgotten to mention to bring lots of sweaters—but was ignoring them in favor of today's crossword puzzle.

She nearly fell backward in her chair when the alarm went off. A shrill cutting tone from monitor twenty-seven. Its little green blip had vanished. "No, no, no, no, no, no. Shit!" Reaching for the phone, she knocked her books and the newspaper to the floor, but before she could even dial, the blip came back as if it was there all along.

She dialed anyway.

The phone rang. "Hello?"

"Mr. St. Pierre?" she asked frantically, a quiver in her voice.

"Yes?"

Jane's brain was still reeling from the adrenaline rush. Was it some computer glitch? Had she made a mistake on her first day? "BHPD Tracking and Monitoring. We seemed to have had a momentary loss of transmission."

"Sorry. I went downstairs to get my mail."

She exhaled in relief. "Probably lost transmission in the elevator," she reasoned. A more authoritative tone returned to her voice. "You must report in any time you are leaving the apartment."

"Right. Sorry. I'm new at this. It won't happen again."

"Good." Crisis averted, the rookie hung up the phone and tried to catch her breath.

⌘

A small black duffel was packed and sat ready on the front hall table. Michael was on the living room floor belly rubbing Hawk, the portable phone still cradled on his shoulder. Thinking. Thinking hard.

He tossed the phone on the sofa and used both hands on his dog. He stretched out his right leg and studied the ankle monitor on it. His tools were spread about the floor. He had removed the cover of the ankle box and—as a test of its capabilities—momentarily removed an internal wire. He needed to know how far he could push before he brought the whole police force down on his head.

"All right, my canine friend," he said aloud. "How am I going to get out of this?"

⌘

Simon, bag in hand, looked at his watch. A plane taxied on the tarmac in the distance. Michael had said he would be there waiting. Well, that was the first lie—should he expect less? Maybe, Simon thought, he should go on his own. He had recovered many items for the Church in the past and had performed services of a far more lethal nature in the name of God. Why had he pursued Michael in the first place? Was it for the keys? Or out of wounded pride? Never had he failed before. The thought crushed him. Why had he come here? He never needed, nor had he ever sought, help before. And why from the man who had deceived him, stolen from him? A man he knew deep in his heart was untrustworthy. Simon prayed this wasn't the first mistake of many.

This is the second call for Flight 1225 to Berlin.

⌘

Jane sat back, eating her McSandwich dinner. The rookie's heart had stopped racing with fear an hour ago. Now, it was racing for other reasons. He was six one, hair blond as corn silk, and his jaw—well, she loved a strong jaw. She had seen Doogy only once at the Academy—no one messed with him about his name, he was just one of those confident people who could carry it off without ridicule—but he had burned a hole in her mind. She had no idea he was assigned to the same precinct until he had walked in.

"Hey, how's it going out there?" she asked, putting on a buddy voice, trying to be just one of the guys.

"Hard to tell. Awfully quiet my first day out. How'd you draw the bad straw of Siberia?"

"Beats the streets."

"Yeah, right," Doogy said. "All that training going to waste."

"I volunteered; they said I can pick my next rotation. That training will be put to good use soon enough."

"Seriously?" He looked around at all the computers. "Yeah, maybe this isn't such a bad gig. None of the dirty work thrown at you by senior officers, a comfortable seat to avoid the sweltering heat. How come I didn't know about this?"

She loved the way his face scrunched up in disappointment. "Pays to be in the know."

He nodded, then pointed at the monitors. "So, tell me about it."

"I watch the movement on parolees, detainees, house-arrests. Exciting stuff."

"Looks like a bad video game. Those dots don't move much." He pulled up a stool.

Got to stay focused, she decided. "They're either sleeping or watching TV. Never much movement. Hungry?" She offered him some of her fries.

"Sure." He reached over.

Big hands; she was trying to shake that myth out of her mind lest he notice. She was running out of small talk. "So . . ." she stammered.

"Get a lot of reading done, I imagine." He gestured toward her books.

Yeah, he was interested, his body language screamed it.

"Now, what is that person doing?" He pointed at a little green dot racing all over the place like a video game gone berserk.

It took Jane a moment to snap out of her lust, she wasn't sure what he was talking about at first. But then she saw it. Monitor twenty-seven. Again. This time, she knocked her sandwich clear across the room as she lunged for the phone.

⌘

Busch and Thal knocked on the front door. No answer. From inside the apartment came a loud crash, like something falling over. Thal raised his foot to kick in the door but Busch stopped him midway, dressing him down with his eyes. Busch flashed a key and opened the door.

"Mike?" he called out.

Everything seemed normal. The apartment was clean, there were fresh flowers on the hall table. Thal headed to the den while Busch checked the living room.

Another crash, this time from the bedroom. Busch eased toward the bedroom door, his gun drawn now. "Mike?" Another crash, glass breaking. "Quit screwing around!" the big cop hollered. But there was no response. He spun in the doorway, gun raised. Busch nearly screamed as something flew in his face and he staggered backward. His heart hammered in his chest as he holstered his gun. "Fucking cat."

CJ tore into the living room, streaking up on the couch. Seconds later, Hawk came running out hot on her trail, screeching to a halt as he saw Busch. The dog sniffed his hand as Busch reached out to pet him. But he caught the scent again and growled at the cat on the couch. CJ hissed and took off. The two animals raced about the room in comical circles until the cat finally jumped up to the high bookshelf, the dog barking and jumping at her tail as it swung just out of reach.

Thal walked back in the room. "How can he not be here?"

And that's when they saw it hanging from the dog's collar: the security anklet.

"Smart son of a bitch," Busch muttered.

⌘

Thal was flipping papers around on Michael's desk. He found an open book and several newspaper articles. Picking one up, he started to read.

Busch was on the phone. He kept his back to Thal; he could no longer bear to look at the man. Busch had checked everywhere: the hospital, the precinct, the security shop. No one had seen Michael. The last time anyone had heard from him was when the rookie at the parole-tracking desk had called at 5:07 that afternoon, admonishing Michael for leaving his apartment to get his mail.

What scared Busch the most was when he called and spoke to Mary. She said that Michael had to go away for a few days. That was information he wasn't about to share with Thal, or anyone for that matter. Busch's ass was in a holy sling of shit now. The house arrest had been his idea; it had been his decision not to arrest Michael on the spot yesterday. If he didn't find the man and quick he'd be in a lot more than shit. How could Michael do this to him?

Busch hung up the phone and turned. Thal was still reading. Busch looked about the surface of the cluttered desk. Michael was working on something, of this Busch was sure.

"Looks like he's had company." Thal pointed to two glasses and the empty bottle of whiskey. "I think your *friend* has an obsession going." He tossed a copy of *International Business* to Busch; Finster was on its cover, his charismatic smile shining under friendly dark eyes.

Busch found it hard to disagree with Thal's obsession reference. Everything upon the desk was about this Finster guy: newspaper articles, magazines, pictures.

"You"—an accusatory finger was in Busch's face—"let him *go*."

Busch grabbed Thal's digit and nearly snapped it in two. He'd had enough of this crap. "Point that at me again and I'll do more than break your finger."

Thal's body twisted toward the floor in pain, yelping. The irony struck Busch square in the mouth: Thal couldn't handle pain. The man thrived on tormenting, on giving it out. But he couldn't handle it. But then a wash of emotion flowed over Thal's face and as he looked up at Busch, he smiled. And Busch realized his conclusion about Thal was completely wrong. Thal enjoyed pain, he enjoyed it whether he was giving it . . . or receiving it.

⌘

Simon watched the redheaded flight attendant pull the 747's door closed. He had resigned himself to the fact that he was going it alone. He threw his carry-on in the upper compartment and took his window seat. The transatlantic redeye was one of the few pleasures he could grasp right now. He'd enjoy not only the sunset but the sunrise from high upon the clouds. He liked this particular flight, it shortened his night. The darkness still scared him though he hid it well. Nighttime was when the distractions of his life vanished, leaving him alone with his thoughts and fears; with the knowledge of what he knew was out there. And that terrible knowledge was impossible to fight, like a cough that rises up each time you lay down to sleep. No matter how hard you try to avoid it, it still creeps up and grabs you.

And so he cherished these moments when the night was abbreviated. Each sunrise was always like a baptism for him, washing away the evils of darkness. It was no legend that the wicked only come out at night: it was a fact. There was more to the meaning and relationship of light and day and dark and night than most people realized.

Now that he was looking out at the soon-to-be-setting sun, he realized he had literally missed the world, passed her by like some ship in the night. Never once had he stopped and tasted her splendor. His life had always been based on devotion, devotion to his work. Never had it allowed him a wife, children, family. Since that horrible afternoon in his childhood, he had been set on this path, a path he had always freely and willingly accepted. A path that had led him to this moment when he questioned it all. Was his merely a life of vengeance? He did not know love or friendship, never had the benefit of a lover or a close friend, someone to talk it through with. His was a monastic, military life. One to be lived alone. One where he would die alone.

He had never sought help before, why now? He'd shared valuable information with a man he couldn't trust, priceless information about the true meaning of the keys. Michael St. Pierre had stolen from him; Michael had been the catalyst for this entire mess, a mess that could have the ultimate consequence for all. And yet he'd been willing to seek the thief's help. It had been a grave mistake he was glad never came to fruition. It was a stroke of luck that the man had decided not to show. Simon considered himself lucky, this once.

"Hi."

Simon looked up.

Michael stood in the aisle, bag in hand.

⌘

Earlier that afternoon, after Michael left Mary's side at the hospital, he took a quick detour by his shop. It was a risk, he knew, but one he had to take. He didn't know how he would get out of the bracelet but whatever the solution he arrived at, he would need his tools. He grabbed the pliers set, a mini drill and saw, a few rolls of wire, and the electronic kit he used to tune security systems.

The security bracelet was a simple design. The GPS worked while out of the house, but it did not provide accuracy when someone was indoors, the signal having difficulty penetrating masonry walls. As a result, a secondary system sent out a signal to a transponder, in this case, one that had been placed in Michael's closet. The strength of the bracelet's signal determined his location in his apartment: that information was relayed to the police station monitor. The power source for the bracelet itself was a small internal battery whose wiring ran the circumference of the security device. The power was activated upon closure about the ankle. To remove it, one would have to cut the bracelet, irreparably severing the internal wiring.

Michael was not only a security specialist, he was a thief—though he considered himself retired despite recent events. He had beaten many alarms, many a security system, when he was active. There had always been a way to do so. Now he set out drilling the bracelet on opposite sides, two pin-sized holes, careful not to slip and drill his ankle. As Hawk watched, he inserted two rigged electrical pins, each attached to a ten-millimeter wire, creating a secondary circuit route, a bypass line. The current now had two routes to follow; when one became inoperable there was a backup. With the ankle bracelet defeated, he snipped it easily off his ankle. Then he called Hawk over and attached it to the dog's collar.

Once safely on the plane, he didn't bother explaining what he had done to Simon, who sat in stiff silence beside him. They had taken off an hour ago and Simon seemed more preoccupied with the setting sun than with the fact that Michael had broken out of his house arrest.

⌘

Captain Delia was pacing; it was a cliché, but he had no other way of expending his nervous energy and he didn't know how to yell from his chair. "You let him go!" he raged.

Busch was used to it. The captain was a screamer and it didn't bother Busch much except that this time the man was right. This time, Michael had gotten the better of him.

"Thal said the guy left the country. Is this true? Do you mind telling me how one of your parolees *leaves the country*?"

"He hasn't left the country. His wife is dying." Busch wasn't a very good liar but he was trying.

"Thal swears he's split town. Either he did or he didn't."

"Thal's not his case officer. I am."

"You get too close to your parolees, Paul you can't be their friend. You're clouded on this issue. I'm thinking of giving this to Thal—"

"Thal?! He's a fucking psycho. I'm warning you, I'm going to break his neck if he doesn't keep his nose out of this—"

Delia slammed his office door and turned to Busch, glaring and red-faced. "That wouldn't be real good for your career right now." The captain sat down, gathering himself, weighing whether or not to share information. After a moment he decided. "Thal's Internal Affairs. And he's on your ass in a big way, my friend."

A thirty-pound sledge hit Busch square in the gut. No way. Couldn't be. Busch had been betrayed again, this time by someone on the inside, another cop. And by his boss, too. "Why didn't you tell me?" He could barely get the question out.

"What is it you always say, 'the law's the law'? Well, this is the cop police. Cop law. If they tell me to shut up, I shut up." Delia's anger boiled in his eyes.

"Why you telling me now?"

"I thought the IA probe was bullshit. You've always been lily white, I didn't think twice about it. I figured they'd find you clean. Now look what you've done to me, the position you put me in—"

"Ah, spare me, you know I did nothing wrong. I'm innocent." Busch never thought he'd be making that statement. "And I'm telling you, St. Pierre may be gone but there's more to it than we're seeing."

"We don't make that call. *You* don't make that call. That's up to the courts."

Busch hated when his own words were thrown back at him. "His wife is knocking on death's door. He's not going to fuck up and land himself back in jail on her dying days."

"You're not thinking straight. Who do you think you're talking to?

You're supposed to watch these guys, ease them back into society. And ride 'em if they don't toe the mark. If they fuck up, you report it and bring 'em in. But no: you become their friend, coddle them, invite them over for tea. Jesus, Mary, and Joseph, couldn't you find a buddy who wasn't a felon?"

"You know that's a load—"

"Spare me the excuses." Delia cut him off in frustration. "Thal said you let him go."

"Sir, that's shit. St. Pierre left of his own free will, without my help."

"You put him on a house monitor and he cut through it like—"

"Sir, I know this man. He is reformed—"

"Reformed men don't break parole, don't cut their security anklets, don't go on the run. What scares me is *why*? What is he running from, Paul? Or . . . running to? Do you know? This guy's breaking the law and I'll bet in a big way. And when he does we're all fucked."

"No, sir! He won't break the law. I'll find him. He's my responsibility."

"You've already blown your responsibility. Tell me why I shouldn't take your badge right now?"

" 'Cause I'm the only one that can find him."

Captain Delia had known Paul Busch for too many years to count. As bad as things looked, he knew deep down that Paul wasn't the type of guy to lie, to risk his career in this fashion. Delia had asked Thal who put the complaint in on Busch, but the powers-that-be were silent. The captain's job was to cooperate and cooperate he would, but only to a point. He never liked cops investigating other cops. And he didn't like Thal to begin with.

"He goes down; you go down," Delia told Busch, bluntly.

Busch said nothing, he just nodded. That was the biggest vote of confidence he could expect out of his captain, all things considered. He stormed out of Delia's office. "Where's Thal?" he yelled to the whole world.

Everyone looked up, shaking their heads. Busch headed straight to Thal's desk. His *empty* desk: no personal effects, not even a scrap of paper. He turned to Judy Langer at the next desk over. They never shared a great love for one another and she was knee-deep in paperwork.

"You see Thal?" he demanded.

"He left." Judy didn't even bother to look up.

"For?"

"I'm not Thal's keeper, Paulie," she mumbled.

Busch studied the desk. This wasn't the desk of someone who had just cleaned up, this was the desk of someone who'd left and wasn't planning on coming back. His head was spinning. Internal Affairs. What the hell? He had lived his life by the law—now he was under investigation like the criminals he had spent his life picking up. And to make matters worse, he was under Thal's microscope. There was something going on here, something that didn't fit, something that went much deeper— Who had fingered him to Internal Affairs? If Busch had any chance of figuring it out, of saving his career, he had to find Thal. But first, he had given his word to Delia: he'd find Michael.

"I overheard something about a family emergency," Judy added, hoping to God Busch would leave if he got what he needed.

"Do you know where?"

"I think I heard him say something about Germany. Berlin, I think."

⌘

Mary's medication left her feeling frail and sick. After Michael left, she was hoping to deal with the after-effects by curling up on her bed and sleeping, but she arrived back in her room to find *him* there.

He never said what he really wanted; she thought that more than a little odd. He claimed he was Paul's new partner, Dennis. . . . She couldn't remember his last name. He just dropped by to see how she was feeling and ask a few questions about her husband's relationship with Busch. He said it was for a citation for Busch's parole work, said he'd stop back after Busch got his most-deserved honorarium. She never mentioned the visit to anyone.

But there was something about him. She felt it as if it was an invasion of her soul. Dennis scared her more than the cancer.

⌘

The fact that Busch was under internal investigation had floored him. There was absolutely no way. At no time in his life that he could recall did he become compromised with any of his charges, most particularly Michael. Busch was more than aware every step of the way of how he was conducting their relationship. Thal had shown up before Mary was sick, before Michael had reopened "that" chapter of his life. Why? And why did Thal head to Berlin? Was it to capture Michael and further indict Busch? Or was there something more?

Busch sat in a private computer room, one light, one chair, one desk, and one computer. No windows, carpets, pictures, or decorations. The Byram Hills Police Department's database was enormous. Not only were there criminal records, but the department had access to a vast array of computer libraries: FBI, Interpol, periodicals, news organizations.

Finster wasn't hard to find. While the billionaire possessed no criminal record, he did leave quite a trail in both the business and celebrity world. In fact, August Finster was a regular Gates-Turner-Perlman-Trump of the former Eastern bloc. Busch found a video montage of Finster in the archives of Bloomberg News. The video showed an impeccably dressed Finster running a board meeting, surveying his vast real estate holdings, arriving at social galas. What really caught Busch's eye was the footage where the industrialist was dancing the night away with some of the most beautiful women Busch had ever seen. Stunning, jaw-dropping ladies right off the runway.

A voice-over announced, *"A virtual unknown until the reunification of Germany, August Finster has since become the wealthiest of the former East Germans. Successful in every business sector, he has yet to know failure. His background is a mystery. Single, utterly ruthless in business, Finster's only weakness appears to be women."* The flickering images showed the billionaire surrounded by a bevy of beauties. If it wasn't for the women, Busch would be beyond bored.

"Notorious for his nightly exploits, entertaining two to three ladies an evening, Finster has yet to be photographed with the same woman twice. He's always found taking in all the latest social scenes which, combined with his ruling of the business world and last name . . ."

Busch pointed the mouse, about to click-cancel this flashy piece of cinema when . . .

". . . has given him the whispered moniker: the Prince of Darkness."

Chapter 18

August Finster was holding court in his library. His thick leather-wrapped gentleman's den of solitude was quite handy for impressing the easily impressionable. The three ladies sat on opposing couches around the fireplace, their recently freshened drinks in hand. Each was dressed in the finest evening wear from the finest shops in Berlin.

Finster came by his women in different ways. His vast money and charm were always an irresistible aphrodisiac, attracting the attractive to him like bees to honey. Elle, her red hair ablaze, had met him that morning on her way from a photo shoot. Portfolio in hand, the international fashion model spotted him as he looked her way and had been instantly smitten. Lovely June had arrived for an interview at Finster Industries and left with an invitation. And Heidi—well, Heidi had simply arrived this evening uninvited but encouraged by friends who had sampled his charms. But beyond his money, his charm, there was something else. They all felt it, but no one could pinpoint it. It was like they all wanted to reach out for that special something in him that sucked you in but always stayed just out of reach, like the last dream you have before waking, the one that remains just beyond the edge of recollection. It was a kind of magic. And despite the fact that he was known as the king of the one-night stand, the women still flocked to him, it was a bragging right akin to a rock-star liaison. Finster was a regular Elvis with the pelvis to your heart.

When the phone rang, Finster paid it no mind, allowing it to ring three times before it finally stopped. He didn't like to be interrupted unless it was of the utmost urgency.

"We will dine at El Grocia," he announced. He always went to the newest restaurants, rarely frequented the same place twice. "Reservations have been arranged for eight fifteen."

The three arm charms smiled. Mostly it was a smile of acknowledgment, a just-thrilled-to-be-with-you kind of smile. Except for Elle's; Elle knew El Grocia had an eight-week waiting list and instantly appreciated the power that Finster wielded. In her eyes, the other two girls were nothing more than horny, dimwitted eye candy here for a quick fling. *She* was different.

"I would be honored if you ladies would select our destination for dancing." Finster's voice was intoxicating to Elle.

Charles appeared silently in the doorway, in his right hand an envelope. He discreetly passed it to his master while leaning toward the billionaire's ear. Elle wasn't a busybody by nature, but she did take an interest in other people's lives. Though Charles spoke softly, she could make out most of his words. Finster shot a glance Elle's way as if he heard her thoughts. His fleeting smile may have seemed warm but his eyes remained cold, icing her heart. She was suddenly filled with shame. And fear.

It wasn't like she heard anything of interest. It was just something to the effect that "they were coming and how dare they and don't worry they're safe and he would set up an appropriate greeting. . . ."

Outside, Finster's chauffeur gave a staccato beep of the Bentley's horn. Charles glided out of the room. Finster directed the ladies outside and toward the car. Heidi and June were all giggles as the chauffeur held the limousine's doors open. In the doorway, Finster stopped and turned to Elle. He put his arm around her.

Maybe things would be OK. She really should shake her habit of eavesdropping; it had almost gotten her in a world of trouble again. At least the warmth had returned to his eyes. *Thank God,* she thought. She hadn't been scared like that since she got caught stealing lip gloss back in Paris.

"I was thinking maybe we would send these other two . . . children on ahead," Finster told her, leaning closer.

"I would love that" was all Elle could get out of her quivering lips.

"Why don't you wait for me in the library? I'll send them on their way and be back in just a moment. Then we can have a nice quiet dinner here, just the two of us."

Elle smiled as he walked toward the car. She looked up at the stars like she used to as a child, wishing, just as her dad had taught her, on the first one she saw. *May this happiness last the rest of my life,* she prayed.

⌘

Three a.m. Thirty thousand feet. Most slept. Some, with headphones, watched the 1948 film *Abbott and Costello Meet Frankenstein.* Simon, being his insomniac self, read the Bible. While he knew the ending, every word in the entire book for that matter, he always came away with some new insight, some lesson that he hoped he could apply in his life if he was lucky enough to continue to live it.

Michael had taken over the two adjacent seats, his legs stretched out, with a writing pad in his lap. He was sketching a detailed diagram of what he remembered of Finster's mansion. His recollection was detailed and vivid, as he had practiced a one-pass reconnaissance technique in his earlier career days.

"Didn't think I was coming, did you?" Michael said quietly, more to himself than to Simon.

Simon looked Michael's way. "I knew you'd come." And he went back to the book in his lap.

Michael didn't take kindly to brush-offs. "Admit it. You had no idea."

"Actually, I did," Simon replied, his nose still in the Bible.

"I wasn't completely sure myself I was coming, until I boarded the plane."

"You were coming from the moment you learned the position you'd put your wife in. It's in your character. You're an easy read."

"You don't know the first thing about me."

Simon didn't take his eyes off his Bible. "Michael Edward St. Pierre, age thirty-eight. Orphan. Adopted at the age of two by Jane and Michael St. Pierre, parochial school, altar boy. Dislike for the mundane got him into a bit of trouble as a teenager. Thief: jewels and art. High-risk hits. Stole for the thrill, not the money. Did hard time: Sing Sing. Wife: Mary, age 30. Loves you very much, stricken with—"

"Enough!" Michael hated hearing his life boiled down to a paragraph befitting an obituary. He had grown up in the suburbs—Armonk, a small town about an hour outside Manhattan. His adopted parents had sent him to Holy Father Catholic High School, where Father Dan pounded in his daily lessons as if they were sermons. Michael was a relatively good kid. He'd had his share of mischief, but nothing that hinted at his troubled future. He got snagged a couple of times for drinking and smoking and he did spend a month in his room—maybe a precursor to his jail time—for stuffing a pack of firecrackers in Mrs. Collete's mail slot. When he lit the fuse and sent them through the brass-hinged slot of her front door, he could hardly contain the giggles. He and his friends had run like the wind but there was no need. The deaf old lady hadn't heard the machine-gun-like pops and explosions. She hadn't heard a thing; she thought the ashen debris was from her cat tearing up the newspaper again, so she just opened the door, and swept the paper shrapnel out. Michael never would have gotten caught if it wasn't for his accomplice: bragging Stevie Tausigenti; who told Kenny Case; who told his girlfriend, Jen Gillicio; who being a tattletale told her mom; who called Mrs. St. Pierre. Michael accepted his confinement like a man . . . for a couple of days. After that, he would get home from school, grab a snack, head to his room, then sneak straight out the window. His mom was none the wiser and in fact expressed her pride for his doing his time so stoically.

Unfortunately, it wasn't his mother who sent him to Sing Sing and it wasn't for setting off firecrackers. Needless to say, his cell didn't have a window he could sneak out of. Sing Sing was a prison tucked into the hills along the Hudson River. A quiet, out of the way penitentiary that never captured much notoriety except for the execution of Ethel and Julius Rosenberg. The three and a half years Michael spent there were pure torture. It had been Hell on earth to be away from his young bride for so long. His biggest fear until last month was that he would end up back in prison, torn from his life with Mary. His vow to her that he wouldn't break the law was really a vow to himself. He'd sworn he would never be trapped away from her again, confined to a world where she couldn't be with him. Nothing could compromise his vow. Nothing.

Now, deciding that ignoring Simon seemed the best way to avoid conceding defeat, Michael went back to his sketching. He quickly captured most of the details of Finster's enormous home on three pieces of paper. The first sheet showed the exterior of the mansion, including the guards, windows, driveways, and lighting. The interior of the first floor was pretty straightforward. Besides the entrance hall and library, he was able to recall each of the rooms that flanked the hallway on the way to the basement. The dungeon, as Michael had reverted to calling it, was a little more difficult, however. Much of his journey belowground had been in darkness or minimal light at best. The tension he'd felt in his stomach when he was down there had fogged his perceptions. So he wasn't sure if he had captured all of the details he would need. He couldn't pinpoint the distance to the chamber that held the two keys. It could have been one hundred paces; it could have been one thousand.

Michael put his feet on the floor and his head back, reclined his seat, and passed the three finished drawings to Simon. "How do we know the keys are still there? What if he takes them with him?"

"Did you give him the keys? Actually place them in his hands?"

"No, I put them on a pedestal."

"How'd he react?" Simon's tone indicated he already knew the answer.

"In awe . . . ," Michael said thoughtfully as the memory worked its way to the surface. "But . . . frightened, too. He wouldn't even touch them—"

"He can't touch them," Simon interrupted.

"Why not?"

"He was cast out of Heaven, forbidden to come in contact with that which is sacred: churches, holy objects—his powers are utterly useless against God's work. In Jesus's own words, he can not knowingly enter holy ground—'upon this rock I will build my church, and the gates of Hell shall not prevail against it.' " Simon paused. Then he said: "Those keys are of God."

Michael did not reply. He was remembering Finster's expression when the billionaire had first seen the keys.

"This is where they are?" Simon was scrutinizing one of the hand-drawn maps, paying particular attention to the lower level.

"That's the last place I saw them." Michael pondered this, then demanded: "Who are you, Simon? You know so much about me. . . ."

"Who I am is real boring."

"Seven-hour flight, can't get much more boring than that. I'm risking my neck here for your keys. So, go ahead, bore me."

The flight attendant walked by, blonde, legs up to Heaven. Her youth was obvious in not only her taut body but her face; she couldn't have been more than twenty. Michael smirked as he caught Simon watching the shimmy of her rear as she moved down the aisle.

"Remember when you were sixteen and all you wished for in life was to end up with that, never thinking if they had a brain or even if they loved you back?" Michael was hoping to get some kind of reaction out of Simon. But the other man said nothing. "Don't tell me—they locked you up in some monastery when you were sixteen."

"Actually, when I was sixteen, they locked me up in prison. For murder."

⌘

The red ball glided over the green felt, slowing to a stop inches before the corner pocket. It hung there for an eternity before finally falling into the leather netting. Elle restrained her elation at the feat. It was the first time she'd played pool and she thought maybe she really was a natural.

"I have the distinct feeling I'm being hustled," Finster said with a raised eyebrow. "Are you sure you've never played before?" He slid his arm about her waist, pulling her close.

"Beginner's luck, I swear." Elle blushed at the comment. She smiled and stole a quick kiss as she went to line up her next shot. She draped her long body across the table, drew back the cue, and sent the balls scattering.

"Are you enjoying yourself?" Finster asked as he hung his dinner jacket over the back of a chair.

"It's an absolutely perfect evening," she assured him. And it was.

They had dined on orange duck resting upon a bed of wild rice and steamed vegetables. The wine was a '45 Triano Rose from his private cellar. They had taken their dessert in the library—chocolate soufflé and brandy—laughing about the modeling industry and how one had to sell oneself for even a modicum of success. Charles was at their beck and call all evening. The butler always seemed to sense the moment to top off their glasses. *So, this is how the stratospheric class lives,* Elle thought.

She couldn't tell if her light-headedness was from the wine or the giddiness of pure joy. She was falling fast for the man before her. His eyes had captured her heart, mind, and soul.

"Tell me, Elle, do you enjoy art?"

She straightened in surprise, standing her full six feet. "It's one of my greatest passions."

"Truly?"

"I spent two years in Paris studying under François Delacroix. Pastels and oils were my life." Her eyes glowed with pride. "That was actually how I ended up modeling."

"Tell me."

"One of our models quit without notice and François insisted that I pose for his class. I was incredibly nervous and shy, but I did it. One of the sketches caught the eye of a photographer and the rest . . ." She thought about it. "Well, it didn't work out like I had hoped." A hint of regret slipped in her voice.

"Do you still paint?" Finster asked.

"I no longer have the time." She paused, then added, "Nor the money."

"I would love to see your work; we could arrange a showing."

She laughed at that. "It's all gone; believe me, no hint of my former talent exists."

"We'll have to change that. I have a studio on the east side of the grounds. Perhaps you would like to set up there."

She couldn't believe her ears. Set up on the estate—that only meant one thing to her. This marvelous night would continue for days, weeks . . . maybe even years. Her heart was bursting in her chest with elation.

He placed their pool cues against the table and clasped her hands.

"Would you like to see my collection? I share it only with those who have a true appreciation, a true eye for beauty."

"I would be honored."

Finster grabbed the five-flamed candelabra and led her across the vast hall. Opening the massive door which led to the lower level, he headed downward without hesitation, holding the candles high.

"It's so dark," Elle said, hoping the wobble in her voice was not noticeable.

"Stay close."

The shadows danced long and fast against the stairwell walls of stone before vanishing into the darkness. The splash of light from the five flames lit only the area immediately around them. Arriving at the end of what she thought was the passage, he led her to a simple wooden bench. He brushed off what looked like some old tools and removed a long rope, draping it over the back of the bench.

"Please," he said, gesturing for her to sit. He handed her the candlestick, then disappeared into the dark. Elle held tightly to the heavy silver stem, praying it wouldn't slide out of her slippery hand. Her palms were sweating and her heart had started to hammer.

Within moments, he was back. He propped eight frames against the bench, then he leaned in and kissed her, long and hard. Elle lost herself in the moment, her free hand pulling him close. Then she opened her eyes and gasped.

He was staring at her with those eyes, so captivating, so powerful, so . . . There was something else in them but before she could comprehend, before her mind could untangle itself, he kissed her again. This time lustful and ruthless. She returned his passion, her blood racing. Then without warning, he broke away, leaving her hanging there in the moment, gulping for air.

As she trembled with anticipation, he arranged each painting, surrounding her with them. "I want your honest opinion now."

She held the candles up and looked. At first she thought he must be joking. This surely was a mistake. "Are you playing with me?" She held the candelabra higher, looking for him, then recoiled in fear. All around her was a menagerie of dark art she never could have imagined: the meek crushed under the weight of death, distorted faces screaming out of each vibrant canvas. The paintings were everywhere and Finster was nowhere to be seen. "August?"

And suddenly, she realized the candles were burning down to stubs, the first of the five winking out before her eyes. The tortured souls seemed to leap off the canvas at her; the darkness of the place wrapped itself about her stunned mind.

Her childhood fears came rushing forth—darkness, confined spaces, monsters lurking under the bed. "August? Please!" she whimpered, rising from the bench. She took a tentative step forward, raising the dying flames high above her and edging toward what she hoped was the way out. Her steps growing quicker, she stumbled, falling to the ground. The candles crashed to the floor. All but one were instantly extinguished. She clung to the last candle as if she held her heart in her hand and groped desperately for the others. Finding two stubs, she relit them from the lighted flame and pushed them into the ornate silver arms of the candelabra.

Why was Finster doing this? She held the candles high again in her trembling hand, frantically trying to get her bearings. She couldn't believe her eyes. The artwork stretched as far as the flickering light could carry. All an abomination of mankind, all portraying terror, and shock, and cruelty beyond imagination. Who would collect such horror . . . and why?

She was alone with her fears. And that was when she realized what she had seen in Finster's mesmerizing eyes. It all came flooding in—where she was, who he was.

The knowledge was too much for her.

And her mind snapped.

Chapter 19

Simon stared out the airplane window. Painful thoughts were spinning in his head. If he and Michael were to work together, it would come down to trust, opening one's soul to one another. He started off soft and slow as if in a confessional.

"My mother was a nun. It was all she ever really wanted, a life entirely devoted to God. She never dreamed of a husband or family. Being an orphan, she had never felt the warmth of a mother or father; the only love she ever felt was God's love. She bounced around in Roman orphanages without affection or purpose, keeping to herself, just another ward of the state until she settled into the St. Christopher Orphanage. It was run by a woman who cared for the children as if they were her own, guiding them to find their purpose in life. As my mother grew, she spent most of her time tending to the sick with a smile and a gentle hand. At night, she read anything she could get her hands on, most particularly that which pertained to God. She had profound insight into His teachings, as if the Scripture were written directly for her. The more she read, the more she knew where her life must lead; her heart had at last found its match. She entered her Order the day she turned sixteen. She was in love and her bridegroom was the Church. . . .

"Till four years later, when she met my dad: the atheist accountant. The only things he believed in were numbers. It was a quick romance, or so they said; they were wed within six months. Mom worked in the Vatican, even after she left her Order. She was the archive liaison to the Pope himself. In charge of the Church's history: she kept its secrets. We lived in Vatican City, a nice boring life. I had a whole country to myself—me and eight hundred others. It was a pretty normal childhood—I had a bunch of friends, played a lot of soccer." Simon looked out the window as if each memory was coming to him from over the horizon. He pushed any remaining emotion from his mind and continued.

"One day, when I was fifteen, my mother didn't come home from work." He paused. "I figured she was working late. Next day came and went. My dad didn't say a word about her absence; it was like the fear of losing her had rendered him mute. The Swiss Guard, by direct order of the Pope, searched not only Vatican City for her but, with the help of the Roman police, all of Rome. They finally found . . ." Simon closed his eyes. He hadn't spoke of this in years. He needed to suppress the pain, he needed to stand back and watch it like a third party observer, as if it had happened to someone else.

"The hospital wouldn't let me see her. She finally came home a month later. She was sitting in our parlor when I got home from soccer. The Pope was there. They quietly spoke together in Latin; his presence seemed to comfort her, at least for a short while. Her face, the parts of it that weren't bandaged, was terribly bruised, and though her wounds were nearly healed, they still had that sick yellow tinge to them, still swollen, distorting her features. I can't think of my mother now without seeing her like that. All she spoke about was forgiveness. That we must forgive the man who had done this to her if we were to survive, if we were to remain above the animals. No one would ever tell me what had happened. My dad became a shell. He seldom spoke. He was rarely home and when he was, he wouldn't even stay in the same room as my mother.

"She slid into a fantasy world, took to wearing the long black habit she'd worn when she was a nun, even the veil and wimple upon her head. Whenever I was around, her smile was frozen, like it was painted on. My parents had become cold and detached from each other and from me. I tried to comfort them but they had retreated to the safety of their illusions." He paused. "I never felt the warm embrace of my parents again."

Simon cracked open another airline bottle of bourbon, poured it into his cup, and drained it. "One day, about six months after she returned, I came home early from school. I guess my mother didn't hear me. She walked out of her room wrapped in only a towel, and when she saw me . . . I'll never forget the look in her eyes. I finally understood why she had covered her body, why she wore her nun's long dresses. It was to spare my heart. Her torso, her legs—they were grotesquely scarred; her skin had become the tapestry of something evil. My mother ran back into her room in shame, refusing to come out, no matter how I implored her. I ran and found my father in the local pub. I screamed at him until he told me the truth. The tears ran down his face as he described how something twisted and evil had risen up from the depths. That a man in a drunken stupor—a man whom my mother once loved—had violated her in ways I could never imagine. I remember feeling oddly detached at that moment: it was as if I was looking in on someone else's life. I absorbed the words but I didn't understand them until much later. How someone could be so ruthless, so heinous. This thing—this *animal*—had worn a mask. . . . My mother never saw his face but she had known him nonetheless. Afterward, she refused to speak his name, saying it must be part of God's plan and insisting that we couldn't see His great design. The police said this monster had vanished. After revealing this to me, my father never came home again."

Michael wanted to stop this torture. Telling his story was clearly killing Simon. But Michael couldn't find the words; his throat was frozen in compassion.

"I spent the next four months tracking down the son of a bitch who destroyed my mother. Found him in his hole in Rome. Tied him up, tortured him till he told me why. He wanted to know the secrets, he said. He had recently discovered his god and he wanted to devote his life, the way my mother had devoted herself. Said he needed to know the secrets that would make his "god" great.

"When my mother wouldn't answer his questions, he'd raped her. When she refused to talk, he used his knife on her over and over again, upside-down crosses—and still she never made a sound—so he burned it into her. Again and again, till she was covered in them. His god's number: six-six-six."

Michael sat there in total shock; he had seen horror in his lifetime but always from afar. But this . . . This was the first time he had seen how horror affected the ones closest to the victims, the ones left behind.

"The fact that the monster before me used to hold me in his arms as a child did not deter me. He was no longer my father, the man who had raised me, the only man my mother ever loved. He had become possessed by things I didn't understand and didn't want to understand. All I knew was what he had done to my mother, the woman whom he had called his wife.

"They arrested me for his murder. I was only sixteen, the judge took pity, said I'd been driven temporarily insane. But I wasn't insane." For the first time that evening, Simon looked directly into Michael's eyes: "I knew exactly what I was doing.

"I was nineteen when I got out of prison. My dad was dead, my mom . . . My mom had chosen a family over God and she'd been punished for it. When I entered prison, her mind shattered just as her family had. She wished only for escape from this world, so she could find peace in Heaven. She hung herself just before my release.

"Do you know that when you commit suicide, it's an unforgivable sin? The Church refuses to bury you. My mother was buried in a pauper's grave, without the Church's blessing. After devoting her life to the Church, the Church denied her her eternal reward.

"I had nothing, nowhere to go, no family. Went to pick up my things from the place I'd once called home—"

"In Vatican City—" Michael said.

"The priests took pity on me," Simon continued as if Michael had not spoken. "Asked me to stay with them, to seek comfort in God. But I sought my comfort elsewhere: I joined the Italian army, received special training. I had skills, the officers said, skills that could be honed razor-sharp. I traveled a bit in the name of peace but what I did was anything but peaceful. Each kill I made was like a cleansing of my mind, my soul. Every time I pulled the trigger or inserted the knife, I saw only my father's face, not that of the real victim. My commanding officer said that I was killing to protect my country, but he was wrong: I was doing it to protect my sanity. After two years I felt no different; killing provided no release from the neverending nightmare of my mother's scarred body and mind. I requested and received my discharge."

The only sounds were of the jet's droning whine. Michael sat riveted.

"I returned to my mother's apartment in the Vatican. Several priests with whom my mother had been close sought me out. They wanted to know if they could assist me in any way. They knew full well what I had done, not only to my father but while I was in the army. They felt responsible for me, in light of the Church abandoning my mother to an unsanctified grave. They forgave me my sins and saw me often. These priests became the only friends I had. They provided me work and a home and the closest thing that I would ever have to a family.

"These priests had worked with my mother for many years and were part of a small group of clerics that answered only to the Pope. Though not publicized, there had been an increase of crimes and violations against the Church. Not only crimes of greed and hate, but crimes meant to destroy Catholicism. These priests approached me with an offer that they warned would require a lifetime of devotion. It was a path that, they cautioned, I could never leave, but one for which I was uniquely qualified. I agreed to pledge myself under one condition: special dispensation for my mother. . . .

"She received her proper burial. In the Church. A private ceremony, performed by the Pope himself."

Simon turned to Michael; he was no longer looking inward, reliving his tormented life. He was facing the world, facing Michael. Although he had revealed himself to be vulnerable and pitiful, he was now back to the man that Michael had first encountered in his apartment: resolute, determined, and hard. "In my new job, I was permitted to perform whatever service was required to do my job, to protect the Church.

"I became the keeper of the secrets, Michael. The guardian of all the things you don't want to know."

⌘

The plane cut through the night sky, its black shadow riding the waves of the inky moonlit ocean below. It would be dawn soon. The whine of the engines sang like sirens in the darkened cabin. Simon was fast asleep, exhausted, perhaps, from reliving his tormented past. Michael, on the other hand, was wide awake, afraid of the dreams that would rise up from the horrors he'd just seen through Simon's eyes. How could anyone possibly remain sane with such a devastating childhood? But at last he had a deeper understanding of the sleeping man beside him. His suspicions about Simon's ability to kill had been confirmed. The balance of Simon's mind was another matter. Michael had pondered the man's grip on reality and now, judging by not only his actions and history but his parents' mental instability, the possibility of the man being insane was vastly probable.

Michael looked out at the black sea, her depth and mystery, thinking of the dangers hidden just below her shiny beautiful surface. It reminded him of Finster. He opened the compartment above him in search of a blanket. Finding none, he satisfied himself with his jacket. He huddled in his seat, wrapping the sport jacket tightly around himself; he could still catch a hint of Mary's perfume on it. As his mind wandered to her smile, he felt something in the pocket. He pulled out an envelope and tore it open.

Dearest Michael,

For years, this has protected me and kept me safe. I know you found it foolish at times and downright exasperating when we made love. But now I ask that you keep it with you at all times. It has delivered me through many a troubled day. I ask only that you wear it now so it may deliver you home to me safe and sound. Wear it not as a representation of your faith but as a reminder of my unwavering faith in you.

I love you with all my heart—

M.

Mary must have slipped the note in the pocket of the jacket while he had stepped out to make a call and fetch her some ice water. Even in her illness she had found the strength to continue the gestures he loved so much.

Michael poured the contents of the envelope into his hand. And it all came flooding forth as he stared at his palm, all of the emotion, all of the pain of the past month. Tears stung his cheeks. He took a quiet comfort in his grief, something he hadn't allowed himself until this moment, hoping that it would help clear his mind for what lay ahead.

Finally—not out of the fear that Simon had instilled in him this night; not out of a newfound devotion to God and religion, but because of his belief in Mary—he slipped her golden cross around his neck as a reminder of his promise to return to her. He grasped the religious object in his hand as he had seen Mary do so many times before, then released it, letting the cold metal dangle against his chest, the irony of the moment fully in his mind. Without saying a word, Mary somehow knew what he was facing. She had sent her belief in her husband with the cross that now hung around his neck. She had uttered no words of protest or anger at being abandoned by him. She had given him only one simple sentence that would support him in whatever he must do: that she had always had faith in him. She was the single reason why he was heading across the world to enter what he could only imagine to be the manifestation of Hell.

Chapter 20

The 747 skidded down the runway, slicing through the dense morning mist of the Berlin Tegel Airport. The summer morning reflected like crystals off the dew-covered grass surrounding the tarmac. The sun had risen out of the ocean that morning, relit for a new day, chasing the shadows of the waves like a waking child shakes off a nightmare. It had been a night where many feelings long ago driven deep down into his soul had resurfaced, reminding Simon of who he was, of what he had become. And while he had longed for the sunrise, it didn't hold the cleansing effect that he usually experienced and, today more than any other day, had hoped for. He knew the nightmares would begin again soon. And when they did, they would be coming in the light.

He and Michael cleared customs without incident. To Michael's surprise, Simon spoke fluent German, explaining to the customs agent that he and Michael were there on a trip of both business and pleasure; they had nothing to declare. He requested that they be hurried through, as they had an appointment to keep.

Michael had finally fallen asleep in the last hours of the flight. It hadn't been a restful sleep, but at least it got him away from Simon. Michael pitied Simon and yet he feared him. While the horrific loss of a mother would surely be devastating to any child, particularly when the loss came at the hands of his father, this loss had created Simon. And while Simon hid behind the veil of the Church, he was surely even further from salvation than Michael. The enigma that Simon posed baffled Michael. He knew the Church was like any other government. Any religion with over one billion followers wielded enormous power and sought to protect that power no matter the cost or the means. Simon had become the means of the Church. In order to protect it, he would break any and all of the commandments; this man upheld his law by breaking it.

"Meet me at the hotel," Simon told him curtly, passing an envelope to Michael as he hailed a taxi from the virtually empty lot outside the airport terminal. "I need to pick up some supplies."

"Don't be late," Michael warned.

Simon hopped in the cab and took off without replying. Supplies, Michael thought. God knew what that meant. Certainly not a bunch of prayer books. He slung his bag over his shoulder and jogged across Lehrter Strasse. His body felt fatigued from the flight, from being cramped for six hours. It felt good to give it a stretch.

The traffic was light, so it wasn't hard to pick out the limo: about one hundred yards off, headed up the street in Michael's direction. He didn't pay it much mind. Instead, he continued down Wastin Hagen Platz. The limo—a black stretch Mercedes—continued to approach. Michael cut down Silberstrasse, a shop-filled street to his left. He was probably just overreacting. It was lack of sleep and too much stress. He was just being paranoid.

The limo turned down the road behind him. Coincidence. That was all. Michael attempted to ignore the car. Michael, slowing to a leisurely pace, looked in the shop windows. All were closed but their keepers could be seen milling about inside, readying for a busy day. As the limo pulled alongside, he saw its dark reflection in the plate-glass storefront of a butcher shop: the rear passenger window was coming down. He strained to see the outline of a face within. He quickened his pace.

So did the limo. This was no coincidence.

Michael took off.

The car screeched out in pursuit, its back end shuddering as it spewed gravel and black tire smoke. It was gaining fast, fishtailing around the turn. Michael's legs were pumping; the adrenaline surged through his muscles. He had no idea where he was headed, the street signs were all in German. The jet-black car was a blur as it cut the distance to him. The vehicle was intent on running him down, of this Michael was sure. The throbbing of the engine grew louder in his ears. Somewhere in the distance he thought he heard someone scream. He needed a plan and he needed it now. It was only seconds until his death. The black German auto was almost on him. And that's when the question hit him: If he died, what would become of Mary?

Michael cut right. He was in an alley, garbage-filled, medieval and dark. Too narrow for the limo. He heard the tires scream, grabbing the pavement. He didn't look back. Seconds later, the twisting sound of bending, crunching metal echoed through the narrow street. Michael hurled himself atop a garbage bin, two cats scattering as he did so. He vaulted to the adjacent fence. And as he flung himself over it, he stole a glance back down the alley. There was nothing there. Only daylight at the other end. The limo had vanished.

He landed in a patch of wildflowers on the edge of what appeared to be a large city park. There was a lake at its heart, a lush meadow off to the left, a playground in the distance. And there were people. Lots of people. The up-before-dawn crowd, out for their morning jog, strolling with their newborns, enjoying a walk with their loved ones. People in their daily routines. This was a place where Michael could blend. A place he could get lost in.

He finally stopped running at the pond's edge, slumped back against a huge weeping willow. It was an ideal surveillance point. Two means of egress at opposing ends led back out into the city, tall cast-iron gates anchored in white polished marble propped open, affixed to the twenty-foot wall that seemed to run the circumference of the park. Michael wondered whether the original architectural intention of foreboding concrete enclosures and enormous gates was to keep people in or keep people out. He couldn't shake the impression that if the gates were closed, the park would become a grotesque nature preserve, humans trapped within its confines for all the world to view.

Catching his breath, he replayed the last two minutes in his mind. Mercedes limo, German plates. It had picked him out at the airport. It had known his arrival time. It had waited for Simon to leave, had pursued Michael only when he was alone. When the window slid down he had glimpsed the passenger inside. An older man, he couldn't make out his features, they seemed to melt into dense shadows within the car. But Michael had no doubt. The man in the limo had been Finster.

⌘

It was one minute after ten and Anna Rechtschaffen was ready to close for the day, maybe the week. Ten minutes earlier, the tall, dark, handsome hero of her latest lust novel had walked in and Anna swore that if she wasn't seventy-seven years old she would have hurled her one-hundred-and-eighty-pound frame on him for a roll in the hay. She hadn't had a six-thousand-mark sale since the Pope visited in '86.

The man never said why, just that he would take the entire lot, all of them. The gold ones, the silver ones, antique and wood, even the cheap plastic ones she'd bought from the little Spanish man two years earlier that nobody wanted. Didn't matter if they were to be hung from the wall or from someone's neck. He bought every single one in the store. She never asked him why and he never offered an explanation. In fact, he hadn't said much, nothing worth remembering except for that last question. The one right after he paid in cash and thanked her. The man with no name had asked if Freudenshaft was one or two blocks down. When Anna asked him what he was looking for, he smiled and answered, "Stingline's." She'd pointed him in the right direction and helped him load the boxes into his car. As he drove off, she couldn't help but wonder what a man who had just purchased every holy cross in her store would want with a gun shop.

⌘

To everyone else they appeared to be two friends out for a jog in the park, mixed in with the other *volk*, approaching from the southern gate. But the two men stirred something in Michael's stomach and he had learned long ago to trust his instincts. Both men were six-foot-plus. Both wore sweat suits, ran with a sense of power, like professionals, with a military precision. They coasted along the jogging path toward Michael, never removing their eyes from him, maintaining an even pace, he was sure they could run around the world without running out of breath. They were a quarter of a mile off. It was half that distance to the gate ahead of him.

Michael broke into a full-out run, racing for the gates. Against his better judgment, he looked back. The two men had increased their pace to a sprint, their four legs moving in perfect rhythm. And the fuckers weren't even breathing hard.

Michael was only fifty feet from freedom when the black limo reappeared on the street. Its front grill was shattered but that didn't seem to affect its performance, its engine revving like a lion ready to spring.

Michael ran harder, through and out the gate. The limo window was coming down but this time he didn't bother looking inside. He raced along a large mall, vacant and bordered on either side by gleaming, glass-tower office buildings. He could taste bile in his dry mouth. His lungs seemed at the point of bursting.

The sweat-suit twins emerged from the gate seconds later, chasing him down, arms pumping and that was good, there weren't any guns out—yet. Michael imagined it was to be a silent hit: they'd get him in the limo, tarp on the floor, and kill him without witnesses.

The limo sped along the interior service road, her racing accomplices at her side. Michael swung out of the mall and tore into the two lanes of morning traffic. Cars squealed and screeched. He dashed down the sidewalk, his voice pounding in his head, *please, please, please,* over and over again like a mantra in sync with his pounding heart.

The sweat-suit twins were unfazed by the speeding traffic. They pounded along the roadway only ten yards back from Michael. They leaped and hurdled cars and barriers in their way as if such obstacles were mere bumps in a field.

Gasping and winded, Michael looked desperately for a way out, sanctuary. And found it. Drawing on his final reserve of energy, he veered left . . . he could even hear them breathing now; no, heaving like he was.

His pursuers were closing in on him. He braced his running body for their pounce, but the blow never came. With his last bit of waning strength, Michael vaulted the two-meter stone wall—the twins hurtling forward and grabbing for his feet—and missing by inches.

On the street, the limo instantly screeched to a halt. Motionless, it just sat there. The twins didn't bother with the fence, though they could each easily leap it in a single bound. Their faces remained cold and emotionless, their arms hung at their sides. Not a word was spoken as the two men impassively watched Michael race through the open doorway of the stone church.

Chapter 21

The morning sun poured through the open window, flooding the crisp white sheets and landing on Busch's closed eyelids. He was awake but always preferred to let his senses rise in the morning before he did. The smell of the fresh sea air, like a shot of tequila, always got his blood going. He had designed and remodeled the house to take full advantage of its waterside location. His bed faced the easterly window so when he finally did open his eyes he would immediately see the ocean that had captivated him since he was a child. His father was an Old World fisherman who had sailed the great south bay of the Long Island Sound, venturing out into the wide open ocean, trawling along the Atlantic shelf for seasonal fish. When Paul was old enough, he'd become a mate, a linesman, a plebe, whatever his dad wanted. In his youth, it wasn't so much the ocean that attracted him but his father. Hank Busch had been a big man. His hands were powerful, his skin like leather. He had a long mat of sandy blond hair and a full beard—Paul could never figure out where the hair ended and the beard began—which was always wind-whipped and tangled. Paul loved his dad, plain and simple, but he dreaded the weeks that would go by when his father would be at sea. Children of twelve shouldn't worry but Paul did. He knew the dangers of the sea, knew that she could never be tamed and never be appeased and that on occasion she would pull down a ship just to remind the seafaring world that they were always at her mercy. Each time his father did return, Paul would cling to him and refuse to let go, lost in the warmth and security of his embrace.

His father had taught him all the tricks and skills of commercial fishing, hoping one day to pass his boat, *The Byram Blonde,* to his son, who could then follow in the family footsteps. Paul never had the heart to tell him he didn't care for fishing; he knew that would break his old man's heart. And anyway, if spending time with his dad meant hanging with the stinky fish and drunken sailors, so be it. Puking over the side when his dad wasn't watching, that was fine. At least they were together.

Late April. Still a bite of winter chill in the air, it always seemed to linger at sea. It was a four-day trip. Five on board: Paul and his father; Sean Reardon, the twenty-year-old linesman, filled with piss and vinegar; Johnny G., a huge Jamaican even bigger than Paul's dad, his deep voice always sounding like song. In all the years Paul had known him, Paul never learned Johnny G's last name. And Rico Libertore, he fancied himself a little mafioso, all five feet five inches of him including the inch his black slicked-back hair added. Rico talked a good game but fought a better one. Nobody ever fucked with Rico without donating a pint of blood. They'd pulled out of Long Island Sound, swinging around Block Island, heading for the mid-Atlantic shelf. Going for cod. It was twelve-year-old Paul's first overnighter and it was also his rite of passage. When this trip was over, he would be a man.

They threw the lines and sat down for supper: beans and franks, easy to cook and easy to eat. They sat around downing Pabst Blue Ribbons except for Paul, who swigged Coca-Cola. The four men treated the boy as one of them, tossing risqué jokes around and swearing colorfully enough to embarrass a prison guard. Lights out at nine; they had to rise at four. The temperature had really dropped, a bone-chilling thirty-eight degrees. At sea, the cold cut right through your skin, seizing your bones, a chill that can't be shaken, no matter how many blankets. Paul couldn't get warm in his bunk. The snoring was unbelievable, out of control, all of them. When he hopped out of the bunk, none of the men stirred. They were all sleeping off at least a six-pack. Paul knew how to run the heater, just like back home: prime it, light it, close the door, and feel the heat. About a year earlier, his dad had told him not to touch it but that was when he was a kid. He was a man now. He figured it his job, everyone being asleep and all. He pumped the primer ten times, then stuck in the match. Nothing. He pumped it again. Lit another match, but as he did so a swift breeze shot through the cabin; the flame blew out before he got near the heater door. He pumped the primer twenty times. This was it, third time's a charm. He struck the match and cupped the flame in hand. This one wouldn't blow out. He stuck it inside.

And all hell broke loose. A fireball exploded outward, engulfing the heater. Flames shot up its exterior and raced along the floor. Paul screamed in panic, sounding like a girl, the way boys do before they are men. A terrible cry. The cabin filled with the orange glow. The heat was intense. Rico shot out of his bunk and raced across the galley, grabbing the extinguisher. The little Italian desperately tried to aim the nozzle at the heater but the extinguisher wouldn't work. The fire ran across the floor and up Rico's leg.

Paul fell back against the wall. The screams were everywhere; he looked about wildly, not realizing they were coming from his own throat. The flames surrounded him like a pack of animals, an ever-shrinking circle, ravenous to pounce. He caught a glimpse of Rico rolling on the floor, trying to extinguish his flaming leg. The flames danced up the walls. Paul was frozen in terror, nowhere to turn, nowhere to run, and he was screaming, just screaming.

Until, finally, he was lifted and hurled out the door into the night air. His father scooped up the flaming heater and ran out, flinging it into the sea. Paul saw it hit the water, still burning. He watched its deadly glow as it sank away, a murderous red haze sinking into the black depths. Through the cabin window he could see Johnny G stomping out the fire, slapping at the flames with a blanket. His father ran back in the cabin to help Rico. Paul had never seen a grown man cry until that night. The pain in Rico's eyes was unbearable, tears streaming down his face. Overwhelmed, Paul broke down, sobbing at what he had done, how his carelessness had hurt Rico. He cried because the fire had paralyzed him, had almost killed them all.

Johnny G came out on deck and wrapped him in a blanket, carrying him back in the galley, saying his name over and over again in his familiar deep voice. The flames were out but the charred, blackened floor and walls still smoldered. Sean threw buckets of seawater along the deck and picked up a broom, sweeping the debris away. The sick, pungent smell of wet, scorched wood filled the air. Paul watched in hopeless misery as his dad tended Rico. When the bandages were finally secured, Paul's father walked over to Paul and, without saying a word, took him in his arms. To this day, his most vivid memory was his father's hands as they held him that night. They were burned, red and black, the top layers of skin curled and rolled back on his fingers, raw blisters covered his palms. But Busch didn't seem to notice; he just sat there holding his son, rocking him in his arms till dawn.

The Byram Blonde pulled into the dock as the sun rose. Johnny G, Rico, and Sean waited on the boat while Paul was taken home by his dad. They never said a word to each other the entire ride. Paul sat in shock, staring out at the foggy morning, locked under his dad's protective arm till they arrived home.

His father carried him upstairs and tucked him into bed. As he was leaving the room, Paul whispered, "I'm so sorry, Dad." His tears fell on his pillow.

His father turned to him. "It was an accident." And the way that he said it, Paul knew he truly meant it. "I thought I was going to lose you last night. I couldn't live with myself if that happened. The sea's an unforgiving place. My father taught me, like his father before him, that every time you sail out you never know if you'll make it back to port, but every time you do, you must thank God for not only your safe return but for everything He has given you. And when you step onto that steady shore, you must remember that maybe tomorrow you won't be so lucky. But today, you cheated death one more time. So you appreciate life all the more."

His father leaned down, kissing his forehead. "We made it tonight, that's all that matters. I love you, son. Nothing could ever change that."

He headed back out to sea that morning.

It wasn't supposed to be a heavy storm but it came in hard nonetheless. A driving, pounding rain, huge waves, forty feet from trough to crest. Paul's father never returned; *The Byram Blonde* was declared lost at sea. There was a memorial service for Johnny G, Sean, Rico, and for Paul's dad but they never found the bodies.

Now, as he did every morning, Busch stood at the window of his bedroom watching the waves crash the shore. Till this day, he still combed the beach for pieces of the *Byram*.

Robbie and Chrissie charged into the room screaming; they hit the bed and launched themselves through the air into their father's waiting arms. "Daddy, why can't you stay?" his son demanded.

"As soon as I get back we'll spend a whole week together, no work, no phones, no visitors." Busch could count on one hand the number of days he had been away from his kids. He had long ago made a quiet vow to himself that he would never leave his children the way his father had left him; he would spend his time with them making memories. And now he was breaking that vow. The pain he saw in his daughter's eyes as he said good-bye was but a fraction of what he felt in his heart.

As he loaded up the car, Jeannie handed him his passport. "I thought we were going to fill these pages together," she said, fanning the little blue book.

"We'll have plenty of time for that." Paul avoided her eyes.

Jeannie grabbed his lapels. "Listen to me, Paul Busch: you find Michael and bring both your asses home lickety-split, you hear?"

They pulled each other into a hug.

"And hurry," Jeannie added. She was always scared when Busch left home. She was a cop's wife: every ring of the phone sent her heart into distress. She dreaded the day when she'd answer the door and be greeted by two of his fellow policemen, their hats off, their heads bent.

"I love you, too," Busch told her.

⌘

"I really think we should stop for lunch." Jeannie clutched an armful of shopping bags.

"I'm fine, that frappuccino will hold me awhile," Mary replied. "Please, let me carry something."

"You just enjoy the walk."

For the past hour, the two women had wandered the Westchester, another massive concentration of high-end stores with the dreary nom de plume of mall, America's executioner of the local mom-and-pop store. Dr. Rhineheart had recommended the shopping expedition as a terrific way to break the soul-deadening routine of Mary's treatment. It was mid-morning; the halls were filled with a smattering of stroller-pushing mothers and the over-sixty-five crowd. The two friends traveled the floors and escalators talking and laughing like a couple of schoolgirls. And though it had only been an hour, Mary looked as if she had just run a marathon. Her body was weak and frail. The combination of chemo and radiation had not only attacked the cancer but the rest of her body as well. "Attack" wasn't the right word. "Kill" was spot-on. Killing her cancer, her life, her spirit. Her hair hadn't fallen out yet, but where a month earlier there had been a glorious red mane befitting a lion, it was now flat and muted, thinning out to nothingness. Jeannie's original plan had been to carry Mary off for a day of beauty, but she'd decided against it. She couldn't escape the image of the hairdresser washing her best friend's glorious hair away. Mary's situation was humiliating enough, she didn't need it compounded.

"Let me carry that for you," Jeannie said, trying to take the package Mary carried.

"Hey!" Mary pulled the package back. "I'm not a cripple."

"I didn't mean—"

Mary smiled. "I know. I'm sorry. It's just that so many people treat you different when you're sick. They make you feel like some kind of freak. You'd think I sprouted long ears and a tail or something. The outside may have changed a bit, but the inside is still here." She tapped her chest.

"I know it is." Jeannie put her arm around Mary's shoulders.

"It's a terrible way to find out who your true friends are. Did you know that Paul comes by the hospital every morning with fresh flowers and food?" Mary paused, reflecting. "He hasn't missed a day. Hang on to that man, Jeannie: you've got a keeper there."

"That's debatable." Jeannie let out a laugh. "The man doesn't know what tough is. Dealing with criminals all day is nothing compared to raising two kids."

Quietly Mary said: "I'm going to be fine, you know."

"I know." And while Jeannie took comfort in Mary's conviction, she had trouble with the lie, desperately trying to hide the tears that stung her eyes.

"I'm so worried about Michael, though," Mary continued. The more she thought about Michael's abrupt departure the more frightened she became. She knew how he cared for her and that he would never abandon her unless . . . unless it was something worse than what she was facing. And she was facing death. "I don't know where he is or when he's coming back. He's in trouble, Jeannie."

Jeannie took her hand and spoke from her heart. "Paul's gone to get him. Don't be angry, Mary."

In all the years the two women had known each other, there had been an unspoken bond between them. Like sisters, they were irrevocably connected and upon Jeannie's marriage, Paul had become Mary's surrogate brother. Like Jeannie, he had always been there for her. The fact that their husbands—one a cop and one a thief—had become best friends had warmed her heart. "How could I be angry?" she asked Jeannie.

"Everything will be fine. Please don't worry. Paul will take care of it."

Mary's thoughts kept running to her wedding vows. She had repeated them to herself again and again back when Michael was on trial: *through good times and bad, through good times and bad.* They had become her theme song. She figured she and Michael were getting the bad times out of the way first. And they had survived the bad times. Of course, now it was *through sickness and in health,* something that usually comes much later in life. But not for them. All of their vows were being tested far too early.

"I've had these dreams," Mary told Jeannie. "Horrible dreams. I'm terrified, Jeannie. I keep thinking that he's not coming back."

"If Paul said he's bringing Michael back, he's bringing him back. Of course, they may stop off and play a little golf on the way, but they'll be back."

Mary smiled but inside she remained frightened. Michael was in trouble, she was certain of it, and all she kept thinking was . . .

Till death do us part.

Chapter 22

The street outside the little stone church was relatively empty, relatively silent. This twist of fate wasn't lost on Michael as he stood looking out through one of its stained glass windows. Alone in this silent place which smelled of incense and wax, he couldn't help but remember a time when it all meant something to him. When he could recite the Mass like it was something out of his high school football playbook, mouthing the prayers spoken by Father Damico, the stooped old priest with the penchant for gnocchi and sambuca. Entering his parish church had once provided Michael with a sense of relief, of comfort, of somewhere he could always come to pray, to ask for help or a favor, or just to talk. There he had spoken to God. And He listened. As a child, Michael could swear He had even talked back. It had been his own little private miracle.

But as Michael had gotten older, he found that God didn't listen much anymore. In fact, from what he had seen, He didn't listen at all. As his world opened up and he saw it for what it really was, he had felt betrayed: he had never experienced a miracle. What he thought was God's voice had just been his own subconscious, talking back to him, producing the answers that he already knew deep down.

Everything he was taught as a child, everything he believed in growing up, was a lie, like those titans in Greek mythology or the Norse tales of Thor and Odin. God was just another fairy tale that the fearful clung to in times of need, giving them a phony anchor to hold on to, providing slick answers to the unexplainable. All the pomp and circumstance, all of the holier-than-thou attitudes of the priests: they had become the very essence of the hypocrisy to him, they were just the manifestation of the lie, perpetuating a cruel myth like all other myths in an uncaring world. Everyone was so sure that their God was true, that they were the righteous ones, that they and their followers were the only ones on the planet who would find peace and comfort in the afterlife.

But then he had met Mary and he'd indulged her beliefs, never daring to tell her his true feelings. He was in love and, well, the things we do for love. He would sit through weekly Masses not in prayer but in thought, his own little ritual, time to think about Mary and life, children and work. He went through the motions he had learned so well as a child, all the while keeping his opinions to himself. But when he had learned of her diagnosis, he could pretend no longer. He was right. God didn't exist.

Yet, here he sat. In church. Running from something, from someone, he couldn't explain. He reached up and fingered Mary's gold cross. He felt nothing spiritual in it, but he did feel *her*. The little gold trinket was Mary's and she had asked him to wear it, had begged him never to take it off. And he wouldn't: not because he believed in what the cross stood for, but for what the necklace meant. It was Mary's. And maybe it would protect him, not because of any divine meaning, but because it would remind him why he was sitting here in Germany, hiding here in this church: for love. Here, not because what he believed, but for what Mary believed.

Noon. A few of the daily faithful had come in throughout the morning, lighting candles, kneeling in silent thought and prayer. Michael worked his way behind the altar and found the red neon exit sign eerily out of place in the two-hundred-year-old sanctuary. He slowly eased the door open. No one around. He headed down the stairs.

There was a vendor on the corner selling pretzels and soda; it had been ten hours since his last bag of airplane peanuts. He was hungry, thirsty, and tired. Sleep could wait but his stomach couldn't. A little one-block detour wouldn't be of any consequence.

He never even made it across the street. A dozen police cars screeched to a halt in front of him, disgorging trigger-happy policemen—*Polizei*—of all shapes and sizes. They encircled him screaming in German, waving their nine-millimeter custom-SIG-Sauers. Michael didn't need a translation. It was pretty clear in his mind what they wanted. He raised his hands in surrender.

⌘

Hotel Friedenberg overlooked Tiergarten Platz. Sixty years old, she'd fallen into utter disrepair in 1961. When the Berlin Wall went up, she went down. The Omega Group had purchased her in '90, spent close to ten million in refurbishments. Not real fancy but nice: spacious rooms, big swimming pool, health club, and room service. The minibars were stocked with liquor, nuts, and those little five-dollar Cokes that you end up cracking open at three in the morning, and which you completely regret when you get the bill.

The business-class suite was broken into separate sleeping and working areas. Two king-sized beds were set toward the back of the room, while near the door was a small conference table, desk, and seating area. The room was tastefully decorated for a hotel room, but you wouldn't remember the muted maroon, brown, and yellow leaf pattern four minutes after you checked out.

"Michael?" Simon called out as he heaved five large duffel bags on the bed; the double-tip would never compensate the bellboy for his ruined back.

Simon opened the blinds, stealing a moment to soak up the sun as it poured in on his face. He checked the phone: no blinking light, no messages. He grabbed his briefcase off the bed, sat at the table, and pulled out the hand-drawn plans of Finster's house that Michael had labored on during their flight. Simon could barely focus. He was beyond exhausted, it had been at least twenty-four hours since he'd slept. He had so much work ahead of him; if he couldn't stay sharp he would fail. It would be his first failure but in what he did, you failed only once. And a failure now would not only reap consequences for himself.

He debated. Study the plans? Unpack? Sleep? He would do it all but not necessarily in that order.

After buying all the crosses in the tiny religious shop, Simon had found Stingline's right where the nice shopkeeper had said it would be. He had frequented the place several years back when in need of "certain" equipment. Today, he was in need again. Stingline's was a gun shop but it was also a Gun Shop. The kind that you went to when the other gun shops wouldn't or couldn't sell you something. The display cases were filled with hunting rifles, bows and arrows, and, for the military wannabes, fatigues. The real stuff, however, was kept out of sight. Herr Stingline was ex-Red Army, Baader-Meinhof, or IRA, depending on who you spoke to. Word was he was fifty-two. Simon knew for a fact that he was sixty-eight; he always put together a thorough dossier before dealing with unknowns. And whether Stingline was fifty-two, sixty-eight, or eighty-five, the man could still kick the lungs out of you before you even had a chance to breathe. The German was soft-spoken and oddly hairless. The fever took his hair when he was eight and the taunting he'd received had been enough to make him tough as a junkyard dog by the age of nine. He had operated since '86, which meant that he had to have some kind of quid pro quo with the former East German government and their enforcers, the Stasi. The Stasi were the secret police, the East German form of the KGB, poking their noses in everyone's lives. Privacy was not a factor in the former Republic; it simply didn't exist . . . anywhere. Meaning that Stingline's op was known and probably even supplied by the government. But as long as Simon had known him, since just after the fall of the Wall, the old man was never a snitch.

He didn't ask how, but Stingline had pulled together Simon's shopping list in less than fifteen minutes: four hands-free radios, four nine-millimeter Glocks with custom silencers; fifty boxes of ammo; two Heckler and Koch PDWs that fired eighteen rounds per second; two Israeli Galil sniper rifles; four head-mounted nightscopes, four bowie knives, six stung grenades, and a box of Power Bars. Simon always bought in fours and twos and he always paid in euros—the least traceable currency at the moment. He'd left Stingline's with everything he wanted and without a question asked or answered.

The knock at the door pulled him back to the moment. "Yeah?" He quickly headed for the bags on the bed.

"Room service."

Simon pulled out one of the Glocks and a box of ammo, no time to check the weapon; he just loaded a couple of rounds and prayed. He hugged the wall, working his way carefully to the door. He didn't bother with the peephole: no sense in turning his eye into a bull's-eye. He swung open the door to slowly reveal . . .

A busboy with a cart of food. The kid couldn't have been more than nineteen, the cover-up Clearasil barely hiding his acne. "It is our custom to present each new guest vith a complimentary food and beverage cart," the kid said in a thick accent. He fidgeted with the silver cart, his sweaty palms leaving fingerprints.

Simon stared at him while slipping his gun into his back waistband. He motioned him inside, leaving the door open. "Sorry. I'm a little tired. This really isn't necessary."

"Sample vines and cheeses for your pleasure, sir." The busboy rolled the cart into the room, uncovering a selection of soft and hard cheeses, some smoked sausage, fruit, and two bottles of red wine, which on closer inspection Simon found to be of decent vintage. Maybe a glass wouldn't be a bad idea after unpacking; it might at least help him sleep.

"May I open the vine for you?" The boy smiled, pleased that his English was being understood.

"That's OK, I've got some work to do first, I can manage." Simon slipped the kid a couple euros and led him toward the open door.

And that's when it happened. The door slammed shut. The shutters smashed closed. The blinds came crashing down. The room was instantly drenched in blackness. As Simon looked around, he cursed his eyes, trying to force them to adjust to the absence of light. He crouched low and rolled away from the last spot he'd seen the busboy. Unsure if anyone else had entered, he held his breath, reaching out with his mind, trying to feel. How many were there? He strained his hearing; there was no further movement. Slowly his pupils grew, shadowed images started to appear, the conference table, the couch . . . Across the room, near the desk, a crack of light squeezed through the shutters. Obscured in shadow, the busboy stood gaping at him as if the room was lit with two-hundred-watt bulbs. The kid knew exactly where Simon was, but made no move.

Seconds, long as hours, ticked by. Neither said a word. Simon could now make out more than shapes, he could see enough to move freely, enough to see the young boy's face. And suddenly as if the shadows and light were playing tricks, it was the face of Finster.

Reflex took over. Simon fired both rounds, emptying the gun, hitting Finster square in the left eye.

Simon stepped up and back from his crouch. Finster was bleeding, of this Simon was sure. Blood and gore poured down his face like buckets of scarlet tears. Yet the German didn't fall. He didn't move at all.

And in a casual motion Finster reached up . . . and reached into his eye. His forefinger and thumb plucked first one then the second bullet from his mutilated socket. Where once an eye stared out at Simon, there was now nothing more than torn flesh and splintered bone, a crevice awash with blood. An opaque fluid separated itself from the redness, the pupil within still reacting to the light. The bullet should have passed clear through his brain but he was still standing.

Simon watched as the wounded man placed the two nine-millimeter slugs on the conference table and pushed them toward Simon.

"Please," Finster said, politely. "Keep them."

A sound softly rumbled. It was a sickly, moist sound, a flesh-on-flesh rubbing and tearing sound from somewhere deep inside Finster. It was his eye—it was re-forming and Finster acted as if this were a nonevent, like hair growing back on a shaved head, a severed limb rejuvenating on a newt.

And suddenly it was whole. His two eyes again fixed on Simon, never blinking, never moving, always terrifying.

"How are those secrets, Simon?"

The emptied gun flew out of Simon's hand, ripped away by some unseen force. The power was everywhere, filling the room, Simon could feel it, growing, overwhelming him like an electrical charge at maximum voltage. He looked around desperately for his duffel bag, the big blue one, the one filled with the crosses. He should have unpacked first. . . .

"That's right. You should have unpacked first," Finster said, as if reading his mind, "instead of nodding off, losing focus."

"You will not have my—"

"Soul?" Finster cut in with a laugh. "But I already do, Simon. You forfeited your soul long ago. Those hunched-over, Bible-thumping men in white collars couldn't come close to offering someone like *you* absolution." He raised a finger, as if sharing something precious. "Little hint here, Simon, my friend, kind of a trade secret: you must be *sorry* for your sins to receive *forgiveness*. . . .

"But I digress, that is not why I'm here. Your soul is not the prize I seek. My realm is nearly filled with the pitiful souls of this world. I'm returning to whence I came. I am going home."

With that, Simon charged Finster, slamming into him, unleashing blow after blow to his body, to his face. Finster turned his head away and when he turned back, he was an old man, his clothes in shreds, his wrists bleeding from some kind of constraints. Grotesque white scars covered his face, some barely healed. Abruptly, Simon stopped his barrage of fists. He recoiled from the old man in fear. He gasped as if struck by a mighty fist.

"I begged your forgiveness, Simon. I knew not what I had become, my mind was gone when I had attacked your mother. She forgave me, why can't you? Why can't a son forgive a father?"

Simon drew back his fists and rained down blow after blow on the old man. "You raped my mother; you stole the life out of her. You left me alone." He continued the assault as the old man began to collapse. "You are nothing more than a bad dream, just a terrible nightmare."

And suddenly, without warning, the old man under his battering fists vanished. Where he once stood, there was a dark-haired lady in a sheer black dress, her alabaster skin shining through, the scars plain as day upon her. She recoiled away from Simon, stumbling backward, falling helplessly beneath his blows.

"Son, please . . ." she pleaded.

An icy shiver ran through Simon as he realized he had struck his mother, thrown her crippled form brutally to the floor.

"Your heart is cold, Simon. Join us, unite us as a family again." She picked up Simon's gun, holding it out. "I am just an instant away, my son. Join me." In her left palm lay a gleaming single bullet.

Simon crumpled to his knees, staring at his mother, the pistol in her hand. He could feel his mind slipping. His mother, who had taught him to be strong, was telling him it was time to stop, to give up, to follow in her footsteps and take his own life. He was a mess. But then he looked up, looked her right in the eye, and as he did so, he swiped the gun out of her pale hand. His tear-filled eyes overflowed with hatred. "Everything you say is a lie. You will be stopped."

And the figure before him started to flicker, the image alternated between his tortured mother and his monstrous father, like a picture struggling to take focus. But the eyes never changed: they remained lifeless, cold—evil.

"You couldn't stop me before. What makes you think you could stop me now?" came the hissing words from the lips of his father.

And with that, Simon slammed back against the wall. The old man was gone and Finster stood once more in his place. Simon dangled eighteen inches above the floor, his face twisted with pain. Deep below his skin, eruptions started to form like tiny bubbles in a pot of water hovering just below boiling. His flesh started to heave, to twist about. And the small bubbles grew, rising just below the skin, contorting his face. Simon screamed in his head but refused to give Finster the satisfaction of crying out aloud.

Finster picked up the gun, examined it, then walked over to Simon. "Do you think it will be hard to find your mother's soul?" He fingered the rising bubbles under Simon's flesh, seemingly fascinated with his handiwork. He peered closely at the gun, examining it, feeling its weight, the deadly power of it. "I love toys." He raised the Glock, pointing it at Simon . . . but then thought better of it. Walking close, he leaned into Simon's ear, whispered in a soft, fatherly tone: "I *will* return to Heaven from which I was banished. Why merely conquer the world, when I can rule eternity?"

⌘

Simon bolted upright from the desk, heart pounding, sweat beading his brow. The shades were open, night had fallen. He looked about. His bags were still on the bed, unopened. His face was unblemished.

"Michael?" he called out. Glancing at his watch: half past eight. He couldn't remember falling asleep. His neck ached from his facedown position over the floor plans. He stood; his body protested from his awkward sleep and the long plane ride. He yanked open the minibar. Only about six of those two-ounce bottles of whiskey, not enough to trash a rat. He grabbed the phone.

"Room service," the voice answered. "How can we help you?"

"I need a bottle of whiskey: Jack Daniel's. And some ice."

"Right away, sir," the master of efficiency replied. "Was the cheese platter to your liking, sir?"

Simon caught a glimpse of the room service cart. Not a scrap of food was touched, the wine was unopened. "Yeah, it was fine."

He hung up, still staring at the cart. He ran his hands about his face, nary a bump or blemish. Yeah, the dreams were getting worse. But then he turned his head and his heart leaped. He tore open his duffel bag and pulled out the boxes of ammo: all sealed. It had been nothing but a bad dream, a frightening nightmare. But then how did he explain the items on the table? There, on the table's edge, lay two crumpled nine-millimeter slugs.

Chapter 23

Before the fall of the Berlin Wall, there existed a building where many went in and few came out. Dunkel Gefangnis was a six-story stone structure out of the Dark Ages. Its enormous iron-plate doors—all three metric tons—swung on twelve-foot hinges. These had well-earned their acquired name: the gates of perpetual torment. The building was surrounded by a two-story-high iron fence, capped in rusted concertina wire. And while the structure was terrifying in appearance, it was her lower level, all seven substories, that contained the true horrors.

During the height of their reign, the Stasi—the vampiric East German security force—were known by all, but their dealings behind this building's great stone facade, which they ruled with an unrelenting bony fist, were only rumored. So, when tales of torture, of maimings, and of slow death circulated, people shuddered in fear, as they were meant to. Dunkel Gefangnis became a useful control on the public, a symbol to terrify them into submission. And it was better for them that they never learned the truth, for the truth of what happened within its walls was far worse then the rumored horrors.

Dunkel Gefangnis was converted in 1996 to the Berlin United Police Headquarters and Jail System. And while trees were planted, lights added, and the imposing iron fence removed, she was still Dunkel Gefangnis, the sinister jail, her hallways perpetually haunted by death.

The prison levels were belowground and it was evident that the refurbishment money was meant only for those levels where the sun shined. The stench of urine permeated the cold moist air of sublevel five, block six. Michael tried to protect his senses from the onslaught, but to no avail. He lay on the granite slab in the gray jumpsuit provided when they'd taken his clothes. The cell was eight-by-eight, three solid granite walls and an iron-bar front; more like an animal cage than a jail cell. A chill pierced the place and the only source of heat he'd found was intense exercise that left him exhausted. He had lost all sense of time since his arrival and they had yet to ask him a single question. The neighboring cells were empty but somewhere off the main hall he could make out the murmur of foreign tongues. Sing Sing, his prior prison home, had been a palace compared to this.

Michael debated asking to call the American Embassy, but in the end he realized the embassy would check stateside and all too soon find him to be a fugitive. Besides, who was to say the local police hadn't contacted them already or, for that matter, that he'd been picked up at the request of the U.S.? No, he wouldn't call. And anyway, they hadn't even offered a phone.

The outer cell-block door crashed open. Down the hallway came the same harsh-looking guard who had silently strip-searched him and thrown him his jumpsuit. But this time, the guard wasn't alone. Michael heard two sets of footfalls. And when the surly guard came into view, Michael's senses were confirmed; behind him stood a man who remained back in the shadows.

"Got a visitor."

Michael rose, straining to make out the second figure. The guard left as the stranger stepped into the faint light.

"Hello, Michael."

Michael stared.

"How did you end up in here?" Finster was visibly shivering as he looked around. "It's so cold. I could have sworn it was summertime."

Michael was looking at him with new eyes, suspicious eyes.

"I tried to bail you out, but they say you're to be extradited."

"Why are you here?" Michael demanded.

"You are my friend—"

"To kill me?" Michael cut in.

Finster looked at him through the bars, confused, finally breaking out in laughter. "Where did you get— It's that pious prick, Simon! Is he filling your head with nonsense? He's a lunatic, been making up stories for years about my being some kind of demon. Do I look like a demon?" The merriment bubbled in his voice. "It's the money, Michael." Finster leaned closer. "*And the women,*" he confided. "People love to associate riches and sex with evil. Why, it's the most ridiculous thing, don't you agree? You'd think we lived in the Dark Ages, the way some people fear it. If I had a nickel for every person that called me wicked . . . As for your new friend Simon, he's a fanatic. He's been spouting that drivel for years now. Why so quiet, Michael? Are you not glad to see me?"

"Why are you here?" Michael repeated.

"I've heard that you came back for the keys. You weren't going to take my keys . . . were you, Michael?" Finster's voice was that of a parent admonishing a child.

Michael hesitated. Maybe he was wrong, maybe Simon was a fanatic. Maybe he'd been too quick to believe him. . . .

"I knew you wouldn't double-cross me, Michael." Finster rubbed his hands together for warmth, then cast down his eyes in sorrow. "I heard about your wife . . ."

Michael bristled.

". . . taking a turn for the worse."

Anxiety clenched Michael's gut like a sickness.

"I'm sorry, Michael," Finster continued. "I know how much you want to be with her in her last moments. I'll see what I can do to speed this process up to get you home. You know—pull some strings."

"I want nothing from you."

"Excuse me? I'm truly sorry about your wife." Finster never sounded more sincere. "And Michael . . . I am sorry for you, too. There is nothing worse than losing a loved one."

"You *damned* my wife. Why didn't you tell me?"

"Tell you what?"

"Who you were." Michael stared a challenge.

Finster eyed Michael, studying him, taking his time before replying. "Have you found God?" he asked, softly.

"I'm not afraid of you." Michael stepped up to the cell door.

Finster's face came within inches of the bars, within inches of Michael's face. Michael stood his ground. The two looked at each other, as if for the first time.

"Who do you think I am, Michael?"

Michael did not answer.

"Be afraid for your wife, Michael. Push this, and she'll die alone, calling your name, and you'll rot away the remaining years of your life right here." Finster gestured about the dank place. "All because of a stupid decision. I can help you, but if you so much as come near my keys—"

"*Your* keys?"

"I paid you in good faith, *we* had a deal."

"Deal, my ass! You never revealed all the terms!"

"You're telling me, you—the man who has no faith—that you believe some wop of a religious freak rather than me? Simon tells you I'm *the Devil,* and you instantly become a true believer. Hallelujah. Has he delivered anything on his word? Did *he* pay for your wife's treatment? Did *he* come up with a quarter of a million dollars? I gave you a bonus: he didn't even say a *prayer* for her!

"Did he tell you that little sob story about his ma and pa? How daddy desecrated mommy in the name of the Devil? Bullshit, all bullshit. He's got you made for a stooge. He wants you to steal the keys for him, then he's gonna sell them on the black market. Save *Heaven,* my ass. Who do you trust, Michael? Someone who's helped you? Or someone who tried to kill you?"

Michael stared at Finster, confusion ripping his mind. Could he be so wrong? Despite everything Simon had said, the truth surely lay with the words of the man standing before him. Could he really have become the pawn of Simon, chasing after stupid religious trinkets while his wife lay alone and dying? Finster had been nothing but help: money, kind words, offers of assistance. Simon had offered nothing.

Who could he believe? Simon? Finster? His own suspicions? He wasn't in this place for Simon, he wasn't here for himself—he was here for Mary. And for what Mary believed. Faith: the ability to believe in the intangible. Putting everything aside to acknowledge the possibility of something greater. He could believe in Mary, she had always believed in him. He trusted her. Mary was his faith. "Fuck you," Michael said, his face inches from the German's.

Finster's eyes took on a feral quality. Michael couldn't help but flinch as the older man reached through the thick bars; his long manicured fingernails trailed lightly against Michael's cheek. "*If* I was who you think I am, do you think I would take this insolence from someone so insignificant as you? No. Think about it. If I were who you think I am, I would hurt you where you are most vulnerable. Her soul would be lost to me. I would make her my bride for all eternity. Ah, the fun I would have, fucking your Mary senseless. Is she a *limber* girl, Michael?"

Finster leaned in as close as the bars permitted and hissed, "If—I was that whom you feared most."

Michael stood there, ashen, silent, defeated.

⌘

The stench assaulted his senses again, rousing Michael from his sleep. He had no sense of time; there were no clocks here, no windows. The cell block was dead quiet, not even a stirring rodent could be heard. The two naked bulbs provided barely enough light to see. His thoughts and dreams had run to Mary. How long since he'd last seen her? He couldn't remember. He had to get out of here; he had to speak to Mary, to hold her in his arms. He had to finish what he came here for.

The crashing gate startled him, its metallic clang echoing and re-echoing off the chill stone. Another cell door screeched, then slammed shut. Ten quick strides reverberated and then Ivan Crusick, the Interpol officer who had processed Michael, stood on the other side of the bars. Crusick pulled out his jumble of keys, finally locating the right one and unlocked the cell. "Your extradition papers have been completed," he said, his English thickly accented.

"You're too kind," Michael sneered.

Crusick did not reply.

Michael followed Crusick down a long dank hall to the first of several large gates. He had no idea what papers Ivan was referring to but as long as they got him out of here, that was fine; he wouldn't miss this place. As they walked, he noticed not a single cell was occupied. Surely the night before, he could have sworn he heard several other prisoners. At no time had he heard the loud clang of the gates releasing them; it was a sound you couldn't miss. He didn't want to know the others' fate. He wished them peace, whatever their crime. This was no place for anything human. Up the stairs they went, Ivan's flashlight leading the way. The passage was narrow, reflecting the building's ancient heritage. There was no light in here, the stone was obviously too thick to run wiring. It was a long climb, far more flights than Michael expected. It was two minutes before he began to see light flooding down from above. He and the silent guard finally emerged into a modern facility abuzz with activity. As old as the lower level was, this was clearly modern: computers, cameras, electronic gates, all attended by a twenty-first-century police force.

Michael was escorted to a holding desk. There he was given his clothes and the few personal possessions he arrived with. He signed for everything, and they allowed him a private changing room. Then, with Ivan at his side, he walked through several more gates, arriving at the last one between him and freedom.

"Please turn and face the wall."

Michael was used to the routine as he was frisked. Not that he could have picked up a weapon in the last thirty seconds, it was just a routine precaution.

"Face me," the guard commanded. Michael turned. "Hands in front." The handcuffs slammed shut about his wrists, the metal biting cold against his flesh. Ivan opened the last remaining gate and mutely directed Michael out the door into a long narrow vestibule, then slammed the gate shut behind him. He said nothing as he left Michael, heading back once more into the bowels of the station.

If Michael was confused before, he was baffled now. Here he

stood, handcuffed, outside a police station in the very heart of Berlin. Protocol dictated that he would be escorted to the airport and back to the U.S. But then again protocol dictated that he be told what was going on. There were only two doors to the vestibule: the iron gates behind and the main door ahead. If Hell was behind him . . . Michael figured he'd go for a walk, at least to the door—and that's when it opened. Standing in the doorway was Busch.

⌘

A heavy rain fell. Umbrellaless, Busch escorted a handcuffed Michael through the enormous, rain-swept police parking lot. Both men were instantly soaked to the bone. Visibility was down to a few feet—not that either man was looking around at the scenery; they weren't even looking at each other. Not a word had been spoken.

"Why'd you run?" Busch finally asked.

Michael said nothing. Instead, he looked at his cuffs. He was just as trapped as he had been in prison.

"I was going to help you." Exhaustion crept into Busch's voice. The only available flight to Berlin was an indirect which had taken him through London; his trip had been over twelve hours long.

"Spare me, will you, Kojak? Mr. Law's-the-law."

The silence continued. Busch was conflicted already, he was putting everything—his job, his integrity, his life—on the line for this man and he had the nerve to lash out at him? "How could you put Mary through this?"

"Don't go there."

"Oh, I'm going there, whether you like it or not. She's back home fighting just to stay alive and you're screwing around over here. Wake up, pal—her life is slipping right through your fingers."

"Fuck you." Michael turned without warning and snarled, "*Fuck you.* You have no idea what I'm dealing with." He slammed Busch against a car, hitting him hard with his cuffed fists. Busch took it, his size absorbing the impact. The blows kept coming until finally, friend or no friend, the parole officer had had enough. He hit Michael once, square in the jaw, knocking him backward into a '99 Beetle.

Michael slumped back on the VW, the rain pouring down his face. "I had no choice. Can't you understand that? No choice. *I love her.*"

And then, drenched to the bone and handcuffed, he ran.

Busch stood there, watching him vanish into the darkness and pouring rain.

And that was when the shots came.

A whole clip-full, fast and furious. Ricocheting off the wet tarmac, off the cars.

Busch tore after Michael, caught a glimpse of him, two rows of cars away, head down, moving fast. The gunshots continued. The shooter was off to the left. Surging forward, Busch yanked Michael down, covering his body with his own.

And the shots stopped.

Nothing could be heard but the storm. Busch dragged Michael between two cars, then peered out in the direction of the assailant, out across the flooded lot, seeing nothing through the sheets of rain. No one. Not a thing. At the first shot, Busch had automatically gone for his gun but he was unarmed, no way he could carry aboard the plane. "Michael—what the fuck is going on—?"

"Cut me loose," Michael insisted, indicating his cuffs. "Cut me loose! I'm a sitting duck with these."

Busch was desperately trying to assess their situation. If the shooter was a professional, he'd move positions, judge his prey, finish the kill. "You'll run again," he said.

"I'll die if you don't." Michael looked at him with impassioned, desperate eyes. "Please . . . for Mary."

Busch grabbed Michael and hunkering down, they raced aisle to aisle, using the cars for cover. "I see you managed to piss someone off as usual," Busch said, still on the move.

Michael glimpsed a shadow move, ten yards off. He hit the pavement near a BMW, Busch right behind him. The whole thing smelled like a setup. They couldn't kill him in prison, there'd be too many questions. Why not set him free, loose him in the killing fields, in close range of the hunter? He was cuffed and utterly defenseless. Busch was probably just a patsy, unaware of his purpose in the matter.

"We've got to make it back to the station," Busch told him. His words were almost drowned out by the rain.

The shots resumed, this time from the right. Busch and Michael darted left, bent low, racing through the puddles, the occasional bolt of lightning illuminating their way. Suddenly, the shots shifted. They now came from the left.

There were two shooters.

They were trapped, being herded like sheep to the slaughter. Busch tried to open the door of the gray Citroën they were crouched behind. No use—locked—they couldn't even break the window; the alarm would alert their pursuers to their location, only hastening their death.

The shots stopped again. Michael didn't know which was worse: the rainy silence or the rattle of the guns. As the bullets whizzed by his head, his body ran on instinct, survival his only thought. But the silence . . . The silence created an anticipation that tore at his very soul. It was worse than any slow death. The fear of what might happen was paralyzing. The assassins knew this and were using it for the crippling psychological pressure it wrought. And the pressure was working.

Busch and Michael looked at each other; the desperation of their situation was clear. Busch hadn't come here to die and he wasn't about to let Michael die, either. On the threshold of death, Busch's perspective changed. The need to survive had cleared his mind, refocused it. He knew now that Michael was right. Restrained, he didn't have a chance.

Busch pulled out the key to the handcuffs . . .

As the cuffs fell to the tarmac, the shots resumed, closer now, tightening the noose. Michael stabbed a finger toward a narrow passage between some cars and they took off in unison. The ricochets skipped behind their heels, shattering car windows, exploding tires. *This must be what war is like,* Busch thought. They dove for cover by an abandoned ticket booth. The rapid-fire shots halted abruptly. Five seconds of silence . . .

. . . and then one single shot rang out.

It suddenly occurred to Busch that the rain was a blessing. These shooters were professionals. Both he and Michael should be long dead by now. Not only did the downpour shield them, obstructing the assassins' sight, it affected the trajectory of their bullets in unpredictable ways.

"We've got to keep our distance from both of them. If we can do that, we just might be able to get out of here," Michael said grimly.

"Nein."

Busch turned. Less than five feet away, a .44 Magnum pointed right at them. The man's dark blue sweat suit was soaked through. His long blond hair was matted against his skull; his lips were pursed in a frustrated grimace. Busch got the impression the killer lacked the muscles to smile. He took aim at Michael but before he could shoot, Busch slid in front of Michael, a human shield.

"My bullet will tear through both your hearts," the assassin promised. He called out, "Anders?!"

Behind him there was a shuffling sound—the other assassin was approaching. They were trapped. "My brother will be disappointed. He bet me five euros that he would get the kill."

He steadied his aim and . . .

A gun barrel came to rest against his temple, a choke hold around his neck. He gurgled for air.

"*Nein,*" a voice whispered.

"My brother will take you down before you can pull the trigger," the first blond threatened.

"*Nein.* Your brother won't be taking *anyone* down." Simon twisted the German around, forcing him to look. On the ground lay Anders, a bullet through his forehead. "Now, drop the gun."

He didn't and, without hesitation, without emotion, Simon shot the man through the temple, then eased his body to the wet ground. The blood ran, washing away in the rivulets on the pavement. Simon looked up and though his heart and soul belonged to God, his eyes were those of a mercenary: cold, lethal . . . deadly. "Let's go," he told Michael and Busch.

"What about the bodies?" the big cop demanded.

Simon walked into the gray, rainy night.

"What about the bodies?!" Busch demanded.

But Simon was already out of sight, engulfed by the swirling rain and fog.

⌘

One thing about Berlin, even after the reunification, it still had its alleys. Deep and dark. The occasional rat scampered for food but other than that no living thing willingly entered. Which is why an alley was a good place to hide the rental car. Simon couldn't afford to draw the attention of a curious policeman. In hindsight, he realized that that shouldn't have been a great worry: not a single man in blue was evident even in the police parking lot. So, assassinating two assassins didn't create the stir one would expect. He had lain in wait outside the prison for thirteen hours after learning of Michael's arrest. To break him out was impossible: his intention was simply to kill whoever finally picked Michael up for extradition, and then to continue after Finster.

The rain had stopped, leaving puddles the size of lakes everywhere. Simon sat behind the steering wheel of the idling car, as Michael and Busch stood in the middle of the alley and argued. While the rain had washed away the accumulated grime, it had had no effect on the putrid smell: it seemed to permeate even the brick walls of their surroundings.

After Simon had killed the two assassins, they had sped off from the police station in Simon's rental car without further incident. The silence was unbroken during the drive, each man stewing, biting his respective tongue from lashing out in anger at the others. It finally all spilled out when Michael and Busch stepped from the car and right into a puddle.

"What are you going to do?" Michael asked Busch.

"What should I do?"

Simon, his arms draped over the steering wheel, said quietly, "You should leave."

Busch whirled around. "I didn't ask you," he snarled, then looked back to Michael. He was waiting for an answer to his question.

"I put you through enough already," Michael said.

"I didn't come all the way over here for my amusement."

"What I told you before, about this man Finster—"

"—is true," Simon finished, drumming his fingers impatiently on the wheel.

"Did you fill his head with this frigging nonsense?" Busch's anger made his voice tremble.

"It isn't nonsense." Simon slid out of the car.

"What are you, some kind of Bible-banging fanatic or something?"

"In so many words—"

Busch never let him finish. "Well, in so many words—no, in four words: *Shut. The. Fuck. Up.*"

"I'm a priest."

Busch was silenced. He was a devout man, so strong in his beliefs that another man's commitment to faith shouldn't be a surprise, but Simon's words stunned him nonetheless. Not only had he spoken viciously to him, but Busch had just witnessed this priest shoot a man dead, a bullet through the side of the head, with an efficiency befitting a machine. The sweat-suited assassin had no chance, not that he would have given them one. This priest didn't kid around.

Busch turned to Michael. "I didn't come here to drag you back against your will."

"No? You're the one who had me arrested."

"No way. I never told anybody you left the country—either time. You left me slack-jawed at the airline security gate, by the way. What the fuck was up with that? You lied right to my face." The big man's eyes were on fire again. He took a deep breath, trying to regain composure. "I didn't have you arrested; my new ex-partner fucked me over. You remember the preppy prick who clubbed you back at your apartment?"

Michael nodded.

"His name's Thal and he was running his Internal Affairs cattle prod up my ass for God knows what reason, and now he thinks I let you go. He wants to bring you in so they can hang me high. That boy's in the know, I'll give him that. He knew where you were going even before you left. He contacted Interpol with your exact location an hour before you were picked up."

"Then why the cuffs, *buddy*?" Michael sneered, still angry.

"Well—*buddy*—if you're picking someone up on an international warrant, handcuffs are the rule. You were to be picked up by Thal and flown back to the U.S. sometime later tonight. If you'd like I can take you back. And listen"—Busch leaned in—"the cuffs were for your benefit. I needed you to listen, needed you to hear me out."

"There is nothing you can do to help us," Simon impatiently interjected. "Michael, we are out of time here."

Busch shifted his gaze to the priest. "I see you and I are going to get along just great, Father." Simon glared at Busch, but Busch was unfazed; he ignored him and turned back to Michael. "I don't believe this bullshit, Michael, but . . ." He pulled out a file and threw it on the hood of the car. "That's everything about this man Finster." He turned to Simon. "And he's just a *man*." He turned back to Michael. "His businesses, habits, pleasures, his taste in women. His profile comes up a bit short, but I'd be willing to bet it's far more than you have already."

As if his anger was suddenly washed away, the cop broke out into a huge smile. He was here, so he might as well make the best of it. He slapped his hands together, rubbing them vigorously. "You guys got a plan?"

"Working on it," Michael said.

"*Working* on it?" Busch's grin vanished. "Some team. What were you going to do, go in, flash a cross and say, 'Hand over those keys'?"

The storm returned, the hard rain washing away the last remnants of fog. Simon was placing multiple crosses around the hotel room, praying as he went. Candles with a Latin inscription carved into them were burning in one corner, casting a luminous glow that gave the impression of some holy force field encircling them. The hotel room's spartan decor had been vanquished by an extreme Gothic feel, one that Busch would have found laughable if the other two men weren't so damn serious.

"May I ask what you're doing?" Busch said, stretching out on one of the beds, beer in hand. He'd decided his drinking moratorium was over for the time being, in light of the insanity going on around him.

"Protecting us," Simon responded, in a hushed tone.

"From?"

"You never see darkness where there is light. Evil avoids that which is holy."

"Not where I come from. Who you trying to keep out—Dracula?" Busch rolled his eyes.

Simon didn't bother looking up from his work. "Let's just say it's much worse than that."

"You really believe those candles will keep 'em out? Protect us from the boogeyman?"

Simon nodded.

Busch sighed. "Yeah, and it keeps us in. Trapped." He rose from the bed, stalking around the room, examining the crosses; he had never seen such a wide variety. "And what if you're wrong? What if this rich Finster guy isn't who you say he is? What if he is really just a tough billionaire industrialist with some warped obsession for keys and some big-ass bodyguards?"

"Then it won't be so difficult," Simon replied. "But, just in case . . ." He walked over to his bag, pulled out a Heckler & Koch submachine gun.

"OK." Busch looked over at Michael for some help, but he just sat there in his chair, silent and still. "What kind of priest are you?" he asked Simon.

Simon returned to placing crosses. "Some priests care for the sick, others hear confessions, celebrate Mass, spread the Word. They perform duties where their strengths are best utilized, where the Church requests their services. Me? My talents lay on a different path. I *protect* God. If I had killed him"—Simon gestured toward Michael—"back in Israel when I had the chance—"

"Killed him?" Busch was outraged. "You tried to kill Michael?"

"You're a lawman. You uphold the law of your town, your society. Well, I'm a lawman, too; the law I live by is the law of God. I'll uphold His law and if an execution is necessary, then . . ." He shrugged. "Am I so different from you?"

"Don't compare us," Busch spat through gritted teeth.

"You were going to arrest Michael just for leaving the country, send him to prison for trying to save his wife. He is your friend and yet you would do that to him?" Simon turned his back on Busch and continued placing crosses. "You obviously value your law more than your friendship." Setting the last cross down, he picked up his bourbon. "I value my law more than life. If I took his earthly life, he still had eternal life, we all had eternal life. But now . . . Well, I didn't take that from him. Finster did."

In a strange way Busch understood Simon, he knew exactly what the lunatic was saying. Busch didn't agree with the priest's methodology yet somehow he understood it. But that didn't change things. "Don't you mean *Satan* did?" Busch asked with half a laugh, shrugging off Simon.

Simon hated to be mocked. "You're here to help? Then you better believe what I am telling you. August Finster is *darkness*."

"Really?" The condescension in Busch's voice couldn't have been thicker. "You run around preaching your bullshit story, treating my friend like some kind of pawn. Whose bidding is Michael doing now, Padre? Huh? You're playing his emotions, taking advantage of his situation with his wife. Exactly like Finster did." Busch's accusing finger came dangerously close to Simon's nose. "At least Finster *paid* him."

"Paul?" Michael sat up in his chair. He had seen Busch explode too many times and while he appreciated his defense, he couldn't afford things getting ugly again. They needed to work together, to remain focused on the task at hand.

"He's playing you for a fool, can't you see it?" Busch demanded.

"I know what I'm doing," Michael answered.

"Do you? Mary needs you, she needs you *bad*. I know you're not thinking straight right now but I am. I got to get you home before you get killed."

"Paul, I believe what I'm doing is right. I'm asking you as my friend: Trust me."

It was killing Busch; he knew that he was here for all the wrong reasons. He and Michael had almost been killed, they were holed up in this room with no plan, and somewhere out there was someone or something who wanted them dead. But he saw the overwhelming conviction in Michael's eye. "All right . . . But I still don't believe all this Devil, Hell, eternal damnation crap—"

"Do you believe in Heaven?" Simon interrupted softly.

"That's not the point."

"Do you believe in Heaven?" Simon roared.

"Yes!" Busch shot back, furious.

"Then why is it so hard to believe in Hell? They are just opposite sides of the same coin." Simon paused, calming himself. "You joke about that which you don't comprehend. Hell is real and it is eternal." Simon had his finger in Busch's face now. "Hell is not some picture on a wall, some actor in a movie. I wish he *was* just a cloven-footed beast with horns." The priest's intensity grew, his conviction growing with every word. "Man has envisioned Satan and created Hell with his own thoughts: Dante's Inferno, the nine circles of Hell, fire and brimstone—they're all just bullshit. That is all man's imagination. As we can not comprehend the beauty and salvation of Heaven, we cannot hope to comprehend the torment and agony of Hell. It is dark, unrelenting, and viciously evil. Hell," Simon laughed, "it's undeserving of any name. You have no concept of pure evil but you will. . . . Before we are through, you will know better than any man who walks this earth what true evil is."

Chapter 24

At about the same time Busch and Simon were arguing, Dennis Thal was showing up at the Berlin United Police Headquarters. When he presented the papers for the release of Michael, confusion seemed to run through each successive officer he spoke with. The fact that each pretended to need a translator annoyed the shit out of him, particularly since the answer was always the same. St. Pierre was gone, picked up, signed for, no longer their problem. Each time, Thal politely nodded his head, then asked to speak to the next in the chain of command. When the chief gave the final word, Thal concealed his rage and left. The description of the man who'd picked up Michael was vague, but one detail made the man's identity obvious: Michael's escort was *ein riesig grosse bär*: an enormous big bear.

The rain stopped as he walked across the parking lot. The stakes had just been raised. Paul Busch was clearly one step ahead. Thal's quarry of one had doubled and the more he thought about it, the more excited he got. His job was Michael and his pleasure would be Busch. Individually, their downfalls would have been supreme. But to get them both together . . . that would be an indulgence of the senses.

His thoughts were interrupted when he saw the two corpses; the white stripes on their jogging suits had turned red with blood. One still clutched a nine-millimeter automatic. Thal looked about; no one seemed to be around. He leaned down, checking the bodies. Rigor mortis had yet to set in. He cursed himself: Busch had gotten the jump on him. These two guys were obviously a European-side backup. The fact that it was presumed he, Thal, needed a backup, that the chance existed he could fail, pissed him off. He made a mental note to address the issue once he achieved success. He examined the bodies closer, checking the bullets' entrance and exit points. The wounds were professional: each had been shot cleanly in the head. Someone was protecting Michael. Well, good, that just ratcheted things another notch.

Thal's initial assignment wasn't to kill Michael St. Pierre. It was only to watch him, keep an eye on him, know his every move. Once it was learned that Michael was on parole, Thal simply started an internal investigation on the ex-con's parole officer. It was absurdly easy to put himself next to the man who was closest to Michael.

For five years, Thal had hidden behind the mask of Internal Affairs. The undercover division provided him mobility and the freedom to slip away on a moment's notice under the pretense of a confidential investigation. He was fair to mediocre in his performance and that was just how he wanted it. Mediocrity was always ignored in this world. People found nothing of interest in the average. Only the outstanding, the successful, the popular, or the dismal failure drew attention. And so he lost himself deliberately in the middle. He couldn't afford any attention or he would risk his passion:

Killing.

Dennis Thal was outstandingly good at it and was outstandingly paid for it. He didn't find much humor in the world, but the fact that he was paid so generously for his one true love always struck him as funny. He was requested by his handler to find a suitable job that would make him inconspicuous. Internal Affairs was just that. An undercover cop among the undercover cops. It allowed him to monitor the progress on any investigation that might lead to him and provided him with the unique ability to manipulate the investigations when necessary. He actually liked Internal Affairs. Sniffing in others' dirty laundry; he had the power to ruin lives. What could be better? But the job he relished most was moonlighting for the faceless individuals who employed him. The pay for that was outrageous, the pleasure was stunning. He had found his vocation in life and he excelled at it.

He'd slipped into the Byram Hills Police force under the pretense of an Internal Affairs investigation of their parole system—namely, Paul Busch. Captain Delia was so flustered at the situation and scared for his own skin that he gave up everything on his number one cop in a heartbeat—Busch's history, records, everything. And most importantly, one file in particular, a file on Thal's actual mark: Michael St. Pierre.

Thal was to keep an eye on Michael; the assignment didn't involve killing, just watching, but Thal being Thal, his urges ran in other directions. He despised Busch, his cozy little life, his perfect morals and codes. From the moment Busch dissed him, not wanting to work together, Thal had looked for an opening, a way to tear Busch and his perfect life down. After all, Thal policed the police. He was absolutely empowered to remove any cop from the system who was deemed corrupt. How fitting that Busch's downfall would come out of his foolish, honest gesture of helping his best friend break parole! And Thal would be right there to call him on it. First, he would destroy Busch's career. Then he would destroy his life.

Now, as Thal stood outside the Berlin police station, he knew he should have followed his instincts; he should have killed Busch when he had the chance. Now things were out of control. Busch had Michael and they had slipped away. Thal knew that he couldn't fail. If he did, he would end up unemployed, replaced, and, most disagreeably, dead.

Michael had slipped out of the U.S. before Thal could stop him. And so Thal had received a new directive. His heart nearly skipped a beat. He could throw restraint to the wind. He hated babysitting, watching, keeping an eye out. He was like a shark, in need of constant motion, always on the hunt, an unsatiated bloodlust; when restrained, motionless in his environment, he would smother and drown.

Thal was no longer to watch Michael: he was to kill him. And not only Michael. Busch, he decided, would die also. And if either of them gave him a hard time, maybe he would go back afterward and pay a visit to their families. That sweet Mary wouldn't have to worry about the cancer anymore. . . .

⌘

The footsteps echoed off the damp stone walls. The match flame cut through the blackness, the fat cigar glowing as its smoke billowed upward into the cavern where it danced around stalactites fifty feet overhead. The single flame grew into many as he lit the succession of candles, one hundred candles, lining the walls. Finster dipped his fresh Cuban in his brandy as he contemplated his bizarre collection of religious artwork. He walked slowly past each masterpiece with a reverence befitting a king. Each piece had been meticulously researched, located, acquired, catalogued, and restored. Pride was his favorite deadly sin. Pride was just self-esteem emboldened by one's accomplishments, and he so liked his accomplishments.

There were three thousand two hundred and eighty-one works of art stacked one against the other here, with his favorites out front. Many purchased outright from galleries and auction houses. For the occasional piece that he found in private hands, collections, or homes, a piece he found that he could not do without, Finster employed other means of procurement. There were thirteen of this type, and of this thirteen, nine had been secured from houses of worship.

Finster found particular fascination with the lesser gods and demons of those early religions which have since become looked upon as mythology by today's "modern" faiths. Hades and Persephone, the gods of the Greek netherworld; Anubis, the Egyptian god of the dead; Proserpine, Roman goddess of the underworld; and Loki and Sigyn, the trickster Norse gods. And what most intrigued him was the fact that these "dark gods" were believed to be part of a balancing force in their particular realms. They were not gods to be vanquished and cast away. While feared, they were also respected—and even admired—looked upon as necessary in daily life. The fact the "modern faiths" had done everything in their power to denigrate their sole lord of darkness baffled and infuriated him.

Shrines and temples had been built to the Hindu god Shiva, one of the darkest of the feminine gods, and they were still worshipped at today. Appeasements made, offerings given. The goddess was spoken of with reverence and many sought help from her. Her followers were not looked down upon. When something tragic was performed by a man, it was not blamed on Shiva possessing his soul, it was ascribed to the individual who had performed the act of his own free will. Finster loved the masterpiece before him, removed under cover of darkness from a temple outside of Jaipur. Shiva's six arms outstretched to her screaming minions, who were engulfed in flames below.

Vlad the Impaler, a magnificent oil painting by Rukaj, stolen from Ceausescu. The Romanian prince of Wallachia struck a deep chord in Finster. Vlad Dracul was never a god. He was just a man in whom the coldest form of evil ran. A military genius who struck fear into not only the hearts of his enemies but those of his countrymen. A count, hailing from the northern mountain regions, Dracul had a hunger for power and an unquenchable thirst for blood. A victorious general who savored the ritual of impaling his victims by the thousands on pikes, their blood running in virtual rivers as a warning. And with men like him in the world—ordinary men with a propensity for violence and evil springing from their own self satisfaction—there was no need to introduce wickedness into the world. Man's evil ways were man's evil ways.

Man had always found evil more fascinating than good. The young girl was always attracted to the rebel, the guy with the leather jacket and motorcycle who defied the law. What allure was there to the nerd, the computer geek goody-goody? And it followed throughout life: actors always wanted to portray the bad guy, the villain was always the more intriguing character in literature. Ask anyone to name ten interesting good guys and ten interesting bad guys. He'll have those ten marauders in twenty seconds flat but after five heroes he'd be hard-pressed.

And with all this confusion, Finster had grown tired. People had become so predictable. Wave a little money in front of their faces, flash a little sex before their eyes, and their will bent like a sapling in a breeze. Finster was merely the tempter, never the hand that wielded the gun.

He continued his stroll down his off-color-Louvre, finally arriving at the door to the key chamber, with the painting of the Gates of Heaven propped beside it. Charles came down the stairs carrying a long black bag and a large knife.

Finster's eyes never left the painting as he spoke to the butler. "And he looked and he saw that it was good," he murmured.

Charles stood in the corner by the hanging body. He laid the black body bag on the floor, unzipping it to prepare it for its latest arrival. The odor of death flowed off the corpse: decay had already set in. With much effort, Charles lowered the body to the ground. He pushed Elle's red hair away from her once beautiful face, and removed the noose from her swollen and bruised neck.

Finster continued to stare at the painting of the Gates of Heaven, deep in thought. And a slight smile began to form on his lips.

"I'm going home," he said.

Chapter 25

Crosses covered the windows, the doors, the walls, thou- sands of crosses, everywhere. Barely an inch of space had escaped the priest's handiwork. It reminded Busch of the serial rapist he had caught eight years back; pictures, culled from magazines, torn from newspapers, had covered every inch of the psychopath's bedroom. All of prepubescent girls. And the sicko, scarcely nineteen years old, had just sat there as Busch arrested him, confused at what he had done wrong, protesting "but Zeus told me to do it."

Busch and Simon sat in the middle of the floor, a bottle of Cutty Sark on the carpet between them. There couldn't have been more than an inch of whiskey left in the brand-new bottle. The two men had finally found something in common: both were within a shot of passing out.

"So, Father, what do you do when you're not out fighting the Devil, killing people, that holy thing you do?" Busch's slurred question was barely understandable.

"I . . . play chess." Simon's voice was clear but he was obviously in no better shape.

"Chess is good. Little too cerebral for me."

After much thought and furrowing of the brow, Simon blurted out: "Football."

"Ah . . . Now we're getting somewhere." Busch perked up.

"Not *American* football. Soccer."

The cop's elation ebbed. "We"—he pointed to Michael, who seemed lost in a game of solitaire on the bed—"play football. Good old *American* football."

"You any good?"

"Yeah, we're any good," Busch shot back.

"Got to be strong for that."

"Yeah, strong." Busch's pride was swelling.

"Quick?"

"Quicker the better."

"Smart?"

"Sharp as a tack." He had second thoughts. "Well, the quarterback's got to be smart."

"You the quarterback?"

Busch laughed. "No. Just quick and strong."

Simon lay on his stomach, extended his arm, offering his hand in challenge. "How strong?" he demanded.

Busch grinned, stretched his arms several times, loosening them up, then sprawled out on the floor in front of Simon. "All right, padre. You confident?"

"Confident." Simon flexed his hand for a good grip.

"Then let's make it interesting. Say one hundred U.S. dollars."

"One hundred bucks," the priest drunkenly agreed.

They pulled out their money, throwing it on the carpet.

Michael kept glancing over at the two drunks, lost in their macho posturing. He got up from the bed and walked over to the food cart. There he picked up two long-stemmed wineglasses and, clearing his throat for effect, turned to the two rug rats. "Bullshit, guys. Want to see who's stronger? Let's make it really *mean* something." And with that, he raised the glasses and brought them down on the edge of the metal food cart, shattering the goblets so only the stems remained. The very jagged, knifelike glass stems.

Michael walked over and placed the broken glasses in the fall line of each of their arms. The loser would be impaled on the dagger-like crystal, the glass piercing the back of his hand, running it through. He smiled. "That's a little more motivation than one hundred bucks."

Simon and Busch exchanged glances.

"Go on," Michael taunted. "You're both so confident. If you don't have faith in yourselves . . ."

Neither man moved.

"This is too good." Michael shuffled his cards several times, flourishing them like a true magician. "I've got to get in on this." He had learned only two card tricks in his youth and remembered only one; fortunately, it was this one. Like Mandrake, he expertly fanned the cards and held them out. "Pick one."

Simon and Busch looked at one another and finally reached out. Each drew a card, not sure where this was going. The alcohol was clearly getting the better of both as they sat there, card in hand, stupefied.

"You have to look at it . . ." Michael admonished them.

Busch could hardly focus but he was certain he was holding the king of clubs. Simon glanced at his jack of spades, swiftly drawing it to his chest, hiding it from the world.

"Now put it back." Michael held out the deck and each man slid his card back in. He shuffled several times, bridging the cards, rolling them along his hand for effect, then placed them on the floor. "If you would be so kind," he said to Busch, "cut the deck."

Busch did as he was told.

Michael turned to Simon. "Give me the top two cards."

Simon complied, handing the two facedown cards to Michael, who took them and placed them under the bottom of the two broken glasses.

"I've put the winner's card under the loser's glass." Michael threw down a hundred-dollar bill. "Count me in."

Simon and Busch looked to the jagged glasses upon the cards, questioning themselves and the insane choice before them.

"What, you scared, holy man?" Busch mocked Simon drunkenly.

"Not of you. *Peaches.*"

Busch's dander was up. They gripped their right hands, each going for the best hold possible. They braced their left arms against the floor for leverage and . . .

"Call it!" they yelled in unison.

Michael grabbed their clasped hands in his, assuring they were even and, more importantly, that they were lined up with the deadly spikes. Then in a voice scarcely above a whisper, he ordered: "Go."

Both were strong, muscles bulging, eyes determined. Their entwined arms seemed to hang there for eternity, trembling like a revving car engine. Almost imperceptibly, Busch began to win, only by a fraction, but the braced arms were definitely canting in his favor. His brow wrinkled in concentration as his whole body quivered, but then . . . ever so slightly, Simon gained the advantage. Busch had never, absolutely never ever, lost to anyone in an arm wrestle. And yet this drunken priest was beginning to get the advantage.

One minute gone.

Their eyes locked, an intensity building like Michael had never seen: sweat beaded their brows. Their breathing came in fits and heaves. Two men unaccustomed to losing, each fiercely determined not to fail. And while it started as an alcoholic challenge, the whiskey evaporated in the heat being generated by the two combatants who now appeared to be as sober as the day was long.

And then, slowly, it started to go Busch's way again. Imperceptibly at first, but as the seconds ticked by, Simon's hand continued inch by inch down toward the jagged glass. Busch would rather die than lose. The priest's hand was halfway to being mangled and even with this bloody inevitability, Busch gritted his teeth and pushed on. Their eyes still locked upon each other, neither glanced at the glass shards.

Suddenly, Simon's descent stopped. The tendons in his neck were distended. His hand hung motionless in the chilled air inches above the glass. Their eyes dared each other toward defeat.

Two minutes ticked by. Their stamina was beginning to wane.

Somewhere deeper Busch descended, finding that extra bit, again inching Simon's hand toward defeat. He continued pushing Simon, bit by bit, fraction by fraction.

Simon's hand was almost upon the jagged stem; he could feel its knife-like edge flicking the hairs at the back of his hand. And yet there was no fear in him—only steadfast determination. The pain of the wound would pale next to the unfamiliar agony of defeat.

Michael had been sure that neither would go through with the ordeal and yet here he stood, eyes transfixed on what would surely be a gruesome conclusion.

It was Busch who broke eye contact, if only for an instant. His eye was irresistibly drawn for a fleeting moment to the lethal crystal edge before he hastily looked back to his opponent.

Simon didn't flinch, his glare didn't waver. The glass now pressed against his skin, the slightest motion would begin the slice. His hand was almost impaled when . . .

Busch pulled out of the match. Simon's hand snapped up like a spring released from its ruthless clasp. Not a word was spoken. Busch stared at the carpet, rubbing his arm. Simon's eyes alternated between the glass and his hand.

"Well." Michael leaned down, scooping up the pile of money. "That was easy." He stuffed the cash in his pocket.

Busch and Simon looked up at Michael, uncomprehending. Busch was the first to realize what had just happened; he grabbed his card from under the broken glass and flipped it over. Five of spades. Simon grabbed and flipped over his . . . Eight of hearts. Neither card was the one they'd pulled. They looked up at Michael a bit confused, a lot pissed.

"What are you—nuts?" Busch demanded.

"I knew your humanity would outweigh your egos," Michael said crisply.

"Wait a minute. Wait a goddamn minute. You don't win shit, my friend. You may think you're smart but you blew the bet, you didn't get either of our cards right." He held out his hand. "Cough it up."

Michael ignored the cop's outstretched hand. "Give me your knife," Michael said to the priest.

Simon paused only a moment, then he pulled his right pant leg up. He unsheathed the bowie knife strapped to his calf and passed it to Michael.

Michael handed the deck of cards to Busch. "Throw 'em in the air."

Busch glared at Michael. If the liquor hadn't fogged his mind, he would have smacked him by now.

"Go on. Throw them high," Michael pressed.

Exhaling in exasperation, Busch tossed the cards in the air, creating a flurry of red and black. They floated there for an eternity until . . . With blinding speed, Michael threw the knife through the center of the falling mist of fifty . . .

Fwack. Nailing two cards to the wall. The jack of spades and the king of clubs. The impaled cards that Bush and Simon had drawn hung there plain as day, the knife still shivering from impact. The room was silent until Busch finally cracked a huge smile and started to laugh. "That's why *he's* the quarterback," he told Simon.

"Son of a bitch," Simon murmured. And for the first time in a long time, a grin lit up his thin dark face.

Michael sat back down and kicked his feet up, a broad Cheshire-cat smile on his face. You could see it in his eyes; it was like he had cracked the code to Fort Knox. While Simon and Busch were locked in their inebriated combat, trying to break each other's arm, Michael had finally come up with the answer he was looking for, that they were all looking for.

He knew how to get the keys.

⌘

Two a.m. The rain still falling. The hotel lobby was deserted. Torre Ericson had come down to Berlin from Sweden to work during his summer vacation. Torre had never traveled Europe but vowed to before next year when he hit twenty-one. Berlin had seemed as good a place as any to base from, and besides, the Hotel Friedenberg was the only place that offered him a job with two consecutive days off. Of course, it took a bit of adjustment to get used to the dead shift but Torre didn't really mind. Dead was the operative word around here anyway, except maybe for the occasional caller seeking a late-night hooker, snack, or both. Nothing ever happened at the Hotel Friedenberg between midnight and six.

So he was a bit surprised when the man stumbled in, soaked to the bone. The stranger coughed uncontrollably as he spun around, trying to get his bearings. This guy was in need of some coffee and a cell to sleep it off in in a bad way, Torre decided. He wasn't worried, his six-foot frame was solid as granite from rock climbing and rugby. He had tossed many a drunk and this wouldn't be his last. However, courtesy was the order of the day. "May I help you?" he offered in perfect German.

The drunk stumbled toward the desk, seemingly oblivious to the question.

Torre switched to English. "Some rain out there, huh?"

Once again, the drunk didn't answer. He staggered to the desk, draping his wet body over the counter, soaking the courtesy newspapers and guest register. "John S-Smith," he slurred.

"I'm sorry, all guests are sleeping now," Torre said with more than a hint of annoyance.

"Smith's expecting me."

Yeah, right, Torre thought. He knew a line of bullshit when he heard one. "Perhaps you would like to leave a message; we could have Mr. Smith call you in the morning."

Torre didn't see it coming; he was more worried about the man throwing up all over his counter. Before he could blink, the drunk whipped out a gun, pressing the barrel an inch above Torre's stunned eyes.

"I'd like to see the register, please," the drunk demanded, in a clear ringing voice.

There was no doubt in the young Swede's mind that this man before him would rob him of his life in an instant if he didn't immediately comply. But being twenty and cocky and still not having tasted his mortality, there were alternatives. Torre was quick, too.

The drunk who was not a drunk didn't flinch as Torre's hand blurred out of nowhere, ripping the gun away.

"Pull a gun on me, motherfucker?" The young concierge's adrenaline pumped up his success. "You're lucky I don't shoot you where you stand." He pointed the pilfered gun straight at the man's heart.

"Pretty quick," the stranger said, drawing an embarrassed smile of pride from Torre.

"When you fuck with best—"

But Torre never finished the sentence. His body stumbled backward to the floor while a good portion of his head exploded, smearing the wall behind him. He never even saw the man draw the second gun, never saw him pull the trigger.

Dennis Thal leapt over the concierge desk, ran his finger down the register's sign-in, and stopped at *Jude Iscariot.*

How obvious, he thought.

⌘

Two fifteen a.m., Michael and Busch were passed out on the couch and floor, respectively. The alcohol they'd polished off left them incapable of traveling the three feet to the bed. Simon was a different story: he had spent too many nights sitting up in wait for the inevitable problem and this night would be no different. The priest paced the room restlessly, having spent the last hour checking and rechecking his guns, all loaded, all ready. Michael had explained his plan, a solid one that could be adopted and executed if the three of them all worked together. Simon had worked out the logistics, mentally reviewing and modifying them several times over so as to play out every situation, every possibility. There would be no room for error and . . . no second chance.

⌘

Thal stepped off the elevator. The hallway was empty. On each hotel room door hung a do-not-disturb sign along with a breakfast order. Several empty food carts littered the hall awaiting busboy pickup.

Room 1283. Down the hall and to the left. Thal checked and rechecked both guns. That boy hadn't even realized the safety was on. How foolish. If he hadn't tried to be Superman, he would still be alive, albeit a little sore from being rendered unconscious. Everyone has to be a hero.

Holstering his Glock, Thal walked with the Magnum dangling from his left hand. Three in the room: St. Pierre, Busch, and some priest. He hadn't confirmed it, but the information came straight from his handler. Beware the priest, he was told. Thal found that amusing.

Room 1283. He stood before the entrance, turning inward, gaining focus. His breathing grew shallow, his shoulders relaxed. He raised his leg to kick in the door.

⌘

Simon lay silently on the bed, the effects of the alcohol still slightly with him. He needed to rest, but rest would have to come with his eyes open. Only two candles remained burning, their glow casting flickering stripes across the shadows. After this, he was done. He couldn't lie to himself anymore, he was past burnout. Having built a wall around himself all these years, he had never looked for friendship; he couldn't afford friends. For a brief moment earlier this evening, he had seen that one day things could be different. He could find a life where he wouldn't always be alone; he could find companions and maybe even a woman to share his life with instead of living the cloistered, celibate existence of a priest. All these years of pain, of avenging his mother—maybe that pain was finally dissipating. Maybe he could even redeem himself.

He shot up from the bed. Something startled him. He looked to the sleeping men—no movement. He spun out of the bed, grabbed his pistol from the night table, and covered the door. His blood raced, pounding in his ears. The silence was deafening. Had it been his imagination? Paranoia was creeping in and that would lead to failure, he knew he must never question himself and his judgment. He was a solo operator and yet here he was with two accomplices, two passed-out, inebriated accomplices.

He heard it again—subtle, someone was moving about. His body tensed. He raised the gun, aiming it head-high at the door he'd hung with crosses hours—it seemed a lifetime—ago. Those holy objects weren't helping in the least.

⌘

Thal had both guns drawn now. It would only take three shots, of that he was confident. He didn't expect much of a commotion; his guns were silencer-equipped, the halls were deserted. In less than a minute, he would be on his way. He would catch the six a.m. flight and be back in the States by nightfall. His employer agreed if he rid the world of the three on the other side of this door, he could retire with a fee that couldn't be spent in ten lifetimes.

And with a blurring motion he drove his foot into and through the doorknob. The door exploded inward. Thal rolled, guns at the ready.

Chapter 26

Two days now. Not a word from Michael. Despite Jeannie's assurances, Mary was scared. Deep down she knew that he was in dire trouble. If he were able to call, he would.

And she was dying. Quicker now. The tumors were spreading like wildfire. The pain came in fits and starts—as much as she hated to admit it, she was growing dependent on the morphine.

She had checked herself out of the hospital this morning, against everyone's wishes and every doctor's order. She wanted to be home among her things. She wanted to be home waiting for Michael when he returned. She'd picked up Hawk and CJ from Mrs. McGinty. The old lady brought Mary a pot of soup and a green salad and never once did she allude to Mary's illness. She was a woman who had witnessed the pains of dying: she walked this road with experience.

As Mary stepped into the den she saw the papers covering Michael's desk: newspaper articles on a German businessman, photos, magazines . . . Michael's desk was a mess, so incongruous with his anal nature. He'd obviously left in a hurry. She had suspected he'd gone back on his word. Years ago, when she was confronted with the reality of Michael's clandestine life, she'd felt betrayed and angry. And while she eventually found forgiveness, it was a long way back to trust. Now, seeing these papers before her, her suspicions increased that Michael may have broken his promise. Still, she knew he loved her and would never betray her. She was certain whatever he was doing, his intentions were honorable.

"Hello?" Jeannie called from the hallway.

"Be right there." Mary scooped up Michael's papers, shoving them into the bottom desk drawer. As she turned to leave the room, she saw something sitting on the desk chair. Not knowing what it was, she picked it up. Her heart stopped when she saw the imprint on the security bracelet. *Property of the Byram Hills Police Dept.* Michael was in far more trouble than she had ever imagined.

"Brought you some food," Jeannie said as she approached.

Mary didn't know what to do; she couldn't let Jeannie know about Michael, not yet at least. It crossed her mind that maybe she did know and that was why Paul had gone after Michael. She shook off the thought and stuffed the security anklet in her pocket.

⌘

The kitchen was one of Mary's favorite places. It wasn't large but it was big enough for her. She loved its oak cabinets and its polished aluminum appliances. She loved to cook, viewed it as an art form: like painting or sculpting, it was something perfected with time and talent and patience. It possessed a bit of the sciences, chemistry in particular—a little too much of this or not enough of that could create a disaster. There was nothing she enjoyed more than having dinner ready for Michael when he arrived home from work. It may have been old-fashioned and out of sync with the whole women's movement, but she didn't care; it was what she took pleasure in.

"My God," Jeannie gasped. "Where'd all the food come from?"

Mary had been cooking all afternoon, finding it one of the more relaxing things she had done in a month. So the fridge was near bursting. "I told you I cooked up a storm."

"Who's going to eat all this?" Jeannie asked.

Mary started to answer, *Michael,* but the name died on her lips.

Jeannie instinctly regretted her question. She took Mary's arm. "Paul called."

"Did he find Michael?"

"Yeah, I spoke to him early this afternoon; they're at a hotel in Berlin."

"Berlin? What did he say?"

"Not much. Paul was in a rush, said they were fine, back in a couple days, that's about it."

"Do you have the number?"

"He wouldn't tell me," Jeannie said with a sly smile.

"And?" Mary knew Jeannie well enough to know she had something up her sleeve.

"Well, let's just say he's not the only detective in the house."

"You're so sneaky." Mary grinned. "Can we call them?"

"It's the middle of the night there."

Mary looked at her, a bit disappointed, but relieved, too. "We'll call first thing," she decided. "At least we know they're safe."

Jeannie wasn't so sure. Paul had said that everything was fine but that he and Michael had to take care of one quick thing and that didn't sit well with her. Her husband had no business over there except bringing Michael back. There was nothing to take care of unless . . .

Mary set the dining room table for dinner and served up a garlic rib roast with new potatoes and the huge green salad that Mrs. McGinty had brought. Conversation was infrequent as the two women ate, mostly centered around the exploits of the Busch children and the recent heat wave that blew into town.

It was eight o'clock but it might as well have been midnight, the way Mary felt. Exhaustion came on quickly; she no longer had the stamina of even a week ago. The drugs had stolen even that.

Jeannie brought the conversation to the living room couch where they had their dessert. The words were coming hard now for Mary; she wanted so much to speak to Michael and while she took comfort in the fact that Jeannie said he was safe with Busch, her doubts would only be dispelled by the sound of his voice.

Her friend's anxiety was obvious. Impulsively, Jeannie opened her purse and pulled out a slip of paper. She reached for the phone.

"It's too late to call," Mary protested.

"Yeah?" Jeannie said with a tilt of her head. "I don't know about you, but my husband has woken me in the middle of the night for less important things. He'll get over it." She finished dialing and passed the phone to Mary. "It's a direct line to their room."

Mary got that tingling in her stomach from anticipation; once she knew her husband was safe, she knew she would finally get some sleep tonight. The phone rang with that flat dual European ring. It rang a second time. Mary felt like a kid again waiting to open the door to the living room on Christmas Day. Again it rang. She looked to Jeannie. Her smile became forced. Concern was seeping in. How big a room was it? Two fifteen in the morning. Why wasn't Michael answering?

Jeannie looked at the number in her hand, 100 percent sure she'd dialed right. "They're probably out for a drink," she lied.

The fear in Mary's heart grew. She couldn't hide the tears in her eyes. The two men weren't out for a drink. Something was wrong, something was very wrong.

The phone rang, unanswered.

❖

Die Hühle der Härte—the Den of Iniquity—dance club started pumping at midnight. It was one of Berlin's older clubs but well-known and frequented by the European elite. An exclusive playground for the rich, it had everything to offer, from nice to nasty. The club—one of the few buildings to survive both world wars—was a converted opera house dating back to the days of King Wilhelm I. Its multiple tiers alternated between dance floors and lounges. Its heart was the grand stage whose motif was changed nightly like the set of a play. It could be a rolling countryside one night, a dark medieval village the next. Tonight it was ancient Rome: backdrops of a looming coliseum, gladiators squaring off against a pride of ferocious lions, toga-wrapped women swooning in the arms of triumphant warriors. Strobes, spots, and flashing lights danced over the tapestries and crowds, illuminating an almost surreal orgy of two clashing millennia. This was a decadence the caesars never dreamed of.

Photographers stalked the balconies, hoping to catch a private moment that could be sold and revealed to the world. Young beautiful couples, of all persuasions and orientations, were swallowed by the huge plush couches, locked in deep passion. Values were loose here and morals were looser.

The music, pumped through tractor-trailer-sized speakers strung from the ceiling, was an eclectic mix of disco, new wave, and techno-punk—all of which was lost on Finster as he danced with two stunning ladies, Audrey and Vaughn. They had met at the door and had been attached at the hip since. While Vaughn had no idea who the older man in the custom Armani blazer was, Audrey had pegged him on his approach to the club from half a mile away. August Finster: suave; enormously successful; and, her favorite part, fabulously rich. The two girls—best friends since their London childhood—were virtually identical: blue and black Prada dresses, Gino pumps, Cartier diamond teardrop chokers; identical in every respect, that is, except their long flowing curls. Audrey's were black as night; Vaughn's, blonde as English straw.

All the girls could think about was how much they could score with their sexual three-way routine. They never thought of themselves as hookers, they were entertainers plying a trade to the gentlemen prey of the week—or sometimes just the weak gentlemen prey. They loved the men who possessed the power and the money, the so-called masters of the universe, but they had power, too: a power more primal, more preternatural than any man they'd ever met could match. These two knew how to make even the most powerful man kneel and beg like a child.

But this man was different. Most thought they had power, flaunting it to hide their insecurities. This one possessed a quiet air, a confidence unlike any other; he knew he had power, but he would demonstrate it only in the worst of circumstances. And for a moment, Vaughn had thought maybe tonight she should walk away. A heavy pit sat in her stomach and it wasn't the 'ludes she'd bought from Phillipe in the bathroom. This guy was different, somehow, seeing through her sexual manipulations to her heart, his eyes seeming to carve away her flesh to look into her soul.

But it was only a fleeting thought, what with the price of clothes and drugs these days. Besides, her gut was never right anyway.

Finster moved with a grace that belied his age, in time and motion with his female companions. He was dancing a victory dance; the adrenaline rush of success flowed richly through his veins. He danced without a care, for his goal was in sight; soon, he would be free of any impediments. He had given the order to kill—he'd been reluctant to do so, but he could no longer take the chance. He despised Simon and if he could have—if he was permitted, if he was *capable*—he would have rejoiced at pulling the trigger himself. Finster and this priest had crossed paths on more than one occasion and this particular man of the cloth had seemed to make it his quest to eradicate Finster from the world. Well, no more.

Michael was another matter; he had actually grown fond of the man. Most men cower away when faced with supreme obstacles. Michael was different, he possessed a drive that was on a par with Finster's. Unfortunately, Michael had become an adversary, the worst kind; one motivated by something beyond greed or lust. Michael St. Pierre was motivated by love. And for that, Finster ordered his death.

Finster had no grievance against the big cop, but Thal was so vehement about including him in the mayhem, he'd acceded. Thal was one of the most perfect machines of evil that he had ever found in a man. Absolutely no regard for others or for life. His pleasure was derived only from human suffering. To date, he'd been every bit the ideal employee: timely, efficient, thorough, and merciless. He wondered at Thal's reaction if he were to find out his employer's true identity.

He wasn't troubled in the least at the order he had given. After all, death was just a step in life that everyone experienced eventually. These three men were more like flies to be squashed than human beings; in the end, the only consequence of their deaths would be the removal of Finster's last obstacle to going home.

The music continued to pound as Audrey brought a round of drinks. Never once did they stop moving as they each downed their fourth Zima of the night.

"You girls are dangerous." Finster smiled as he watched them grind against one another.

"Practice makes perfect," Vaughn shouted over the music.

"How much practice have you had?"

The girls smiled in unison.

"I guess we'll just have to see how perfect you really are," Finster shouted.

And they danced on.

Chapter 27

The door exploded open, splintering as it slammed full-force into the wall. Thal spun into the darkly shadowed room, his trigger finger hardwired to his brain. His eyes darted left to right, scanning for targets as he went.

But no one was there. Not a soul. The suite couldn't have been emptier. Thal methodically checked the room, the closets, the bathroom, under the bed, every nook and cranny, keeping his guard up. But there was no one there. It was as if no one had ever been there. How did they vanish? How did they know? He ran the last ten minutes through his head. The concierge: dead before he could alert anyone. The lobby: empty. He hadn't seen a soul but the concierge. This was unacceptable. To his employer, it would be a problem. To him, it was his worst nightmare. He knew only too well the price of failure and it was a payment he wasn't prepared to make. He had tracked the three here. He could track them again.

The silence of the darkened room was shattered by a ring. A phone ringing at two fifteen in the morning somewhere else in the hotel but . . . not far.

When the door smashed in, Simon rolled right and drew a bead, his gun hand never wavering. He would empty the entire clip into whatever intruded into their room. Simon wouldn't wait to discern friend or foe; no friend crashed the place at two fifteen in the morning.

But he never got the chance. There was nobody there; in fact, the door hadn't even opened. . . . The sound came from the floor above.

Simon had booked three rooms in the hotel under three different names. A prudent idea, it turned out. A one-in-three chance. Whoever was stalking them went for the obvious religious cover name. *Jude Iscariot*. It was an old trick. Book at least two rooms, one under a subtly obvious name and the other surnames as common as a leaf in a forest.

Simon lowered his gun. They wouldn't have much time. The ruse would only provide a couple minutes at best.

Simon's heart nearly jumped out of his chest when the phone rang. Michael and Busch—out cold—bolted upright from their sleep. Michael dived for the phone. But Simon intercepted him before he had a chance to answer it. His hand held down the receiver as he shook his head no. The phone rang again.

Busch and Michael finally noticed the gun in Simon's hands.

"What's up with that?" Busch whispered, pointing to the guns.

Simon put his forefinger to his lips, shaking his head. The phone rang a third time. Busch held his hands out, palms up, still looking for an answer. Simon pointed at the ceiling and whispered, "We have to go."

As confused and groggy as they were, Busch and Michael didn't need another word. They grabbed their stuff and helped Simon pack up the duffel bags of weapons.

⌘

Simon raced down the autobahn, redlining the car on one of the few legal public raceways of the world. Only a BMW 8 series had passed them in the last hour, otherwise he and the Audi Turbo left the world behind.

"Where to?" Busch asked from the backseat, his nerves a little frazzled as he watched Germany speed by.

"We'll grab a motel outside of the city." Simon's eyes were glued to the road.

"And how do we know they won't track us down there?"

"We don't."

Busch had never seen the law from this point of view. And he didn't like it. Not that he didn't feel a certain adrenaline rush in response to all the subterfuge. He would just rather be the hunter than the prey; the adverse consequences of a hunter's actions were always minimized.

"So this is how you lived your life?" Busch said to Michael, who was hunkered down on the backseat next to him, eyes closed.

"That was Mary calling, guarantee it," Michael said more to himself than anyone else.

"You'll see her soon enough. 'Forty-eight more hours, we'll be back home.' Those were your words."

Michael opened his eyes and turned to Busch. A smile crept across his lips. "Never thought we'd be running together like this, did you?"

The irony wasn't lost on either of them.

"You sure about Finster's move? You're sure you know where he'll be tomorrow night?" Simon asked.

"I guarantee it," Busch answered confidently before turning back to Michael. "Got a job for me at your shop when I get busted off the force?"

"Shut up, nobody's gonna get busted off of anything. I just need you to trust me."

"Yeah, I did before and look where that got me." Busch raised his arms, alluding to their present one-hundred-and-ninety-kilometer-per-hour situation.

"So I owe you."

"You'll get my bill." Busch leaned over the seat to Simon. "Any idea who whacked the guy in the lobby?"

"No."

"You realize they are going to have a field day with that hotel room we left behind, what with more crosses than a Bible convention."

"Mmm hmm."

"And now the cops are probably looking for us. . . ."

"Mmm hmm, but they have no idea who we are."

"No idea . . . ," Busch repeated, unconvinced.

"I have a little experience with this kind of thing and I'm sure your friend has, too."

Busch looked to Michael, who raised his eyebrows in hesitant agreement.

"Finster really wants you dead." Busch pointed out the obvious.

"Makes me feel so warm and fuzzy to get all this attention," Michael remarked.

"Don't get cocky. I would imagine he wants to take us all out," Simon said, gripping the wheel, his foot to the floor.

"That's comforting." Busch watched the countryside whiz by.

"Take comfort in the little things. We got out of there alive," Simon joked.

For a humorous guy, Busch was quickly losing his sense of mirth. He was marked for death, something he never would have comprehended three days ago. He would do a lot for his friend—hadn't he always said he would lay down his life? But this was too real. Until tonight, he had never been on the run before.

⌘

At 2:17 a.m. Thal stood in the middle of a hotel room staring at the serious collection of crosses strewn everywhere. He held tightly to the pistol in each hand as his brain tried to process the sight before him. The unanswered ringing phone was like a homing signal, leading him from the room above down into this religious retreat that seemed to have lost its way. The phone finally fell silent. "What the fuck?" was all he could mutter.

At least he knew he had the right room this time. How ridiculous were these crosses? Like a cross would keep him out. And for a moment he wondered if maybe they were keeping someone or something else out. Dracula and the werewolf were fiction but these crosses still hung there. And they weren't for praying—you only needed one for that, his Episcopalian upbringing was clear on this fact. These were for protection. He had given up his faith long ago; God was merely for the weak, the big brother hero to turn to when darkness was around the corner. But still the thousands of crucifixes were to ward off something, something that the conventional weapons of man couldn't defend against. But what?

Before he had a chance to really consider the possibilities, a voice screamed out behind him, "Halt!!!"

Thal did nothing of the sort. The German policeman was dead before his riddled head hit the carpet. As the smoke from his two guns cleared, Thal scolded himself for getting lost in thought.

No time now for a search, he grabbed some of the crosses in hopes of IDing them later, and took off.

He hustled down the hall, stowing his guns in the back of his waistband, and hit the elevator button. If the cops were downstairs, better to act casual and try to head out the front door in hopes that the lobby commotion over the dead body would be overwhelming. When the elevator door opened, however, his plans took a dramatic turn, one that would make headlines for days and be remembered for years to come.

The three policemen drew their guns on Thal, who threw his trembling hands in the air in mock fear.

"He's dead . . . *Dead,*" Thal said in English. His voice quivered as he pointed down the hall.

Two of the cops ran to the room, guns ready, and bisected the door for cover.

"I'm an American. They ran down the stairs"—tears streamed down Thal's face—"down the stairs." Thal took pride in the way he could assimilate himself into any situation or mood. But what thrilled him at this very moment was the burning in the small of his back where the two red-hot gun barrels burned his flesh. He could swear he was beginning to smell something.

The policeman in front of him, a rookie by the name of Schmidt, radioed down for help. "Cover the stairs, officer down," he said in German. He stepped closer to Thal. "What did they look like?"

Thal debated giving the description of Simon, Michael, and Busch, but that would send them to ground. No, Thal needed them relaxed; he couldn't afford anyone else hunting his quarry. He began to blubber, his arms trembling with his whole body.

"You can put your arms down—" the flustered young policeman said.

His words were interrupted by the gasps of his partners, who had entered the room where the murdered officer lay. The young rookie's curiosity drew him slowly down the hall, while his gun remained trained on Thal. He glanced in to see his former training buddy Jon Reiberg in a pool of blood, his left foot spastically twitching. As hard as Schmidt tried, it took him a good fifteen seconds to pull his eyes away from the horrid sight. And when he did so, he saw the lean American holding a small holy cross in his right hand, unconsciously thumbing its edge as he leaned against the wall directly opposite the suite, crying like a baby. Schmidt looked back in the room to see one of the other cops puking in a corner. The whole scene felt like an out-of-body experience as the astonished rookie watched the third cop pirouette and fall.

Schmidt never felt the bullet pierce his heart, the gunshot sounded so far away. Time crawled as he watched his two partners spin about and fall under the barrage of bullets coming from the two guns held high by the man in the doorway. Schmidt found it so strange to watch the man rapid-pull the triggers of two monster-sized guns as tears still sat upon his cheeks. Whatever happened to that cross he was holding? Schmidt fell to his knees, feeling so tired but not the least bit of pain. And he at last noticed them. They were everywhere; all about the room. Why didn't he notice them when he first looked in? No matter. He fell to the floor, the last remnants of life escaping through the bullet holes in his chest. He died there, among the three thousand crosses.

Thal ripped the badge off Reiberg and sprinted three floors up the stairwell. He ran to the end of the hall to one of the few doors with a do-not-disturb sign and pounded on room 1474.

An annoyed English accent cried out from within, "Jesus Christ, what the hell?"

Thal remained silent, waiting as the man within stumbled through the room. After thirty seconds, the door parted just an inch and Thal thrust Reiberg's badge in the man's face. "Excuse me, sir," Thal said in a strained German accent.

"What the bloody hell is going on? A fire or something?"

"I'd just like a moment of your time."

Chapter 28

Dawn. In the Bavarian countryside just beyond a field of barley, the knee-deep blanket of fog was beginning to burn off in the early morning sun. Michael and Busch sat on a split-rail fence watching a herd of grazing Black Angus. There must have been three hundred head in the lush green pasture all gorging themselves, unaware of their pending demise. Michael couldn't help thinking that the cows had gone through their existence unaware of their future, unaware that it was controlled by something higher in the order of life.

Simon had checked them into a small motel next to the meadow at three thirty that morning. The ancient wrinkled clerk and the priest had conversed for quite a while about the diminishing faith in the world and the loss of an entire generation to television. Simon's German was dead-on and the added touch of the priest's collar—Simon apparently wore it only when absolutely necessary—deflected any possible suspicion of Simon's travel at such an hour. The small lobby hadn't seen a paintbrush in twenty years and that was just fine—the more inconspicuous the place, the more inconspicuous they would be. Simon took the key and gently pulled shut the front door.

The motel rooms were situated along a strip of sidewalk bordered in fresh begonias planted by the clerk's equally ancient wife. Simon had asked for the room furthest from the road under the pretense of the need for quiet prayer and meditation. Confident in their seclusion, the priest motioned the hidden Busch and Michael from the car into the room, locking the door behind them. The room was sparse—two single beds, a dresser, and a bathroom.

While the others slept, Michael took the first watch. No crosses this time, just guns.

Their plans would not change as a result of their near-demise and relocation. Within the next twenty-four hours they were going to steal the keys back. They each had their roles but once they began the job, Michael would be in charge. It was his plan and the other two were riding on the coattails of his experience.

The morning was crisp and clear; Michael inhaled slowly, forcing himself to remember the moment. But for the faint smell of cattle, the air was the cleanest he had ever known. He'd run his plan over and over in his head all night, playing out every possible scenario; he never left anything to chance and always hoped for luck.

"Did you get Mary?" Busch asked, his legs hitched up on the middle post rail. If he had a ten-gallon hat he could have passed for John Wayne keeping watch over the herd.

"She checked out of the hospital."

"That's great. Is she home?"

"I'm assuming. It's one in the morning there, God knows she needs her sleep. I'll try her after lunch."

"Sure you don't want to head home now? We could ditch the priest. Be home by tonight."

Michael had run that possibility through his head more times than he wished to remember. It was something that had gnawed at him since he'd arrived three days ago. He was chasing shadows and myths. What good was it possibly doing? He and Busch could leave and let Simon try to steal the keys back on his own. All Michael wanted was Mary. They didn't have much time left in the world and what little they had he was pissing away here thousands of miles away from her. His guilt was crippling. It wasn't fair to either of them. Mary needed him and he needed her. But what had pulled back his resolve as he sat guard last night was pulling him back now. Michael couldn't face the possibility of Mary dying in limbo, trapped forever in Purgatory, her faith destroyed, her eternity left in shambles, all at his hands. Doubt about Mary's eternal peace would devastate him for the rest of his days.

And it would be his fault.

Michael finally looked at Busch. "If you want to back out, I understand."

"In for a penny . . ." Busch grinned. Despite everything, he felt more alive with the risk laid out before him. He finally understood what his father felt every time he headed out to sea. It was the thrill of never knowing what was over the horizon. It was the risk that made a man really feel alive.

⌘

Mary woke at dawn. Unable to fall back to sleep, she forced her body out of bed and into the shower. The hot water across her back, the steam filling her head, helped to cleanse the nightmares from her mind. The dark dreams had returned with a vengeance. And though she had not recognized it, it was one of the main reasons she checked herself out of the hospital. She needed to be back in a world she could control, a place where her mind would be at ease, somewhere she could suppress the unconscious images of dread and terror that had tormented her.

They always started the same, she and Michael in happy, healthy times. Laughing and dancing at the Country House, their favorite dinner and dance club. The images so vivid, her heart soaring next to Michael's. And then they were at home, in bed, the clothes strewn about, she in Michael's arms making love while soft music played on the stereo. It was a joy that had taken her to new heights . . . only to come crashing down into the darkest, blackest place she had ever seen.

And while there was a complete absence of light, she knew He was there. That same man. Circling her, sniffing at her hair, his pungent breath on her neck. The words he whispered, taunting her in a vile tone, "Mary, Mary, where did your husband go?"

Her mind screamed yet her lips remained powerless, stitched shut with black bloodied sutures, her voice trapped in her head. She was paralyzed, unable to fight back, to strike at this thing that just kept circling. And she felt another presence. The cop, the one whose words were so empty, so false in their caring. The one who had visited her in the hospital three days ago: Dennis. *He never said what he really wanted; wasn't that odd? He said he was Paul's new partner, he was just seeing how she was and what her husband's relationship with Busch was based on. So why did he terrify her so?*

Dennis was in the background waiting, standing there waiting at His side. They were laughing. A mocking hyena cackle that surrounded her, drowning out her very thoughts. Knife-like, their laughter reached out, sharp and deadly, to perform a task she would never have dreamed. It cut her soul from her body.

She felt it detach as their mockery grew louder and crueler. It left her utterly empty, as if her body were withering into a swarm of insects. She watched as her soul drifted away, dimly glowing like diffused light in a blinding fog. And he swallowed it, like a beast tearing at the flesh of a young child. The unseen man who was no man.

And every night what snapped her out, what sent her eyes flashing open, was the brief sweep of light coming from far above, passing through the dark earthen room. It passed over the thing that ate her soul, the man who had always seemed so familiar yet whose face she could never remember upon waking. The light continued moving, shining over her shriveled cancerous body, finally stopping, landing on the one thing that shook her to her core: Michael. He was lying faceup on the earthen floor staring at her, only not with his eyes—with vacant sockets pooled with blood. His mouth was frozen in a terrifying, soundless scream.

She woke, bolted upright in the bed night after night, sweat flowing from every pore. Only under the spray of hot water was she able to wash away the terror.

As she stepped from the shower this dawn, she wrapped herself in a large towel and her oversized robe; she refused to look at her hands, her feet, her body. She had removed or covered all the mirrors in the house, preferring to avoid her wasting reflection at all costs.

She ate her breakfast with a hunger she hadn't known in days—she had only picked at food the night before. She dressed and headed out for the day.

Wanting to have their home filled with fresh flowers for Michael's return, she had stopped by Troy's Nursery to pick up several bunches of flowers. Though she hadn't gotten through to Michael the night before, she did not panic. No news is good news, she told herself. Jeannie had convinced her that Michael and Paul were fine. They had either checked out or moved to another hotel. They would be home in two days, she had said so confidently, and Jeannie never lied.

As she headed down Maple Avenue, for reasons she did not understand, Mary felt energized, ready to tackle the world, whatever she faced. She noticed sights that in all her years in this town she had never paid attention to. The symmetry of the fir trees at the duck pond. The timelessness of the white gazebo. The beauty of the old church, its spire reaching toward Heaven. And all the people everywhere who always smiled, nodding hello. They had hope in their eyes and it infected her. Despite everything she had gone through, there was always hope.

It is said that the human spirit is the strongest force in nature. It has conquered every type of adversity known to man: physical, mental, spiritual. It is what has driven progress and innovation. It brought man out of the caves and onto the moon. Mother Nature has thrown every obstacle, every curveball—yet time and time again, she has been beaten back. It infuses optimism, it empowers strength, it drives the will to live and succeed. But most of all, it is what gives us hope. The human spirit carries man forward and never has it been defeated.

It has also been said that there is a serenity before the final adversity; that a calm always precedes a storm; that a light bulb always burns brightest before winking out.

At four o'clock that afternoon, Mary checked back into Byram Hills Memorial Hospital for the last time.

⌘

Finster looked out the leaded glass window of his grand mansion. Many had called it a castle but its design really bore no resemblance to those whimsical structures. The building was more befitting the robber barons of the late 1890s. He looked across his miles of wooded property, across the valley toward the mountains that rose so high they were lost in the clouds. He watched as the gardeners and groundskeepers tended to the huge estate, trimming bushes, cutting grass. None of them found the sidearms at their waists or the communication earpieces cumbersome. After all, in their prior careers they carried sixty-pound packs through jungles and deserts as gunfire crackled overhead and mortar shells crashed on all sides. All in all, this was more peace than any of them would ever know. It was a precaution Finster had always taken. Always wary of an assault, he took no chances. And tonight would be no different; in fact, he had already requested Charles see that all twenty members of his security staff were on duty. He wanted guards at the front gate, multiple patrols walking the perimeter walls, snipers on the roof equipped with nightscopes. It would be a lockdown more thorough than any prison had ever seen. There must be no room for error, no room for defeat. No one would take back what was rightfully his. Nothing would be left to chance on this, his final night.

It was the same precaution he'd taken when he'd assigned Thal to clean up. He hadn't heard from his hired gun in two days, nor had he read of the untimely demise of his three suitors. There had been word over the newswire of a shooting spree in the Hotel Friedenberg, which confirmed that Thal was on the job, but Finster wanted proof. He wanted *bodies*. Thal was a good find, far better than his past employees. Thal had spent the last five years in the service of the disembodied voice of Finster. Most of the jobs were performed in the interest of business, in the interest of correcting a betrayal. And though August Finster would have liked to perform these tasks himself, it was something he could not do.

He was forbidden.

It was one of the few powers he didn't possess: he could not directly take a life. Bargain for a soul, yes; perform a miraculous act, absolutely; but not directly end a life. No matter, he would still be there to receive the fruits of death. And death always came, sooner or later. And besides, if he did possess the power to annihilate uncounted numbers, where would the fun be in that? If there were no more people to corrupt, there would be no more souls to reap.

His was a deeper goal, one with a far longer-lasting impact.

And that's where Thal came in. It was a simple way around Finster's problem: man could kill man. If anyone was to renege on a deal or go back on a promise, Thal would be there to add that little bit of umph that would shorten their stay on terra firma.

Never had they met, Finster would never take that chance. But he watched. Thal was the closest thing he had ever seen to a creature without a soul. No remorse, no hesitancy at any task. Thal's was a spirit buried deep down within the most malevolent primal area of the human heart. But of late, Finster was seeing a weakness. The cop, the one called Busch. Thal seemed fixated on him, driven by a personal desire that Finster had not seen before in his private assassin. And it ate at his mind, clouding Thal's abilities. Finster sensed a momentary failure on Thal's part. His efficiency had never before been in question, but this day it was. The simple hit should have been completed and Finster should have received word by now. No matter, Finster's confidence in Thal may have been shaken but it still remained. Thal would succeed and, worse-case scenario, if he kept the three alive and busy until tomorrow, that would be just as well. For tomorrow, Finster would be gone.

There would be no good-bye, no adieu, no auf Wiedersehen. Come tomorrow, he would simply vanish. No trace of his whereabouts. His disappearance would surely come to be known as one of the world's great mysteries. Like Amelia Earhart, nary a clue left behind. There would be no heirs, no will for the vast fortune created in less than ten years. Not a relative would be unearthed, no parents, no birth records. No friends from childhood, no close associates, no wives or children. Of course, many a pretender would surface, but no legitimate kin would ever lay claim.

No answers. Only questions.

Chapter 29

The woods around Waldberg were darker than night. These were the forests of the Brothers Grimm, where Hansel and Gretel strode the same path as Red Riding Hood, the wolf always lurking just beyond the bush. It was no wonder that the dark legends and fairy tales were born here. The forbidding canopy blocked any view of the sky. The giant branches of ancient trees reached out to steal the breath from your lungs. The ghostly stillness stoked a primal fear that brought forth witches, trolls, and goblins of the wood. It was fitting that Finster's estate sprang from this ground. Its entrance gates were five kilometers up the road, the only sign of civilization for the next ten.

Paul Busch emerged from the Mercedes C-Class, the unmarked car of choice for the German police. A portable flashing light was affixed to the roof right above the driver's door, the spinning red glow casting wicked shadows on the evergreen trees. Busch sauntered up to the scarlet convertible. The driver was a beautiful woman in a pair of black Vuarnet sunglasses. Her black hair was, surprisingly, only slightly tousled from the wind. Up close, she was more than beautiful; she was stunning.

"Guten Abend, Fraulein," Busch said, with a pathetic attempt at a German accent.

Audrey didn't look up as she rifled her purse for her license and registration. *"Guten Abend, Herr Kommissar. Gist es cin Problem?"*

"Sprechen sie Englisch?"

"Yes, as a matter of fact—" But the words froze in her throat when she recognized Herr Kommissar.

"License, please." She handed it to him with just a hint of disgust. "How did it go?" Busch asked.

"He went home with Vaughn, I haven't heard from her yet."

"Did he suspect?"

"Look, I know what I'm doing. All you asked me to do was meet him, tease him, lead him on, and leave him dry."

"So how did you do?"

"I'm back for seconds, aren't I? I made him desire that which he did not attain last night. Just like you asked."

"Like I paid for," Busch admonished. He glanced at the name on the license and chuckled. "Miss Charm?"

"Give me a break."

"Isn't it a crime to impersonate someone?"

"I was going to ask you the same thing," she shot back. Busch's eyes knocked her down. Audrey was her real name it, but her last name . . . Well, she was saddled with the unfortunate moniker of Lipschitz and that wasn't something she was about to share.

Busch had hooked up with Audrey just before he picked up Michael from prison yesterday. She came on a good recommendation from not only the Berlin police but the dean of the club circuit, someone by the name of Christian Croix. Busch really wasn't sure if Christian was a boy or a girl—he/she was some kind of gendernaut hovering in-between macho and pretty, a muscled torso stretching an angora T-shirt. Christian was the de facto head of the clubbies, the German twentysomethings who ruled the night. What they said was in was in and what they said was out was finished, dried up, shut down. Audrey and Vaughn were well-known clubbies worshipped for their dancing, their matching clothes, their sexual talent, and their ability to make a living off of the weakness of others. Christian gave up Audrey's number—after throwing a tantrum—upon threat of arrest for possession of mescaline.

Busch met her in a pub, explained the situation, how she could make a fast buck for doing what she did best and at the same time keep herself out of prison. Not that he could act on the threat: his jurisdiction ended on the other side of the Atlantic. Busch had researched Finster's habits, his tastes. He had memorized the dossier on the plane; it was all so well documented. Audrey would make fitting bait. Busch paid her an even grand to get into Finster's pants but not touch. She wouldn't have a difficult time finding him. Finster loved clubs and there was always a buzz created by the clubbies as to the in place for the night.

Audrey didn't breathe a word of it to her friend Vaughn, who was more than a bit surprised when Audrey bowed out of last night's after-dance activities with Finster. She feigned illness but kept up the seductive charm, securing a rare second date with the industrialist.

"I don't see you writing a ticket," Audrey pointed out to Busch.

"Time for Part Two," he replied. "I need my last and final favor."

"Shall I use my hand or my mouth?"

"Bribery? That's a very serious offense. Worse than speeding, worse than prostitution."

"I'm all out of favors." She rubbed her fingers together, expecting payment.

"It would be a shame if you had to spend the night in jail."

"What do you want?"

"I want you to take him somewhere."

"Who?" she asked, knowing full well who they were talking about.

"Enough with the games." Busch flashed a roll of cash.

"Where?" she asked in a tired voice, her eyes glued to the money.

He handed her a sheet of paper.

She glanced at the club flyer. "What, is there going to be a raid or something?"

"Nothing of the sort. No police action, no harm to anyone. It's a new place, my friend owns it," he lied. "It's hot, impossible to get in, and he's better than a ticket."

"If I refuse?"

"There'll be consequences."

"What'll you do: arrest me?"

"I'll tell him that you were spying on him. For some reason, I don't think he'll take kindly to that." He let his answer hang in the night for a moment.

Audrey sat there stewing. Between what Busch was paying and what she could get out of Finster, she could go to Nice for the rest of the summer and that did have its appeal. She knew the cop's money was too good to be true—if he was a cop, which she sincerely doubted. Her mother always told her that if you dance with the Devil you pay the price. "How am I going to get him there?"

"I don't think you'll have a problem with that. Just use your feminine prowess." He handed her the wad of bills. "For your trouble."

Without so much as another glance, she started up the convertible and drove off toward Finster's.

⌘

Four and a half kilometers up the road, the black Audi was tucked into the woods, the engine cool, its body covered in pine boughs. Simon had taken up a position behind a berm, his binoculars fixed on a pair of forbidding black gates. The gates were of a classic design, decorative black iron hinged into massive stone columns. The ornamentation ran to the Gothic, cherubs dancing through wrought iron gardens, gargoyles riding the upper rails. Twin pairs of gas lanterns were mounted upon the columns. Their flames cast only a dim glow, long shadows shimmering up and down the winding drive. Simon had never seen this entrance's equal. These were security gates in every sense of the word.

It had been two hours since the gates had swung open to admit the fire-engine red Fiat, a raven-haired beauty behind the wheel. Simon fought to keep his mind in check. While he had never broken his vow of celibacy, he'd spent many an hour saying the Act of Contrition for his thoughts. The gates had slammed shut quickly behind the Italian roadster. It was a two-second window of opportunity for entrance, but that wasn't necessary yet. Busch had assured them that the woman would cooperate; she'd lure Finster out of the house. It was only a matter of time. Anyway, they weren't going in through the gate.

The property was bordered by a fifteen-foot stone wall that ran along its perimeter. When Michael had visited Finster just one week earlier, he had noted that Hiencen laser monitors ran along the wall's interior wall. Tough to beat, but not impossible. He knew the house security system was produced by Hughes Aircraft, the same system used by the United States military for their high-clearance-level locations. The encryption changed daily. It was a bitch of a system, but again, not impossible. However, there was one element of security he wasn't ready for; it was not in his training, in fact it was something he had always carefully avoided. On Michael's previous visit to Finster's estate, he had noted the staff working about the grounds. Their shoulders were wide, their hips slim, bodies trained and honed by the military. And they were armed to the teeth.

Now he sat patiently with Simon behind the Audi and, though a warm summer breeze blew up the road, a chill ran through him. It was the forest, wilderness all around, yet something was missing: life. There were no sounds of the wild, no birds in the air. The summer nights, usually alive with the crickets' song, were dead silent. No animals lurked in these trees, nothing crept along this ground. But what caused the greatest dread of all was the absence of bugs. There were no worms in this earth, no flies, no mosquitoes seeking blood. You could usually find a spiderweb, the weaver lying in wait, tucked into the base of most trees, but none were visible here. The insect world was always present. Through feast or famine, war or peace, they were the only living thing present on the planet since the dawn of time. Nothing could wipe them out or drive them away. And yet they were banished from the forests of August Finster.

Hearing a low whistle, Michael spun about just in time to see a black limo—the same limo with the same license plate that pursued him from the airport, her front end repaired and painted—approach down the long road. The halogen lamps cut through the night, lighting up even the deeper reaches of the forest. The giant gates silently yawned open and the Mercedes shot through, picking up speed, entering the road, and flying away into the dark.

⌘

The forty-five-minute drive flew by with the help of some alcoholic lubrication. The limo bar, freshly stocked, was nothing but top-shelf: Dom Perignon, Chivas, Moët, and Gray Goose. No beer here. Ice jingled in Tiffany crystal tumblers as the silent outer world of the countryside flew by at one hundred and eighty kilometers per hour. The lights of downtown Berlin were coming into view through the smoked glass like stars cutting through a hazy night sky. Four passengers sat in the limo's spacious backseat, laughing, that is, all except one. Finster was distant, his mind somewhere else as he watched the night rush past. Finster was filled with a mixture of joy and sadness. The impending realization of one's dreams can be sobering.

But the mood didn't last; back to the moment he came, putting his arm around Joy, she of the copper locks. Her bosom was warm and full under his right hand, the cleavage a tad too firm beneath her sheer gingham dress. Silicone. But this didn't bother Finster; he was well aware of life's illusions and the masks we all wear. Zoe, a flaxen-haired vision, sat across from Finster, her long legs stretched across the floor, her bare feet squarely in his lap, sipping her third sea breeze of the night. She was a swimmer from the German Olympic team. He loved the way her shoulders filled out her silver lamé blouse.

He was looking forward to tasting the fruit tonight. Joy, the red; Zoe, the blonde; and Audrey, the black-haired beauty seated on his left. Three different flavors for his farewell tryst.

"Where are we headed?" Joy asked.

"Ladies, I leave that to you."

"Let me pick!" Zoe begged like a child. She was a little drunk.

"No! Me!" Joy pleaded.

Audrey stroked Finster's cheek, while caressing his body with her own. "I know the perfect place. Brand-new, sensuous, utterly decadent. Heaven on earth."

"My kind of place," Finster said.

"Rapture?" Joy's eyes lit up.

"Rapture?" Zoe hoped.

"Do you think you could get us in?" Audrey purred in Finster's ear, knowing he could, and, more importantly, knowing he couldn't resist the challenge.

He sat there silently staring at his mini-harem, their minds loosened, their bodies willing. He was undecided where they would go. Rapture was definitely *in*, the place to be seen, but Finster wasn't sure if it should be his last memory of Germany, the land he had grown to love. It was so new he had yet to sample its wares. Was it a night for new or a night for nostalgia?

⌘

Dr. Rhineheart sprinted down the hall, two nurses flanking him. An orderly steered the rattling crash cart, fighting to keep pace. They burst into the private hospital room to the sound of high-pitched alarms and hyper pinging. The heart monitor next to the bed was a green static line. Mary St. Pierre was in cardiac arrest, her body motionless upon the bed.

Four hours earlier she was in her car on the way back from the garden nursery, planning to head home for lunch. Instead, she stopped by St. Pius Church in Byram Hills, where she lost herself in prayer. She thanked God for her friends and her life; for the love she felt. She thanked Him for her husband, a man who had put aside his life to pursue her heart. She prayed for strength. Not her strength, but for Michael's strength, that he would see things through, that he would find the will to carry on after she was gone. She prayed that he would find love again. He was too kind a man to go through life alone, he had too much love to share. She wished him children and happiness and patience. She longed for the chance to live along with him, standing by his side, but she knew now that wasn't to be. And she wished for the day many years from now when they would be united.

It was only one sneeze, a small one, petite and silent. She covered her mouth as taught so many years before. She teased herself a little as she rummaged in her purse; she'd meant to pick up a small pack of tissues. She'd felt a hint of a cold coming on the night before and knew it could wreak havoc on her weakened immune system. And now that was coming to pass.

She hurried to the car; the glove compartment was always well stocked. She didn't notice her hand until she opened the car door and reached for the small compartment latch. It wasn't a lot, just enough to be noticed. Small speckles, freckle-like, already darkening. It was her right hand, the one she had covered her mouth with.

Driving straight to the hospital, she could barely control herself, her hands shaking, a cold sweat breaking out on her neck. Her fear was back, this time with a vengeance. She needed Michael here, now.

Dr. Rhineheart admitted her, got her set up in a private room. He said it would be a few hours before the test results came back. He said not to worry. Expelling blood orally wasn't uncommon. The constriction pressure caused by a sneeze created a rupture of the capillaries in the lungs. No other symptoms had manifested themselves, but he would keep her overnight just as a precaution. Again, he told her not to worry, all the signs pointed to a stable condition, she could go home in the morning.

Now, three hours later, Rhineheart affixed the automatic defibrillator to her chest. Flipped the switch. A unisex electronic voice droned from the machine: *"Three . . . two . . . one . . . CLEAR."* A Klaxon alarm sounded and a surge of electricity shot through Mary's body. Her unconscious form arched up in the air; her arm still dangled off the mattress.

In a fraction of a second, she slumped back down in the bed, her eyes still closed, the color drained from her face. Rhineheart leaned in with a stethoscope. Nothing. The heart monitor readout was green and straight, its whine uninterrupted.

He flipped the switch again.

"Three . . . two . . . one . . . CLEAR."

Again, her body lifted off the bed, this time a fraction higher.

While Mary lay there with her heart as dead as dead could be, her mind raced on. She was lost not in the classic white room with a bright light before her, but rather a dark, cavernous hall. Nondescript and quiet. She felt nothing—no pain, no joy. Nothing. She could vaguely hear the calls of Dr. Rhineheart somewhere far away. He was working feverishly on someone—she hoped he was successful. She walked the hall trying the various doors, finding each locked. Somewhere close by she heard the murmur of voices, hushed and nondescript. She wandered toward the sound, the tone and cadence growing more distinct as she advanced. She came to the end of the hall where it ended in a classic T. The crowd—it was surely that—sounded as if it was behind every door, there must be thousands of people. Left or right, she wasn't sure which way to go when a terrific sharp pain struck her, racing through her veins. Like a fire wire, the pain laced its way through her skin.

And just as quickly, the agony was gone. She still stood at the T. Left or right? The voices growing, like the roar of a stadium: the sound of men and women, the cries of scared children. All sounded confused, crying out to her for help like a city of lost souls. She went right, meandering for what seemed like hours, the frightened voices blotting out her own thoughts, confusion tearing her mind apart. She arrived at last at a door that stood out from the rest: black as ebony, old as dirt. She reached for the rusted knob. She entered.

The face shocked her, terrified her. You never had to meet him to know instantly who he was.

Her body was hit by that sharp force again, pain so great it seemed to lift her in the air, the white lights so brilliant they were blinding.

Rhineheart leaned over Mary, a hint of a smile on his lips. "Not going to lose you that easily."

Mary lay there unconscious but alive, her heart returned to normal rhythm. The doctor looked up. "Let me know when she wakes up," Rhineheart told the attending nurse.

He turned to Nurse Schrier, who stood with a hint of mist in her eyes; he took the big woman by the arm and led her to a corner. "I don't care what you do, you find her husband." He headed for the door. "Her body's failing fast. I don't know how long she'll last."

Chapter 30

Simon and Michael were hunkered down in the forest twenty-five yards from the monstrous black gates of Finster's estate. It had been two hours. They were at a disadvantage; Simon didn't like it and neither did Michael. They had no idea of the exact count of men they would have to deal with before getting to the house. They made a rough estimate at twelve. That number would apply based on Michael's intel from his first visit if the basic security points were manned. But those would be the minimal points covered by someone with limited resources. Finster didn't fit that profile.

And what if the keys weren't there? If the man-count was at a minimum, they would have their answer. But if the keys were inside, well, then they would be facing an army. The trick was getting to the house before being detected. It was like capture the flag; the knack of the game was getting in the vicinity of the prize without being caught.

"We're running out of time," Simon whispered. His earpiece contained a subvocal mike wired into his cell phone.

"Patience," Busch replied over the cell phone, his voice tinny, far off, the signal breaking up occasionally on account of the poor spread of cell towers in rural Germany. *"He'll show."*

Simon wasn't so sure now—too much time had elasped—but he'd never admit defeat.

⌘

Twelve thirty a.m. and the line outside the club was still growing. The maroon velvet rope held back the hundreds of nobodies as the Somebodies were greeted and escorted in. The whole scene was frantic, reminding Busch of New York City's golden age. Studio 54, The Tunnel, The Palladium. It was different then, the music was better—every generation possesses superiority about their music—the snobbery was less, and it didn't cost you two weeks' salary to have a good time.

He stood near the door, having identified himself to the bouncers earlier as a New York cop working with Interpol to bring back a fugitive. There would be no raid, no bust for drugs, underage patrons, or lewd behavior. Busch would quietly watch his man and when the time was appropriate, he would discreetly make his move. The bouncer was only too willing to cooperate, after Busch's assurances. The five hundred euros didn't hurt, either.

Busch was not looking forward to entering; he hated the techno scene, the thumping music, the incoherent lyrics mixed with inane rapping. He was a Springsteen-or-nothing kind of guy. He had to get Finster into the club unsuspecting, unaware of where he really was. It was the only way if Michael and Simon were to have any chance of success.

"*Busch?*" Simon said in Busch's earpiece.

"Yeah."

"*Why Peaches?*"

"It's killing you, isn't it?" Busch leaned against the club's doorway.

"*Just killing time.*"

"Old girlfriend from Georgia, loved the Allman Brothers' album *Eat a Peach*, she always called me her New York Peach."

"*Really?*" Simon's voice came back with suspicion.

⌘

"Allman Brothers story?" Michael whispered to Simon. He was lying in the grass watching the gates through the binoculars. Simon nodded. Michael shook his head. "It's his wife's name for a certain part of his body."

Simon stifled a laugh.

Busch was beyond upset. Though Michael didn't have an earpiece in, he could hear the raving coming from Simon's ear. "*What did he say? Did he say—*"

"Hey, relax." Simon cut Busch off.

"*Relax, my ass—*"

But then there was silence. Obvious silence. "Busch? He's only pulling your chain." Nothing. "Paul, you there?" Simon tapped his earpiece, "Can you hear me?" Michael looked over, eyes questioning. "Quit screwing around." Simon was suddenly deeply serious.

Finally, after what seemed like an eternity, Busch's voice came in, clear and grim. "*He's here.*"

⌘

The limo pulled up and out stepped the three arm charms, Audrey, Zoe, and Joy, each sensuous, breathtaking, their rainbow of hair blowing in the summer breeze. The three women flanked the car door as all eyes watched. Finster emerged to the kind of oohs and ahhs usually reserved for celebrities at the Academy Awards. The crowds parted like the Red Sea before the entourage as the quartet walked up the red carpet. Whispers, cheering, and catcalls mixed into the reverie as the velvet-rope hopefuls craned their necks to see the industrial giant and his beauties.

Busch slipped silently into the club from his perch at the door, parked himself in a corner, and monitored through the doorway as the bouncer held back the velvet rope and bid the celebrity party welcome. Busch watched as they stepped through the door and straight to the dance floor. An invisible barrier seemed to precede them as they did so, dancers stepping aside as if out of respect. People either stared or ignored Finster, enamored with his presence or completely oblivious to it. An oblivion entered into by drink, drugs, or ego. The charisma that Finster possessed was overwhelming; it was as if he owned the club, the people, the world.

Busch leaned against the far end of the bar and ordered a straight Jack Daniel's on the rocks. He was out of his element now; his plain khaki pants and denim shirt made him a bull's-eye right out of a Gap ad. He had never seen so many pierced body parts in all his life. Ears, noses, lips, and brows; bellies, nipples, cheeks, even chins. His mind wandered to the gutter and easily imagined several more spots ripe for piercing. And the tattoos . . . he had seen an awful lot of felons in his time and they had painted their bodies with untold numbers of works, none too creative, themes mostly running to mother, sweethearts, or fantasy. But here the money ran deep: these people could buy a Mona Lisa for their body mosaic.

Busch flipped open his phone, stuffed the earpiece in his ear, hit redial. He saw the connection made but could barely hear Simon on the other end over the deafening music. He sipped his drink and merely said in a loud clear voice, "We are a go."

Busch didn't wait for a reply; he flipped the phone closed and stuffed it in his pocket. He leaned with his back against the bar and tilted his chin up. The ceiling soared one hundred feet above, he could make out the thick wooden rafters that were placed two hundred years earlier. The smoky haze was thick up there. He imagined the original architect's shock had he lived to see the day where his masterpiece was desecrated by this unforeseen future. The music pounding as bodies writhed in a clothed sexual orgy. Drinks flowed. Drugs abounded. A modern-day Sodom and Gomorrah. This was hedonism at its best.

Busch stayed at the bar; not for drink, but rather because it placed him directly between Finster and the exit. The only exit. Busch couldn't believe the bodies crammed into this place; there had to be five hundred strong and easily double that waiting outside. A firetrap for sure—and that did give him pause, what with his fear of the flame and all, but he could overcome it for now—still, it was the only way out. There was no way Finster could leave without Busch knowing. The plan was rolling now, he even began to feel hopeful. Simon and Michael were surely well into their endgame. It had been a risk. Finster could have gone several places this night but here, this place called Rapture, was fitting in more ways than anyone realized.

Finster was in. And as far as Busch was concerned, he wasn't leaving.

⌘

Al Graham did a stint in the National Guard and was in Desert Storm, although he landed on February 28, 1991, the last day of fighting, and never saw any action. In point of fact, Al had never once fired his gun in a combat situation. He had fallen under the command of Colonel T. C. Roberts, a mean-ass, leather-necked, sand-fucker marine who could stare down a scorpion. The colonel had called him just four weeks ago enticing him with this cushy assignment with amazing pay. And if he was lucky, maybe he would get to shoot his gun at a live target for a change.

Al stood point with Javeed Waquim twenty-five yards up the driveway. They were the gatekeepers, but it was a pretty sturdy gate in their estimation, so the two men didn't pay much attention to it. No one had ever made an attempt on their employer, Mr. Finster, and anyway who would be foolish enough to challenge the estate's security precautions and guards? The colonel had informed them earlier that evening that this would be their last night and that as a result of their outstanding service they would each receive a bonus of five thousand American dollars come morning. To top it off, the colonel had offered them each a position as "peacekeepers" for some African military dictator who was looking to start an uprising. Six months pay upfront and a guarantee that on this assignment they would get to fire their guns. But Al and Javeed never got the chance. They were both dead before they hit the ground.

Michael had made quick work of the Hiecen laser monitors, quickly patching in a by-pass. He and Simon scrambled over the fifteen-foot wall and pulled the bodies into the woods at the side of the drive. Simon ripped off Al's headset, shaking the blood away. Then he pulled Al's radio from his waist and set it down on the ground next to his knapsack. Simon reached in and pulled out a small black box the size of a paperback book with a speaker and several LEDs. He hadn't used a frequency analyzer/scrambler in years, but it was still pretty basic. He put on Al's blood-encrusted headset and hit a button. The slight static cut out as the radio went into talk mode; it was still working. Simon flipped on the little black box and pulled up its antenna. He hit the talk button again. The black box went into scan mode. After about three seconds, a green LED lit up and the screen displayed the radio's frequency; Simon clipped the box to his belt.

The woods of Finster's estate were thick and dark as pitch. Simon wore a nightscope on his left eye, moving slowly as he scanned back and forth. Michael was right behind, doing his best not to lose sight of Simon. The closer they got to the house, the worse his stomach felt. The bad feeling that had started with his first kill grew with every step. They both held HK MP5s; Simon had taken the liberty of modifying the chamber and installing a silencer on each. They were dual-mode weapons capable of firing either a single shot or, when the trigger was fully depressed, fourteen rounds per second. The priest had spent a good part of the late afternoon and early evening teaching Michael how to use their assortment of weapons. How not to let the machine gun ride up as you shot, how to steady the gun, how to mark your target and not hesitate. The nine-millimeter Glock pistols they each wore contained seventeen rounds per with one in the chamber. Simon didn't waste time teaching Michael the Israeli Galil sniper rifle; it took years of practice to become a marksman. And an expert marksman, that had to be a gift.

The radio squealed in Simon's ear. *"Checkpoint."*

"Alpha," a deep voice said.

"Bravo," came the next.

"Charlie . . . Delta . . . Edward . . . Francis . . . Gary . . ." Each voice was different, each responded in a rehearsed fashion. *"Hooper . . . Isaac . . . Jack . . ."*—there was a brief pause, then—*"Luke . . . Mark . . . Nathan . . . Oscar . . ."*—another pause—*"Quint . . . Richard . . . Steven . . . Thomas."*

A different voice, one with authority, spoke. *"Kevin? Paul? Come back."*

Simon immediately hit the frequency jammer on his belt, two quick hits sending a static signal across the band.

"Come again?"

Simon again hit the jammer, this time intermittently while saying, "Signal problem." Of course it came across the headset as "Sig— . . . lem."

"Hold your position, I'll send someone down."

Simon responded only by hitting the jammer. He grabbed Michael by the arm and they moved toward the road. In the distance they heard a motorcycle start up, its engine kicking in loud. "We've got eighteen, plus whoever is in charge," Simon reported as he took up a position by the side of the road. He pulled out the Galil rifle with its fat high-powered nightscope.

"Nineteen guards," Michael repeated. "And how are we going to get past nineteen?"

Simon screwed the silencer on the end of the barrel and did not answer.

The motorcycle was nearer. Simon lay flat in the grass. He unfolded the buttstock, flipped down the bipod, and attached it one-third back from the muzzle propping up the rifle. The light of the approaching cycle sliced through the trees. He slammed in the twenty-round cartridge and drew a bead on the middle of the road.

"Nineteen," Michael said again.

The whine of the bike was growing louder by the second, its pitch increasing courtesy of the Doppler effect. Simon kept his focus on the road. The glare of the cycle's light lit up the drive in front of them. The biker was almost there. Simon shrugged his shoulders, flexed his fingers, twisted his neck. He put his eye back to the lens piece. The biker was twenty yards off. Going at least sixty. Simon inhaled deep and held his breath. And, without fanfare, he pulled the trigger.

The muted rifle sounded like the pop of a toy gun. The guard slammed backward off the bike, the bullet catching him square in the forehead. He hit the ground, tumbling and cartwheeling like a sack of bones. The bike continued on, veering wildly before crashing out into the woods. The guard ground to a halt just feet from them, his body torn worse than his clothes. Simon wasted no time throwing the rifle over his shoulder and grabbing the corpse. With Michael's help, they dragged it into the woods.

⌘

The smoke hung sour in the air, the stink of cigarettes and other smokables would permeate his clothes for days. Busch hated this scene: the loud music with no coherent lyrics seemed to him the sounds of a pounding rivet factory; the flashing lights left heavy black spots behind his eyes. Was it really that much different when he was younger? He never felt a generation gap like he was feeling right now in this bastard descendant of a German beer hall and Studio 54.

It had been an hour and the silver-haired mogul with the energy of a teenager was still pumping and grinding on the dance floor with his three ladies of the evening. Not a drink, not a rest. The guy had to be flying on something, no one could last that long, moving with that intensity. None of them looked worse for the wear, though, appearing as fresh as when they first arrived.

Busch was tempted to call Michael for an update but was afraid a ringing phone would be a distraction. His sole job tonight was to make sure that Finster didn't leave. As long as he was within the walls of the club, Finster was powerless. Judging by the rapturous dancing, he wasn't going anywhere. Michael and Simon would have all the time they needed. And as he nursed his drink, looking at the beautiful women, Busch thought he may have gotten the easier task of the night.

Finster and the girls continued to dance. Working the crowd. Moving through the dance floor. Pumping everyone up. He occasionally turned to the other dancers, hip-swaying in a seductive way with the gorgeous women of the club. And that was what Busch found so amazing: the women were completely captivated, no one ignored this white-haired guy as he drew closer, all entirely forgot their boyfriends for the moment. Yet no one lashed out, it was like the night owls of Germany held Finster in reverence. Maybe they all hoped that a little bit of his magic would rub off. Busch suddenly realized the source of the billionaire's unending energy: he fed off of this—the envy, the lust, the way they were enamored of his presence.

As the music built to a frenzy, everyone, the dancers, the drinkers, the druggies, all were pulled toward Finster like he was a magnet relentlessly drawing their attention to him. Busch studied this strange quirk in human behavior and for the life of him couldn't figure it out. But he knew one thing. This was what Finster craved; it was a kind of power, one he flexed at will, supremely confident in its strength. He could be the worst kind of cult leader, his charisma pulling in followers by the thousands, making a Jim Jones retreat or any of those fanatical suicide cults seem like a Cub Scout meeting. Perhaps that was how he held sway in business, charming his way through deals, his allure a deceptive knife, a lethal ally in taking down his opposers.

The song reached fever pitch and everyone was drawn, staring from the sidelines and balconies, dancing about Finster as if he was the chief of the tribe. All eyes were upon him, Finster felt them. The bartenders, the DJ, the entire crowd. All eyes except one pair.

Audrey's. She was looking to the bar. Finster followed her gaze as he slowed his dance pace. And that's when he saw Busch. Looking way too obvious among this retro Aryan crowd.

The spell broke within the club, the connection shattered, all went back to their own little worlds. Finster turned to Audrey, who trembled as if she was about to face death, a cold sweat of terror beading upon her beautiful face. He had been tricked, lulled into a false sense of security. Finster needed no introduction to know that the stranger was Paul Busch. What the cop from America was doing here he didn't know, but he certainly wasn't dead and if he wasn't dead, then neither was Michael or that fucking priest.

He would deal with Thal's failure later.

He had to get to his keys.

Audrey flinched as if preparing for a blow, waiting for death. Zoe and Joy continued to dance, not realizing Audrey's terror; their hands were still upon Finster, trying to pull him back into the mood. Cursing, he pushed them away and raced for the exit, shoving any and all from his path. This time there was no parting of the sea as he pushed the dancing throng aside. The wall of people seemed to grow at his approach. His eyes were ablaze; his anger the match that lit a fire of rage. He would pummel anyone in his tracks who obstructed him. He had to get out and get home no matter the cost.

Busch was caught, panic welled within him. He stood frozen at the bar watching his quarry successfully fight his way through the crowd. The music that assaulted his ears only seconds earlier seemed to vanish into deadly silence as he watched his plan unravel before his eyes. If Finster got out the door, there was no possible way Michael and Simon could finish.

⌘

They emerged into the English gardens south of the mansion, the periphery lit up with floodlights. Michael hadn't realized the enormity of the home on his first visit. It was truly vast, stretching out like a primordial beast on the land. The stone facade was etched with the distorted shadows of the manicured topiary. Suddenly he understood the allure of the place to a thing like Finster: not only was it a statement of power, but it was a dare to those who might be foolish enough to attempt to penetrate her.

Simon flipped down the pair of V-shaped legs from the Galil rifle, setting them on a shadowed stone wall. The area seemed deserted. The priest turned on his frequency jammer, cutting all radio signals between the remaining eighteen mercenaries. It would only be a matter of time before they fell into isolation panic, one of those afflictions experienced by soldiers. They needed to be in constant touch with command and, to achieve military precision, they acted only upon direct orders. But when the command fell silent and was thought lost, they became like rudderless ships, spinning in helpless circles, always on the brink of sinking.

Simon swept the scope back and forth, examining the front of the mansion, studying its detail, its windows and doors. His surveillance moved to the second and then the third floor. Something caught his eye. Up on the blue slate roof. Multiple movements. There were three of them. Tucked behind the decorative frieze and low parapets. Snipers. Each tapping their ear, murmuring to one another, probably concerned about the abrupt loss of communication.

Simon set his sight on the one farthest away, the foolish man wearing a white painter's cap, its brim facing backward. It flew off in what could have been mistaken for a breeze if not for the hat's sudden change in color. The bullet had ripped clear through the man's head.

Simon swung the rifle onto the middle sniper, who had turned to see what the noise was. The sniper's eyes registered the death of his comrade just before he joined him. Fortune turned with the third. He was onto the assault, hunkering down behind the stone facade, swinging his rifle back and forth, looking for a target.

It was at that point the other guards began to congregate in front of the mansion. Milling about like cattle, confusion in their movements as they tapped their earpieces and spoke in hushed tones. The sniper saw the men below and leaned over the edge to alert his fellow guards, but he never got a word out. The priest pulled the trigger. The man teetered on the parapet and then fell, his rifle clutched in his hand as he silently spun end over end. The guards below recoiled in shock, scattering and cursing as the body splattered in a broken heap at their feet.

Simon wasted no time. It was total confusion as the routed guards ran for cover, Simon's bullets ripping into the ground and walls. Bodies fell and blood flew.

Word traveled fast, and some obviously had experience in keeping their wits about them. They pinpointed Simon's position from the flame licking out of his barrel. Taking up positions behind cars and walls, they returned fire.

Michael huddled behind the wall as the bullets whizzed overhead, shattering rock, embedding in trees. He understood now the fear of the soldier, the one who became paralyzed, unable to move, unable to return fire. No matter how much basic training a soldier received, you could never tell a man's mettle in battle until he was under fire. Michael glanced over: Simon hadn't flinched, his lethal assault continued. The priest was brutally efficient, like a pitcher in touch with his perfect game. Firing off round after round with deadly precision, his hand sweeping in a new cartridge in perfect rhythm as the spent case ejected to the ground.

Michael's mind kept running to the Knights Templar, warriors for God, the first to attack and the last to retreat during the Crusades. But hadn't it been so all through history—Moses killing Ramses's men with the Red Sea, the knights crusading for Christianity, the Spanish Inquisition? Throughout history hadn't the Church in practice and the Church in preaching seemed diametrically opposed? Yet it was always in the name of God. Always for a perceived greater good. And those who fought for the Church all believed with every fiber of their souls that they were fighting the good fight. Michael saw that fervor in Simon as he slew the men before him. No remorse, no hesitancy. Simon had one objective and one objective only: to regain the keys of his Church.

It was the red dot that caught Michael's eye, unnaturally sweeping back and forth looking for a target in the darkness, like an errant, bright fly seeking a perch. The dot landed on Simon's back, creeping up his neck. Simon was oblivious to his death mark, continuing his attack unaware. Michael's fear washed away. Raising his HK, he fired, the cascade of bullets splintering the woods as he swept his weapon back and forth in the dark direction of the unseen stalker. He emptied his cartridge at the invisible assailant, then slammed a new one in the stock, his nose burning from the acrid cordite smell. The red dot vanished. The smoke cleared; Simon hadn't flinched, his eye still glued to the gun sight, pulling off shot after shot. Eight bodies littered the lawn. "There are probably more," the priest whispered without looking up.

Michael looked to the woods; he had always loved the dark, the way it enveloped him, hugged him, protected him. But now it was protecting others, cloaking them as they lay in wait to kill him. Reluctantly, he checked his gun, then belly-crawled toward the trees.

"Keep track of your kills," Michael heard Simon say as he crept deeper into the shadows.

Keep track of your kills. Sure. Does that include me? Michael thought, as he got to his feet. The lights of the mansion had disappeared behind the trees. Cautiously looking about, he held his gun like Simon had taught him, his knuckles gone white from his clench. He had drawn a line in his mind from the priest to the red beam's point of origin. "One," Michael murmured, as his boot toe touched his first kill.

He leaned down to the body, not knowing what he was looking for, when the tree to his right exploded with gunfire, the flying wood chips slicing his cheek. He tumbled left, taking up position behind a large oak tree, blasting his gun in the general direction of his attacker. His volley was answered with a furious onslaught of gunfire. His arm suddenly burned as a bullet grazed it. He was pinned down and inexperienced. This wasn't his game: he knew alarms and electronics, he was a thief, and way out of his element.

He pressed his back against the tree, hoping its size proved just a slight bit of protection. Simon had taught him how to shoot cans. Small unmoving cans: Pepsi and Coke. These targets were mobile and unseen. And they shot back. He didn't know if others were gathering and if he couldn't fell them here, Simon was surely dead. And that's when he looked up. He slung his rifle over his back. He paused, listening for movement. Hearing nothing, he straightened and started climbing.

⌘

Twelve. Simon felt a strange comfort, something he hadn't felt in years. As quirky as it seemed, he was at home. And while he should have felt conflicted, he didn't; these were men protecting an evil. They were the worst kind of soldier, whose loyalties ran to the highest bidder. He felt no remorse as they fell. He would leave their judgment to the afterlife—if the afterlife existed after tonight.

All the shooting had cleared his mind, forcing his senses to react by instinct. It had been fifteen years since he served in the Italian army but it felt like yesterday. He hadn't come under fire like this but thrice in his life and it energized him; he thrived under pressure. And if this wasn't pressure, the word didn't exist. Throughout it all, he never forgot his vocation, that of a priest. One with a special sanction to protect the Church and its beliefs, at all costs. Each pull of the trigger was accompanied by a simple prayer of praise, for renewal and forgiveness. It was the same prayer he always said when he felled a man. A prayer he had said more times than he could ever count.

He fought to ignore the pain in his right shoulder. The bullet had passed clear through; its heat had partially cauterized the entry wound, but the exit wound was a different matter. He could feel the blood soaking into his shirt. The shooting had stopped, silence all around. His tactic of drawing the guards out had worked. He had eliminated a good portion, but the remaining guards were now at the ready and they were doing the hunting. It was the last few who proved the hardest to kill and it was always the one final opponent that posed the greatest challenge.

⌘

Colonel T. C. Roberts stepped from the house, a solid six feet, his upper body almost as wide. He looked about, seeing the bodies; he had no idea how many were down or how many were left. The blasted radio was out of commission, something was jamming the signal.

No longer in the U.S. Marines, Roberts held on to the title anyway as it immediately established command and respect among his men. Of course, he didn't have the title when he left, having been stripped of it at his court-martial. His treatment of that simpleminded soldier hadn't gone over well with the high command, particularly as he'd meted out punishment up to and including death. The fact that he administered the killing blow to the young Southerner's temple with the butt of his rifle and then blamed it on his sergeant provided him few allies during his trial. But escape from military prison was easy and finding soldiers of fortune easier. Roberts knew of many from his Desert Storm command who just weren't satisfied by that abbreviated fight. They weren't always the most talented soldiers, but they were driven. Driven by a lust beyond money; driven by a lust for blood.

Roberts scratched at the scar along his nose. It ran from his left eye across his bridge to his right cheek and had caused him trouble since his run-in with that drunken street bum two years prior. Of course, the bum hadn't scratched anything since, but Roberts cursed the creep's soul daily for the disfigurement. No one would breach this house, that was a promise he made to Finster and a promise he would keep. He debated notifying him on the cell phone but thought better of it. Get the situation in hand, mitigate the damage, and end the assault. There would be plenty of time for reports later.

He set the house alarm and stood in the opening of the porte cochere looking out at the well-lit grounds. He couldn't see beyond the lights' reach, though, and cursed his men for their stupidity. They might as well have been wearing neon bull's-eyes and blindfolds. Roberts pulled his Colt and in quick succession shot out the lights; one bullet per was all he needed. They exploded in a hail of sparks and winked out. The estate fell dark. He had just equalized the playing field a bit. It was time to turn the tables.

Chapter 31

Busch raced through the dancing crowd, the music pounding in his ear; it was like wading through mud, the progress he was making. The young and the beautiful gave no quarter. They were oblivious to his mounting panic. An occasional few even threw a swing or an elbow at the out-of-place American.

Finster had figured them out and had gotten the jump, shoving all from his path easily as he fought to get out of the murky club and get home. The billionaire had allowed himself to get lost in the moment, enjoying his last night of fun. All the lust, all the greed—he had become just like those he manipulated. And though there was an armed force of twenty-one standing in the way at home, he was certain they could fail. He wasn't about to lose everything he had fought for now. Those keys were his destiny.

Finster had the advantage on the American policeman; he was off the dance floor, only twenty meters to the door. He had lost sight of the cop, not that he was of any consequence. No man had ever really created worry in Finster, he was sublimely confident in himself and his abilities. His only thoughts now were on his keys and keeping them out of the hands of the thief and the priest. Ten meters to the door and he hit a wall. A human wall. Busch was there, all two hundred and sixty pounds of him. "Move!" Finster screamed over the music, his voice the sound of breaking glass.

Busch was silent. He stared at this man who so many held in awe. A man who had created such fear in Michael.

"Do you realize who I am? I'll blind you before you can blink." Finster could barely contain his verbal rage, yet his body remained calm, without motion.

Busch finally saw the man—not his picture, not some televised broadcast, this was Finster up close. There was something frighteningly unnatural about him, a foreboding in his stillness which contrasted oddly with his boiling wrath. He possessed an aura that felt like a repulsive field around him. And it occurred to Busch when he looked into Finster's eyes that they were *wrong*. Like nothing he had ever seen before. He couldn't explain it, but they didn't lie. They weren't the eyes of a man; they were the eyes of evil. Against all logic, Busch finally believed what Michael and Simon had fought so hard to convince him of. Whatever one's religion, this was the embodiment of darkness. But, at this particular moment, he didn't care. "You can't blind me. Not here," Busch replied.

Finster didn't comprehend: he tried to barge straight through Busch. But the giant wasn't about to budge.

"You have no idea where you are," Busch said with confidence.

Finster stepped within inches of Busch's face. "Out of my way before—"

"You're on holy ground." Busch cut him off. "This place"—he waved his hands around—"used to be a church. Consecrated in the name of God. Sanctuary."

Finster looked around, baffled, and began to seethe. Lo and behold, it was a church. The fifteen-foot windows depicted the Stations of the Cross in stunningly detailed stained glass. At the far end, upon a raised platform, was a marble altar on which the DJ spun his music. The seats: old wooden pews. The balcony: a choir loft. The club's shape was now obvious: that of a cross.

"Personally, I think it's sick, but tonight it serves my purpose," Busch said, cracking the beginning of a Cheshire smile.

"Which is?" Finster's anger was finally manifesting itself physically, his face going red, his body quivering.

Busch's arm snapped out, grabbing the older man's arm, squeezing it tightly to emphasize his point. "To keep you here, blind and powerless." Finster struggled but couldn't break Busch's grip. "You're trapped in the one place you have been forbidden to enter . . . and . . . there is no way out for you."

Busch smiled ear to ear. He had beaten the one they said couldn't be beaten.

⌘

Michael was fifty feet up and moving through the trees. His movement was effortless but stealth proved difficult. The control he mustered to remain silent within the flexing branches sapped his energy. He was taking advantage of darkness and the distant gunfire to work his way across the treetops. The wound to his arm was minor; only a little blood seeped from it. Still, his fingertips sore, his feet on the verge of failure, he wondered if he would ever get back to getting the keys before Finster returned home.

The sound of crunching leaves rose up from the forest floor. Michael froze. Moving in the shadows below, he could make out the shape of a man, hunkered on the ground, hiding tree to tree. One of Finster's soldiers. Michael propped himself between two branches, wedging himself silently in place. He drew his rifle off his shoulder and pointed downward. It would have to be the first shot. He needed to preserve his position from any other stalkers. If he gave himself away, he was surely dead; there was no other place to go now that he was up here. Briefly, he debated letting the guy pass and then climbing down. He hadn't realized how compromised he was. Sitting fifty feet up, he'd become a restricted, stationary target.

The man stopped directly below him. Michael braced himself, aimed at the crown of the guard's head.

The guard fell where he stood, the bullet careening downward through his skull, through his throat, through his body. Michael looked about. "Two," he whispered. His personal body count.

He waited a brief moment, then descended. He loved to climb but had gotten so used to brick and stone buildings he had forgotten about the joy of trees from his youth. Terrific handholds, branches for footholds. He thought it would be nice to be a child—then at least he wouldn't be here. He jumped the last eight feet, landing next to the body. He leaned in to check the soldier.

"Don't move." Michael couldn't tell where the voice was coming from. "Hands in the air." Someone behind him removed the rifle from his back. The butt of a gun crashed his head, tumbling him forward. "How many?" the soldier snarled.

Michael said nothing and was rewarded with another blow to the head.

"Answer me, you son of a bitch." The soldier's name was Jax but he never offered it up.

The gun rammed Michael's lower back, sending him crashing to his knees. Sharp pain shot up from his kidneys. Michael lost his breath. He heard the loud metallic ratchet of the rifle being cocked. The soldier jammed the gun in his ear, pressing him in the dirt, the smell of pine needles everywhere.

"You got ten seconds," the mercenary spat.

"OK." Michael's mind was racing. "I'll show you where they are."

"Get up."

It was an effort, but Michael made it to his feet and headed in what he prayed was the right direction. "Got some operation here, my friend," he said, trying to lighten the mood. The soldier said nothing. "Must have a whole army in there, huh?" Michael continued, his arms in the air. The mercenary's footfalls were heavy in his ear. Michael had no doubt that the man would shoot him in the back given the slightest excuse. They emerged in the clearing where Simon had been, but of course, he wasn't there now. The smell of gunfire hung heavy in the air, shells scattered the ground. You could see the scorched rock where Simon's rifle had rested.

"Well?" Jax snapped, suspecting he had been had.

Michael looked about, no idea where his partner in mayhem had gone. He looked toward the darkened mansion, nothing more than a monstrous shadow blotting out the night sky.

"Keep moving." The mercenary jabbed him with the gun barrel in the direction of the house. As they stepped on the drive, others stepped from the shadows. Five of them, armed to the teeth: sidearms and rifles, a survival knife strapped to each of their legs.

"Anyone else?" Jax called out to his comrades.

"Nobody," some buzz-cut soldier shot back. "Figure there was only one?"

"At least two," Jax replied grimly.

Michael couldn't tell who was doing the talking, but none bore the air of a leader. Hope sprang up a little in his heart: at least they didn't have Simon. Then again, the priest could be lying somewhere swimming in his own blood.

"Where's the colonel?" Jax asked.

"Haven't seen him since before the firefight."

"What're you going to do with him?" One of the mercenaries pointed to Michael.

"Squeeze him, find out what he was up to, then use him for target practice." Jax turned to Michael. "So what's so important about this house that you took on twenty-one of us?"

"It's not twenty-one anymore, is it?" Michael retorted. As his face hit the driveway, he regretted the macho statement. He didn't know who hit him, but this time it was more than one. He curled into a ball as the blows rang down. The kicks to his sides were the worst; he could feel the cracked ribs floating about, the pain relived with every excruciating breath. The metallic taste of blood rose in his mouth as he fought to hold on to consciousness. The mercenaries had gathered around him like a pack of ravenous hyenas, laughing and cackling as they took cheap shots at their helpless prey. As Michael barely clung to consciousness, he realized their foolish questions told more about them than they'd ever learn from him.

"How many?"

"Who do you work for?"

"What are you after?"

"Why hit a peaceful businessman?"

They're clueless, thought Michael. These men knew nothing of Finster, thinking him the mild-mannered business mogul. They had no idea what sat below the house. Michael craned his neck upward, defiantly staring at Jax, his interrogator. It was a cold face, lifeless, what little hair the soldier possessed fell in gray wisps about his ears. And his eyes . . . his eyes were a little south of sanity. Michael heard Jax mumble something about a rope and his neck, but it all turned to white noise as he blacked out.

Chapter 32

Busch and Finster were toe to toe, eye to eye. Busch's smile would have done his dentist proud. The entire club was oblivious to their confrontation. The music still pounded, the dancers still gyrated. Busch hadn't succumbed to Simon's beliefs earlier and thought Michael's plan foolish. Yet here he stood, crushing the man's arm and all Finster could do was struggle uselessly.

A panic had overtaken Finster, one that he had never known in all his years. His mind raced, fruitlessly seeking a solution. He had never felt so weak, so powerless. He was trapped in this oppressive place. The images on the stained glass were screaming at his dark heart, the marble walls were closing in. This huge man's smile of contempt was choking the life out of him.

And then it hit him. Finster lifted his slumping head in triumph, stared into Busch's soul . . . and smiled. And then Finster started to boil. Literally. His eyes flickered, rolling back in his head, nothing but the whites showing. His hands trembled and shook, his mouth fell open, slack-jawed, foam forming on his lips. His body began to quiver violently, like a dance bordering on an epileptic seizure. His head snapped back and forth. And then he was down on the floor. Viciously shuddering like a pad of butter on a hot skillet, fists clenched, head thrashing side to side, slamming against the dance floor. People started to take notice, stepping out of the way, making room for what they thought was another overdose.

Busch's eyes went from arrogant triumph to utter fear. He didn't know what to think as Finster spasmed uncontrollably at his feet. A crowd started to gather, forming a circle, some fascinated, some frightened. A woman's scream cut through the music. Busch was shoved out of the way by three burly bouncers who picked up Finster, carrying the spasming man to a couch in one of the grottoes. This was obviously routine to these guys, probably a few went down each night, overdosed, on the verge of death. Their job was to make sure the death didn't happen within the club. They could ill afford the questions of an investigation, what with the forms of recreation partaken of here.

The swelling crowd followed them with morbid curiosity to the lounge, fascinated by the poor sod who so entertained and enraptured them earlier. Here was a celebrity in their midst and maybe, if they were lucky, they could say they saw him die. Busch was shoved back and back, farther from the action.

Quicker than Busch could ever have imagined, a stretcher appeared. The bouncers effortlessly lifted Finster and strapped him to the gurney. The crowd was huge now, nearly half the club crammed around; gaping, they stood twenty deep and Busch was the twenty-first out. He shouted to be let through but what could be heard over the still-pounding music was ignored. He was a powerless American cop in a foreign land; he was working without sanction, authority, or jurisdiction, and he could not have been farther away from Finster as they wheeled him out the door. More bouncers materialized out of nowhere, holding back the curious as the medics made way for the famous stricken industrialist.

Busch fought his way through the sea of people emerging onto the street, past the paparazzi, past the throngs of gawking velvet-rope hopefuls, finally reaching the sidewalk only to watch the taillights of the ambulance, and Finster's limousine right behind it, vanish into the night.

⌘

Michael awoke to carnage. Blood ran in scarlet mini-rivers along the driveway. His body and mind were numb. Unsure if the blood was his own, he dared not move as he recognized the sound of hissing bullets overhead. As his eyes focused, he saw fresh soldiers' bodies strewn about: two down, three remaining. And those three were firing in all directions.

Jax was to Michael's right under cover of a green Peugeot. Wild-eyed, the mercenary was strafing the gardens, his body shaking with the rapid recoil of his assault rifle. One of the soldiers flew back, landing in a heap. Michael heard the last gasps of his breath through the nickel-sized hole in his neck.

"Where is the colonel?" the other guard shouted over the sounds of gunfire.

"Don't know," Michael's captor said.

"A little firefight and he hides? I thought he was supposed to be this brave and glorious leader."

Jax spun about, his gun aimed at his comrade. "Keep your attention on the enemy out there." He pointed into the darkness beyond.

Michael waited silently as the dissension escalated. These men weren't soldiers. They were military rejects, weekend warriors hovering at the very edge of sanity, and they were armed. Simon was somewhere out there, picking them off one by one. As far as Michael was concerned, it wasn't fast enough.

Jax turned to see Michael lying there awake among the corpses, and what few viable brain cells the soldier had started spinning. "Look who's up." He grabbed Michael by the hair, dragging him to his feet.

"Well. I'll be goddamned. . . ." the other guard said, as he stumbled to his feet.

"Shhh." Jax cut him off. "Get down."

"Hey, who made you God?" the guard snapped, as he stood squinting, trying to see into the darkness. A rifle shot cracked from somewhere off in the gloom, the report echoing through the valley. "Shit," was all the soldier said as Michael and Jax watched him fall dead.

⌘

Simon lay behind an old stone water well, his nerves on fire. The hired guns never had a chance, each tumbling to the ground, their lives snuffed out by a single shot to the head. Simon never lost his center, never lost concentration.

By Simon's count, there were only two remaining, the leader and one soldier. The soldier with the gray wisps of hair was still hiding behind the Peugeot, but where the other one was was anyone's guess. Simon scanned the driveway through his rifle scope and found Michael. He stood on wobbly legs behind the Peugeot, badly beaten, his right eye blackening and swelling shut. The wispy-haired guard stood behind him, ramming the barrel of his rifle under Michael's chin. Simon desperately tried to line up a shot but the guard wasn't stupid; he moved Michael to and fro, leaving no room for a clear shot. One hundred yards in a crosswind, at a small, moving target. Simon couldn't take the chance. He moved in fifty yards.

He lay down on the exposed ground, flipped out the rifle's legs, and removed his pistols. He flexed his fingers, working out the kinks. Then he wrapped his right hand around the rifle's stock, snuggling the butt in his left shoulder, slipped his index finger around the trigger, and nestled his eye in the sight. He swept the gun back and forth in infinitesimal amounts, finally settling the crosshairs on the hood of the green French car. He gradually raised his aim, lining up the shot, a spot inches to the left of Michael's right shoulder. The guard's head moved in and out of position for a good second and a half before withdrawing, then, an instant later, passed through the target range once again. Simon judged for the slight wind, drew a bead . . . Counted off . . . Exhaled . . . And began his prayer. As the guard's head began to slide into position, Simon readied his finger.

The foot caught Simon square in the temple; the rifle flew out of his hands, discharging in the woods. He rolled with the impact, instinctively trying to cushion the blow. His skull throbbed as he leaped to his feet. Standing before him was a man with one of the worst scars he had ever seen, dressed as an officer in tan fatigues—of what army was anyone's guess. But it was the confidence of the man that gave Simon pause. This "colonel" was armed with pistols—both hips—yet no weapon in hand. This soldier for hire possessed the confidence to kill, even without the benefit of his guns.

They were squared off, eyeing each other across an invisible barrier. The colonel struck first, a hard spin-kick to the ribs. Simon stumbled backward, but regained his footing just in time to avoid the follow-up. He threw a barrage of punches—all were blocked. It was if his opponent could read his mind. Simon was overmatched and knew it. The assault came in a salvo of kicks and strikes delivered without so much as a breath. Simon was steadily forced backward with each blow, farther away from his own weapons. He came in low, assaulting the colonel's legs and stomach, beginning to make a dent, strain showing in the mercenary's eyes. Simon continued his attack, pouring all his energy into each blow as if it was his last. But like a chess game gone wrong, he realized his bad move too late in the match. The colonel was letting him waste his energy, feigning pain and defeat when in reality he was the constant aggressor. And as Simon realized this, the colonel came back hard, raining down blow after blow.

Simon's body began to weaken and fail. He parried what he could, but the blows were getting in, brutally assaulting his face and gut. He continued backing up, away from his opponent and away from his guns, until he was stopped in his tracks, his back against a wall. He could feel the coolness of the stone at his waist; it was a well; Simon could smell the dampness wafting up from below.

Without warning, the colonel lunged; his hands gripped the priest's throat. Simon tried desperately to pry them off, but his body was spent. He had come up against an adversary who bested him with not only strength but mind and strategy. The colonel leaned his body weight against Simon, bending his back over the lip of the well. Simon could see the depth of the scar, the white calloused skin running deep into the gouged bone. As powerful fingers relentlessly cut off his air, he could hear the throbbing of his pulse mixed with the echoes of pebbles falling deep into the pit over his shoulder, their echoes splashing at least seventy-five feet down. The night grew darker as he felt his world slipping away.

And then the fingers about his neck were gone. As Simon gasped for air, he felt the full weight of the colonel collapse against him. A migraine of proportions he had never known rushed in, as the oxygen returned to his blood. He squeezed out of his wedged position, bewildered and wheezing. The colonel slumped over the lip of the well, a knife in his back.

Michael stood there bruised and bloody, barely managing a smile as Simon slumped to the ground against the cool musty stone. Michael walked up to the colonel and pulled the long knife out of the mercenary's back, the tan fatigues already darkened beyond maroon. Without hesitation, he grabbed the soldier's legs, flipped them up in the air, and the dead weight did the rest, pulling him into the darkness. It was a good five count before the head of Finster's security force hit the water far below.

Simon never asked Michael how he escaped the other guard but he had just gained a new respect for the man he had thought about killing just over a week ago.

Michael sheathed the knife in an ankle holster he'd lifted off one of the dead guards. It was the same knife he used to kill his captor, Jax, the repulsive mercenary who'd played chaperon for the last half hour.

As Michael was being held captive, spun back and forth as a shield, he had heard the single rifle shot. Jax threw Michael to the ground and drove his heel into the back of Michael's neck as he took cover behind the Peugeot. Michael, weak and powerless, looked to the dead bodies for a weapon but could barely move his head under the weight of his captor's heavy black boot. Then he remembered. They all had them. Strapped to their leg. Jax ground his foot into Michael's neck hard, forcing his face into the asphalt drive. Michael reached up, felt the knee, the calf... And there it was. Michael quickly pulled it from its sheath and made three quick slices. The first was up and over, severing Jax's right hamstring and femoral artery; the second drew the blade in the same motion behind the left leg. The wispy-haired guard collapsed as the blood from each leg spewed like a faucet turned to full-bore. Free of the restraint to his neck, Michael made the third and final stroke.

⌘

Busch had never driven over one hundred and twenty mph. Tonight, he didn't drive below it. It had taken him ten minutes to get his car and another five to fight his way out of the Berlin side streets, all the while dialing his cell phone like a man possessed. Every time, it came back with a female German voice that he could only imagine was saying, *"We're sorry, the mobile customer you are trying to reach has traveled out of the coverage area. Please leave a message at the tone."*

Busch had left a message, not knowing if they would ever get it. It was simple: "Get out, get out now! He's coming!!!!"

In a matter of minutes their well-conceived plan had gone to Hell—literally. Busch had no doubt Simon could get past the guards and into the mansion. Michael would snatch back the keys and they'd be at the airport and in the air before anyone was the wiser. All Busch had to do was keep Finster in the nightclub formerly known as a church.

He hit redial. "Come on, come on, come on—"

"Es tut mir—"

"Shit!" Busch slammed the phone closed. Why didn't they have the phone on? He wove in and out of the traffic like a madman, juggling the phone, flashing his lights, laying on the horn. Five kilometers out of the city, he spotted the ambulance at the side of the road, doors ajar, lights still flashing. He didn't need to stop to know that the driver and the medic inside were dead.

Busch had only one thought: Finster was loose, pissed, and headed for home.

Chapter 33

Jeannie Busch was sitting vigil. The drone of the respirator combined with the sterile hospital smell had brought on one of her massive migraines and that was two hours ago. The last minutes of the setting sun painted the little room orange: Jeannie was thankful for any color after staring at the antiseptic white of intensive care for so long.

Mary was in a drug-induced sleep. The medication kept not only the pain at bay but her consciousness as well. Her face had gone pale, bloated from the treatments, her hair a faded memory of its former brilliance. She was withering before Jeannie's eyes; the doctor couldn't give any estimate on how long she had, but it wasn't much. Jeannie knew Mary's greatest fear: she was terrified to die alone. If Michael wasn't here to honor her friend's last wish, she would. Jeannie left the kids with her sister and wouldn't leave until Michael's return, no matter how long.

She had checked with the hotel that Paul had named. Her fear escalated when she was transferred to an over-inquisitive policeman whose line of questioning frightened her. Did she know who her husband was traveling with? Something about gunshots and dead bodies. Did she know where he'd gone? The questions scared her into slamming down the phone. They were supposed to be back by now, that's what Paul had told her. He'd be in and out, promise. As the wife of a policeman, a life she knew so well, she blocked the thoughts from her mind. Mary needed her now.

Mary's heart rate began to climb, the beep of the heart monitor quickened. She started to stir, legs twitching, head pressing back in the pillow. Jeannie saw the rapid eye movement: Mary was dreaming. Mary started to moan, incoherent at first. The sweat began on her brow and spread out from there.

It was a nightmare. And Jeannie knew Mary's nightmares; she had shared her fears with her best friend too often. They always revolved around Michael, his going back to crime and paying the price horribly with his life as Mary helplessly bore witness. Jeannie knew the only way the nightmares ended was when Mary bolted out of the bed, frightened into reality. Jeannie leaned in, taking a moist washcloth, dabbing her forehead. "Shhh," she whispered as if to a child, "it's OK, I'm here for you." She cursed the drugs for imprisoning her friend in her nightmare world.

Mary's body stiffened. Gently, Jeannie took her hand. Her feeling of helplessness grew. She could do nothing to ease her friend's suffering. Mary's head swung side to side as if trying to outrun whatever was haunting her mind. She was trapped in a realm she couldn't escape. Mary had told her that the dream never played through to its conclusion; she always broke out to consciousness at the last moment, to reality, mercifully released from the terror. Tonight, however, Mary would have no choice other than to live the nightmare through, seeing it play out to its devastating conclusion.

Jeannie's life had been linked to Michael and Mary's for years; now, she felt herself crumbling with them. Mary was dying, Michael was in trouble, and now Paul was missing. She loved her husband for his gruffness, the way he lived for his kids, the way he had morals others had abandoned decades ago. She hoped against hope that Paul and Michael were safe but somehow knew that whatever they had to face was still before them.

She watched as Mary's vitals climbed, her body spasming, the sheets soaked in sweat; her dream was cresting. *Please make it.* Jeannie prayed for them all.

⌘

The front door to the mansion swung open. A loud beeping in one-second increments came from somewhere inside.

"Can we hurry it up?" Simon whispered.

"Relax. I've got sixty seconds."

"Fifty-eight now."

Michael stepped into the foyer; all lights were out, the house was as dark as dark could be. He flipped on his penlight, opened up the mahogany closet near the doorway, and whipped out his knife. He threw aside the vast collection of coats, revealing a smooth white security box, and stared at the readout: counting down from forty-five in glowing red lights. There was no keypad, only a magnetic card-swipe slot. And Michael had no card. "OK," Michael said.

"OK, what?" Simon called, over his shoulder.

Michael paused, exhaling a great gasp of air. He had thirty-eight seconds. "See, this is—"

"Don't explain." Simon cut him off. The last thing they needed was a local police drive-by. Twenty-one dead bodies would be hard to hide and even harder to explain. The place would swarm with law enforcement, leaving them no way out.

Michael focused, stuck his penlight in his mouth, twirled his knife, and slid it behind the alarm panel. He pried off the cover and stared. The host of wires looked more like a plate of spaghetti than a security system. Twenty-nine seconds. The beeps were now coming in double-time.

He pulled from his pocket a pair of wires with alligator clips. He thumbed through the twenty-odd wires searching—there was never really a blue wire and a red wire—this system was coded, each color bearing an individual number that matched to a codex. The odds on finding the correct wires were three hundred and eighty to one. Unfortunately, they were a little short on time. Nineteen seconds. The beeps sounded like a drumroll now. Michael just stared, lost in thought.

"Uh, not that we are in a hurry or anything," Simon reminded him. There was a hint of nerves in his voice.

Nine seconds. If only he had an hour . . . maybe he could crack this. And then he found his solution. He traced out the wires to the timing display, following their jumble of a run through the box to a small black chip. He clamped on one of the alligators. Four seconds.

"We don't have all day." Simon's stress was worse now than when he was under fire.

"Actually"—Michael paused as he clipped on the other alligator clip—"we do."

The readout flashed and where it had previously read two seconds, it now counted down from ten hours. "When you can't reset the alarm, reset the clock," Michael explained, with a sigh of relief.

He led Simon into the heart of the mansion. As they moved deeper into the house past the entrance hall and library, faint light filtered in from the side rooms and stairwells. It wasn't much but it allowed them to avoid using their flashlights. Michael wasted no time staring into the various rooms; everything carried a different meaning this time. Before he'd felt wonder and amazement at the vast wealth possessed by the man who owned these rooms, but now . . . he felt nothing but disgust.

They finally reached the enormous old wooden door. It stood slightly ajar. Michael wrapped his hand around the large black iron handle. The screech of the hinges as they protested were worse than any alarm. Simon spun about, gun at the ready, braced for someone to come running at the sound.

The rank smell floated up from the stone recesses, instantly assaulting their senses, reigniting Michael's fear. Simon took point, his pistol waist-high as they were swallowed by the darkness. They left their flashlights off so as not to make an easy target, but at the expense of traveling the two hundred feet down blind with nothing but slippery stone and a splintered handrail to guide them. Deeper into the earth they traveled, down the moss-covered stairs. Michael couldn't help remembering the parallels between this place and the lowermost cells of the German prison: an intangible menace hung in the air of both.

They hit the bottom step, coming out onto the hard-packed dirt floor. There was no more handrail to lead them as they searched for direction. They stood there momentarily, the inky blackness like a mask over their eyes, the smell running to something south of decay.

"How about some light—" Michael started to say before Simon tackled him violently to the ground.

The shot came out of nowhere, an explosive crack stabbing their ears as it echoed off the damp stone walls. They hunkered down, unsure of their bearings or the location of the guard they never expected to find here.

"I'm going to roll right. Try to draw his fire," Simon whispered from the darkness.

"Gee, thanks."

Simon silently scooted away, leaving Michael alone in the place that had caused him such nightmares. *Draw his fire. Great.*

He crept back up several steps, groping along the wall for a shelf. His fingers sunk into an area six feet up, where the mortar had grown soft. Quietly, he dug in with his knife, clearing a recess, then he jammed the butt of his penlight in. It was high and away as a target—the same trick he used with Simon in the graveyard. It was all a matter of perspective, sleight of hand, magic; make them see what you want them to see.

Ducking low, he reached up, flicking on the penlight, its naked, narrow glow falling upon the host of immoral artifacts. He kept his body out of the light's wash but before he could take a step, gunfire exploded again. Five shots in rapid succession, seemingly from all directions.

The flashlight shattered. Suffocating darkness descended. The silence that followed was maddening. And there was no sign of Simon. A faint scratching came from deeper within the hold. Drawing on what memory he could conjure up, Michael edged into the room. He held his Glock before him, heading in the direction of the soft, scratching sounds. They seemed to be low and near the ground, nails against stone. With each step, a new sound emerged from the blackness. A slow gurgling wheeze, like someone trying to breathe through a shallow puddle, was right in front of him. Michael swiftly crouched. Leading with his gun, he poked the darkness. An arm's length in front of him the barrel abutted something soft, frail. The breaths were shallow and weak. Michael searched about, felt a head, and rested his gun on the ground. His fingers kept exploring: the hair was fine, almost brittle; the skin, paper thin. A hand clutched Michael's shoulder from behind, startling him. The priest flipped on his flashlight and found Michael crouched down next to the body of a man, well past ninety.

Michael glanced up. "He was just an old man."

Simon lowered his pistol. "Who is he?"

"Charles . . . Finster's butler" was all Michael could say as the elderly man let out his final, shallow breath.

Simon stood over the corpse, blessed himself, and said a quick prayer for the dead. The irony wasn't lost on Michael that Simon was rendering last rites to someone he had just murdered.

They stepped away, walking deeper into the gallery. The shadows hung heavy, the musty stench of decay everywhere. As he shined his light across the room, Simon was stunned by what he saw. A mother screamed in anguish as she clutched her blood-soaked children. A warlord disemboweled those who cowered in surrender. Tapestries glorified death; canvases depicted decaying bodies, their souls crying out for release; mankind ruthlessly subjugated by evil. Thousands of pieces of art, each more terrible than the one before. It was as if he had crossed into Hell itself.

The thought entered Simon's mind that before they left this hole in the world it all must be destroyed. This was not art; this was something far worse than anything he had ever seen or imagined. No eye should ever be cast upon this collection again; these horrific pieces had all been created by man, not by evil gods or Satan. These were wrought by the hands of artists possessed by thoughts Simon could never comprehend.

"Hurry up!" Michael insisted as he continued through the gallery. He stole a quick glance at the light licking up the walls; the dark rock tinged with a natural rust gave the sense of blood dripping downward. The stalactites, barely visible in the ceiling, hung like daggers ready to fall upon them. "I'm not staying in here any longer than I have to."

Simon tore himself away and followed, but was drawn back by the last painting in the lineup. It rested up ahead, near the door, propped up against a stack of others. Four feet high and wide, it stood out among the rest, incongruous in its presence. The one shining piece of light among the darkness. The beautifully rendered Gates of Heaven. Simon stared at it reverently, reminded that there was always hope, no matter how grave the situation. And he was reminded . . .

Finster wasn't concerned about gaining a soul here or there, he wanted it all, he wanted the land from whence he was cast out before time began. Simon seethed, gaining new focus, and charged down the corridor.

Michael stood at the key-chamber door; the gleaming wood was ebony, polished to a high oily sheen, six feet high, the low sill compelling you to duck. He made easy work of the ancient lock, and grabbed the rusted iron ring for a handle. As Michael pulled the creaking door open, Simon shined in his light.

Upon the central stone pedestal in the small crypt, the two keys sat upon a blood-red pillow, looking as plain and harmless as they did on the day Michael stole them. The simple carved box that had held them was set aside on a stone shelf next to hundreds of candles, most burned down to their nubs. Michael felt a surge of hope. For the first time, he was close to righting the wrong that so endangered his wife.

The two men stood on either side of the pedestal; the room was so confined, their backs nearly touched the walls. Michael looked about the pedestal, checking for alarms or traps, running his fingertips along the stone base and wood column, up to and then under the red pillow. All clear. As he stood, a slight flashing caught his eye. He looked at Simon and then at the cell phone at his waist. The tiny green message light was blinking. Simon flipped it open, the display glowed: *1 message, 19 missed calls. No signal.* Busch was the only one with the number.

They may have been two hundred feet below the ground, with thousands of tons of dirt and rock over their heads, but the thundering noise made its way down into the bowels of the earth nonetheless. It was like the crash of a military jet slamming into a mountainside, concussive and threateningly low. The soil and stone literally shook out of the ceiling, crashing in a choking mist about them. They were sure the world would collapse at any second.

⌘

The enormous front door blew off its hinges and landed on the main stairs, the force of the blow instantly collapsing the grand flight of steps into a pile of splintered scrap. Finster, in an absolute fury, flew through the house. It was as if an invisible wave preceded him: the wooden walls fluttered and distended like a balloon around him, the pictures crashed down, statuary tumbled to the floor. Anything caught in his way was destroyed.

Five minutes into his ambulance ride, he had come fully to his senses. He had never been so utterly fooled, done in by his lust, vanity, and greed. It would never happen again, he swore. To the shock of the attending medic, he ripped off his gurney restraints, flung open the rear door, and leaped from the ambulance as it sped down the autobahn. His chauffeur, attuned to the situation, had trailed the emergency vehicle, watching with a smile as Finster flew out onto the road. Closer than a hairbreadth, the driver swerved around the cartwheeling body. Then he sped alongside the ambulance and broadsided it with the limo, forcing its terrified driver to the side of the road. Finster rose from the ground and dusted himself off.

It wasn't Finster who took out the medics; the chauffeur did the deed. The two EMTs died with countless questions swirling in their heads about their last pickup.

As the limo tore through the gates, ripping them from their stone moorings, Finster saw the first two victims. He had underestimated Michael and the priest and overestimated his little mercenary outfit. His years as a powerful industrialist had made him forget the power of a man facing death. And the even stronger will of a man trying to save the one he loves. As the limo reached the top of the drive, the carnage was laid out before him. Dead soldiers everywhere, the blood splattered about as if by a paintbrush. His wrath grew exponentially, escalating with each stride toward the house; his pent-up fury finally exploded forth as he blasted into the stone mansion, destroying the front doors in his way.

Within seconds he was at the cellar door, tearing it from its hinges. He descended the stairs in a flash; there was no need for light, he knew the way by heart. He was home.

⌘

Finster, stalking, more animal than human, moved through his gallery, his back hunched over, his footfalls silent, looking about cautiously as he faintly sniffed the air. He sensed something off to the right, behind the stack of Russian warfare paintings, but passed it by. He loved the hunt, the way you seek and flush out your quarry, toying with them, allowing them to believe they were smarter, that they could deceive you, when in fact they were hopelessly trapped.

He continued through the darkness toward the door of the key chamber, passing the Gates of Heaven painting: his motivator. The picture had driven him, kept him focused on his goal, like a prisoner who kept a photograph of the mountains taped to his cell wall to remind him to stay attuned to freedom. The painting gave him something to strive for, it almost gave him hope. No one would take that from him and anyone who dared try would pay the price. He took the rusted door ring in his cold hand and pulled, the black door reluctantly creaking open.

Without warning, he spun about, reaching out violently with his left hand, seizing the night. The room started to shake, the air became charged; blue sparks erupted out of the blackness. Statues toppled, pictures crashed to the ground; the seemingly inanimate room came suddenly alive with confusion and mayhem. Out of the darkness, two bodies rose: Simon and Michael. Floating upward carried on an unseen wind. Higher and higher, twenty feet up, until they were crushed to the cavern's ceiling, dangerously close to the razor-sharp stalactites. Hands and legs splayed out, the two men were pressed upward, as if gravity had somehow reversed itself. With a flash, the weapons that each carried flew from their bodies. Guns, knives, all tumbled to the ground.

"Why?" Finster raged. "Did you really think you could beat ME?" He stepped beneath them, looking upward, guiding them with his hand like helpless puppets on an invisible string.

Where doubt had swirled in Michael's head about the true identity of his former employer, utter and complete fear now took up permanent residence. He saw candles and torches coming to life, igniting spontaneously all about the perimeter of the cavern, illuminating everything. He had not known the depth of depraved art that Finster had amassed: tenfold to what he had previously glimpsed, all lit eerily by the orange glow of the torches. Bigger than a football field, the area below him held a sea of artifacts, stretching out as far as the light carried, filling the largest cavern that anyone had ever witnessed. The ceiling undulated wildly, the stalactites pierced the shadows like teeth from the mouth of a beast. Finster paced below. His custom-made clothes tattered and torn, his posture a coiled spring. Even at a distance, Michael could see his eyes had gone red, deep and menacing as they reflected the candle flames.

"Give me what is mine!" Finster bellowed. "Give——me——my——*keys!*"

Simon was in obvious pain, the side of his face sliced by a stalactite, the blood pooling on his cheek before falling like rain to the earthen floor below. But his eyes never conveyed fear as he struggled against the invisible hand. "They never were *your* keys," he spat.

"They are now, priest! As is everything that goes along with them. Now, give my keys to me before I rip out your hearts."

Michael's face was contorted in agony as he breathlessly uttered, "You . . . made . . . a promise." Simon looked to Michael, confused by his statement. "You said you never break a deal."

"Point?" Finster sneered.

"You promised me no harm."

And Finster smiled. "Aren't we the wise one? Such foresight." He looked to Simon. "I'm afraid you don't have a similar arrangement." Simon was crushed further into the ceiling, the air forced from his lungs, an invisible vise about his chest.

"Now, give them back," Finster growled, his voice holding but a fraction of its former timbre and elegance. He stalked away, but paused before the key chamber door. Turning back, he sneered: "You are right, Michael. I did promise I would not harm you, but that is why *he* works for me. I don't recall *him* making any such promise."

Down the shadowy stairs came Finster's driver, the one who'd picked him up off the highway. A pistol in his left hand, the same gun used to kill the paramedics.

Dennis Thal was finally going to redeem himself in the eyes of his boss.

⌘

He had arrived earlier that night. Finster was standing in his library enjoying the joys of Joy; the billionaire said not a word when he entered, only stared at Thal for his apparent failure. Thal had never imagined that it was this renowned billionaire who had pulled his strings, who was the mysterious voice giving orders over the phone. Finster's eyes intimidated the assassin so much that Thal couldn't verbalize his failure for fear that he would be dead before the final words left his lips.

And so Thal said the only thing he could think of that would prolong his life: "They are dead."

Finster's eyes softened as he heard this. The last real obstacle to his success—Michael St. Pierre and that madman priest—had been removed. But he still was the consummate businessman, cautious and shrewd. He would leave no room for error. He'd armed and protected his home with every resource, every man he had at his disposal. All of his private army including his driver were mobilized for the continued protection of his keys. To this end, Finster ordered Thal to be his chauffeur for the evening.

As Thal guided the limo through the night with Finster and his gaggle of cackling golddiggers in the back, he waited for the bullet to shatter the back of his skull. The shot never came. He thought the blatant lie about succeeding in the assassination had been written on his face: he was certain he would be found out. For two hours, he had waited outside the dance club, wondering how Finster might carry out his demise when the truth was learned. But as the time passed, he convinced himself that Finster would never learn the truth, or maybe . . . Maybe he would kill Finster.

His schemes were interrupted when his commander in chief was carried out on a stretcher. Thal raced to the limo and followed. When Finster tumbled out of the rear of the ambulance, Thal selfishly wrote the man off as dead, rammed into the emergency vehicle, and exacted vengeance on the two paramedics with a bullet each. He turned from the carnage to see Finster rising from the road, dusting himself off, not a scratch on him. That's when Thal realized there was far more to his employer than he could ever have imagined. His thoughts raced as they sped through the gates to the estate, as he saw the bodies littering the property. When the doors blew off their hinges with a mere flick of Finster's wrist—well, Thal was ever so enamored of his employer.

⌘

Thal stood looking up at the two men crushed high overhead against the cavernous ceiling; he knew at last whose bidding he had been doing these last five years. No fear arose in his loins; his heart didn't miss a beat.

"You'll be stopped," Simon said. The priest was flattened to the ceiling, his face flushed crimson, the tendons in his neck distended. It was hard to tell if it was the grinding of his body against the rock or the grinding of his bones that echoed about. "You can't—"

"Of course." Finster humored him as he pushed open the door to the key chamber.

"You can't steal Heaven," Simon gasped.

"I already have. Now put my keys ba—"

Finster stopped mid-sentence, the creaking door of the chamber opened to its fullest extent, flames flickering in the darkened vault. He stared in. A glint on the crimson pillow caught his eye. He cocked his head, squinting. A smile of triumph painted his face.

And with that, Simon and Michael fell from the cavern's ceiling, tumbling two stories to the earthen floor below.

Finster was mesmerized by his keys: the thieves hadn't gotten them after all, they'd been interrupted mid-crime. He straightened. Standing tall, palms to his temples, he pushed back his long white hair, regaining his former composure. "Take them out of here," he said to Thal without even turning to glance at the bodies of the two men who had opposed him, his triumphant voice again mellifluous like a song, "and do that which you do best."

Chapter 34

Thal marched Simon and Michael out the front door, guns at their backs, past the fallen soldiers on the driveway, to the black stretch limo. The two men were bruised and bloody, their dazed minds still refusing to come to grips with the terrible power they had just witnessed.

Thal pulled out two pairs of cuffs, secured their hands behind their backs, opened the front passenger door, and pushed them in. He got behind the wheel of the still-running vehicle, his gun pointed at Simon's head. He drove off into the night, past the vast gardens and towering stone walls, off the driveway, and across the field. The high beams cut through the dark, until they finally came to a stop twenty feet in front of the old well.

Thal stepped from the vehicle, ripped open the passenger door, reached in, and violently tore Michael out by his hair. He threw Michael against the stone structure where he collapsed in the blinding light of the car's headlights, illuminated as if on stage. Thal returned to the car and was back in seconds, a nasty-looking knife held to Simon's throat.

"Never killed a priest before." Thal threw Simon down on the ground face-first, the priest putting up no struggle, his body still weakened from Finster's assault.

It was brighter than daylight under the car's fierce halogen beams, the shadows falling long and severe. It was as if they were in a bright operating theater surrounded by an audience of darkness. Thal tucked his gun in his waistband and laid out on the dew-soaked grass a vile assortment of knives: serrated and butterfly, fillet, scallop, and bone. A collection that would look natural in a butcher shop, but in this arena had a much different, much more evil purpose.

"Have you ever witnessed the removal of flesh from a freshly killed deer?" Thal asked Michael matter-of-factly.

Michael, his voice lost in his throat, helplessly stared.

"No? Well, now you will know what to expect." Thal picked up the fillet knife. "This blade is the sharpest of the bunch. Cuts through skin like silk. It's so sharp you barely feel it as it does its job. You're only aware of your missing flesh when the cool air hits those freshly exposed nerves." Thal pressed his knee to the back of Simon's head, completely immobilizing him. "So, I heard that story about your mom and it really inspired me."

"Save your soul," Simon mumbled, his face crushed into the grass.

"Is that a standard line they teach you at the seminary?"

"You are in league—"

"Oh, boy. Here we go. Hallelujah, amen, Lord Jesus, save me Lord, et cetera, et cetera . . ." Thal rolled his eyes. "Spare me. Will ya? You're hurting my concentration." With the experience of a surgeon, he sliced the shirt from Simon's back.

Michael struggled against the stone of the well, moans coming from deep within his chest.

"This particular knife is an artisan's blade, held delicately, like a paintbrush, between the thumb, forefinger, and middle finger." Thal demonstrated.

An odd thing caught Michael's eye. Thal's pinky and ring finger stuck out abnormally, not curling under as they should. He hadn't noticed it before, but now . . . His heart sank even lower. He had seen these tools before. He remembered that night. He remembered his own knife, how it had dug into his shoulder, into the bone, how he'd been dragged across the floor of an art studio by a maniac. How the pain stayed with him to this day, flaring up with the changing weather. And he remembered it was the first time he wanted to kill someone, a creature so vile, so disgusting, a man who had been poised to perform inhuman acts on a woman.

"How's the shoulder?" Thal smiled.

Everything came flooding into Michael's mind. Who Thal really was . . . How Finster had heard of Michael and his skills . . . Why Thal despised him from the day they met.

The tools that were laid out on the grass before him now were the same tools on the windowsill of a Fifth Avenue apartment five and a half years before. It was Dennis Thal who had assaulted Helen Staten, prepared to perform some heinous act upon her naked body. Thal was the reason Michael had aborted his escape from the Akbiquestan Embassy. He was the man whom Michael fought in Helen Staten's apartment. And he was the reason that Michael was caught and sent to prison.

"You can see why you interest me so," Thal said cheerfully as he set back to work. "This will only be practice, give you a little taste of things to come. Anticipation is so much greater than realization, don't you think? I have contemplated the designs for your demise for some time now. I had hoped when I recommended you to Finster to steal the keys that I would be rewarded in the end. You will be my Sistine Chapel."

Bound, Michael squirmed helplessly against the well; bile flooded his throat.

"Please, sit still," Thal admonished. "You might startle me. If you do, my hand could slip, plunging this metal beauty into the heart of your friend."

Simon buried his mind deep down, cutting himself off from all sensation. His mind swirled with images of his father performing this same horrible act on his mother. She had endured her fate without any training, without the hardened mind brought on by the military. His respect grew for what she suffered, for now he was about to endure the same fate. The rape of his soul.

Thal was lost in concentration, hunched over Simon, poised to cut flesh from muscle. He was living completely in the moment—and that was his downfall. He never heard the whistle of the foot cutting through the air, never saw the giant shadow of the enraged man.

The steel-shanked toe of the boot caught Thal square in the ear. The force of the blow sent him sprawling, his body sliding in the slick grass. Blood poured from his ear. He couldn't hold a coherent thought but this much he did know: the giant silhouette was killing him. With the adrenaline-induced energy of a cornered animal, Thal leaped to his feet; his hand snapped to his waist. But quick as he was, he wasn't quick enough. The two policemen, the parole officer and the assassin, locked eyes. Each held a gun—leveled directly at the other. It was a Mexican standoff.

"A little out of your jurisdiction," Thal sneered.

"This has nothing to do with the law." Busch's Sig Sauer pointed at Thal without wavering.

For the second time in Thal's life he came face to face with fear, real shake-your-hand-drop-you-into-oblivion fear. It ran from his feet through his heart and landed square in his eyes. Thal fed off the fright he induced in others, a delicacy to his senses, but until this moment had never experienced it for himself. And it was crippling, his legs reduced to Jell-O, his mind jumbled. He did the only thing he could think of. He dove left, simultaneously rapid-firing his pistol.

Busch drop-rolled, returning fire shot for shot. Thal disappeared into the darkness beyond the headlights. Michael and Simon were sitting ducks, painted, handcuffed targets for Thal, and Busch would have none of that. The big cop grabbed his friend and pulled him into the shadows behind the well. Then he ran back into the blinding light of the car, racing for Simon. When the bullets erupted behind him, tearing up the ground at his feet, Busch didn't stop, dive-rolling and rising. He grabbed the priest by the legs and dragged him through the onslaught of Thal's gunfire.

Back in the shadows, Busch tucked Simon up against the well wall. He turned and grabbed the cuffs behind Michael's back. He held the cuff chain against the stone of the well, and ordered: "Don't even breathe." Busch placed the barrel of his gun to the cuff chain and fired, pulverizing it. In short order, Simon's cuffs were also shattered. "Stay here," Busch growled, before heading back into the darkness.

⌘

Busch crept through the field, holding tight to the darkness. The night was silent but for the low drone of the idling limo. If he could get to the driver's seat, he could drive around, grab his friends, and fly out of here. Even if Thal shot out the tires, they could put enough distance between them and their assailant to make it to safety. Busch worked his way behind the black car, mindful of the fact that he could be shot dead at any moment. His mind was a bundle of confusion. There was no coincidence in Thal's involvement with him or with Finster. Busch's instinct always served him well: now, he regretted turning a deaf ear when it had warned him about Dennis Thal. There would be no hesitation this time, no words of venom. He would shoot Thal dead in his tracks, law be damned.

Gunfire ripped into the front of the limo, puncturing the metal body. Busch was pinned down, five shots left in his clip, but that wouldn't matter if Thal succeeded in hitting him. He raced for and tore open the driver's side door.

The bullet ripped into his right shoulder, his arm falling dead at his side as the force of the impact spun him against the car. Busch lost his footing on the grass and tumbled. His left hand scrambled for his gun. He clawed the grass, ignoring the pain in his arm, his pistol almost in reach . . .

The booted foot came down hard, two of his fingers instantly on fire, their bones cracking under the brutal impact. Thal crouched down, picked up Busch's gun, then hurled it into the darkness.

"Hello, Peaches." Blood cascaded from Thal's ear. "Mistakes, mistakes, mistakes. Some easily overlooked, some fatal. What happened to the law?" he taunted Busch. "Remember the law, your law? No compromising, no way around it?"

The accusation stung Busch as much as the pain wracked his

body. He was still a cop. And although Thal accused him of forsaking his code of the law, he had not. He had merely set the law upon a shelf, while a higher law stepped in, one of friendship and loyalty. Moral compromise. Sometimes there were circumstances, and sometimes one had the power and the need to turn a blind eye while life took a temporary turn. But always there was a price to pay.

Grinding his foot deeper into Busch's hand, the taillights carving bloodred shadows upon his face, Thal slammed a new cartridge in his pistol and chambered a round. He aimed square at the head of the man he had grown to despise, and smiled. "Your wife's death will be as slow as yours is quick."

Busch's face went white as his worst fears were upon him.

Thal gripped the gun with two hands, steadying his aim. He wouldn't miss.

And then, all at once, the wind was crushed out of Thal like a deflating balloon. He crashed backward into the limo with no time to recover, no time to shield himself from the second and third blows. Michael and Simon were upon him, moving with a blinding speed, and then, just as swiftly as they had struck, they backed away.

Thal could barely stand. His gun gone, his body grievously injured. For the second time that endless night, he waited for death to come from a gunshot. But it didn't. They just stood there staring at him, Busch, Simon, and Michael, not moving, not making a sound, watching, waiting. Thal didn't know what to make of them. But he couldn't breathe. He didn't know why. He clutched his stomach. And his hand came away sticky, oily. In a blur of memories, faces of all of his victims came back to him. Helen Staten, James Staten, the women, the men, dozens of victims, all silently staring, mutely bearing witness to his demise.

He hadn't felt the incision—the scalpel was that sharp—he never even saw Simon actually make the cuts, but he did feel his intestines spill out; they slipped through his fingers like a greased eel, as he desperately tried to hold them in his body. They poured out of his sliced belly onto the midnight grass. He scooped at them, trying in vain to force them back into his vacant cavity. He staggered and fell. Then the cold tendrils of death wrapped themselves about him.

And he died.

Chapter 35

Finster's shadow danced on the wall of the small private chamber; the remaining candles were reaching the end of their life. He was again a calm, reserved man of culture admiring his keys upon their pillow. His momentary fears of failure put to rest, he had possession of them now and he would soon be going home.

Despite what he had said, he had never taken the time to admire his prize but for that first night he acquired it. In fact, he could care less what the keys looked like, it was what they stood for that really mattered. But his ego stepped in and his vanity forced him to gloat. He stood there reverently staring; nothing stood in his way any longer.

Out in the gallery, in the section dedicated to the Hindu god Kali, tucked in the corner behind the stacked paintings, the red glow of a timer ticked digitally down toward zero. There were five timers scattered about the cavern set to go off in thirty-second increments. Incendiary bombs, compact but powerful—flame-bringers. They were not concussive devises but rather chemical sprayers. When activated they would pop up in the air ten feet and spew out a sticky gel-like substance that would ignite instantly upon contact with the air.

Finster paid no attention to the popping sound beyond the heavy black door nor the whoosh of what he was sure was fire. Instead, he stepped around the pedestal and leaned in closely, as if he was studying the keys' details for the first time. His leather shoes crunched the earthen floor, as he circled around and around. A loud hiss came from under the door; the air was being sucked out of the small chamber in giant gulps to feed the growing inferno in the cavern. The last few candles about the key chamber started to burn out from lack of oxygen. Only a few remained to light his trophy, their glow reflecting off the precious metal. And to illuminate Finster's baffled face.

Something was not right. And it wasn't what was beyond the door that concerned him. Michael and Simon had come within moments of success. Men so driven would never give up, never surrender. Michael's love for his wife was as strong as anything Finster had ever seen but then why did he relent, giving up so easily, unless . . .

Finster looked closer. Hesitantly, he reached out for the silver key, well aware he was forbidden to come in direct contact with that which is holy. His fingers moved nearer. It was the only way to be sure. The only true test. With a sudden overcoming of fear, his hand covered the keys. And that's when it happened. He exploded, a whirlwind of anger. He screamed at the top of his lungs—not in pain but in anger. In furious recognition that he'd been tricked. For on the gold key, worn down by time but still visible, was an engraving stamp, subtle, damning: *585*.

Finster spun about and tore open the door. He was met by a whirling fireball, pluming upward, its flaming tendrils lashing back down from the ceiling. The entire cavern was engulfed. The canvas of the paintings had ignited, filling the room with an oily black mushroom cloud; waves of heat melted metal sculptures. The last of the incendiary bombs exploded, its napalm-like gel spewing out, torching anything it touched. The flame's roar was deafening, but that was nothing compared to the inhuman shriek from Finster's lips.

Chapter 36

Busch was a mess. Simon and Michael had wrapped his hand and patched his shoulder. He was propped uncomfortably upon the hood of the limo but as far as he was concerned, things were just fine. He would live to see another day.

"Hmph, you did get 'em." Busch's voice was barely above a whisper.

Simon nodded, admiring the keys he held reverently in his palm, as if they were made of glass and might shatter if he breathed on them.

"So simple . . ."

"Yeah."

"Gentlemen, we've got to fly," Michael interrupted.

But Busch continued to stare at the keys. He couldn't help himself. "May I?"

Very, very gently, Simon placed them in his hand. They were larger than Busch had thought they would be and not as dramatic. As he held them, he expected to be enlightened, filled with the Lord, so to speak, but that didn't happen. Instead, he was filled with wonder and amazement that two objects so small in the scheme of things could mean so much. Michael had risked his freedom, his life—everything—to return these two pieces of shaped metal. And what struck Busch was not their symbolism but the power of the heart that they inspired. A belief in the intangible, one so powerful that men were willing to go to war for it, die for it, to sacrifice everything on the conviction of a promise. It was a miracle, a miracle of faith, one that he understood well but until this moment had not truly experienced. And because of it, everything would somehow be all right, he felt it.

"Let's go, guys." Michael's impatience was growing.

Busch handed the keys back to Simon, who wrapped them up tightly in a velvet cloth before placing them in his pocket. A quiet relief washed over Busch. Despite the odds, he and Michael were going home.

The library's French doors crashed open. Flames exploded outward. The enormous stone house had become an inferno. Windows shattered from the heat, spewing smoke and flame, lighting up the night. A figure burst from the firestorm and raced toward them. Like some dark feral beast, it crossed the two hundred yards in seconds.

"You'll return nothing!" The voice bellowed from everywhere. And before they could react, he was standing there right in front of them, his clothes nothing but ash, an odd contrast with his skin, which was pure and unwrinkled, not a burn or blemish, impossible for someone who just came through a twelve-hundred-degree blaze.

Michael stepped forward, his body braced for an attack. "What makes you think—"

But before he could finish, Finster flicked his wrist and sent him sprawling. "I will visit upon you suffering that you could never imagine—"

"You gave me your word," Michael moaned from the ground.

"I wasn't talking to you." Finster had turned to Busch. "No. More. Sanctuary," he roared at the wounded policeman.

Busch recoiled, trying desperately to get away. He tumbled off the car's hood, his injured shoulder breaking like a thousand shards of glass as he collapsed to the ground, paralyzed. He refused to make a sound but in his mind he let out a bloodcurdling scream. His nightmare had become real: he was burning up; his skin felt afire, yet there was no flame. He was back on the boat—his father's boat—the flames dancing about the deck, racing up his legs, licking greedily at his torso. He was once again a helpless child, powerless against the monster. The agony was unbearable as he writhed in the grass.

"Stop!" Michael shouted, scrambling to his feet.

"Give me the keys!" Finster bore down on Michael, his voice as deadly as the blaze that now engulfed his stone mansion.

Finster's eyes were cold, dead, black like the deepest end of the ocean. Michael was filled with a fear he had never imagined possible, a fear not just for him or Mary, but for Busch, for Simon, for everyone. He turned to Simon, bewildered and looking for answers. The priest shook his head emphatically at Michael.

"Hand them over or I will bring suffering to everyone you know and love," Finster snarled.

"Never!" Simon shouted.

Helplessly, Michael watched Busch thrash about in the moist

grass, slapping at his own face, hugging his big body, desperately attempting to put out the invisible flames.

"No! Stop!" Michael screamed, unable to bear the big policeman's suffering. "If I give them to you, do you promise to stop this? Do you promise that you will not bring suffering to anyone—"

"I will not!" Finster roared.

Michael's heartfelt whisper was barely audible. "Then no deal," he said, knowing that with his words he was sealing the death of his best friend.

Busch fought to speak. "Michael! Don't deal with him."

"THE KEYS!" Finster came nose to nose with Michael; his hot breath was nauseating.

Busch twisted, rolling this way and that. "I will not—be—a bargaining chip." And then he saw something on the grass. Painfully, he reached for it.

Michael could see Busch out of his peripheral vision. "Paul. No. Jesus Christ—"

"He is not here," Finster sneered.

Busch's fingers closed around his gun; he raised it, aiming at Finster.

"You cannot harm me with that," Finster hissed, not bothering to turn toward the weapon pointed at the center of his back.

But shooting Finster was not Busch's intention. The big cop pressed the gun to his own head. "Promise me you'll take care of Jeannie and my children—"

"Paul!!!" Michael screamed.

"Don't make your efforts or my sacrifice be in vain—"

The clarity of this moment was clearer than anything Busch had ever experienced in his life. It was as if the pain he felt was a baptism of fire, unbearable yet somehow cleansing. He believed in Michael, he believed in Simon. Most of all, he believed in the keys.

"Paul, don't—"

"Promise me," the policeman pleaded, his eyes crying to Michael.

Michael's anguish filled the air, his heart fought the words in his mind, but he said them nonetheless. "I promise," he whispered, knowing that he was agreeing to his best friend's death sentence.

Busch's finger wrapped the trigger and with a Herculean effort pulled, but his hand fell away. The gun was silent. His body arched, gasping, his eyes widening as his heart seized. He slumped to the ground.

"You killed him!" Michael screamed.

"No," Finster said. "Don't you wish I had? That would be so convenient. His body couldn't take it; he's had a heart attack. I imagine, if he doesn't get to a hospital quickly, he *will* die. . . . Give me those keys, Michael, and I will let you go. Give me those keys and you can save him, you still have time. Are you willing to trade his life? If not, his death will be on your conscience."

Michael felt paralyzed: Paul's life? Or Mary's soul. No matter how he chose, Finster was right: he would be burdened with an unbearable guilt for the rest of his days.

And then Michael's mind filled with rage, wiping all logic and reason away. He charged and swung at Finster. A taunting laugh was the only response. Overcome with anger, Michael grabbed Finster around the neck, squeezing.

And then she was there.

Standing in Finster's place.

Mary St. Pierre.

Michael's hands choking the life out of her.

"Michael . . . please . . . don't kill me," Mary gasped.

Michael froze in fear as his wife struggled for breath. "Mary! Mary, I'm sorry—"

"Close your eyes, Michael. It's a trick," Simon warned softly. "You know in your heart that's not your wife. Don't give in." It was the first hint of sympathy Michael had ever seen in him.

Michael's hands dropped to his sides. He crumpled to the ground, his head bowed, sobbing, a beaten man. Mary placed her hand on his shoulder and when Michael looked up, she had transformed back into Finster. "If you give me the keys, Michael, you can still save your friend from death and I will let your wife into Heaven. That's what she wants, that is why you are doing this. I'll guarantee that she has everlasting peace." Finster paused. "I give you my word."

Michael was never so lost. He looked to Simon.

"His word means nothing," Simon cautioned.

Michael got to his feet in silence. Tears stained his face. He walked toward Simon and demanded, "Give me the keys." Michael could not meet the other man's eyes.

"What?" The priest couldn't believe Michael's words. "I didn't come this far to—" He could barely control himself. "It doesn't matter what happens to us, Michael. This is for *God*—"

The frustration finally exploded out of Michael. "We came all this way on our own! No help from God. Where was He? If He wants these keys back, why doesn't He help? Why doesn't He give me a sign?" His voice filled with contempt. "He can get them Himself. I have no use for Him. He did nothing for me, nothing! And nothing—nothing—for my wife."

"Michael, no—"

"Yes, Michael. Finster seized the opening. "He abandoned you long ago."

"No, He didn't, Michael. Your name: St. Pierre. St. Peter. Do you think it's a coincidence? You were meant for this."

"No!" Finster raged. "That is not true. Think, Michael." His voice oozed charm. "If it is, then God brought this suffering upon you. And if it's not"—he stepped closer and said quietly—"then He has abandoned you."

Finster's words rang damningly in Michael's ear. He turned back to Simon. "Give me the keys."

"You'll have to kill me first."

"Don't make me do that—"

"—Let me help." As Finster made the offer, suddenly Simon's body spasmed in agony. His hands stretched out to his sides in the shape of a cross.

"You remind me of someone. Hmmm, who could it be?" Finster crooned, with his hand to his chin.

Simon's words came on a waning gasp. "Michael, you have betrayed God. You will not see the Gates of Heaven."

"Neither will you." Finster smiled.

Michael reached out and removed the velvet cloth from Simon's pocket.

He turned to Finster as he unwrapped the keys. "If I give you these keys, my wife's soul belongs to God, she will have eternal life in Heaven, she will rest in peace." And, turning to Busch's crumpled body, he added, "And you will not get in the way of our trying to save him. You'll let Simon be. You will not bring suffering to anyone I know. Promise me this."

Finster reached greedily for the keys.

"Promise me!" Michael snarled, pulling the keys back.

"You . . . have my word," Finster relented.

Simon fell to the ground half dead . . . but half alive.

Michael moved forward, his hand outstretched. The two keys lay in his palm.

Shuddering, Finster stepped back hastily. "Wait. I can not touch them."

"Then I'll put them someplace safe."

"Michael, reconsider," Simon gasped. "Forgiveness, Michael. You must remember there is always forgiveness."

"Then forgive me, Simon."

And then to the shock of Finster and Simon, he walked over to the stone structure still lit by the halogen headlights and, without giving it another thought . . .

Dropped the keys down the well.

"What have you done?!?!" Finster raced to the well, instantly frantic.

"It's your well. I'm sure you'll think of a way to retrieve them."

"But I can't touch them," Finster protested, through gritted teeth.

"Not my problem."

Michael walked back and opened the door of the limo. He reached down for Simon, who batted his help away in anger. Saying nothing, Michael stepped to Busch and picked his big friend up under the shoulders, dragging him. Without a word, Simon joined him, picking up Busch's legs. The two men placed his body in the rear of the limo and raced off into the night.

Chapter 37

The Bavarian mountain forest is more primal than anywhere on earth. It's no wonder the great Germanic tales of Siegfried the Dragon Slayer come to life here. Sunlight only makes its way through the canopy to the forest floor on the sunniest of days and even then it is scarcely enough to read a book by. The decaying mulch and underbrush created a soft bed, home for the abundant insects, birds, and wolves. Civilization is only an afterthought and in many regions here, man hasn't set foot since the great logging days of old. Ancient, moss-covered logging roads serve as the sole route for the small primeval villages, all that remained of the tree-cutting boom days, now barely surviving on local trade.

On the southwestern edge of the forest, twenty kilometers from the nearest town, was a cluster of old buildings. A stone and wooden fence ran about the perimeter, a half mile in total, covered in a tangled snarl of vines and weeds. The log and stone huts dated back centuries and were gathered around an enormous fieldstone structure that rose four stories, from the forest floor, competing with the treetops for dominance. The castle-like building sat upon an outcropping of granite and it was impossible to tell where the natural environment left off and the man-made structure began. Rumors prevailed that the entire town had grown out of the earth, the next step in Mother Nature's evolution. And yet there was not a soul in sight, as if everyone packed up and ran back to civilization, unable to deal with the wild, untamed world.

On the edge of the abandoned community, hidden in the evening shadow, was a stone pub. The ramshackle, wooden shake roof was moss-covered with snippets of grass sprouting on it. It was a squat building tucked back into the forest itself. A sign welcomed weary travelers in for a mug of ale.

The interior was as simple and old as the outside. There were a handful of tables and benches on a slate floor and old leaded windows, cracked and in need of a paint job. On the walls hung a host of medieval tapestries depicting knights, dragons, and landscapes. Michael sat alone at a bare wooden table, grim, sipping a beer.

No one else was there except the bartender, who kept his back to Michael and his nose in his work, cleaning glasses. Michael had desperately tried to reach Mary back in the States, to tell her he was on his way but was left in shock, his heart skipping a beat, when the switchboard connected him to her room and the nurse answered, "Intensive Care. How can I help you?"

The nurse implored him to hurry home. His wife had been calling for him, she said, and time was running out. Mary had slipped into a coma fifteen hours ago.

Michael had wanted to tell Mary he had put things right. Instead, he told the ICU nurse he would be home in twenty-four hours. There was still one thing left to do.

⌘

The door slammed open. A gale force howled through the little pub, blowing everything into a frenzy. Michael held tight to his glass as the wind fanned the flames in the fireplace, kicking up dust clouds everywhere. And then he walked in. Seething. His eyes burned into Michael as he stalked across the room and took a seat directly across the table. Dressed entirely in black, his white hair pulled back into a severe ponytail, his hands balled up into fists. The light seemed to be sucked out of the room, vanishing into Finster's body as if he were some sort of black hole. An eerie darkness emanated from him, spreading like the plague. "Give me my keys," he hissed.

Michael sat motionless, his heart thundering in his ears. He had foolishly thought that Finster wouldn't go down the well, that he could put this whole nightmare behind him, but now he realized how ridiculous that was. Michael had taken a chance and he'd lost. It had been a foolish move, and it had done nothing but postpone the inevitable. He had raced out of Finster's estate with Simon giving Last Rites to his best friend, Paul Busch, whose body was sprawled across the backseat, barely alive. They had charged into a hospital on the outskirts of Berlin, carrying Busch into the emergency room. As soon as the doctors began working on Busch, Michael and Simon were back in the car. They drove south, redlining the limo down the autobahn for twelve hours, knowing that running was simply postponing fate.

"Excuse me?" Michael didn't know what else to say. He gripped tighter to the glass as if it was a life preserver.

Finster's face had gone an ugly red; he rested his hands upon the table, opened, palms up. His eyes pierced Michael. Michael wouldn't break eye contact, he didn't need to, he knew what the man before him held. In each hand: a single key, one of gold, one of silver.

Michael nodded. "Ah . . . Somebody went down the well."

Finster glared, the hate brimming inside him, and then hurled the useless metal forgeries at Michael. "I want *my keys*. Now!"

Michael just sat there.

Finster lunged across the table, grabbing Michael by the throat and lifting him effortlessly into the air. "Your wife's soul is mine."

His hands were squeezing the life out of him. Michael struggled, to no avail.

"I'm going to rip Mary's soul right out of her body and ravage it every single day for all eternity. Do you understand?" He shook Michael violently. "Give me my KEYS!"

Like a rag doll, Michael was hurled against the wall. He crumpled, bloody and dazed, the wind knocked out of him. He didn't have the strength to move. He was certain another rib was broken. He looked for the bartender, praying for help, but the man must have slipped out at the first sign of trouble. Finster walked about the room, cocksure. It was clear that he'd get what he came for and be gone in moments.

"Smart son of a bitch." He picked up Michael's beer. "Never renege on a deal, Michael. Didn't your mother ever tell you that? And if you do, be prepared for consequences." He emptied the mug in one gulp, wiping the foam from his mouth. "I gave you what you wanted. You got the funds for her treatment, not my fault it didn't take. That wasn't my fault, you know. I have no power like that, despite what the storybooks tell you. Giving life is beyond anyone's means. But taking it . . ." He let the threat hang in the air. "I helped you, Michael, and you betrayed me. I agreed to your terms, I let that delusional priest live, I swore to you your wife would have her eternal life. And you betrayed me a second time; you broke your word to me, Michael. So now Mary's mine."

The hatred in Michael's eyes blazed as he struggled to stand.

"Don't bother." Finster motioned Michael to sit down. "You're finished." He flicked his wrist and a table upended itself, careening across the floor into Michael. "You had two sets of keys." Finster spat.

"Three actually." The cheerful voice came from behind the bar. "But you were never known for your intelligence, were you?"

Finster swung around to see the bartender leaning over the bar. The man was bandaged, a sling holding up his right arm. The wounds on his face would heal in time, but the scars would be a reminder for the rest of his life. Without another thought, Finster grabbed Simon by the hair, smashing his head into the bar, then lifted and threw him against the wall of bottles.

From across the room, Michael's voice came. "You were in too much of a rage to think clearly—"

"I want the *real keys* and I want them now!" Finster screeched. He flashed to Michael, a blur as he sped through the room, violently ripping him off the floor, pulling him in close. "Only *one* of you can have them, so only *one* of you is protected by them." He discarded Michael in the corner.

Finster closed his eyes. He was starting to shake, more beast now than human. As his frustration built, any hint of humanity washed away. The wind continued to howl through the place, the raging fire in the fireplace refracting like broken rainbows off the shattered bar glasses. Looming shadows danced off the ceiling.

Simon was on his feet, dazed, fighting to recover. He pressed his good shoulder into the side of the bar, pushing with all his might. And slowly, slowly, the bar moved. Not much, only a couple of inches, but it moved. It slowly slid across the floor, as the silent priest put every ounce of his remaining strength into it.

Finster, perplexed, again grabbed Simon, lifting him into the air. "What are you—"

"Did you ever hear the expression, 'Fool me once shame on you' "—Michael's ragged voice come from across the room—" 'fool me twice shame on me'?"

Finster ignored Michael. Squeezing Simon's throat, he snarled, "Nothing is going to save you this time, holy man—no guns, no knives. No God is going to step in and pluck you from death. And when you die, you will have nowhere to go—no Heaven, no eternal reward for the life of sacrifices you have made to your God." He hurled Simon into the wall. "There will be only *me*."

Michael struggled to his knees. "At any rate, I'd say I've fooled you three—"

Finster stretched out his hand and Michael was dragged into his grasp, flying across the room like steel to a magnet. Michael struggled to free his throat from the vise-like grip.

"Four," Simon said, correcting Michael as he gasped for breath.

"Four times fooled," Michael agreed, his voice ebbing along with his consciousness. Bloodied and battered, he pressed on through gritted teeth. "Tricked you into that dance club, which was really a church. That's one." The words were coming in a faint whisper. "Tricked you with the first set of fake keys I put in your gallery. Two."

"The second set of keys into the well," Simon added.

"Three," Michael agreed, looking toward the priest. "And number four—"

Finster had reached his limit. Nobody toyed with death, particularly malevolent death, and he personified it. He was finished with Michael's and Simon's games; his would be the last game this pair ever played. "No number four for you. I'm going to chain your soul to my feet so every single day you will witness the torment I will bring to your wife." He hurled Michael against the far wall, but this time Michael didn't fall, he hung there affixed like a picture. The blood flowed freely from his nose and a gash in his head.

Finster reached out with his left hand and from Michael's belt shot his knife. It flew across the room straight to Finster and with only inches to spare, it turned and landed in his outstretched hand. He rolled the handle to and fro in his palm, admiring the blade's glimmer, the way the edge had been honed to a deadly point. Again, Finster stretched out his left hand. Michael's shirt ripped open, buttons flying. His chest was naked and completely exposed.

Finster stepped to Michael and held the blade before his eyes. "You will take your own life."

Michael was silent, his lips trembling.

"I can't do it," Finster sneered. "I can remove your will, bring you within seconds of death, torture you until you plead for death's release, but I can't bring you over that edge. You seemed to have learned this secret so well from your dying friend there." Finster pointed the knife at Simon. "I cannot commit the final act; so you will do it for me. You will give me the keys. Then you will take this blade and plunge it into your own heart. And if you aren't willing to give them to me alive, I have no problem removing them from you when you're dead."

The terror rose in Michael's eyes. His body was unable to respond to his mind's command. Any reply he might make to Finster's threats was lost, replaced with fear—fear that he had failed Simon, that he had failed his wife. And—Michael finally admitted it—fear that he had failed God.

Finster dragged the blade down Michael's bare chest. The point came to rest over his heart. He reached across Michael's body and grabbed his left hand, effortlessly pulling it toward him. Against his will, Michael's fingers opened, pried by an unseen force. Finster placed the knife in his hand as Michael's fingers wrapped around the hilt. A pinprick of blood drooled down his chest from where the blade's tip pressed over his heart. Finster stepped back, admiring Michael's form against the wall, hovering at the edge of suicide.

Michael fought with all his spirit. His arm trembled from exertion, sweat broke out on his brow, but he could not pry the knife from his body. Even with all his might, muscles distended in effort, he failed to halt the dagger's will.

And then, without warning, his arm snapped away like a catapult released, his knife hand arcing back, slamming into the wall. Astonishingly, he had regained control of his arm. He slid slowly down the wall, bewildered and not knowing why. Until he looked at Finster. He was staring at Michael, or more precisely, at his shirt pocket. His concentration broken, no longer concerned with Michael's immediate death. A smirk creased Finster's face. For sticking out of Michael's pocket was Mary's cross, on a long gold chain. And dangling next to it were the two keys.

Finster reached out for them.

Michael blanched. "You can't touch them."

"Fool." Finster laughed. He leaned over and without fanfare, pulled them from Michael's pocket by the long chain. As they dangled there in the air, Finster felt the all-too-familiar nausea sweep over him. His body jerked as the keys drew nearer. Yes, these were the right ones. And despite the pain that new flooded his body, he felt a wave of triumph wash over him. "Mine," he said, with naked satisfaction.

Michael looked down at his chest where Mary's cross had hung. Gone now. He had worn it not out of reverence for God but out of reverence for his wife. She had insisted it would keep him safe, that it would protect him and bring him home again to her. He didn't believe her at the time. But he did now. "All yours," Michael said.

And with that, he ripped the chain that held Mary's cross—and the keys—out of Finster's hand and forced the chain over Finster's head and around his neck. Finster tried to pull away but it was too late, his brain was fogged and his body weakened from being in the presence of the true keys.

With the chain about his neck, the keys fell against Finster's chest. An ungodly cry from the absolute depths of Hell erupted. The pain unbearable, Finster spun about the room bouncing off walls and tables, whirling in a frenzy, falling to the floor, where he writhed in unspeakable agony. Fire and blood oozed from his black shirt as the keys burned into his flesh, embedding in his skin.

Michael scooted back toward the wall doing his best to stay out of the way. Simon watched through impassive eyes, witnessing what he had striven for for so long. And then Finster was still, stock-still, not a movement, not a sound. Smoke rose from his scorched chest, his eyes rolled back in his head. Tables and chairs were upended, claw marks scarred the floor before him. Life had slipped away from the billionaire.

Michael looked to Simon. The priest was barely hanging on to consciousness. They each spilled a fair amount of blood and had their share of bruises and broken bones. And Michael thought: To Simon, this must be old hat, but for me, this is the first and last time.

Michael approached Finster; he looked at the keys embedded in his chest, at the burnmarks around his torso. No one would believe what he had borne witness to. He had seen more than enough to last ten lifetimes. But in the end he had gotten what he had come for with a bonus: he would survive.

Michael crouched down over the body, the stench of burned flesh assaulting his senses. The keys were hot to the touch; he wrapped a cloth about them and pulled. They didn't budge. They had burned into the flesh and into the very bone of Finster's sternum. Michael braced his foot, took a tighter grip around the keys, and pulled with all his might.

Finster's eyes flashed open. Michael froze in shock as Finster leaped to his feet, spinning, frantically clawing at his chest. Tearing, ripping into his own skin. Desperately trying to rid himself of his death sentence. His skin peeled away as his fingers sunk into his flesh trying to free the keys from his body. Then it happened. In a frantic last-ditch effort, he caught the chain and ripped the keys free. They sailed through the air end-over-end, across the room, skidding under a table.

Finster lunged. His hand clawed around Michael's throat. Michael was choking, dying. And all he could think of was the scorched flesh before him, the shape of the keys burned into Finster's chest.

"No more tricks." Finster's voice was pure evil now; there was no hint of the seductive German tone that the captains of industry had grown to know over the last ten years.

Michael gasped. His eyes fluttering, darkness creeping in the periphery of his vision. He fought to muster just one last scrap of energy, just one final push to bring an end to this insanity. And with his last breath he uttered . . . "Number four."

Michael reached up and ripped a tapestry from the wall. It depicted a knight upon a black steed driving his lance into the heart of an enormous, snarling dragon. The handcrafted weaving tumbled to the ground to reveal an altar recessed back into a vestibule. There was only one thing on it: a crucifix. It was a simple thing, made of wood and stone, and dated back centuries.

Finster's eyes went wide.

Michael continued with newfound energy. "This time there is nobody here to carry you out or expected for a long time."

Finster fell to a fetal position, unable to control the pain that ravaged him. One last clear thought ran through his mind, before it burned to ash. He had come so close to avenging himself before He who had cast him down. Finster cursed himself for taking human form, for falling for a human's vices and pleasures. He had fallen prey to the frailty of man, addicted to the lust and greed that infects so many. The only way he had been lured into this church was through the weaknesses of this body. It had dulled his senses, blinded him to the truth. And now as this human shell dissolved around him, his spirit no longer shielded by flesh, the pain blazed within him like an inferno. His soul was awash in light: it was like being forced to look at the sun, unable to avert your eyes. Finster's body was shriveling, beginning to smoke, bursts of small flame erupting from his flesh.

The shell that was August Finster was burning away.

Michael struggled to stand and helped Simon to his feet. The two men put the simple chapel back in order. They pushed the phoney bar out the front door and removed the stacked pews from the rear, remaking the neat rows where parishioners gathered to pray. With great care they reset the altar with its chalice and candles, ready for a service that would never come.

Simon lifted up the tapestry depicting the valiant knight from the floor and passed an end to Michael. They carried it across the little church and stood over what little remained of Finster's body. Simon laid his end over the feet. As Michael reached down to cover Finster's head, a hand snapped up, snatching his wrist. The hand was blackened, charred, more claw than finger.

What could barely be called eyes shone up from the shadows of the floor, bloodred and vengeful, from a face that was gone, darkened into nothingness unlike anything that Michael had seen. This was truly a monster that lay before him, no longer the facade known as August Finster.

The voice was not from lips, nor did it carry to the ears of Simon. It spoke solely in Michael's head. And Michael knew it delivered the truth. *"I can never die."* The voice came from everywhere. *"Without darkness there can be no light."* Michael looked deep into the thing's eyes as it continued, *"I will always be."*

Without another thought, Michael removed Finster's pitiful fingers from his wrist, walked across the room, and picked up the keys. He held them reverently in his hand, running his fingertips over the ancient metal. Like Mary's cross, they were objects of minimal design, unassuming in their simplicity, yet the faith and power they invoked was far greater than anything Michael had ever imagined. To the world they represented faith; to Mary, they represented hope. And to Michael, they represented love.

He removed the keys from the chain, leaving only Mary's cross upon it. He passed the keys to Simon, then stepped to Finster, crouching down. Finster was motionless, his feral eyes frozen open, the smoke continuing to smolder from his charred body. Carefully, Michael placed the necklace around the corpse's neck, setting the cross in the center of the blackened chest.

Chapter 38

Five minutes later, two men stepped from the chapel. Night had fallen, deeper and clearer than any they had ever experienced. The forest seemed alive around them, crickets and owls, tree frogs and cicadas. A sliver of moon crept up over the trees, providing just enough light to see by.

Simon had helped Michael lay the medieval tapestry over the scorched remains of Finster and then pushed him before the altar. They snuffed out the fire in the hearth and stacked the tables and chairs in the corner, leaving the place as ordered as they had found it.

Michael stood in the moonlight as Simon removed the fake German beer house sign they had hurriedly crafted and pulled the true sign from the underbrush. The carved words were German, but Simon had translated them for Michael:

CHAPEL OF THE HOLY REDEEMER
NO SERVICES SCHEDULED
ALL TRAVELERS WELCOME TO PRAY
OR SEEK SANCTUARY.

It had been a hastily conceived plan, one crafted on the fly in sheer desperation—not Michael's favorite method, but he was getting good at it. The allies they had contacted were more than accommodating, actually preparing the chapel, window-dressing it as a bar hours before Michael and Simon had even arrived.

As Simon replaced the church sign, there was an almost imperceptible movement around and within the other buildings, as if they were coming to life. People, scores of them, stepped from the buildings and converged on the chapel. They moved silently, their cassocks and skirts brushing the earth as they walked. Others came from the darkness, bringing wheelbarrows and tools. A large ancient handcart was pushed by a monk; within it were loads of brick and sand.

In hours, the new walls were built; within days, the building was completed. A brick-and-mortar structure now entirely encased the chapel. There were no doors, no windows, no way in or out. The dirt took a bit longer. About a month. It was wheeled in by hand and, when they were done, a giant mound of earth covered the entire building. Trees, flowers, and grass were planted on it so that it blended with its surroundings. At the apex of the mound, a marble statue was placed. It had been sent from the Vatican, coming from the Sistine Chapel itself. Handcrafted by Michelangelo in the year 1530, it had been blessed by the Pope and revered by the Church for its poignant rendering: Jesus handing a pair of keys to the Apostle Simon Peter.

Chapter 39

The humid air was condensing on the hospital windows. It was ninety-five and only seven in the morning, truly the dog days of summer. The shifts were changing; bleary-eyed doctors and nurses replaced by bleary-eyed doctors and nurses. A bruised and battered Michael walked the vacant white halls, past empty rooms and empty stations. He had the distinct feeling there was only one patient in the entire hospital.

He had boarded the first flight he could find out of Munich, at dawn, racing the sun; he'd flown across the ocean perpetually at sunrise, the luminous glow floating on the eastern edge of the world. Dead tired, up for at least seventy-two hours, he couldn't will himself to sleep for even a moment. His eyes remained fixed on the watery horizon, the skies above it clear with that mixed blue and pink that the world has just before it awakens. Michael willed the plane to fly faster.

He stepped quietly into the room expecting to find Mary still and deep in a coma. She was awake, lying in wait as if she knew he was coming. If her frail appearance shocked him, he gave no sign. His eyes filled with tears of relief at the sight of her. Without a word, he took her in his arms and held her forever. They reveled in the miracle that each was still alive. "Sorry I'm late," he murmured, stroking her cheek.

"You made it back," she answered softly. "That's all that matters."

"I'm taking you home."

Mary smiled, not moving from her husband's embrace.

"I was thinking maybe . . . we could head out to the Cape for a week, stay at the Ship's Bell Inn, make love in the dunes," Michael whispered, his head buried in her shoulder.

"Mmmm. Eat Portuguese soup, fresh lobster." Mary's heart was swelling.

"Run on the beach, splash in the waves. The sun warm on our backs . . ." Michael cradled her as the morning rays of sun washed through the window, lighting his beloved's face.

Chapter 40

To everyone's surprise, Paul Busch survived. The German doctors told him he was very lucky not to have been killed by his heart attack and advised him to cut back on the red meat and cholesterol. They stitched up his shoulder and set his two fingers. Any questions about the origins of his wounds were silenced by the five thousand euros Simon gave them. Busch was well enough to fly home five days later and walk off the plane into Jeannie's arms. She hugged him for ten minutes before finally chewing half his ass off for the worry he had caused her.

He sat on the chair in Captain Delia's office while his boss stood over him and chewed off the other half of his ass. "And you're telling me that you're withdrawing the parole violation?" Delia thundered.

"The guy's wife was dying, he did some honest work to try and save her," Busch answered.

"Then why such a big deal before?" Delia was pacing. "Putting him on house arrest?"

"I overreacted; he's a good friend; I thought he was taking advantage. That changed when I learned all of the circumstances. He didn't break a single U.S. law except a minor parole infraction for leaving the state. I couldn't live with myself if I had the guy thrown in jail for a little thing like that. Could you?"

"No more making friends with the parolees, Paul. I mean it." Delia took off his jacket, hung it on the back of his chair, and sat down heavily. He looked at Busch's bandaged fingers. "Care to explain that?"

"Kids, car door, my fingers and an unbelievable amount of pain."

Delia smiled. "You're really falling apart. Word around here is you were having some heart trouble. At the rate you're going, do you figure you'll last the year?"

"I'm fine. Too much red meat. Jeannie's pressing me to leave, though."

"And how do you feel about that?"

"Thought about being a cliché and opening a bar. I don't know. I don't think I could bear not seeing your cheerful face every day." Busch got to his feet and opened the door.

But Delia stopped him. "Have you seen Thal?"

"Thal?" Busch turned back.

"Yeah, Thal. You remember. Internal Affairs. You're under investigation."

"He could be dead, for all I care."

"Hey, we don't kid around with stuff like that."

"If I see him, I'll let you know." Calmly, Busch walked out of the captain's office.

Chapter 41

The living quarters are located in the easterly section of the Vatican Palace with a host of windows overlooking St. Peter's Square. Unseen by the world, it has always been a place of solitude for the Pope, a place where the leader of the Catholic Church can have a vague sense of living a normal life. The library contained five thousand volumes within its mahogany shelves. It was his private room where he could absorb the books, magazines, and newspapers of the current earthly world while keeping with the ancient traditions of his spiritual calling. Three large televisions sat in a corner picking up news-feeds from around the globe. A man who mastered eight languages, the Pope was at home in any country and enjoyed viewing the news that shaped human opinion.

Simon was seated in the crimson receiving room, eyes cast down. The sofas and chairs were of crushed red velvet, accented in gold borders, transporting one back to the days of the Renaissance, when this place had been the very heart of the political world as well as the spiritual one. Simon's black cassock and white collar contrasted sharply with the richly colored decor. His vestments always made him uncomfortable, as if he didn't deserve to wear them; though the traditional priest's clothing did have a calming effect upon him. It was as if he absorbed the spiritual intentions of the material. His hands in his lap, he solemnly held the wooden key box, carved by a carpenter two thousand years ago. He lifted the lid, admiring the keys one last time.

An inner door opened. "His Holiness will see you now, Father," a short bald man said in Italian. Archbishop Baptiste, the Pope's personal secretary, was dressed in the traditional purple vestments of a man of his office.

"Thank you, your Eminence." Simon genuflected. "Did you tell His Holiness of my request?" In Simon's mind there was only one true safe place for the keys: in the possession of the most heavily protected man in the world.

"Our Holy Father found it amusing," the cardinal replied. "He has never worn a key-ring before."

They entered the inner sanctum where the Pope humbly awaited.

Chapter 42

The leaves were in their last days of full greenery, change was just around the corner. The colors would all too soon be transformed into a mosaic of scarlet and gold as they have been since time could remember. The flowers that he planted last month were still in full bloom, they were her favorite: marguerite daisies. Michael knelt at a simple headstone, the winds of September blowing over him, and read the words for the thousandth time.

Mary St. Pierre
God's gift to Michael
Michael's gift to God

They had three weeks, uninterrupted. Mary had rallied. Her smile bright, her green eyes clear and radiant. They spent the time doing absolutely nothing. They disconnected the phone, the TV, and the computer. All food and essentials were delivered to the house. Life was talking, eating, and laughing, taking comfort in the presence of the other. Their love was not expressed through words, but looks and deeds. There is a comfort to a great love that only those that truly know it feel. It is warm and secure, free of anger and jealousy. It is euphoric beyond drugs and renders one immune to life's cruelty.

And then without warning, without pain, she died.

In her sleep, her husband at her side.

Michael lay there next to her for hours, holding her hand in his as he silently wept.

Chapter 43

Michael sat at his desk, his bank statement in front of him. The account in the Cayman Islands held two hundred and seventy-six thousand dollars. But it was all for naught. Mary was gone; all of his efforts, all of the risks a waste. All he really wanted was the money to save her and that had led him down a path that had left the question of Mary's eternal life unanswered. Simon had assured him things were put to right. But he didn't know.

And the money. It came from Finster. It was tainted and evil, bounty money to undermine God and the Church. It had brought only suffering.

Hawk barked, startling Michael, and as the dog charged out of the room, the doorbell rang. Michael tucked the bank statement in his back pocket and walked out of his den. He opened the door. Standing before him was a tall woman of indeterminate age.

"Mr. St. Pierre?" the woman asked in an accent that Michael couldn't place.

Michael studied her. She could have been in her late thirties or a well-preserved fifty.

"I'm so terribly sorry about your wife." She handed Michael an ornate envelope. "The Vatican sends its deepest condolences and prayers in your time of mourning."

Michael averted his eyes, he really didn't know where he stood with the Church, after all the chaos he had caused them.

The woman smiled, seeming to sense his shame. "Mr. St. Pierre, please understand, the Church comprehends the trappings of temptation. But, more importantly, the Church always believes in forgiveness."

Michael looked at the card. "Are you a nun?"

She smiled and let out a small laugh. "No. My name is Genevieve. Simon is an old friend of mine. I run an orphanage in Italy and I'm in town seeking donations."

Michael remained silent, looking at the Vatican envelope.

She smiled. "Not from you, of course. I am attending a fundraiser here in the city. Simon asked me to check on you, to see how you were doing."

"I'm fine," he told her. But they both knew it was a lie.

"If there is anything I can do . . ." She reached out her hand. "Everyone deals with grief in their own way. Sometimes, those who have been there can help."

He took her offered hand; it was soft and unexpectedly delicate. For a moment, he felt comfort from this woman's presence. He wasn't sure if it was her gentle way or the fact that she ran an orphanage that had touched him. Though he was adopted as a baby and raised by loving parents, he'd always felt a kindred spirit with those who were orphaned. They were the ones who were truly alone in the world. And this was a woman who cared for those forgotten children, helping them to realize that they were not alone, bringing the power of love into their world.

Michael tucked his hand in his back pocket, feeling the bank statement, and he thought: *Maybe some good could come from this.* He knew what he would do with the money.

But that wouldn't bring him peace, no one could truly bring Michael peace. Not this woman, not Simon, not Busch, not even the Church, no matter how mighty it was. For none of them could answer the question that still haunted his dreams. He didn't know if Mary was at peace. Had she truly found the Heaven of her prayers?

Chapter 44

It was late into the night. Michael was curled in Mary's favorite den chair, Hawk snoring at his feet, CJ nestled in his lap. He was beyond exhausted, falling at last into a desperately needed deep sleep. He had volunteered to help Busch coach his son's football team. The season was a few weeks old and they had won the day's game 18–12. Still undefeated.

Michael was hoping for a routine, something that would give his life structure, help fill the void. Work and kids' football. That was all he could come up with for the moment. It was a start.

Although the silver and gold keys had been returned and he had borne witness to sights he could never explain, he still carried his doubts. They haunted his days and his dreams. It was the what-if that gnawed at his heart.

The question of a hereafter.

And he desperately needed an answer: the ramblings of his mind had torn him apart the last several weeks; he couldn't imagine what would happen with the passing of years.

He had been out cold nine hours, hadn't moved a muscle, it was the longest he had slept in months. Ever so quietly, Mary stepped into the room, her hair once again a glorious mane. Her skin like alabaster, her green eyes filled with light. She stood there looking down at Michael, smiling at his sleeping form. She sat at the desk and quietly opened the drawer; her hand vanished inside, searching for something. She pulled it out. She stood at the bookshelf, absorbing the memories in the pictures before her, her eyes glowing as the happiness washed over her.

She placed it on the wall—the nail was still there—fiddling with it before finally stepping back, admiring the completeness that filled the void that had too long been there.

The simple crucifix hung there in all its cheap tackiness, in all its meaning.

She returned to Michael's side and, bending, gently kissed him.

His eyes slowly opened as if he knew she would be there and for an instant they shared a warm, intimate smile until the first rays of the morning sun filtered into the room and she dissolved into the shafts of light.

Michael stretched his body fully awake; CJ skittered off onto the couch. He stood and walked to the wall.

He straightened the cross and smiled . . .

. . . for he knew she was at peace.

His question had been answered with a miracle.

Chapter 45

In the heart of the Black Forest, in a region frequented by few, there is an area closely guarded within the confines of a once-abandoned monastery. Five Swiss Guard on permanent assignment from the Vatican man the watch. Mixed in with the monks, brothers, and priests, these soldiers are not obligated to wear their traditional outfits of blue, maroon, and yellow. They guard a five-hundred-year-old statue. Or, more precisely, they safeguard the tomb below it.

It is the only place in the world where the Swiss Guard are stationed outside the Vatican.

About the Author

Richard Doetsch is currently the President of WRMC, Inc., a commercial real estate management and investment firm based in Greenwich, Connecticut.